THEIR FAVORITE FANTASY STORIES

"I loved the story because it was both a Pratchett story and a story that asks so many of the questions I always ask when the covers of the book have closed, the last battle has been fought, and the harbor to the west is empty."
—Michelle West on "Troll Bridge"
   by Terry Pratchett

"His stories brimmed with ideas that no one had ever thought before. 'This is how it is!' you tell yourself on discovering Lafferty, delighted. awed, changed."
—Neil Gaim⋯
   by R. A. ⋯

"In a field whe⋯ ⋯like, Jack Vance's v⋯ ⋯e is a storyteller, a st⋯ ⋯on his names alone⋯
—George R. R. Martin on "Liane the Wayfarer"
   by Jack Vance

"You think: this is how it could have been, this is how it would have to be. When an author spins your head like that, you're in the presence of genius."
—Terry Pratchett on "The Gnarly Man"
   by L. Sprague de Camp

"I think all Zelazny stories tend to be special, but some more so than others."
—Fred Saberhagen on "Unicorn Variations"
   by Roger Zelazny

"This is a simple, heart-felt tale that will linger for a long time in the hearts of those who under-stand that great and marvelous wonders can, indeed, come in small and subtle packages."
—Charles de Lint on "Homeland"
   by Barbara Kingsolver

MY FAVORITE FANTASY STORY

EDITED BY

Martin H. Greenberg

DAW BOOKS, INC.

DONALD A. WOLLHEIM, FOUNDER

375 Hudson Street, New York, NY 10014

ELIZABETH R. WOLLHEIM
SHEILA E. GILBERT
PUBLISHERS

First Printing, August, 2000
1 2 3 4 5 6 7 8 9

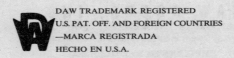

DAW TRADEMARK REGISTERED
U.S. PAT. OFF. AND FOREIGN COUNTRIES
—MARCA REGISTRADA
HECHO EN U.S.A.

PRINTED IN THE U.S.A.

ACKNOWLEDGMENTS

"Ghosts of Wind and Shadow" was first published by Triskell Press, 1990. Copyright © 1990 by Charles de Lint. Reprinted by permission of the author.

"Mazirian the Magician" by Jack Vance. Copyright © 1950, renewed 1978 by Jack Vance. Reprinted by permission of the author and his agents, Ralph M. Vicinanza, Ltd.

"Troll Bridge" by Terry Pratchett. Copyright © 1992 by Terry Pratchett. Reprinted by permission of the author.

"The Tale of Hauk" by Poul Anderson. Copyright © 1977 by Poul Anderson. Reprinted by permission of the author.

"In Our Block" by R. A. Lafferty. Copyright © 1965 by Galaxy Publishing Corp. Reprinted by permission of the agent for the author's Estate, the Virginia Kidd Agency, Inc.

"The Gnarly Man" by L. Sprague de Camp. Copyright © 1939 by Street & Smith Publications, renewed 1966 by L. Sprague de Camp. Reprinted by permission of the author.

"Homeland" by Barbara Kingsolver. Copyright © 1989 by Barbara Kingsolver. Excerpted from *Homeland and Other Stories*. Reprinted by permission of the author and her agent, the Frances Goldin Literary Agency, Inc.

"Stealing God" by Debra Doyle and James Macdonald. Copyright © 1995 by Debra Doyle and James Macdonald. Reprinted by permission of the authors.

"Shadowlands" by Elisbeth Waters. Copyright © 1990 by Elisbeth Waters. Reprinted by permission of the author.

"Liane the Wayfarer" by Jack Vance. Copyright © 1950, 1978 by Jack Vance. Reprinted by permission of the author and his agents, Ralph M. Vicinanza, Ltd.

"The Spring" by Manly Wade Wellman. Copyright © 1979 by Manly Wade Wellman. Reprinted by permission of the Executrix for the author's Estate, Frances Wellman.

"That Hell-Bound Train" by Robert Bloch. Copyright 1958 by Mercury Press, Inc. Reprinted by permission of the agent for the author's Estate, Ralph Vicinanza, Ralph M. Vicinanza, Ltd.

"The Dancer From the Dance" by M. John Harrison. Copyright © 1985 by M. John Harrison. Reprinted by permission of the author.

"More Spinned Against" by John Wyndham. Copyright © 1953, renewed 1981 by the Estate of John Beynon Harris. Reprinted by permission of the agent for the author's Estate, the Scott Meredith Literary Agency, LP.

"Unicorn Variations" by Roger Zelazny. Copyright © 1991 by Davis Publication, Inc. Reprinted by permission of the agent for the author's Estate, The Pimlico Agency, Inc.

CONTENTS

INTRODUCTION

As soon as mankind began to tell stories, the concept of fantasy was not far behind. From the ancient myths and legends every culture created to explain natural phenomena to the folktales, fairy tales, and our urban legends of today, our capacity for imagining the fantastic is exceeded only by our desire to find it. As the concept of fantasy literature evolved over the centuries, it has also become more refined, and now encompasses every type of fiction, from mainstream fantasy to epic high fantasy, from sword and sorcery to urban fantasy. But no matter how many types of fantasy literature exist today, the purpose behind the genre remains the same; to escape the real world and explore other places and events that exist only in the imagination.

Unlike science fiction, which required the fantastic to develop before it could even exist, the roots of fantasy fiction stretch back before the dawn of history. The first structured mythologies, of Mesopotamia and Egypt, pre-date the invention of the written word, as they appear already fully developed in the earliest of texts. The very first "novel"— the Mesopotamian epic of Gilgamesh, elements of which probably date back before the fourth millennium BC—in part relates the type of quest beloved of modern fantasy readers as the heartsick king of Uruk searches for the secret of eternal life.

In the second millennium BC, a group of people known as Indo-Europeans migrated from their homeland north of the Black Sea. Eventually this group took over most of Europe, part of the Middle East, and much of the Indian subcontinent, assimilating the local cultures into their own. From this mixture of languages and societies came what is generally believed to be one of the first creation myths, the Rig-Veda, in which Indra, the warrior god and leader of the Adityas, ancient children of the earth, does battle with Vritra, the great dragon and leader of the Danavas, the children of Danu the Restrainer. After many epic battles, Indra destroys Vritra with his thunderbolt, making the creation of our world possible. It is here that the important theme of warrior versus warrior, one concerned with protecting mankind, one concerned with destroying it, emerged.

When the Greeks rose to prominence in this second millennium, they took the best elements of the creation myths of all the indigenous populations and made them their own. Indra, the lightning god, evolved into Zeus, god of thunder and the heavens. The Indo-European god of the sun, named Mitra, became Apollo, and so on. In fact, Hera, Poseidon, and several other gods actually originated on the Indian continent, and were brought into the local Mediterranean cultures when the Indo-Europeans settled in those areas. Several minor gods, including Demeter, Aphrodite, Rhea, and others have their beginnings firmly established in the Mediterranean subcultures.

Although the Greeks had used written language in the second millennium BC, they did not start writing down their stories until the eighth century BC. Add to this the fact that each poet, playwright, or author interpreted the myths in a way most suitable to what they were writing, and the genealogy of Greek mythology becomes even more muddled. The poet Hesiod was the first to actually weave the dissimilar fragments of the Indo-European, Mediterranean, and Greek myths into a cohesive whole. He played a large part in creating the Greek pantheon we know today, chronicling their exploits and genealogy as real beings in his works *Theogony*. It is in his work that we find the myths of Uranus, who mates with Gaea, the earth, creating the Titans, including Cronos, who gives birth to the gods as we know them.

The epic poems of Homer, including the *Iliad* and the *Odyssey*, utilized the myths of the times symbolically in some of the first stories to use a connected narrative element and theme. Homer set the stage for a new, dynamic form of storytelling, solidifying the pantheon's place in history in the process.

The comedic playwright Aristophanes used fantasy in his play *The Birds,* written in 414 BC, which described how a Greek vagabond convinced the birds to build a utopian city in the sky, and eventually made the gods do his bidding. Other Greek playwrights used fantasy for satire and humor in their plays, and fantasy flourished as it never had before.

With the rise of the Roman Empire came an emphasis on a more practical pantheon. The Roman gods existed primarily for the use of the people, to be venerated on their particular festival days or at designated physical locations. However, the creation story of Rome, the tale of the brothers Romulus and Remus, as well as Virgil's *Aeneid* are excellent examples of the Roman fantasy stories, in which larger-than-life characters struggle against the forces of nature to achieve their goals.

The first English fantasy epic is the classic Northumbrian poem *Beowulf,* written down for the first time sometime during the eighth century. Again, this tale of the struggle of the greatest Geatish warrior against the almost elemental evil creature Grendel continues the warrior versus warrior myth, with Beowulf the protector saving the Danes from Grendel the destroyer. The ninth-century poet Cynewulf wrote *Andreas,* often called the "Christian Beowulf," as well as "The Dream of the Rood," an imaginative poetic meditation that was precursor to the dream visions of the Middle Ages.

The next major step in the development of fantasy occurred in the twelfth century, when the Welsh cleric Geoffrey of Monmouth transformed a minor Celtic war chieftain into one of the greatest legendary figures in the English language, King Arthur. Originally published in Latin in the twelfth century, Monmouth's partly legendary *History of the Kings of Britain* was translated into French by historians Geoffrey Gaimar and Robert Wace of Jersey. The English priest Layamon then retold the tale in English in 1205 in his poem, *The Brut,* the first Anglicized version of the story of King Arthur. Again the theme of protector versus destroyer is set down, King Arthur versus Mordred, with the sorcerer Merlin in the middle.

In the fourteenth century, Geoffrey Chaucer advanced the fantasy story even further by incorporating legends and myths into his seminal *Canterbury Tales.* Among the stories of the various pilgrims traveling to Canterbury is the Pardoner's tale of three thieves who each meet Death personified in appropriate ways. One of the first to use the frame story device, Chaucer combined the myths and folktales of his time with archetypes of real people, making his work accessible to the common man.

The Elizabethan Age brought an explosion of literary fantasy to the forefront of public consciousness. Beginning with Christopher Marlowe's *Doctor Faustus,* perhaps the first deal-with-the-devil story in which the church has only a secondary role next to the tangled web that entangles the power-hungry doctor. At the same time, William Shakespeare was starting his meteoric rise to glory, with his historical, tragic, and comedic plays sweeping the imagination of England like no one had before him. Fantasy was a major element in several of his plays, in particular *A Midsummer Night's Dream, The Tempest,* and *Macbeth,* and he paved the way for the fantasists of the following centuries. Another important author of the time was Edmund Spenser, whose romantic masterpiece *The Faerie Queene* was dedicated to Queen Elizabeth.

The eighteenth century was a period when fantasy blossomed once again, beginning with Jonathan Swift's political satire *Gulliver's Travels,* and ending with William Blake's fiery rhetoric and powerful verses in *Songs of Innocence, Songs of Experience,* and *The Marriage of Heaven and Hell.* By rejecting the standards of then-contemporary life and writing about his driving passions, Blake blazed a new trail for fantasy writers to follow. Horace Walpole wrote the precursor to the Gothic romance, *The Castle of Otranto,* in the latter half of the century.

The dawning of the nineteenth century brought with it the seminal novel *Frankenstein* by Mary Wollstonecraft Shelley, which straddled the boundary between fantasy and science fiction. Later, in the repressive Victorian age, was Charles Dickens, whose novel *A Christmas Carol* is perhaps one of the best known fantasy novels the world over. The first half of the 1800s also witnessed the development of America's great fantasist, Edgar Allan Poe, whose melancholy, macabre works weren't fully appreciated until decades after his death in 1849. During the last years of the nineteenth century, two wrote novels that prophesied the shape of things to come: Jules Verne, with his fantastic sea adventure story *20,000 Leagues Under the Sea,* and H. G. Wells, whose novels *The Time Machine* and *War of the Worlds,* while cloaked in the trappings of early science fiction, opened the door for dozens of future fantasy authors to step through.

Which brings us to the twentieth century, a time in which a book that came out of nowhere defined fantasy for several generations of readers. That book, of course, is *The Hobbit.* John Ronald Reuel Tolkien's charming fable, originally conceived as a serial bedtime story for his son, made fantasy accessible to every reader, and continued the cycle of warrior protector (however unlikely a hero Bilbo Baggins is, he is still a hero) versus warrior destroyer, in the guise of the ancient dragon Smaug.

With Tolkien's work sweeping America, and coupled with the rise of the pulp magazine era, fantasy enjoyed a renaissance in America. Authors such as Robert E. Howard, H. P. Lovecraft, August Derleth, Jorge Luis Borges, Lewis Carroll, and Ray Bradbury rose to prominence during this era. Dozens of fantasy worlds were created and explored during this ascendancy of the fantasy genre.

In the latter half of the twentieth century, the emphasis of the fantasy genre has shifted somewhat. Instead of the single novel, we now see trilogies, or perhaps multivolume works that span thousands of pages along with thousands of years of imagined history. Authors such as Tad Williams, Robert Silverberg, Roger Zelazny, Melanie Rawn, Stephen R. Donaldson, Ursula K. Le Guin, Marion Zimmer Bradley, Robert Jordan, Lloyd Alexander, George R.R. Martin, David Eddings, and Mercedes Lackey reinvented the fantasy novel as the epic series, covering their created worlds and characters in exhaustive detail, yet still leaving enough surprises to keep their readers coming back from more, volume after volume. Of course, the legions of writers who are still tackling fantasy in all its myriad forms are too many to count. Authors such as Michael Moorcock, Harlan Ellison, Charles de Lint, Jonathan Lethem, Orson Scott Card, Joan D. Vinge, and Lucius Shepard are taking the fantasy story to bold new plateaus.

With such a rich and varied history to draw upon, choosing one story would seem to be an impossible task. Yet that is what we asked several of today's preeminent fantasy writers to do, pick the one fantasy story that spoke to them, touched them, made them reexamine the genre in a new light. And they answered, with the results in this book you're holding right now. From the ornate passages of Charles Dickens to the lean, understated, yet richly evocative prose of Roger Zelazny, some of the best fantasy of two centuries is represented here, chosen by the very people who know it best—those who write it. Each story is preceded by a brief (or not so brief, in some cases) introduction by the author who selected it, telling why they still remember that particular story. So prepare yourself for a journey of imagination unlike any you've ever experienced, as you read these stories chosen by today's top fantasy authors as their favorites.

From the first piece by Charles de Lint I read, I felt he knew something the rest of us didn't. I can't actually define what that is, but it keeps me eagerly reaching for every new story. "Ghosts of Wind and Shadows" is a favorite for two reasons. First, for the seamless way he weaves his world into ours, making room for a traditional Faerie, the Oak King's Daughter, and her small cousins beside traffic and raincoats and MTV. Second, for the music. I have no musical ability at all, so I've always considered music to be magical. In this story, it is. It's nice to be right. . . .

—Tanya Huff

GHOSTS OF WIND AND SHADOW
by Charles de Lint

> There may be great and undreamed of possibilities
> awaiting mankind; but because of our line of descent
> there are also queer limitations.
> —Clarence Day,
> from *This Simian World*

Tuesday and Thursday afternoons, from two to four, Meran Kelledy gave flute lessons at the Old Firehall on Lee Street which served as Lower Crowsea's community center. A small room in the basement was set aside for her at those times. The rest of the week it served as an office for the editor of *The Crowsea Times,* the monthly community newspaper.

The room always had a bit of a damp smell about it. The walls were bare except for two old posters: one sponsored a community rummage sale, now long past; the other was an advertisement for a Jilly Coppercorn one-woman show at The Green Man Gallery featuring a reproduction of the firehall that had been taken from the artist's *In Lower Crowsea* series of street scenes. It, too, was long out of date.

Much of the room was taken up by a sturdy oak desk.

A computer sat on its broad surface, always surrounded by a clutter of manuscripts waiting to be put on diskette, spot art, advertisements, sheets of Lettraset, glue sticks, pens, pencils, scratch pads and the like. Its printer was relegated to an apple crate on the floor. A large cork board in easy reach of the desk held a bewildering array of pinned-up slips of paper with almost indecipherable notes and appointments jotted on them. Post-its laureled the frame of the cork board and the sides of the computer like festive yellow decorations. A battered metal filing cabinet held back issues of the newspaper. On top of it was a vase with dried flowers—not so much an arrangement, as a forgotten bouquet. One week of the month, the entire desk was covered with the current issue in progress in its various stages of layout.

It was not a room that appeared conducive to music, despite the presence of two small music stands taken from their storage spot behind the filing cabinet and set out in the open space between the desk and door along with a pair of straight-backed wooden chairs, salvaged twice a week from a closet down the hall. But music has its own enchantment and the first few notes of an old tune are all that it requires to transform any site into a place of magic, even if that location is no more than a windowless office cubicle in the Old Firehall's basement.

Meran taught an old style of flute-playing. Her instrument of choice was that enduring cousin of the silver transverse orchestral flute: a simpler wooden instrument, side-blown as well, though it lacked a lip plate to help direct the airstream; keyless with only six holes. It was popularly referred to as an Irish flute since it was used for the playing of traditional Irish and Scottish dance music and the plaintive slow airs native to those same countries, but it had relatives in most countries of the world as well as in baroque orchestras.

In one form or another, it was one of the first implements created by ancient people to give voice to the mysteries that words cannot encompass, but that they had a need to express; only the drum was older.

With her last student of the day just out the door, Meran began the ritual of cleaning her instrument in preparation to packing it away and going home herself. She separated the flute into its three parts, swabbing dry the inside of each piece with a piece of soft cotton attached to a flute-rod. As she was putting the instrument away in its case, she realized that there was a woman standing in the doorway, a hesitant presence, reluctant to disturb the ritual until Meran was ready to notice her.

"Mrs. Batterberry," Meran said. "I'm sorry. I didn't realize you were there."

The mother of her last student was in her late thirties, a striking, well-dressed woman whose attractiveness was undermined by an obvious lack of self-esteem.

"I hope I'm not intruding . . . ?"

"Not at all; I'm just packing up. Please have a seat."

Meran indicated the second chair which Mrs. Batterberry's daughter had so recently vacated. The woman walked gingerly into the room and perched on the edge of the chair, handbag clutched in both hands. She looked for all the world like a bird that was ready at any moment to erupt into flight and be gone.

"How can I help you, Mrs. Batterberry?" Meran asked.

"Please, call me Anna."

"Anna it is."

Meran waited expectantly.

"I . . . it's about Lesli," Mrs. Batterberry finally began.

Meran nodded encouragingly. "She's doing very well. I think she has a real gift."

"Here, perhaps, but . . . well, look at this."

Drawing a handful of folded papers from her handbag, she passed them over to Meran. There were about five sheets of neat, closely-written lines of what appeared to be a school essay. Meran recognized the handwriting as Lesli's. She read the teacher's remarks, written in red ink at the top of the first page "Well written and imaginative, but the next time, please stick to the assigned topic," then quickly scanned through the pages. The last two paragraphs bore rereading:

"The old gods and their magics did not dwindle away into murky memories of brownies and little fairies more at home in a Disney cartoon; rather, they changed. The coming of Christ and Christians actually freed them. They were no longer bound to people's expectations but could now become anything that they could imagine themselves to be.

"They are still here, walking among us. We just don't recognize them anymore."

Meran looked up from the paper. "It's quite evocative."

"The essay was supposed to be one of the ethnic minorities of Newford," Mrs. Batterberry said.

"Then, to a believer in Faerie," Meran said with a smile, "Lesli's essay would seem most apropos."

"I'm sorry," Mrs. Batterberry said, "but I can't find any humor in this situation. This—" she indicated the essay, "—it just makes me uncomfortable."

"No, I'm the one who's sorry," Meran said. "I didn't mean to make light of your worries, but I'm also afraid that I don't understand them."

Mrs. Batterberry looked more uncomfortable than ever. "It . . . it just seems so obvious. She must be involved with the occult, or drugs. Perhaps both."

"Just because of this essay?" Meran asked. She only just managed to keep the incredulity from her voice.

"Fairies and magic are all she ever talks about—or did talk about, I should say. We don't seem to have much luck communicating anymore."

Mrs. Batterberry fell silent then. Meran looked down at the essay, reading more of it as she waited for Lesli's mother to go on. After a few moments, she looked up to find Mrs. Batterberry regarding her hopefully.

Meran cleared her throat. "I'm not exactly sure why it is that you've come to me," she said finally.

"I was hoping you'd talk to her—to Lesli. She adores you. I'm sure she'd listen to you."

"And tell her what?"

"That this sort of thinking—" Mrs. Batterberry waved a hand in the general direction of the essay that Meran was holding, "—is wrong."

"I'm not sure that I can—"

Before Meran could complete her sentence with "do that," Mrs. Batterberry reached over and gripped her hand.

"Please," the woman said. "I don't know where else to turn. She's going to be sixteen in a few days. Legally, she can live on her own then, and I'm afraid she'd just going to leave home if we can't get this settled. I won't have drugs or . . . or occult things in my house. But I . . ." Her eyes were suddenly swimming with unshed tears. "I don't want to lose her. . . ."

She drew back. From her handbag, she fished out a handkerchief which she used to dab at her eyes.

Meran sighed. "All right," she said. "Lesli has another lesson with me on Thursday—a make-up one for having missed one last week. I'll talk to her then, but I can't promise you anything."

Mrs. Batterberry looked embarrassed, but relieved. "I'm sure you'll be able to help."

Meran had no such assurances, but Lesli's mother was already on her feet and heading for the door, forestalling any attempt Meran might have tried to muster to back out of the situation. Mrs. Batterberry paused in the doorway and looked back.

"Thank you so much," she said, and then she was gone.

Meran stared sourly at the space Mrs. Batterberry had occupied.

"Well, isn't this just wonderful," she said.

* * *

From Lesli's diary, entry dated October 12th:

I saw another one today! It wasn't at all the same as the one I spied on the Common last week. That one was more like a wizened little monkey, dressed up like an Arthur Rackham leprechaun. If I'd told anybody about him, they'd say that it *was* just a dressed-up monkey, but we know better, don't we?

This is just so wonderful. I've always known they were there, of course. All around. But they were just hints, things I'd see out of the corner of my eye, snatches of music or conversation that I'd hear in a park or the backyard, when no one else was around. But ever since Midsummer's Eve, I've actually been able to see them.

I feel like a birder, noting each new separate species I spot down here on your pages, but was there ever a birdwatcher that could claim to have seen the marvels I have? It's like, all of a sudden, I've finally learned how to *see*.

This one was at the Old Firehall of all places. I was having my weekly lesson with Meran—I get two this week because she was out of town last week. Anyway, we were playing my new tune—the one with the arpeggio bit in the second part that I'm supposed to be practicing but can't quite get the hang of. It's easy when Meran's playing along with me, but when I try to do it on my own, my fingers get all fumbly and I keep muddling up the middle D.

I seem to have gotten sidetracked. Where was I? Oh, yes. We were playing "Touch Me If You Dare" and it really sounded nice with both of us playing. Meran just seemed to pull my playing along with hers until it got lost in her music and you couldn't tell which instrument was which, or even how many there were playing.

It was one of those perfect moments. I felt like I was in a trance or something. I had my eyes closed, but then I felt the air getting all thick. There was this weird sort of pressure on my skin, as though gravity had just doubled or something. I kept on playing, but I opened my eyes and that's when I saw her—hovering up behind Meran's shoulders.

She was the neatest thing I've ever seen—just the tiniest little faerie, ever so pretty, with gossamer wings that moved so quickly to keep her aloft that they were just a blur. They moved like a hummingbird's wings. She looked just like the faeries on a pair of earrings I got a few years ago at a stall in the Market—sort of a Mucha design and all delicate and airy. But she wasn't two-dimensional or just one color.

Her wings were like a rainbow blaze. Her hair was like honey, her skin a soft, burnished gold. She was wearing—now don't blush, diary—nothing at all on top and just a gauzy skirt that seemed to be made of little leaves that kept changing color, now sort of pink, now mauve, now bluish.

I was so surprised that I almost dropped my flute. I didn't—wouldn't that give Mom something to yell at me for if I broke it!—but I did muddle the tune. As soon as the music faltered—just like that, as though the only thing that was keeping her in this world was that tune—she disappeared.

I didn't pay a whole lot of attention to what Meran was saying for the rest of the lesson, but I don't think she noticed. I couldn't get the faerie out of my mind. I still can't. I wish Mom had been there to see her, or stupid old Mr. Allen. They couldn't say it was just my imagination then!

Of course they probably wouldn't have been able to see

her anyway. That's the thing with magic. You've got to know it's still here, all around us, or it just stays invisible for you.

After my lesson, Mom went in to talk to Meran and made me wait in the car. She wouldn't say what they'd talked about, but she seemed to be in a way better mood than usual when she got back. God, I wish she wouldn't get so uptight.

* * *

"So," Cerin said finally, setting aside his book. Meran had been moping about the house for the whole of the hour since she'd gotten home from the Firehall. "Do you want to talk about it?"

"You'll just say I told you so."

"Told you so how?"

Meran sighed. "Oh, you know. How did you put it? 'The problem with teaching children is that you have to put up with their parents.' It was something like that."

Cerin joined her in the window seat where she'd been staring out at the garden. He looked out at the giant old oaks that surrounded the house and said nothing for a long moment. In the fading afternoon light, he could see little brown men scurrying about in the leaves like so many monkeys.

"But the kids are worth it," he said finally.

"I don't see you teaching children."

"There's just not many parents that can afford a harp for their prodigies."

"But still . . ."

"Still," he agreed. "You're perfectly right. I don't like dealing with their parents; never did. When I see children put into little boxes, their enthusiasms stifled. . . . Everything gets regimented into what's proper and what's not, into recitals and passing examinations instead of just playing—" he began to mimic a hoity-toity voice, "—I don't care if you want to play in a rock band, you'll learn what I tell you to learn. . . ."

His voice trailed off. In the back of his eyes, a dark light gleamed—not quite anger, more frustration.

"It makes you want to give them a good whack," Meran said.

"Exactly. So did you?"

Meran shook her head. "It wasn't like that, but it was almost as bad. No, maybe it was worse."

She told her husband about what Lesli's mother had asked of her, handing over the English essay when she was done so that he could read it for himself.

"This is quite good, isn't it?" he said when he reached the end.

Meran nodded. "But how can I tell Lesli that none of it's true when I know it is?"

"You can't."

Cerin laid the essay down on the windowsill and looked out at the oaks again. The twilight had crept up on the garden while they were talking. All the trees wore thick mantles of shadow now—poor recompense for the glorious cloaks of leaves that the season had stolen from them over the past few weeks. At the base of one fat trunk, the little monkey men were roasting skewers of mushrooms and acorns over a small, almost smokeless fire.

"What about Anna Batterberry herself?" he asked. "Does she remember anything?"

Meran shook her head. "I don't think she even realizes that we've met before—that she changed, but we never did. She's like most people; if it doesn't make sense, she'd rather convince herself that it simply never happened."

Cerin turned from the window to regard his wife.

"Perhaps the solution would be to remind her, then," he said.

"I don't think that's such a good idea. It'd probably do more harm than good. She's just not the right sort of person. . . ."

Meran sighed again.

"But she could have been," Cerin said.

"Oh, yes," Meran said, remembering. "She could have been. But it's too late for her now."

Cerin shook his head. "It's never too late."

* * *

From Lesli's diary, addendum to the entry dated October 12th:

I hate living in this house! I just hate it! How could she do this to me? It's bad enough that she never lets me so much as breathe without standing there behind me to determine that I'm not making a vulgar display of myself in the process, but this really isn't fair.

I suppose you're wondering what I'm talking about. Well, remember that essay I did on ethnic minorities for Mr. Allen? Mom got her hands on it and it's convinced her that I've turned into a Satan-worshiping drug fiend. The worst thing is that she gave it to Meran and now Meran's supposed to "have a talk with me to set me straight" on Thursday.

I just hate this. She had no right to do that. And how am I supposed to go to my lesson now? It's so embarrassing. Not to mention disappointing. I thought Meran would understand. I never thought she'd take Mom's side— not on something like this.

Meran's always seemed so special. It's not just that she wears all those funky clothes and doesn't talk down to me and looks just like one of those Pre-Raphaelite women, except that she's got those really neat green streaks in her hair. She's just a great person. She makes playing music seem so effortlessly magical and she's got all these really great stories about the origins of the tunes. When she talks about things like where "The Gold Ring" came from, it's like she really believes it was the faeries that gave that piper the tune in exchange for the lost ring he returned to them. The way she tells it, it's like she was there when it happened.

I feel like I've always known her. From the first time I saw her, I felt like I was meeting an old friend. Sometimes I think that she's magic herself—a kind of oak-tree faerie princess who's just spending a few years living in the Fields We Know before she goes back home to the magic place where she really lives.

Why would someone like that involve themselves in my mother's crusade against Faerie?

I guess I was just being naive. She's probably no different from Mom or Mr. Allen and everybody else who doesn't believe. Well, I'm not going to any more stupid flute lessons, that's for sure.

I hate living here. Anything'd be better.

Oh, why couldn't I just have been stolen by the faeries when I was a baby? Then I'd *be* there and there'd just be some changeling living here in my place. Mom could turn *it* into a good little robot instead. Because that's all she wants. She doesn't want a daughter who can think on her own, but a boring, closed-minded junior model of herself. She should have gotten a dog instead of having a kid. Dogs are easy to train and they like being led around on a leash.

I wish Granny Nell was still alive. She would never, ever have tried to tell me that I had to grow up and stop imagining things. Everything seemed magic when she was around. It was like she was magic—just like Meran. Sometimes when Meran's playing her flute, I almost feel as though Granny Nell's sitting there with us, just listening to the music with that sad wise smile of hers.

I know I was only five when she died, but lots of the time she seems more real to me that any of my relatives that are still alive.

If she was still alive, I could be living with her right now and everything'd be really great.

Jeez, I miss her.

* * *

Anna Batterberry was in an anxious state when she pulled up in front of the Kelledy house on McKennit Street. She checked the street number that hung beside the wrought-iron gate where the walkway met the sidewalk and compared it against the address she'd hurriedly scribbled down on a scrap of paper before leaving home. When she was sure that they were the same, she slipped out of the car and approached the gate.

Walking up to the house, the sound of her heels was loud on the walkway's flagstones. She frowned at the thick carpet of fallen oak leaves that covered the lawn. The Kelledys had better hurry in cleaning them up, she thought. The city work crews would only be collecting leaves for one more week and they had to be neatly bagged and sitting at

He gave her another shove to start her moving again. She wanted desperately to break free of his hand and just run, but as he marched her across the park, she discovered that she was too scared to do anything but let him lead her away.

She'd never felt so helpless or alone in all her life. It made her feel ashamed.

* * *

"Please don't joke about this," Anna said in response to Cerin's suggestion that they turn to Faerie for help in finding Lesli.

"Yes," Meran agreed, though she wasn't speaking of jokes. "This isn't the time."

Cerin shook his head. "This seems a particularly appropriate time to me." He turned to Anna. "I don't like to involve myself in private quarrels, but since it's you that's come to us, I feel I have the right to ask you this: Why is it, do you think, that Lesli ran away in the first place?"

"What are you insinuating? That I'm not a good mother?"

"Hardly. I no longer know you well enough to make that sort of a judgment. Besides, it's not really any of my business, is it?"

"Cerin, please," Meran said.

A headache was starting up between Anna's temples.

"I don't understand," Anna said. "What is it that you're saying?"

"Meran and I loved Nell Batterberry," Cerin said. "I don't doubt that you held some affection for her as well, but I do know that you thought her a bit of a daft old woman. She told me once that after her husband—after Philip—died, you tried to convince Peter that she should be put in a home. Not in a home for the elderly, but for the, shall we say, gently mad?"

"But she—"

"Was full of stories that made no sense to you," Cerin said. "She heard and saw what others couldn't, though she had the gift that would allow such people to see into the invisible world of Faerie when they were in her presence.

You saw into that world once, Anna. I don't think you ever forgave her for showing it to you."

"It . . . it wasn't real."

Cerin shrugged. "That's not really important at this moment. What's important is that, if I understand the situation correctly, you've been living in the fear that Lesli would grow up as fey as her grandmother. And if this is so, your denying her belief in Faerie lies at the root of the troubles that the two of you share."

Anna looked to Meran for support, but Meran knew her husband too well and kept her own council. Having begun, Cerin wouldn't stop until he said everything he meant to.

"Why are you doing this to me?" Anna asked. "My daughter's run away. All of . . . all of this . . . ?" She waved a hand that was perhaps meant to take in just the conversation, perhaps the whole room. "It's not real. Little people and fairies and all the things my mother-in-law reveled in discussing just aren't real. She could make them *seem* real, I'll grant you that, but they could never exist."

"In your world," Cerin said.

"In the real world."

"They're not one and the same," Cerin told her.

Anna began to rise from the sofa. "I don't have to listen to any of this," she said. "My daughter's run away and I thought you might be able to help me. I didn't come here to be mocked."

"The only reason I've said anything at all," Cerin told her, "is for Lesli's sake. Meran talks about her all the time. She sounds like a wonderful, gifted child."

"She is."

"I hate the thought of her being forced into a box that doesn't fit her. Of having her wings cut off, her sight blinded, her hearing muted, her voice stilled."

"I'm not doing any such thing!" Anna cried.

"You just don't realize what you're doing," Cerin replied.

His voice was mild, but dark lights in the back of his eyes were flashing.

Meran realized it was time to intervene. She stepped between the two. Putting her back to her husband, she turned to face Anna.

"We'll find Lesli," she said.

"How? With *magic?*"

"It doesn't matter how. Just trust that we will. What you have to think of is of what you were telling me yesterday: her birthday's coming up in just a few days. Once she turns sixteen, so long as she can prove that she's capable of supporting herself, she can legally leave home and nothing you might do or say then can stop her."

"It's you, isn't it?" Anna cried. "You're the one who's been filling up her head with all these horrible fairy tales. I should never have let her take those lessons."

Her voice rose even higher in pitch as she lunged forward, arms flailing. Meran slipped to one side, then reached out one quick hand. She pinched a nerve in Anna's neck and the woman suddenly went limp. Cerin caught her before she could fall and carried her back to the sofa.

"Now do you see what I mean about parents?" he said as he laid Anna down.

Meran gave him a mock-serious cuff on the back of his head.

"Go find Lesli," she said.

"But—"

"Or would you rather stay with Anna and continue your silly attempt at converting her when she wakes up again?"

"I'm on my way," Cerin told her and was out the door before she could change her mind.

* * *

Thunder cracked almost directly overhead as Cutter dragged Lesli into a brownstone just off Palm Street. The building stood in the heart of what was known as Newford's Combat Zone, a few square blocks of night clubs, strip joints, and bars. It was a tough part of town with hookers on every corner, bikers cruising the streets on chopped-down Harleys, bums sleeping in doorways, and winos sitting on the curbs, drinking cheap booze from bottles vaguely hidden in paper bags.

Cutter had an apartment on the top floor of the brownstone, three stories up from the street. If he hadn't told her that he lived here, Lesli would have thought that he'd taken her into an abandoned building. There was no furniture except a vinyl-topped table and two chairs in the dirty kitchen. A few mangy pillows were piled up against the wall in what she assumed was the living room.

He led her down to the room at the end of the long hall that ran the length of the apartment and pushed her inside. She lost her balance and went sprawling onto the mattress that lay in the middle of the floor. It smelled of mildew and, vaguely, of old urine. She scrambled away from it and crouched up against the far wall, clutching her knapsack against her chest.

"Now, you just relax, sweet stuff," Cutter told her. "Take things easy. I'm going out for a little while to find you a nice guy to ease you into the trade. I'd do it myself, but there's guys that want to be first with a kid as young and pretty as you are and I sure could use the bread they're willing to pay for the privilege."

Lesli was prepared to beg him to let her go, but her throat was so tight she couldn't make a sound.

"Don't go away now," Cutter told her.

He chuckled at his own wit, then closed the door and locked it. Lesli didn't think she'd ever heard anything so final as the sound of that lock catching. She listened to Cutter's footsteps as they crossed the apartment, the sound of the front door closing, his footsteps receding on the stairs.

As soon as she was sure he was far enough away, she got up and ran to the door, trying it, just in case, but it really was locked and far too solid for her to have any hope of breaking through its panels. Of course there was no phone. She crossed the room to the window and forced it open. The window looked out on the side of another building, with an alleyway below. There was no fire escape outside the window and she was far too high up to think of trying to get down to the alley.

Thunder rumbled again, not quite overhead now, and it started to rain. She leaned by the window, resting her head on its sill. Tears sprang up in her eyes again.

"Please," she sniffed. "Please, somebody help me. . . ."

The rain coming in the window mingled with the tears that streaked her cheek.

* * *

Cerin began his search at the Batterberry house which was in Ferryside, across the Stanton Street Bridge on the west side of the Kickaha River. As Anna Batterberry had remarked, the city was large. To find one teenage girl, hiding somewhere in the confounding labyrinth of its thousands of crisscrossing streets and avenues, was a daunting task, but Cerin was depending on help.

To anyone watching him, he must have appeared to be slightly mad. He wandered back and forth across the streets of Ferryside, stopping under trees to look up into their bare branches, hunkering down at the mouths of alleys or alongside hedges, apparently talking to himself. In truth, he was looking for the city's gossips:

Magpies and crows, sparrows and pigeons saw everything, but listening to their litanies of the day's events was like looking something up in an encyclopedia that was merely a confusing heap of loose pages, gathered together in a basket. All the information you wanted was there, but finding it would take more hours than there were in a day.

Cats were little better. They liked to keep most of what they knew to themselves, so what they did offer him was usually cryptic and sometimes even pointedly unhelpful. Cerin couldn't blame them; they were by nature secretive and like much of Faerie, capricious.

The most ready to give him a hand were those little sprites commonly known as the flower faeries. They were the little winged spirits of the various trees and bushes, flowers and weeds, that grew tidily in parks and gardens, rioting only in the odd empty lot or wild place, such as the riverbanks that ran down under the Stanton Street Bridge to meet the water. Years ago, Cicely Mary Barker had cataloged any number of them in a loving series of books; more recently the Boston artist, Terri Windling, had taken up the task, specializing in the urban relations of those Barker had already noted.

It was late in the year for the little folk. Most of them were already tucked away in Faerie, sleeping through the winter, or else too busy with their harvests and other seasonal preoccupations to have paid any attention at all to what went beyond the task at hand. But a few had seen the young girl who could sometimes see them. Meran's cousins were the most helpful. Their small pointed faces would regard Cerin gravely from under acorn caps as they pointed this way down one street, or that way down another.

It took time. The sky grew darker, and then still darker as the clouds thickened with an approaching storm, but slowly and surely, Cerin traced Lesli's passage over the Stanton Street Bridge all the way across town to Fitzhenry Park. It was just as he reached the bench where she'd been sitting that it began to rain.

There, from two of the wizened little monkeylike bodachs that lived in the park, he got the tale of how she'd been accosted and taken away.

"She didn't want to go, sir," said the one, adjusting the brim of his little cap against the rain.

All faerie knew Cerin, but it wasn't just for his bardic harping that they paid him the respect that they did. He was the husband of the oak king's daughter, she who could match them trick for trick and then some, and they'd long since learned to treat her, and those under her protection, with a wary deference.

"No, sir, she didn't," added the other, "but he led her off all the same."

Cerin hunkered down beside the bench so that he wasn't towering over them.

"Where did he take her?" he asked.

The first bodach pointed to where two men were standing by the War Memorial, shoulders hunched against the rain, heads bent together as they spoke. One wore a thin raincoat over a suit; the other was dressed in denim jacket, jeans, and cowboy boots. They appeared to be discussing a business transaction.

"You could ask him for yourself," the bodach said. "He's the one all in blue."

Cerin's gaze went to the pair and a hard look came over his features. If Meran had been there, she might have laid a hand on his arm, or spoken a calming word, to bank the dangerous fire that grew in behind his eyes. But she was at home, too far away for her quieting influence to be felt.

The bodachs scampered away as Cerin rose to his feet. By the War Memorial, the two men seemed to come to an agreement and left the park together. Cerin fell in behind them, the rain that slicked the pavement underfoot muffling his footsteps. His fingers twitched at his side, as though striking a harp's strings.

From the branches of the tree where they'd taken sanctuary, the bodachs thought they could hear the sound of a harp, its music echoing softly against the rhythm of the rain.

* * *

Anna came to once more just as Meran was returning from the kitchen with a pot of herb tea and a pair of mugs. Meran set the mugs and pot down on the table by the sofa and sat down beside Lesli's mother.

"How are you feeling?" she asked as she adjusted the cool cloth she'd laid upon Anna's brow earlier.

Anna's gaze flicked from left to right, over Meran's shoulder and down to the floor, as though tracking invisible presences. Meran tried to shoo away the inquisitive faerie, but it was a useless gesture. In this house, with Anna's presence to fuel their quenchless curiosity, it was like trying to catch the wind.

"I've made us some tea," Meran said. "It'll make you feel better."

Anna appeared docile now, her earlier anger fled as though it had never existed. Outside, rain pattered gently against the windowpanes. The face of a nosy hob was pressed against one lower pane, its breath clouding the glass, its large eyes glimmering with their own inner light.

"Can . . . can you make them go away?" Anna asked.

Meran shook her head. "But I can make you forget again."

"Forget." Anna's voice grew dreamy. "Is that what you did before? You made me forget?"

"No. You did that on your own. You didn't want to remember, so you simply forgot."

"And you . . . you didn't do a thing?"

"We do have a certain . . . aura," Meran admitted, "which accelerates the process. It's not even something we consciously work at. It just seems to happen when we're around those who'd rather not remember what they see."

"So I'll forget, but they'll all still be there?"

Meran nodded.

"I just won't be able to see them?"

"It'll be like it was before," Meran said.

"I . . . I don't think I like that . . ."

Her voice slurred. Meran leaned forward with a worried expression. Anna seemed to regard her through blurring vision.

"I think I'm going . . . away . . . now. . . ." she said.

Her eyelids fluttered, then her head lolled to one side and she lay still. Meran called Anna's name and gave her a little shake, but there was no response. She put two fingers to Anna's throat and found her pulse. It was regular and strong, but try though she did, Meran couldn't rouse the woman.

Rising from the sofa, she went into the kitchen to phone for an ambulance. As she was dialing the number, she heard Cerin's harp begin to play by itself up in his study on the second floor.

* * *

Lesli's tears lasted until she thought she saw something moving in the rain on the other side of the window. It was a flicker of movement and color, just above the outside windowsill, as though a pigeon had come in for a wet landing, but it had moved with far more grace and deftness than any pigeon she'd ever seen. And that memory of color was all wrong, too. It hadn't been the blue/white/gray of a pigeon; it had been more like a butterfly—

doubtful, she thought, in the rain and this time of year

—or a hummingbird—

even more doubtful

—but then she remembered what the music had woken at her last flute lesson. She rubbed at her eyes with her sleeve to remove the blur of her tears and looked more closely into the rain. Face-on, she couldn't see anything, but as soon as she turned her head, there it was again, she could see it out of the corner of her eye, a dancing dervish of color and movement that flickered out of her line of sight as soon as she concentrated on it.

After a few moments, she turned from the window. She gave the door a considering look and listened hard, but there was still no sound of Cutter's return.

Maybe, she thought, maybe magic can rescue me. . . .

She dug out her flute from her knapsack and quickly put the pieces together. Turning back to the window, she sat on her haunches and tried to start up a tune, but to no avail. She was still too nervous, her chest felt too tight, and she couldn't get the air to come up properly from her diaphragm.

She brought the flute down from her lip and laid it across her knees. Trying not to think of the locked door, of why it was locked, and who would be coming through it, she steadied her breathing.

In, slowly now, hold it, let it out, slowly. And again.

She pretended she was with Meran, just the two of them in the basement of the Old Firehall. There. She could almost hear the tune that Meran was playing, except it sounded more like the bell-like tones of a harp than the breathy timbre of a wooden flute. But still, it was there for her to follow, a path marked out on a roadmap of music.

Lifting the flute back up to her lip, she blew again, a narrow channel of air going down into the mouth hole at an angle, all her fingers down, the low D note ringing in the empty room, a deep rich sound, resonant and full. She played it again, then caught the music she heard, that particular path laid out on the roadmap of all tunes that are or yet could be, and followed where it led.

It was easier to do than she would have thought possible, easier than at all those lessons with Meran. The music she followed seemed to allow her instrument to almost play itself. And as the tune woke from her flute, she fixed her gaze on the rain falling just outside the window where a flicker of color appeared, a spin of movement.

Please, she thought. Oh, please. . . .

And then it was there, hummingbird wings vibrating in the rain, sending incandescent sprays of water arcing away from their movement; the tiny naked upper torso, the lower wrapped in tiny leaves and vines; the dark hair gathered wetly against her miniature cheeks and neck; the eyes, tiny and timeless, watching her as she watched back and all the while, the music played.

Help me, she thought to that little hovering figure. *Won't you please—*

She had been oblivious to anything but the music and the tiny faerie outside in the rain. She hadn't heard the footsteps on the stairs, nor heard them crossing the apartment. But she heard the door open.

The tune faltered, the faerie flickered out of sight as though it had never been there. She brought the flute down from her lips and turned, her heart drumming wildly in her chest, but she refused to be scared. That's all guys like Cutter wanted. They wanted to see you scared of them. They wanted to be in control. But no more.

I'm not going to go without a fight, she thought. I'll break my flute over his stupid head. I'll. . . .

The stranger standing in the doorway brought her train of thought to a scurrying halt. And then she realized that the harping she'd heard, the tune that had led her flute to join it, had grown in volume, rather than diminished.

"Who . . . who are you?" she asked.

Her hands had begun to perspire, making her flute slippery and hard to hold. The stranger had longer hair than Cutter. It was drawn back in a braid that hung down one side of his head and dangled halfway down his chest. He had a full beard and wore clothes that though they were simple jeans, shirt, and jacket, seemed to have a timeless cut to them, as though they could have been worn at any point in history and not seemed out of place. Meran dressed like that as well, she realized.

But it was his eyes that held her—not their startling brightness, but the fire that seemed to flicker in their depths, a rhythmic movement that seemed to keep time to the harping she heard.

"Have you come to . . . rescue me?" she found herself asking before the stranger had time to reply to her first question.

"I'd think," he said, "with a spirit so brave as yours, that you'd simply rescue yourself."

Lesli shook her head. "I'm not really brave at all."

"Braver than you know, fluting here while a darkness stalked you through the storm. My name's Cerin Kelledy; I'm Meran's husband and I've come to take you home."

He waited for her to disassemble her flute and stow it away, then offered her a hand up from the floor. As she stood up, he took the knapsack and slung it over his shoulder and led her toward the door. The sound of the harping was very faint now, Lesli realized.

When they walked by the hall, she stopped in the door-way leading to the living room and looked at the two men that were huddled against the far wall, their eyes wild with terror. One was Cutter, the other a businessman in suit and raincoat whom she'd never seen before. She hesitated, fingers tightening on Cerin's hand, as she turned to see what was frightening them so much. There was nothing at all in the spot that their frightened gazes were fixed upon.

"What . . . what's the matter with them?" she asked her companion. "What are they looking at?"

"Night fears," Cerin replied. "Somehow the darkness that lies in their hearts has given those fears substance and made them real."

The way he said "somehow" let Lesli know that he'd been responsible for what the two men were undergoing.

"Are they going to die?" she asked.

She didn't think she was the first girl to fall prey to Cutter, so she wasn't exactly feeling sorry for him at that point.

Cerin shook his head. "But they will always have the *sight*. Unless they change their ways, it will show them only the dark side of Faerie."

Lesli shivered.

"There are no happy endings," Cerin told her. "There are no real endings ever—happy or otherwise. We all have our own stories which are just a part of the one Story that binds both this world and Faerie. Sometimes we step into each others' stories—perhaps just for a few minutes, per-haps for years—and then we step out of them again. But all the while, the Story just goes on."

That day, his explanation only served to confuse her.

* * *

From Lesli's diary, entry dated November 24th:

Nothing turned out the way I thought it would.

Something happened to Mom. Everybody tells me it's not my fault, but it happened when I ran away, so I can't help but feel that I'm to blame. Daddy says she had a nervous breakdown and that's why she's in the sanitarium. It happened to her before and it had been coming again for a long time. But that's not the way Mom tells it.

I go by to see her every day after school. Sometimes

she's pretty spaced from the drugs they give her to keep her calm, but on one of her good days, she told me about Granny Nell and the Kelledys and Faerie. She says the world's just like I said it was in that essay I did for English. Faerie's real and it didn't go away; it just got freed from people's preconceptions of it and now it's just whatever it wants to be.

And that's what scares her.

She also thinks the Kelledys are some kind of earth spirits.

"I can't forget this time," she told me.

"But if you know," I asked her, "if you believe, then why are you in this place? Maybe I should be in here, too."

And you know what she told me? "I don't want to believe in any of it; it just makes me feel sick. But at the same time, I can't stop knowing it's all out there: every kind of magic being and nightmare. They're all real."

I remembering thinking of Cutter and that other guy in his apartment and what Cerin said about them. Did that make my Mom a bad person? I couldn't believe that.

"But they're not *supposed* to be real," Mom said. "That's what's got me feeling so crazy. In a sane world, in the world that was the way I'd grown up believing it to be, that *wouldn't* be real. The Kelledys could fix it so that I'd forget again, but then I'd be back to going through life always feeling like there was something important that I couldn't remember. And that just leaves you with another kind of craziness—an ache that you can't explain and it doesn't ever go away. It's better this way, and my medicine keeps me from feeling too crazy."

She looked away then, out the window of her room. I looked, too, and saw the little monkey-man who was crossing the lawn of the sanitarium, pulling a pig behind him. The pig had a load of gear on its back like it was a packhorse.

"Could you . . . could you ask the nurse to bring my medicine," Mom said.

I tried to tell her that all she had to do was accept it, but she wouldn't listen. She just kept asking for the nurse, so finally I went and got one.

I still think it's my fault.

* * *

I live with the Kelledys now. Daddy was going to send me away to a boarding school, because he felt that he couldn't be home enough to take care of me. I never really thought about it before, but when he said that, I realized that he didn't know me at all.

Meran offered to let me live at their place. I moved in on my birthday.

There's a book in their library—ha! There's like ten million books in there. But the one I'm thinking of is by a local writer, this guy named Christy Riddell.

In it, he talks about Faerie, how everybody just thinks of them as ghosts of wind and shadow.

"Faerie music is the wind," he says, "and their movement is the play of shadow cast by moonlight, or starlight, or no light at all. Faerie lives like a ghost beside us, but only the city remembers. But then the city never forgets anything."

I don't know if the Kelledys are part of that ghostliness. What I do know is that, seeing how they live for each other, how they care so much about each other, I find myself feeling more hopeful about things. My parents and I didn't so much not get along, as lack interest in each other. It got to the point where I figured that's how everybody in the world was, because I never knew any different.

So I'm trying harder with Mom. I don't talk about things she doesn't want to hear, but I don't stop believing in them either. Like Cerin said, we're just two threads of the Story. Sometimes we come together for a while and sometimes we're apart. And no matter how much one or the other of us might want it to be different, both our stories are true.

But I can't stop wishing for a happy ending.

Choosing favorites among the six novelettes that make up Jack Vance's *The Dying Earth* is a disagreeable task. Abandoning "Liane the Wayfarer" means giving up the unforgettable Chun the Unavoidable. Dismissing "Turjan of Miir" loses us the Excellent Primastic Spray and the Omnipotent Sphere. Casting out "Ulan Dhor" robs us of Rogol Domedonfors, the last ruler of Ampritatvir. And so on.

I console myself with the thought that the book as a whole will continue to exist even after one story has been selected for this book, and so we really lose nothing by plucking one forth. You still remain able to run from this anthology to the complete text, something that I would do instantly, if I were you and had never read Vance's lovely fable of an astonishingly beautiful far future that will never happen. Herewith, then, is the rich, profusely colored "Mazirian the Magician"—one of the six best tales from this magical book, one of my six favorite stories out of this group of wondrous fantasies.

—Robert Silverberg

MAZIRIAN THE MAGICIAN
by Jack Vance

Deep in thought, Mazirian the Magician walked his garden. Trees fruited with many intoxications overhung his path, and flowers bowed obsequiously as he passed. An inch above the ground, dull as agates, the eyes of mandrakes followed the tread of his black-slippered feet. Such was Mazirian's garden—three terraces growing with strange and wonderful vegetations. Certain plants swam with changing iridescences; others held up blooms pulsing like sea-anemones, purple, green, lilac, pink, yellow. Here grew trees like feather parasols, trees with transparent trunks threaded with red and yellow veins, trees with foliage like metal foil, each leaf a different metal—copper, silver, blue tantalum, bronze, green iridium. Here blooms like bubbles tugged gently upward from glazed green leaves, there a shrub bore a thousand pipe-shaped blossoms, each whistling softly to make music of the ancient Earth, of the ruby-red sunlight, water seeping through black soil, the languid winds. And beyond the roqual hedge the trees of the forest made a tall wall of mystery. In this waning hour of Earth's life no man could count himself familiar with the glens, the glades, the dells and deeps, the secluded clearings, the ruined pavilions, the sun-dappled pleasances, the gullys and heights, the various brooks, freshets, ponds, the meadows, thickets, brakes, and rocky outcrops.

Mazirian paced his garden with a brow frowning in thought. His step was slow and his arms were clenched behind his back. There was one who had brought him puzzlement, doubt, and a great desire: a delightful woman-creature who dwelt in the woods. She came to his garden half-laughing and always wary, riding a black horse with eyes like golden crystals. Many times had Mazirian tried to take her; always her horse had borne her from his varied enticements, threats, and subterfuges.

Agonized screaming jarred the garden. Mazirian, hastening his step, found a mole chewing the stalk of a plant-animal hybrid. He killed the marauder, and the screams subsided to a dull gasping. Mazirian stroked a furry leaf and the red mouth hissed in pleasure.

Then: "K-k-k-k-k-k-k," spoke the plant. Mazirian stooped, held the rodent to the red mouth. The mouth sucked, the small body slid into the stomach-bladder underground. The plant gurgled, eructated, and Mazirian watched with satisfaction.

The sun had swung low in the sky, so dim and red that the stars could be seen. And now Mazirian felt a watching presence. It would be the woman of the forest, for thus had she disturbed him before. He paused in his stride, feeling for the direction of the gaze.

He shouted a spell of immobilization. Behind him the plant-animal froze to rigidity and a great green moth wafted to the ground. He whirled around. There she was, at the edge of the forest, closer than ever she had approached before. Nor did she move as he advanced. Mazirian's young-old eyes shone. He would take her to his manse and keep her in a prison of green glass. He would test her brain with fire, with cold, with pain and with joy. She should serve him with wine and make the eighteen motions of allurement by yellow lamp-light. Perhaps she was spying on him; if so, the Magician would discover immediately, for he could call no man friend and had forever to guard his garden.

She was but twenty paces distant—then there was a thud and pound of black hooves as she wheeled her mount and fled into the forest.

The Magician flung down his cloak in rage. She held a guard—a counter-spell, a rune of protection—and always she came when he was ill-prepared to follow. He peered into the murky depths, glimpsed the wanness of her body flitting through a shaft of red light, then black shade and she was gone . . . Was she a witch? Did she come of her own volition, or—more likely—had an enemy sent her to deal him inquietude? If so, who might be guiding her? There was Prince Kandive the Golden, of Kaiin, whom Mazirian had bilked of his secret of renewed youth. There was Azvan the Astronomer, there was Turjan—hardly Turjan, and here Mazirian's face lit in a pleasing recollection . . . He put the thought aside. Azvan, at least, he could test. He turned his steps to his workshop, went to a table where rested a cube of clear crystal, shimmering with a red and blue aureole. From a cabinet he brought a bronze gong and a silver hammer. He tapped on the gong and the mellow tone sang through the room and out, away and beyond. He tapped again and again. Suddenly Azvan's face shone from the crystal, beaded with pain and great terror.

"Stay the strokes, Mazirian!" cried Azvan. "Strike no more on the gong of my life!"

Mazirian paused, his hand poised over the gong.

"Do you spy on me, Azvan? Do you send a woman to regain the gong?"

"Not I, Master, not I. I fear you too well."

"You must deliver me the woman, Azvan; I insist."

"Impossible, Master! I know not who or what she is!"

Mazirian made as if to strike. Azvan poured forth such a torrent of supplication that Mazirian with a gesture of disgust threw down the hammer and restored the gong to its place. Azvan's face drifted slowly away, and the fine cube of crystal shone blank as before.

Mazirian stroked his chin. Apparently he must capture

the girl himself. Later, when black night lay across the forest, he would seek through his books for spells to guard him through the unpredictable glades. They would be poignant corrosive spells, of such a nature that one would daunt the brain of an ordinary man and two render him mad. Mazirian, by dint of stringent exercise, could encompass four of the most formidable, or six of the lesser spells.

He put the project from his mind and went to a long vat bathed in a flood of green light. Under a wash of clear fluid lay the body of a man, ghastly below the green glare, but of great physical beauty. His torso tapered from wide shoulders through lean flanks to long strong legs and arched feet; his face was clean and cold with hard flat features. Dusty golden hair clung about his head.

Mazirian stared at the thing, which he had cultivated from a single cell. It needed only intelligence, and this he knew not how to provide. Turjan of Miir held the knowledge, and Turjan—Mazirian glanced with a grim narrowing of the eyes at a trap in the floor—refused to part with his secret.

Mazirian pondered the creature in the vat. It was a perfect body; therefore might not the brain be ordered and pliant? He would discover. He set in motion a device to draw off the liquid and presently the body lay stark to the direct rays. Mazirian injected a minim of drug into the neck. The body twitched. The eyes opened, winced in the glare. Mazirian turned away the projector.

Feebly the creature in the vat moved its arms and feet, as if unaware of their use. Mazirian watched intently; perhaps he had stumbled on the right synthesis for the brain.

"Sit up!" commanded the Magician.

The creature fixed its eyes upon him, and reflexes joined muscle to muscle. It gave a throaty roar and sprang from the vat at Mazirian's throat. In spite of Mazirian's strength it caught him and shook him like a doll.

For all Mazirian's magic he was helpless. The mesmeric spell had been expended, and he had none other in his brain. In any event he could not have uttered the space-twisting syllables with that mindless clutch at his throat.

His hand closed on the neck of a leaden carboy. He swung and struck the head of his creature, which slumped to the floor.

Mazirian, not entirely dissatisfied, studied the glistening body at his feet. The spinal coordination had functioned well. At his table he mixed a white potion, and, lifting the golden head, poured the fluid into the lax mouth. The creature stirred, opened its eyes, propped itself on its elbows. The madness had left its face—but Mazirian sought in vain for the glimmer of intelligence. The eyes were as vacant as those of a lizard.

Mazirian shook his head in annoyance. He went to the window and his brooding profile was cut black against the oval panes . . . Turjan once more? Under the most dire inquiry Turjan had kept his secret close. Mazirian's thin mouth curved wryly. Perhaps if he inserted another angle in the passage . . .

The sun had gone from the sky and there was dimness in Mazirian's garden. His white night-blossoms opened and their captive gray moths fluttered from bloom to bloom. Mazirian pulled open the trap in the floor and descended stone stairs. Down, down, down . . . At last a passage intercepted at right angles, lit with the yellow light of eternal lamps. To the left were his fungus beds, to the right a stout oak and iron door, locked with three locks. Down and ahead the stone steps continued, dropping into blackness.

Mazirian unlocked the three locks, flung wide the door. The room within was bare except for a stone pedestal supporting a glass-topped box. The box measured a yard on a side and was four or five inches high. Within the box—actually a squared passageway, a run with four right angles—moved two small creatures, one seeking, the other evading. The predator was a small dragon with furious red eyes and a monstrous fanged mouth. It waddled along the passage on six splayed legs, twitching its tail as it went. The other stood only half the size of the dragon—a strong-featured man, stark naked, with a copper fillet binding his long black hair. He moved slightly faster than his pursuer, which still kept relentless chase, using a measure of craft, speeding, doubling back, lurking at the angle in case the man should unwarily step around. By holding himself continually alert, the man was able to stay beyond the reach of the fangs. The man was Turjan, whom Mazirian by trickery had captured several weeks before, reduced in size and thus imprisoned.

Mazirian watched with pleasure as the reptile sprang upon the momentarily relaxing man, who jerked himself clear by the thickness of his skin. It was time, Mazirian thought, to give both rest and nourishment. He dropped panels across the passage, separating it into halves, isolating man from beast. To both he gave meat and pannikins of water.

Turjan slumped in the passage.

"Ah," said Mazirian, "you are fatigued. You desire rest?"

Turjan remained silent, his eyes closed. Time and the world had lost meaning for him. The only realities were the gray passage and the interminable flight. At unknown intervals came food and a few hours rest.

"Think of the blue sky," said Mazirian, "the white stars, your castle Miir by the river Derna; think of wandering free in the meadows."

The muscles at Turjan's mouth twitched.

"Consider you might crush the little dragon under your heel."

Turjan looked up. "I would prefer to crush your neck, Mazirian."

Mazirian was unperturbed. "Tell me, how do you invest your vat creatures with intelligence? Speak, and you go free."

Turjan laughed, and there was madness in his laughter.

"Tell you? And then? You would kill me with hot oil in a moment."

Mazirian's thin mouth drooped petulantly.

"Wretched man, I know how to make you speak. If your mouth were stuffed, waxed and sealed, you would speak! Tomorrow I take a nerve from your arm and draw coarse cloth along its length."

The small Turjan, sitting with his legs across the passage-way, drank his water and said nothing.

"Tonight," said Mazirian with studied malevolence, "I add an angle and change your run to a pentagon."

Turjan paused and looked up through the glass cover at his enemy. Then he slowly sipped his water. With five angles there would be less time to evade the charge of the monster, less of the hall in view from one angle.

"Tomorrow," said Mazirian, "you will need all your agility." But another matter occurred to him. He eyed Turjan speculatively. "Yet even this I spare you if you assist me with another problem."

"What is your difficulty, febrile Magician?"

"The image of a woman-creature haunts my brain, and I would capture her." Mazirian's eyes went misty at the thought. "Late afternoon she comes to the edge of my garden riding a great black horse—you know her, Turjan?"

"Not I, Mazirian," Turjan sipped his water.

Mazirian continued. "She has sorcery enough to ward away Felojun's Second Hypnotic Spell—or perhaps she has some protective rune. When I approach, she flees into the forest."

"So then?" asked Turjan, nibbling the meat Mazirian had provided.

"Who may this woman be?" demanded Mazirian, peering down his long nose at the tiny captive.

"How can I say?"

"I must capture her," said Mazirian abstractedly: "What spells, what spells?"

Turjan looked up, although he could see the Magician only indistinctly through the cover of glass.

"Release me, Mazirian, and on my word as a Chosen Hierarch of the Maram-Or, I will deliver you this girl."

"How would you do this?" asked the suspicious Mazirian.

"Pursue her into the forest with my best Live Boots and a headful of spells."

"You would fare no better than I," retorted the Magician. "I give you freedom when I know the synthesis of your vat-things. I myself will pursue the woman."

Turjan lowered his head that the Magician might not read his eyes.

"And as for me, Mazirian?" he inquired after a moment.

"I will treat with you when I return."

"And if you do not return?"

Mazirian stroked his chin and smiled, revealing fine white teeth. "The dragon could devour you now, if it were not for your cursed secret."

The Magician climbed the stairs. Midnight found him in his study, poring through the leather-bound tomes and untidy portfolios . . . At one time a thousand or more runes,

spells, incantations, curses and sorceries had been known.
The reach of Grand Motholam—Ascolais, the Ide of Kau-
chique, Almery to the South, the Land of the Falling Wall
to the East—swarmed with sorcerers of every description,
of whom the chief was the Arch-Necromancer Phandaal. A
hundred spells Phandaal personally had formulated—
though rumor said that demons whispered at his ear when
he wrought magic. Pontecilla the Pious, then ruler of Grand
Motholam, put Phandaal to torment, and after a terrible
night, he killed Phandaal and outlawed sorcery throughout
the land. The wizards of Grand Motholam fled like beetles
under a strong light; the lore was dispersed and forgotten,
until now, at this dim time, with the sun dark, wilderness
obscuring Ascolais, and the white city Kaiin half in ruins,
only a few more than a hundreds spells remain to the
knowledge of man. Of these, Mazirian had access to
seventy-three, and gradually, by stratagem and negotiation,
was securing the others.

Mazirian made a selection from his books, and with great
effort forced five spells upon his brain: Phandaal's Gyrator,
Felojun's Second Hypnotic Spell, The Excellent Prismatic
Spray, the Charm of Untiring Nourishment, and the Spell
of the Omnipotent Sphere. This accomplished, Mazirian
drank wine and retired to his couch.

The following day, when the sun hung low, Mazirian
went to walk in his garden. He had but short time to wait.
As he loosened the earth at the roots of his moon geraniums a soft rustle and stamp told that the object of his desire
had appeared.

She sat upright in the saddle, a young woman of exquisite
configuration. Mazirian slowly stooped, as not to startle her,
put his feet into the Live Boots and secured them above
the knee.

He stood up. "Ho, girl," he cried, "you have come again.
Why are you here of evenings? Do you admire the roses?
They are vividly red because live red blood flows in their
petals. If today you do not flee, I will make you the gift
of one."

Mazirian plucked a rose from the shuddering bush and
advanced toward her, fighting the surge of the Live Boots.
He had taken but four steps when the woman dug her

knees into the ribs of her mount and so plunged off through the trees.

Mazirian allowed full scope to the life in his boots. They gave a great bound, and another, and another, and he was off in full chase.

So Mazirian entered the forest of fable. On all sides mossy boles twisted up to support the high panoply of leaves. At intervals shafts of sunshine drifted through to lay carmine blots on the turf. In the shade long-stemmed flowers and fragile fungi sprang from the humus; in this ebbing hour of Earth nature was mild and relaxed.

Mazirian in his Live Boots bounded with great speed through the forest, yet the black horse, running with no strain, stayed easily ahead.

For several leagues the woman rode, her hair flying behind like a pennon. She looked back and Mazirian saw the face over her shoulder as a face in a dream. Then she bent forward; the golden-eyed horse thundered ahead and soon was lost to sight. Mazirian followed by tracing the trail in the sod.

The spring and drive began to leave the Live Boots, for they had come far and at great speed. The monstrous leaps became shorter and heavier, but the strides of the horse, shown by the tracks, were also shorter and slower. Presently Mazirian entered a meadow and saw the horse, riderless, cropping grass. He stopped short. The entire expanse of tender herbiage lay before him. The trail of the horse leading into the glade was clear, but there was no trail leaving. The woman therefore had dismounted somewhere behind—how far he had no means of knowing. He walked toward the horse, but the creature shied and bolted through the trees. Mazirian made one effort to follow, and discovered that his Boots hung lax and flaccid—dead.

He kicked them away, cursing the day and his ill-fortune. Shaking the cloak free behind him, a baleful tension shining on his face, he started back along the trail.

In this section of the forest, outcroppings of black and green rock, basalt and serpentine, were frequent—forerunners of the crags over the River Derna. On one of these rocks Mazirian saw a tiny man-thing mounted on a dragonfly. He had skin of a greenish cast; he wore a gauzy smock and carried a lance twice his own length.

Mazirian stopped. The Twk-man looked down stolidly.

"Have you seen a woman of my race passing by, Twk-man?"

"I have seen such a woman," responded the Twk-man after a moment of deliberation.

"Where may she be found?"

"What may I expect for the information?"

"Salt—as much as you can bear away."

The Twk-man flourished his lance. "Salt? No. Liane the Wayfarer provides the chieftain Dandanflores salt for all the tribe."

Mazirian could surmise the services for which the bandit-troubadour paid salt. The Twk-men, flying fast on their dragonflies, saw all that happened in the forest.

"A vial of oil from my telanxis blooms?"

"Good," said the Twk-man. "Show me the vial."

Mazirian did so.

"She left the trail at the lightning-blasted oak lying a little before you. She made directly for the river valley, the shortest route to the lake."

Mazirian laid the vial beside the dragon-fly and went off toward the river oak. The Twk-man watched him go, then dismounted and lashed the vial to the underside of the dragon-fly, next to the skein of fine haft the woman had given him thus to direct Mazirian.

The Magician turned at the oak and soon discovered the trail over the dead leaves. A long open glade lay before him, sloping gently to the river. Trees towered to either side and the long sundown rays steeped one side in blood, left the other deep in black shadow. So deep was the shade that Mazirian did not see the creature seated on a fallen tree; and he sensed it only as it prepared to leap on his back.

Mazirian sprang about to face the thing, which subsided again to sitting posture. It was a Deodand, formed and featured like a handsome man, finely muscled, but with a dead black lusterless skin and long slit eyes.

"Ah, Mazirian, you roam the woods far from home," the black thing's soft voice rose through the glade.

The Deodand, Mazirian knew, craved his body for meat. How had the girl escaped? Her trail led directly past.

"I come seeking, Deodand. Answer my questions, and I undertake to feed you much flesh."

The Deodand's eyes glinted, flitting over Mazirian's body. "You may in any event, Mazirian. Are you with powerful spells today?"

"I am. Tell me, how long has it been since the girl passed? Went she fast, slow, alone or in company? Answer, and I give you meat at such time as you desire."

The Deodand's lips curled mockingly. "Blind Magician! She has not left the glade." He pointed, and Mazirian followed the direction of the dead black arm. But he jumped back as the Deodand sprang. From his mouth gushed the syllables of Phandaal's Gyrator Spell. The Deodand was jerked off his feet and flung high in the air, where he hung whirling, high and low, faster and slower, up to the treetops, low to the ground. Mazirian watched with a half-smile. After a moment he brought the Deodand low and caused the rotations to slacken.

"Will you die quickly or slow?" asked Mazirian. "Help me and I kill you at once. Otherwise you shall rise high where the pelgrane fly."

Fury and fear choked the Deodand.

"May dark Thial spike your eyes! May Kraan hold your living brain in acid!" And it added such charges that Mazirian felt forced to mutter countercurses.

"Up then," said Mazirian at last, with a wave of his hand. The black sprawling body jerked high above the treetops to revolve slowly in the crimson bask of setting sun. In a moment a mottled bat-shaped thing with hooked snout swept close and its beak tore the black leg before the crying Deodand could kick it away. Another and another of the shapes flitted across the sun.

"Down, Mazirian!" came the faint call. "I tell what I know."

Mazirian brought him close to earth.

"She passed alone before you came. I made to attack her but she repelled me with a handful of thyle-dust. She went to the end of the glade and took the trail to the river. This trail leads also past the lair of Thrang. So is she lost, for he will sate himself on her till she dies."

Mazirian rubbed his chin. "Had she spells with her?"

"I know not. She will need strong magic to escape the demon Thrang."

"Is there anything else to tell?"

"Nothing."

"Then you may die." And Mazirian caused the creature to revolve at ever greater speed, faster and faster, until there was only a blur. A strangled wailing came and presently the Deodand's frame parted. The head shot like a bullet far down the glade; arms, legs, viscera flew in all directions.

Mazirian went his way. At the end of the glade the trail led steeply down ledges of dark green serpentine to the River Derna. The sun had set and shade filled the valley. Mazirian gained the riverside and set off downstream toward a far shimmer known as Sanra Water, the Lake of Dreams.

An evil odor came to the air, a stink of putrescence and filth. Mazirian went ahead more cautiously, for the lair of Thrang the ghoul-bear was near, and in the air was the feel of magic—strong brutal sorcery his own more subtle spells might not contain.

The sound of voices reached him, the throaty tones of Thrang and gasping cries of terror. Mazirian stepped around a shoulder of rock, inspected the origin of the sounds.

Thrang's lair was an alcove in the rock, where a fetid pile of grass and skins served him for a couch. He had built a rude pen to cage three women, these wearing many bruises on their bodies and the effects of much horror on their faces. Thrang had taken them from the tribe that dwelt in silk-hung barges along the lake-shore. Now they watched as he struggled to subdue the woman he had just captured. His round gray man's face was contorted and he tore away her jerkin with his human hands. But she held away the great sweating body with an amazing dexterity. Mazirian's eyes narrowed. Magic, magic!

So he stood watching, considering how to destroy Thrang with no harm to the woman. But she spied him over Thrang's shoulder.

"See," she panted, "Mazirian has come to kill you."

Thrang twisted about. He saw Mazirian and came charging on all fours, venting roars of wild passion. Mazirian later wondered if the ghoul had cast some sort of spell, for a strange paralysis strove to bind his brain. Perhaps the spell lay in the sight of Thrang's raging gray-white face, the great arms thrust out to grasp.

Mazirian shook off the spell, if such it were, and uttered a spell of his own, and all the valley was lit by streaming darts of fire, lashing in from all directions to split Thrang's blundering body in a thousand places. This was the Excellent Prismatic Spray—many-colored, stabbing lines. Thrang was dead almost at once, purple blood flowing from countless holes where the radiant rain had pierced him.

But Mazirian heeded little. The girl had fled. Mazirian saw her white form running along the river toward the lake, and took up the chase, heedless of the piteous cries of the three women in the pen.

The lake presently lay before him, a great sheet of water whose further rim was but dimly visible. Mazirian came down to the sandy shore and stood seeking across the dark face of Sanra Water, the Lake of Dreams. Deep night with only a verge of afterglow ruled the sky, and stars glistened on the smooth surface. The water lay cool and still, tideless as all Earth's waters had been since the moon had departed the sky.

Where was the woman? There, a pale white form, quiet in the shadow across the river. Mazirian stood on the riverbank, tall and commanding, a light breeze ruffling the cloak around his legs.

"Ho, girl," he called. "It is I, Mazirian, who saved you from Thrang. Come close, that I may speak to you."

"At this distance I hear you well, Magician," she replied. "The closer I approach the farther I must flee."

"Why then do you flee? Return with me and you shall be mistress of many secrets and hold much power."

She laughed. "If I wanted these, Mazirian, would I have fled so far?"

"Who are you then that you desire not the secrets of magic?"

"To you, Mazirian, I am nameless, lest you curse me. Now I go where you may not come." She ran down the shore, waded slowly out till the water circled her waist, then sank out of sight. She was gone.

Mazirian paused indecisively. It was not good to use so

many spells and thus shear himself of power. What might exist below the lake? The sense of quiet magic was there, and though he was not at enmity with the Lake Lord, other beings might resent a trespass. However, when the figure of the girl did not break the surface, he uttered the Charm of Untiring Nourishment and entered the cool waters.

He plunged deep through the Lake of Dreams, and as he stood on the bottom, his lungs at ease by virtue of the charm, he marveled at the fey place he had come upon. Instead of blackness a green light glowed everywhere and the water was but little less clear than air. Plants undulated to the current and with them moved the lake flowers, soft with blossoms of red, blue and yellow. In and out swam large-eyed fish of many shapes.

The bottom dropped by rocky steps to a wide plain where trees of the underlake floated up from slender stalks to elaborate fronds and purple water-fruits, and so till the misty wet distance veiled all. He saw the woman, a white water nymph now, her hair like dark fog. She half-swam, half-ran across the sandy floor of the water-world, occasionally looking back over her shoulder. Mazirian came after, his cloak streaming out behind.

He drew nearer to her, exulting. He must punish her for leading him so far. . . . The ancient stone stairs below his workroom led deep and at last opened into chambers that grew ever vaster as one went deeper. Mazirian had found a rusted cage in one of these chambers. A week or two locked in the blackness would curb her willfulness. And once he had dwindled a woman small as his thumb and kept her in a little glass bottle with two buzzing flies . . .

A ruined white temple showed through the green. There were many columns, some toppled, some still upholding the pediment. The woman entered the great portico under the shadow of the architrave. Perhaps she was attempting to elude him; he must follow closely. The white body glimmered at the far end of the nave, swimming now over the rostrum and into a semicircular alcove behind.

Mazirian followed as fast as he was able, half-swimming, half-walking through the solemn dimness. He peered across the murk. Smaller columns here precariously upheld a dome from which the keystone had dropped. A sudden fear smote him, then realization as he saw the flash of movement from above. On all sides the columns toppled in, and an avalanche of marble blocks tumbled at his head. He jumped frantically back.

The commotion ceased, the white dust of the ancient mortar drifted away. On the pediment of the main temple the women kneeled on slender knees, staring down to see how well she had killed Mazirian.

She had failed. Two columns, by sheerest luck, had crashed to either side of him, and a slab had protected his body from the blocks. He moved his head painfully. Through a chink in the tumbled marble he could see the woman, leaning to discern his body. So she would kill him? He, Mazirian, who had already lived more years than he could easily reckon? So much more would she hate and fear him later. He called his charm, the Spell of the Omnipotent Sphere. A film of force formed around his body, expanding to push aside all that resisted. When the marble ruins had been thrust back, he destroyed the sphere, regained his feet, and glared about for the woman. She was almost out of sight, behind a brake of long purple kelp, climbing the slope to the shore. With all his power he set out in pursuit.

* * *

T'sain dragged herself up on the beach. Still behind her came Mazirian the Magician, whose power had defeated each of her plans. The memory of his face passed before her and she shivered. He must not take her now.

Fatigue and despair slowed her feet. She had set out with but two spells, the Charm of Untiring Nourishment and a spell affording strength to her arms—the last permitting her to hold off Thrang and tumble the temple upon Mazirian. These were exhausted; she was bare of protection; but, on the other hand, Mazirian could have nothing left.

Perhaps he was ignorant of the vampire-weed. She ran up the slope and stood behind a patch of pale, wind-beaten grass. And now Mazirian came from the lake, a spare form visible against the shimmer of the water.

She retreated, keeping the innocent patch of grass between them. If the grass failed—her mind quailed at the thought of what she must do.

Mazirian strode into the grass. The sickly blades became sinewy fingers. They twined about his ankles, holding him in an unbreakable grip, while others sought to find his skin.

So Mazirian chanted his last spell—the incantation of paralysis, and the vampire-grass grew lax and slid limply to earth. T'sain watched with dead hope. He was now close upon her, his cloak flapping behind. Had he no weakness? Did not his fibers ache, did not his breath come short? She whirled and fled across the meadow, toward a grove of black trees. Her skin chilled at the deep shadows, the somber frames. But the thud of the Magician's feet was loud. She plunged into the dread shade. Before all in the grove awoke she must go as far as possible.

Snap! A thong lashed at her. She continued to run. Another and another—she fell. Another great whip and another beat at her. She staggered up, and on, holding her arms before her face. Sna— Snap! The flails whistled through the air, and the last blow twisted her around. So she saw Mazirian.

He fought. As the blows rained on him, he tried to seize the whips and break them. But they were supple and springy beyond his powers, and jerked away to beat at him again. Infuriated by his resistance, they concentrated on the unfortunate Magician, who foamed and fought with transcendent fury, and T'sain was permitted to crawl to the edge of the grove with her life.

She looked back in awe at the depression of Mazirian's lust for life. He staggered about in a cloud of whips, his furious obstinate figure dimly silhouetted. He weakened and tried to flee, and then he fell. The blows pelted at him—on his head, shoulders, the long legs. He tried to rise but fell back.

T'sain closed her eyes in lassitude. She felt the blood oozing from her broken flesh. But the most vital mission yet remained. She reached her feet, and reelingly set forth. For a long time the thunder of many blows reached her ears.

Mazirian's garden was surpassingly beautiful by night. The star-blossoms spread wide, each of magic perfection, and the captive half-vegetable moths flew back and forth. Phosphorescent water-lilies floated like charming faces on the pond and the bush which Mazirian had brought from far Almery in the south tinctured the air with sweet fruity perfume.

T'sain, weaving and gasping, now came groping through the garden. Certain of the flowers awoke and regarded her curiously. The half-animal hybrid sleepily chittered at her, thinking to recognize Mazirian's step. Faintly to be heard was the wistful music of the blue-cupped flowers singing of ancient nights when a white moon swam the sky, the great storms and clouds and thunder ruled the seasons.

T'sain passed unheeding. She entered Mazirian's house, found the workroom where glowed the eternal yellow lamps. Mazirian's golden-haired vat-thing sat up suddenly and stared at her with his beautiful vacant eyes.

She found Mazirian's keys in the cabinet, and managed to claw open the trap door. Here she slumped to rest and let the pink gloom pass from her eyes. Visions began to come—Mazirian, tall and arrogant, stepping out to kill Thrang; the strange-hued flowers under the lake; Mazirian, his magic lost, fighting the whips . . . She was brought from the half-trance by the vat-thing timidly fumbling with her hair.

She shook herself awake, and half-walked, half-fell down the stairs. She unlocked the thrice-bound door, thrust it open with almost the last desperate urge of her body. She wandered in to clutch at the pedestal where the glass-topped box stood and Turjan and the dragon were playing their desperate game. She flung the glass crashing to the floor, gently lifted Turjan out and set him down.

The spell was disrupted by the touch of the rune at her wrist, and Turjan became a man again. He looked aghast at the nearly unrecognizable T'sain.

She tried to smile up at him.

"Turjan—you are free—"

"And Mazirian?"

"He is dead." She slumped wearily to the stone floor and lay limp. Turjan surveyed her with an odd emotion in his eyes.

"T'sain, dear creature of my mind," he whispered, "more noble are you than I, who used the only life you knew for my freedom."

He lifted her body in his arms.

"But I shall restore you to the vats. With your brain I build another T'sain, as lovely as you. We go."

He bore her up the stone stairs.

J.R.R. Tolkien has fallen out of fashion in the last thirty years, and many, many people blame him for the death of the fantasy genre (which probably means the death of their interest in fantasy, but I digress. I digress a lot). But to those of us who found his opus at the right time, there was something about his mythic work that cut clean to the heart and left its peculiar, indelible scars. I still reread Tolkien every few years, finding things in it that I missed previous times, remembering things I'd forgotten. I always find it moving.

I like to be moved when I read. I have no objection to weeping my way through the end of a story, and have been lost enough in the web of an author's words that I've had strangers on subways stop me to make sure I'm all right. So it's with some surprise that I find myself having chosen a humorous short piece. Given that, it's no surprise at all that the story is written by Terry Pratchett.

What do these two fine authors have in common? Well . . .

I discovered "Troll Bridge" in an anthology of excellent fantasy work called *After the King,* an anthology that was ostensibly a tribute to Tolkien's work. But while the stories chosen were excellent, most of the book could have been lumped into something titled "Excellent short stories by good authors which in reality has nothing at all to do with Tolkien." Pratchett's story was one of the few exceptions.

It was in every possible way a Pratchett story (a Cohen the Barbarian story, for those in the know, and I darn well wish the Horse would show up again, but I digress). The use of language, the situations, the characters, and the affectionate humor with which these are all combined could not be mistaken for anyone else's work. (If it's not obvious yet, I'm something of a Pratchett fanatic, and the answer to the favorite character question is Samuel Vimes.) Pratchett cannot be accused of committing Tolkien pastiche; indeed in many ways he has lampooned some of Tolkien's more ardent readers.

But having said that, there is something about this story that echoes Tolkien in a way that made me think of both authors—Tolkien and Pratchett—as two men sharing a moment in completely different but very British ways, with mutual respect and understanding. I read the story because it was a Pratchett story; I loved the story because it was both a Pratchett story and a story that asks so many of the questions I always ask when the covers of the book have closed, the last battle has been fought, and the harbor to the west is empty.

—Michelle West

TROLL BRIDGE
by Terry Pratchett

The wind blew off the mountains, filling the air with fine ice crystals.

It was too cold to snow. In weather like this wolves came down into villages, trees in the heart of the forest exploded when they froze.

In weather like this right-thinking people were indoors, in front of the fire, telling stories about heroes.

It was an old horse. It was an old rider. The horse looked like a shrink-wrapped toast rack; the man looked as though the only reason he wasn't falling off was because he couldn't muster the energy. Despite the bitterly cold wind, he was wearing nothing but a tiny leather kilt and a dirty bandage on one knee.

He took the soggy remnant of a cigarette out of his mouth and stubbed it out in his hand.

"Right," he said, "let's do it."

"That's all very well for you to say," said the horse. "But what if you have one of your dizzy spells? And your back is playing up. How shall I feel, being eaten because your back's played you up at the wrong moment?"

"It'll never happen," said the man. He lowered himself onto the chilly stones, and blew on his fingers. Then, from the horse's pack, he took a sword with an edge like a badly-maintained saw and gave a few halfhearted thrusts at the air.

"Still got the old knackcaroony," he said. He winced, and leaned against a tree.

"I'll swear this bloody sword gets heavier every day."

"You ought to pack it in, you know," said the horse. "Call it a day. This sort of thing at your time of life. It's not right."

The man rolled his eyes.

"Blast that damn distress auction. This is what comes of buying something that belonged to a wizard," he said, to the cold world in general. "I looked at your teeth, I looked at your hooves, it never occurred to me to *listen*."

"Who did you think was bidding against you?" said the horse.

Cohen the Barbarian stayed leaning against the tree. He was not entirely sure that he could pull himself upright again.

"You must have plenty of treasure stashed away," said the horse. "We could go Rimwards. How about it? Nice and warm. Get a nice warm place by a beach somewhere, what do you say?"

"No treasure," said Cohen. "Spent it all. Drank it all. Gave it all away. Lost it."

"You should have saved some for your old age."

"Never thought I'd *have* an old age."

"One day you're going to die," said the horse. "It might be today."

"I know. Why do you think I've come here?"

The horse turned and looked down towards the gorge. The road here was pitted and cracked. Young trees were pushing up between the stones. The forest crowded in on either side. In a few years, no one would know there'd even been a road here. By the look of it, no one knew now.

"You've come here to *die?*"

"No. But there's something I've always been meaning to do. Ever since I was a lad."

"Yeah?"

Cohen tried easing himself upright again. Tendons twanged their red-hot messages down his legs.

"My dad," he squeaked. He got control again. "My dad," he said, "said to me—" He fought for breath.

"Son," said the horse, helpfully.

"What?"

"Son," said the horse. "No father ever calls his boy 'son' unless he's about to impart wisdom. Well-known fact."

"It's *my* reminiscence."

"Sorry."

"He said . . . Son . . . yes, okay . . . Son, when you can

face down a troll in single combat, then you can do anything."

The horse blinked at him. Then it turned and looked down, again, through the tree-jostled road to the gloom of the gorge. There was a stone bridge down there.

A horrible feeling stole over it.

Its hooves jiggled nervously on the ruined road.

"Rimwards," it said. "Nice and warm."

"No."

"What's the good of killing a troll? What've you got when you've killed a troll?"

"A dead troll. That's the point. Anyway, I don't have to kill it. Just defeat it. One on one. Mano a . . . troll. And if I didn't try, my father would turn in his mound."

"You told *me* he drove you out of the tribe when you were eleven."

"Best day's work he ever did. Taught me to stand on other people's feet. Come over here, will you?"

The horse sidled over. Cohen got a grip on the saddle and heaved himself fully upright.

"And you're going to fight a troll today," said the horse.

Cohen fumbled in the saddlebag and pulled out his tobacco pouch. The wind whipped at the shreds as he rolled another skinny cigarette in the cup of his hands.

"Yeah," he said.

"And you've come all the way out here to do it."

"Got to," said Cohen. "When did you last see a bridge with a troll under it? There were hundreds of 'em when I was a lad. Now there's more trolls in the cities than there are in the mountains. Fat as butter, most of 'em. What did we fight all those wars for? Now . . . cross that bridge."

* * *

It was a lonely bridge across a shallow, white and treacherous river in a deep valley. The sort of place where you got—

A gray shape vaulted over the parapet and landed splayfooted in front of the horse. It waved a club.

"All *right*," it growled.

"Oh—" the horse began.

The troll blinked. Even the cold and cloudy winter skies seriously reduced the conductivity of a troll's silicon brain, and it had taken it this long to realize that the saddle was unoccupied.

It blinked again, because it could suddenly feel a knife point resting on the back of its neck.

"Hello," said a voice by its ear.

The troll swallowed. But very carefully.

"Look," it said desperately, "it's tradition, okay? A bridge like this, people ort to *expect* a troll.

" 'Ere," it added, as another thought crawled past, " 'ow come I never 'eard you creepin' up on me?"

"Because I'm *good* at it," said the old man.

"That's right," said the horse. "He's crept up on more people than you've had frightened dinners."

The troll risked a sideways glance.

"Bloody hell," it whispered. "You think you're Cohen the Barbarian, do you?"

"What do *you* think?" said Cohen the Barbarian.

"Listen," said the horse, "if he hadn't wrapped sacks round his knees you could have told by the clicking."

It took the troll some time to work this out.

"Oh, *wow*," it breathed. "On *my* bridge! Wow!"

"What?" said Cohen.

The troll ducked out of his grip and waved his hands frantically. "It's all right! It's all right!" it shouted, as Cohen advanced. "You've got me! You've got me! I'm not arguing! I just want to call the family up, all right? Otherwise no one'll ever believe me. *Cohen the Barbarian! On my* bridge!"

Its huge stony chest swelled further. "My bloody brother-in-law's always swanking about his huge bloody wooden bridge, that's all my wife ever talks about. Hah! I'd like to see the look on his face . . . Oh, no! What can you think of me?"

"Good question," said Cohen.

The troll dropped its club and seized one of Cohen's hands.

"Mica's the name," it said. "You don't know what an honor this is!"

He leaned over the parapet. "Beryl! Get up here! Bring the kids!"

He turned back to Cohen, his face glowing with happiness and pride.

"Beryl's always sayin' we ought to move out, get something better, but I tell her, this bridge has been in our family for generations, there's always been a troll under Death Bridge. It's tradition."

A huge female troll carrying two babies shuffled up the bank, followed by a tail of smaller trolls. They lined up behind their father, watching Cohen owlishly.

"This is Beryl," said the troll. His wife glowered at Cohen. "And this"—he propelled forward a scowling smaller edition of himself, clutching a junior version of his club—"is my lad Scree. A real chip off the old block. Going to take on the bridge when I'm gone, ain't you, Scree. Look lad, this is Cohen the Barbarian! What d'you think o' that, eh? On *our* bridge! We don't just have rich fat soft ole merchants like your Uncle Pyrites gets," said the troll, still talking to his son but smirking past him to his wife, "we 'ave proper heroes like they used to in the old days."

The troll's wife looked Cohen up and down.

"Rich, is he?" she said.

"Rich has got nothing to do with it," said the troll.

"Are you going to kill our dad?" said Scree suspiciously.

" '*Course* he is," said Mica severely. "It's his job. An' then I'll get famed in song an' story. This is Cohen the Barbarian, right, not some bugger from the village with a pitchfork. 'E's a famous hero come all this way to see us, so just you show 'im some respect.

"Sorry about that, sir," he said to Cohen. "Kids today. You know how it is."

The horse started to snigger.

"Now look—" Cohen began.

"I remember my dad tellin' me about you when I was a pebble," said Mica. " ' 'E bestrides the world like a clossus,' he said."

There was silence. Cohen wondered what a clossus was, and felt Beryl's stony gaze fixed upon him.

"He's just a little old man," she said. "He don't look very heroic to me. If he's so good, why ain't he *rich*?"

"Now you listen to me—" Mica began.

"This is what we've been waiting for, is it?" said his wife. "Sitting under a leaky bridge the whole time? Waiting for people that never come? Waiting for little old bandy-legged old men? I should have listened to my mother! You want me to let our son sit under a bridge waiting for some little old man to kill him? That's what being a troll is all about? Well, it ain't happening!"

"Now you just—"

"Hah! Pyrites doesn't get little old men! He gets big fat merchants! He's _someone_. You should have gone in with him when you had the chance!"

"I'd rather eat worms!"

"Worms? Hah? Since when could we afford to eat worms?"

"Can we have a word?" said Cohen.

He strolled toward the far end of the bridge, swinging his sword from one hand. The troll padded after him.

Cohen fumbled for his tobacco pouch. He looked up at the troll, and held out the bag.

"Smoke?" he said.

"That stuff can kill you," said the troll.

"Yes. But not today."

"Don't you hang about talking to your no-good friends!" bellowed Beryl, from her end of the bridge. "Today's your day for going down to the sawmill! You know Chert said he couldn't go on holding the job open if you weren't taking it seriously!"

Mica gave Cohen a sorrowful little smirk.

"She's very supportive," he said.

"I'm not climbing all the way down to the river to pull you out again!" Beryl roared. "You tell him about the billy goats, Mr. Big Troll!"

"Billy goats?" said Cohen.

"I don't know _anything_ about billy goats," said Mica. "She's always going on about billy goats. I have no knowledge whatsoever about billy goats." He winced.

They watched Beryl usher the young trolls down the bank and into the darkness under the bridge.

"The thing is," said Cohen, when they were alone, "I wasn't intending to kill you."

The troll's face fell.

"You weren't?"

"Just throw you over the bridge and steal whatever treasure you've got."

"You were?"

Cohen patted him on the back. "Besides," he said, "I

like to see people with . . . good memories. That's what the land needs. Good memories."

The troll stood to attention.

"I try to do my best, sir," it said. "My lad wants to go off to work in the city. I've tole him, there's bin a troll under this bridge for nigh on five hundred years—"

"So if you just hand over the treasure," said Cohen, "I'll be getting along."

The troll's face creased in sudden panic.

"Treasure? Haven't got any," it said.

"Oh, come *on*," said Cohen. "Well-set-up bridge like this?"

"Yeah, but no one uses this road any more," said Mica. "You're the first one along in months, and that's a fact. Beryl says I ought to have gone in with her brother when they built that new road over his bridge, but"—he raised his voice—"I said, there's been trolls under this bridge—"

"Yeah," said Cohen.

"The trouble is, the stones keep on falling out," said the troll. "And you'd never believe what those masons charge. Bloody dwarfs. You can't trust 'em." He leaned toward Cohen. "To tell you the truth, I'm having to work three days a week down at my brother-in-law's lumber mill just to make ends meet."

"I thought your brother-in-law had a bridge?" said Cohen.

"One of 'em has. But my wife's got brothers like dogs have fleas," said the troll. He looked gloomily into the torrent. "One of 'em's a lumber merchant down in Sour Water, one of 'em runs the bridge, and the big fat one is a merchant over on Bitter Pike. Call that a proper job for a troll?"

"One of them's in the bridge business, though," said Cohen.

"Bridge business? Sitting in a box all day charging people a silver piece to walk across? Half the time he ain't even there! He just pays some dwarf to take the money. And he calls himself a troll! You can't tell him from a human till you're right up close!"

Cohen nodded understandingly.

"D'you know," said the troll, "I have to go over and

have dinner with them every week? All three of 'em? And listen to 'em go on about moving with the times . . ."

He turned a big, sad face to Cohen.

"What's wrong with being a troll under a bridge?" he said. "I was brought up to be a troll under a bridge. I want young Scree to be a troll under a bridge after I'm gone. What's wrong with that? You've got to have trolls under bridges. Otherwise, what's it all about? What's it all *for?*"

They leaned morosely on the parapet, looking down into the white water.

"You know," said Cohen slowly, "I can remember when a man could ride all the way from here to the Blade Mountains and never see another living thing." He fingered his sword. "At least, not for very long."

He threw the butt of his cigarette into the water. "It's all farms now. All little farms, run by little people. And *fences* everywhere. Everywhere you look, farms and fences and little people."

"She's right, of course," said the troll, continuing some interior conversation. "There's no future in just jumping out from under a bridge."

"I mean," said Cohen, "I've nothing against farms. Or farmers. You've got to have them. It's just that they used to be a long way off, around the edges. Now *this* is the edge."

"Pushed back all the time," said the troll. "Changing all the time. Like my brother-in-law Chert. A lumber mill! A *troll* running a lumber mill! And you should see the mess he's making of Cutshade Forest!"

Cohen looked up, surprised.

"What, the one with the giant spiders in it?"

"Spiders? There ain't no spiders now. Just stumps."

"Stumps? *Stumps?* I used to like that forest. It was . . . well, it was darksome. You don't get proper darksome any more. You really knew what terror was, in a forest like that."

"You want darksome. He's replanting with spruce," said Mica.

"Spruce!"

"It's not his idea. He wouldn't know one tree from another. That's all down to Clay. He put him up to it."

Cohen felt dizzy. "Who's Clay?"

"I said I'd got *three* brothers-in-law, right? He's the merchant. So he said replanting would make the land easier to sell."

There was a long pause while Cohen digested this.

Then he said, "You can't sell Cutshade Forest. It doesn't belong to anyone."

"Yeah. He says that's why you can sell it."

Cohen brought his fist down on the parapet. A piece of stone detached itself and tumbled down into the gorge.

"Sorry," he said.

"That's all right. Bits fall off all the time, like I said."

Cohen turned. "What's happening? I remember all the big old wars. Don't you? You must have fought."

"I carried a club, yeah."

"It was supposed to be for a bright new future and law and stuff. That's what people said."

"Well, I fought because a big troll with a whip told me to," said Mica, cautiously. "But I know what you mean."

"I mean it wasn't for farms and spruce trees. Was it?"

Mica hung his head. "And here's me with this apology for a bridge. I feel really bad about it," he said. "You coming all this way and everything—"

"And there was some king or other," said Cohen, vaguely, looking at the water. "And I think there were some wizards. But there was a king. I'm pretty certain there was a king. Never met him. You know?" He grinned at the troll. "I can't remember his name. Don't think they ever told me his name."

* * *

About half an hour later Cohen's horse emerged from the gloomy woods onto a bleak, windswept moorland. It plodded on for a while before saying, "All right . . . how much did you give him?"

"Twelve gold pieces," said Cohen.

"Why'd you give him twelve gold pieces?"

"I didn't have more than twelve."

"You must be mad."

"When I was just starting out in the barbarian hero business," said Cohen, "every bridge had a troll under it. And you couldn't go through a forest like we've just gone through without a dozen goblins trying to chop your head off." He sighed. "I wonder what happened to 'em all?"

"You," said the horse.

"Well, yes. But I always thought there'd be some more. I always thought there'd be some more edges."

"How old are you?" said the horse.

"Dunno."

"Old enough to know better, then."

"Yeah. Right." Cohen lit another cigarette and coughed until his eyes watered.

"Going soft in the head!"

"Yeah."

"Giving your last dollar to a troll!"

"Yeah." Cohen wheezed a stream of smoke at the sunset.

"Why?"

Cohen stared at the sky. The red glow was as cold as the slopes of hell. An icy wind blew across the steppes, whipping at what remained of his hair.

"For the sake of the way things should be," he said.

"Hah!"

"For the sake of things that were."

"Hah!"

Cohen looked down.

He grinned.

"And for three addresses. One day I'm going to die," he said, "but not, I think, today."

* * *

The wind blew off the mountains, filling the air with fine ice crystals. It was too cold to snow. In weather like this wolves came down into villages, trees in the heart of the forest exploded when they froze. Except there were fewer and fewer wolves these days, and less and less forest.

In weather like this right-thinking people were indoors, in front of the fire.

Telling stories about heroes.

Choosing my favorite fantasy short story of all time turned out to be an astoundingly difficult assignment. In the time it took me to decide on Poul Anderson's "The Story of Hauk," I could have written several of my own stories, with less tooth grinding and hair pulling. I could not, in good conscience, take this duty lightly. While I cannot say for certain that this story is "my favorite fantasy tale of all time," I do believe that Mr. Anderson deserves special recognition for the valuable contributions he has made to the genre.

Although I had read and enjoyed fantasy novels as a child, including the classics such as the complete Oz series, the Narnia chronicles, and Tolkien's work, I did not become reacquainted with fantasy until college. After reading *Dune*, Michael Moorcock's Eternal Champion series, and any story I could find by Robert E. Howard, I rediscovered Norse mythology. A fellow medical student caught me reading it one day and recommended Poul Anderson's *The Broken Sword*. That book not only inspired me to leap back into fantasy reading, but also to begin writing my own stories.

Soon after my first book appeared in print, I had the opportunity to meet Mr. Anderson. I gave him a copy of *Godslayer* and told him how much his novels had inspired me. To my surprise, he ignored me, and I was positively devastated. It was only years later that I learned about his hearing impairment. The meetings that I have had with him since that time have shown him to be a kind and caring, as well as a talented, man. I hope to have the pleasure of his company again soon.

If you have a chance to pick up a copy of *The Merman's Children, The Demon of Scattery*, or any other of Poul Anderson's myriad fantasy and science fiction works, do so. You won't regret it. Meanwhile, I hope you enjoy this story.

—Mickey Zucker Reichert

THE TALE OF HAUK
by Poul Anderson

A man called Geirolf dwelt on the Great Fjord in Raumsdal. His father was Bui Hardhand, who owned a farm inland near the Dofra Fell. One year Bui went in viking to

Finnmark and brought back a woman he dubbed Gydha.
She became the mother of Geirolf. But because Bui already
had children by his wife, there would be small inheritances
for this by-blow.

Folk said uncanny things about Gydha. She was fair to
see, but spoke little, did no more work than she must, dwelt
by herself in a shack out of sight of the garth, and often
went for long stridings alone on the upland heaths, heedless
of cold, rain, and rovers. Bui did not visit her often. Her
son Geirolf did. He too was a moody sort, not much given
to playing with others, quick and harsh of temper. Big and
strong, he went abroad with his father already when he was
twelve, and in the next few years won the name of a mighty
though ruthless fighter.

Then Gydha died. They buried her near her shack, and
it was whispered that she spooked around it of nights. Soon
after, walking home with some men by moonlight from a
feast at a neighbor's, Bui clutched his breast and fell dead.
They wondered if Gydha had called him, maybe to accom-
pany her home to Finnmark, for there was no more sight
of her.

Geirolf bargained with his kin and got the price of a ship
for himself. Thereafter he gathered a crew, mostly younger
sons and a wild lot, and fared west. For a long while he
harried Scotland, Ireland, and the coasts south of the Channel, and won much booty. With some of this he bought his
farm on the Great Fjord. Meanwhile he courted Thyra, a
daughter of the yeoman Sigtryg Einarsson, and got her.

They had one son early on, Hauk, a bright and lively lad.
But thereafter five years went by until they had a daughter
who lived, Unn, and two years later a boy they called Einar.
Geirolf was a viking every summer, and sometimes wintered over in the Westlands. Yet he was a kindly father,
whose children were always glad to see him come roaring
home. Very tall and broad in the shoulders, he had long
red-brown hair and a full beard around a broad blunt-nosed
face whose eyes were ice-blue and slanted. He liked fine
clothes and heavy gold rings, which he also lavished on
Thyra.

Then the time came when Geirolf said he felt poorly and
would not fare elsewhere that season. Hauk was fourteen
years old and had been wild to go. "I'll keep my promise

to you as well as may be,'' Geirolf said, and sent men asking around. The best he could do was get his son a bench on a ship belonging to Ottar the Wide-Faring from Haalogaland in the north, who was trading along the coast and meant to do likewise overseas.

Hauk and Ottar took well to each other. In England, the man got the boy prime-signed so he could deal with Christians. Though neither was baptized, what he heard while they wintered there made Hauk thoughtful. Next spring they fared south to trade among the Moors, and did not come home until late fall.

Ottar was Geirolf's guest for a while, though he scowled to himself when his host broke into fits of deep coughing. He offered to take Hauk along on his voyages from now on and start the youth toward a good livelihood.

"You a chapman—the son of a viking?" Geirolf sneered. He had grown surly of late.

Hauk flushed. "You've heard what we did to those vikings who set on *us,*" he answered.

"Give our son his head," was Thyra's smiling rede, "or he'll take the bit between his teeth."

The upshot was that Geirolf grumbled agreement, and Hauk fared off. He did not come back for five years.

Long were the journeys he took with Ottar. By ship and horse, they made their way to Uppsala in Svithjodh, thence into the wilderness of the Keel after pelts; amber they got on the windy strands of Jutland, salt herring along the Sound; seeking beeswax, honey, and tallow, they pushed beyond Holmgard to the fair at Kiev; walrus ivory lured them past North Cape, through bergs and floes to the land of the fur-clad Biarmians; and they bore many goods west. They did not hide that the wish to see what was new to them drove them as hard as any hope of gain.

In those days King Harald Fairhair went widely about in Norway, bringing all the land under himself. Lesser kings and chieftains must either plight faith to him or meet his wrath; it crushed whomever would stand fast. When he entered Raumsdal, he sent men from garth to garth as was his wont, to say he wanted oaths and warriors.

"My older son is abroad," Geirolf told these, "and my younger still a stripling. As for myself—" He coughed, and blood flecked his beard. The king's men did not press the matter.

But now Geirolf's moods grew ever worse. He snarled at everybody, cuffed his children and housefolk, once drew a dagger and stabbed to death a thrall who chances to spill some soup on him. When Thyra reproached him for this, he said only, "Let them know I am not yet altogether hollowed out. I can still wield blade." And he looked at her so threateningly from beneath his shaggy brows that she, no coward, withdrew in silence.

A year later, Hauk Geirolfsson returned to visit his parents.

That was on a chill fall noontide. Whitecaps chopped beneath a whistling wind and cast spindrift salty onto lips. Clifftops on either side of the fjord were lost in mist. Above blew cloud wrack like smoke. Hauk's ship, a wide-beamed knorr, rolled, pitched, and creaked as it beat its way under sail. The owner stood in the bows, wrapped in a flame-red cloak, an uncommonly big young man, yellow hair tossing around a face akin to his father's weatherbeaten though still scant of beard. When he saw the arm of the fjord that he wanted to enter, he pointed with a spear at whose head he had bound a silk pennon. When he saw Disafoss pouring in a white stream down the blue-gray stone wall to larboard, and beyond the waterfall at the end of that arm lay his old home, he shouted for happiness.

Geirolf had rich holdings. The hall bulked over all else, heavy-timbered, brightly painted, dragon heads arching from rafters and gables. Elsewhere around the yard were cookhouse, smokehouse, bathhouse, storehouses, workshop, stables, barns, women's bower. Several cabins for hirelings and their families were strewn beyond. Fishing boats lay on the strand near a shed which held the master's dragonship. Behind the steading, land sloped sharply upward through a narrow dale, where fields were walled with stones grubbed out of them and now stubbled after harvest. A bronze-leaved oakenshaw stood untouched not far from the buildings; and a mile inland, where hills humped themselves toward the mountains, rose a darkling wall of pinewood.

Spearheads and helmets glimmered ashore. But men saw it was a single craft bound their way, white shield on the mast. As the hull slipped alongside the little wharf, they lowered their weapons. Hauk sprang from bow to dock in a single leap and whooped.

Geirolf trod forth. "Is that you, my son?" he called. His voice was hoarse from coughing; he had grown gaunt and sunken-eyed; the ax that he bore shivered in his hand.

"Yes, father, yes, home again," Hauk stammered. He could not hide his shock.

Maybe this drove Geirolf to anger. Nobody knew; he had become impossible to get along with. "I could well-nigh have hoped otherwise," he rasped. "An unfriend would give me something better than strawdeath."

The rest of the men, housecarls and thralls alike, flocked about Hauk to bid him welcome. Among them was a burly, grizzled yeoman whom he knew from aforetime, Leif Egilsson, a neighbor come to dicker for a horse. When he was small, Hauk had often wended his way over a woodland trail to Leif's garth to play with the children there.

He called his crew to him. They were not just Norse, but had among them Danes, Swedes, and English, gathered together over the years as he found them trustworthy. "You brought a mickle for me to feed," Geirolf said. Luckily, the wind bore his words from all but Hauk. "Where's your master Ottar?"

The young man stiffened. "He's my friend, never my master," he answered. "This is my own ship, bought with my own earnings. Ottar abides in England this year. The West Saxons have a new king, one Alfred, whom he wants to get to know."

"Time was when it was enough to know how to get sword past a Westman's shield," Geirolf grumbled.

Seeing peace down by the water, women and children hastened from the hall to meet the newcomers. At their head went Thyra. She was tall and deep-bosomed; her gown blew around a form still straight and freely striding. But as she neared, Hauk saw that the gold of her braids was dimmed and sorrow had furrowed her face. Nonetheless she kindled when she knew him. "Oh, thrice welcome, Hauk!" she said low. "How long can you bide with us?"

After his father's greeting, it had been in his mind to say he must soon be off. But when he spied who walked behind

his mother, he said, "We thought we might be guests here
the winter through, if that's not too much of a burden."

"Never—" began Thyra. Then she saw where his gaze
had gone, and suddenly she smiled.

Alfhild Leifsdottir had joined her widowed father on this
visit. She was two years younger than Hauk, but they had
been glad of each other as playmates. Today she stood a
maiden grown, lissome in a blue wadmal gown, heavily
crowned with red locks above great green eyes, straight
nose, and gently curved mouth. Though he had known
many a woman, none struck him as being so fair.

He grinned at her and let his cloak flap open to show
his finery of broidered, fur-lined tunic, linen shirt and
breeks, chased leather boots, gold on arms and neck and
sword-hilt. She paid them less heed than she did him when
they spoke.

Thus Hauk and his men moved to Geirolf's hall. He
brought plentiful gifts, there was ample food and drink, and
their tales of strange lands—their songs, dances, games,
jests, manners—made them good housefellows in these
lengthening nights.

Already on the next morning, he walked out with Alfhild. Rain had cleared the air, heaven and fjord sparkled,
wavelets chuckled beneath a cool breeze from the woods.
Nobody else was on the strand where they went.

"So you grow mighty as a chapman, Hauk," Alfhild
teased. "Have you never gone in viking . . . only once, only
to please your father?"

"No," he answered gravely. "I fail to see what manliness
lies in falling on those too weak to defend themselves. We
traders must be stronger and more warskilled than any who
may seek to plunder us." A thick branch of driftwood,
bleached and hardened, lay nearby. Hauk picked it up and
snapped it between his hands. Two other men would have
had trouble doing that. It gladdened him to see Alfhild
glow at the sight. "Nobody has tried us twice," he said.

They passed the shed where Geirolf's dragon lay on roll-
ers. Hauk opened the door for a peek at the remembered
slim shape. A sharp whiff from the gloom within brought
his nose wrinkling. "Whew!" he snorted. "Dry rot."

"Poor *Fireworm* has long lain idle," Alfhild sighed. "In
later years, your father's illness has gnawed him till he

doesn't even see to the care of his ship. He knows he will never take it a-roving again.''

"I feared that,'' Hauk murmured.

"We grieve for him on our own garth too,'' she said. "In former days, he was a staunch friend to us. Now we bear with his ways, yes, insults that would make my father draw blade on anybody else.''

"That is dear of you,'' Hauk said, staring straight before him. "I'm very thankful.''

"You have not much cause for that, have you?'' she asked. "I mean, you've been away so long . . . Of course, you have your mother. She's borne the brunt, stood like a shield before your siblings—'' She touched her lips. "I talk too much.''

"You talk as a friend,'' he blurted. "May we always be friends.''

They wandered on, along a path from shore to fields. It went by the shaw. Through boles and boughs and falling leaves, they saw Thor's image and altar among the trees. "I'll make offering here for my father's health,'' Hauk said, "though truth to tell, I've more faith in my own strength than in any gods.''

"You have seen lands where strange gods rule,'' she nodded.

"Yes, and there too, they do not steer things well,'' he said. "It was in a Christian realm that a huge wolf came raiding flocks, on which no iron would bite. When it took a baby from a hamlet near our camp, I thought I'd be less than a man did I not put an end to it.''

"What happened?'' she asked breathlessly, and caught his arm.

"I wrestled it barehanded—no foe of mine was ever more fell—and at last broke its neck.'' He pulled back a sleeve to show scars of terrible bites. "Dead, it changed into a man they had outlawed that year for his evil deeds. We burned the lich to make sure it would not walk again, and thereafter the folk had peace. And . . . we had friends, in a country otherwise wary of us.''

She looked on him in the wonder he had hoped for.

Erelong she must return with her father. But the way between the garths was just a few miles, and Hauk often rode or skied through the woods. At home, he and his men helped do what work there was, and gave merriment where it had long been little known.

Thyra owned this to her son, on a snowy day when they were by themselves. They were in the women's bower, whither they had gone to see a tapestry she was weaving. She wanted to know how it showed against those of the Westlands; he had brought one such, which hung above the benches in the hall. Here, in the wide quiet room, was dusk, for the day outside had become a tumbling whiteness. Breath steamed from lips as the two of them spoke. It smelled sweet; both had drunk mead until they could talk freely.

"You did better than you knew when you came back," Thyra said. "You blew like spring into this winter of ours. Einar and Unn were withering; they blossom again in your nearness."

"Strangely has our father changed," Hauk answered sadly. "I remember once when I was small how he took me by the hand on a frost-clear night, led me forth under the stars, and named for me the pictures in them, Thor's Wain, Freyja's Spindle—how wonderful he made them, how his deep slow laughterful voice filled the dark."

"A wasting illness draws the soul inward," his mother said. "He . . . has no more manhood . . . and it tears him like fangs that he will die helpless in bed. He must strike out at someone, and here we are."

She was silent a while before she added: "He will not live out the year. Then you must take over."

"I must be gone when weather allows," Hauk warned. "I promised Ottar."

"Return as soon as may be," Thyra said. "We have need of a strong man, the more so now when yonder King Harald would reave their freehold rights from yeomen."

"It would be well to have a hearth of my own." Hauk stared past her, toward the unseen woods. Her worn face creased in a smile.

Suddenly they heard yells from the yard below. Hauk ran out onto the gallery and looked down. Geirolf was shambling after an aged carl named Atli. He had a whip in his hand and was lashing it across the white locks and wrinkled cheeks of the man, who could not run fast either and who sobbed.

"What is this?" broke from Hauk. He swung himself over the rail, hung, and let go. The drop would at least have jarred the wind out of most. He, though, bounced from where he landed, ran behind his father, caught hold of the whip and wrenched it from Geirolf's grasp. "What are you doing?"

Geirolf howled and struck his son with a doubled fist. Blood trickled from Hauk's mouth. He stood fast. Atli sank to hands and knees and fought not to weep.

"Are you also a heelbiter of mine?" Geirolf bawled.

"I'd save you from your madness, father," Hauk said in pain. "Atli followed you to battle ere I was born—he dandled me on his knee—and he's a free man. What has he done, that you'd bring down on us the anger of his kinfolk?"

"Harm not the skipper, young man," Atli begged. "I fled because I'd sooner die than lift hand against my skipper."

"Hell swallow you both!" Geirolf would have cursed further, but the coughing came on him. Blood drops flew through the snowflakes, down onto the white earth, where they mingled with the drip from the heads of Hauk and Atli. Doubled over, Geirolf let them half lead, half carry him to his shut-bed. There he closed the panel and lay alone in darkness.

"What happened between you and him?" Hauk asked.

"I was fixing to shoe a horse," Atli said into a ring of gaping onlookers. "He came in and wanted to know why I'd not asked his leave. I told him 'twas plain Kilfaxi needed new shoes. Then he hollered, 'I'll show you I'm no log in the woodpile!' and snatched yon whip off the wall and took after me." The old man squared his shoulders. "We'll speak no more of this, you hear?" he ordered the household.

Nor did Geirolf, when next day he let them bring him some broth.

For more reasons than this, Hauk came to spend much of his time at Leif's garth. He would return in such a glow that even the reproachful looks of his young sister and brother, even the sullen or the weary greeting of his father, could not dampen it.

At last, when lengthening days and quickening blood bespoke seafarings soon to come, that happened which surprised nobody. Hauk told them in the hall that he wanted to marry Alfhild Leifsdottir, and prayed Geirolf press the suit for him. "What must be, will be," said his father, a better grace than awaited. Union of the families was clearly good for both.

Leif Egilsson agreed, and Alfhild had nothing but aye to say. The betrothal feast crowded the whole neighborhood together in cheer. Thyra hid the trouble within her, and Geirolf himself was calm if not blithe.

Right after, Hauk and his men were busking themselves to fare. Regardless of his doubts about gods, he led in offering for a safe voyage to Thor, Aegir, and St. Michael. But Alfhild found herself a quiet place alone, to cut runes on an ash tree in the name of Freyja.

When all was ready, she was there with the folk of Geirolf's stead to see the sailors off. That morning was keen, wind roared in trees and skirled between cliffs, waves ran green and white beneath small flying clouds. Unn could not but hug her brother who was going, while Einar gave him a handclasp that shook. Thyra said, "Come home hale and early, my son." Alfhild mostly stored away the sight of Hauk. Atli and others of the household mumbled this and that.

Geirolf shuffled forward. The cane on which he leaned rattled among the stones of the beach. He was hunched in a hairy cloak against the sharp air. His locks fell tangled almost to the coal-smoldering eyes. "Father, farewell," Hauk said, taking his free hand.

"You mean 'fare far,' don't you?" Geirolf grated. " 'Fare far and never come back.' You'd like that, wouldn't you? But we will meet again. Oh, yes, we will meet again."

Hauk dropped the hand. Geirolf turned and sought the house. The rest behaved as if they had not heard, speaking loudly, amidst yelps of laughter, to overcome those words of foreboding. Soon Hauk called his orders to be gone.

Men scrambled aboard the laden ship. Its sail slatted aloft and filled, the mooring lines were cast loose, the hull stood out to sea. Alfhild waved until it was gone from sight behind the bend where Disafoss fell.

The summer passed—plowing, sowing, lambing, calving, farrowing, hoeing, reaping, flailing, butchering—rain, hail, sun, stars, loves, quarrels, births, deaths—and the season wore toward fall. Alfhild was seldom at Geirolf's garth, nor was Leif; for Hauk's father grew steadily worse. After midsummer he could no longer leave his bed. But often he whispered, between lung-tearing coughs, to those who tended him, "I would kill you if I could."

On a dark day late in the season, when rain roared about the hall and folk and hounds huddled close to fires that hardly lit the gloom around, Geirolf awoke from a heavy sleep. Thyra marked it and came to him. Cold and dankness gnawed their way through her clothes. The fever was in him like a brand. He plucked restlessly at his blanket, where he half sat in his short shut-bed. Though flesh had wasted from the great bones, his fingers still had strength to tear the wool. The mattress rustled under him. "Straw-death, straw-death," he muttered.

Thyra laid a palm on his brow. "Be at ease," she said.

It dragged from him: "You'll not be rid . . . of me . . . so fast . . . by straw-death." An icy sweat broke forth and the last struggle began.

Long it was, Geirolf's gasps and the sputtering flames the only noises within that room, while rain and wind ramped outside and night drew in. Thyra stood by the bedside to wipe the sweat off her man, blood and spittle from his beard. A while after sunset, he rolled his eyes back and died.

Thyra called for water and lamps. She cleansed him, clad him in his best, and laid him out. A drawn sword was·on his breast.

In the morning, thralls and carls alike went forth under her orders. A hillock stood in the fields about half a mile inland from the house. They dug a grave chamber in the top of this, lining it well with timber. "Won't you bury him in his ship?" asked Atli.

"It is rotten, unworthy of him," Thyra said. Yet she made them haul it to the barrow, around which she had stones to outline a hull. Meanwhile folk readied a grave-ale, and messengers bade neighbors come.

When all were there, men of Geirolf's carried him on a litter to his resting place and put him in, together with weapons and a jar of Southland coins. After beams had roofed the chamber, his friends from aforetime took shovels and covered it well. They replaced the turfs of sere

grass, leaving the hillock as it had been save that it was
now bigger. Einar Thorolfsson kindled his father's ship. It
burned till dusk, when the horns of the new moon stood
over the fjord. Meanwhile folk had gone back down to the
garth to feast and drink. Riding home next day, well gifted
by Thyra, they told each other that this had been an honor-
able burial.

The moon waxed. On the first night that it rose full,
Geirolf came again.

A thrall named Kark had been late in the woods, seeking
a strayed sheep. Coming home, he passed near the howe.
The moon was barely above the pines; long shivery glades
of light ran on the water, lost themselves in shadows
ashore, glinted wanly anew where a bedewed stone wall
snaked along a stubblefield. Stars were few. A great
stillness lay on the land; not even an owl hooted, until all
at once dogs down in the garth began howling. It was not
the way they howled at the moon; across the mile between,
it sounded ragged and terrified. Kark felt the chill close in
around him, and hastened toward home.

Something heavy trod the earth. He looked around and
saw the bulk of a huge man coming across the field from
the barrow. "Who's that?" he called uneasily. No voice
replied, but the weight of those footfalls shivered through
the ground into his bones. Kark swallowed, gripped his
staff, and stood where he was. But then the shape came so
near that moonlight picked out the head of Geirolf. Kark
screamed, dropped his weapon, and ran.

Geirolf followed slowly, clumsily behind.

Down in the garth, light glimmered red as doors opened.
Folk saw Kark running, gasping for breath. Atli and Einar
led the way out, each with a torch in one hand, a sword in
the other. Little could they see beyond the wild flame-
gleam. Kark reached them, fell, writhed on the hard-beaten
clay of the yard, and wailed.

"What is it, you lackwit?" Atli snapped, and kicked him.
Then Einar pointed his blade.

"A stranger—" Atli began.

Geirolf rocked into sight. The mould of the grave clung
to him. His eyes stared unblinking, unmoving, blank in the
moonlight, out of a gray face whereon the skin crawled.

The teeth in his tangled beard were dry. No breath smoked from his nostrils. He held out his arms, crook-fingered.

"Father!" Einar cried. The torch hissed from his grip, flickered weakly at his feet, and went out. The men at his back jammed the doorway of the hall as they sought its shelter.

"The skipper's come again," Atli quavered. He sheathed his sword, though that was hard when his hand shook, and made himself step forward. "Skipper, d'you know your old shipmate Atli?"

The dead man grabbed him, lifted him, and dashed him to earth. Einar heard bones break. Atli jerked once and lay still. Geirolf trod him and Kark underfoot. There was a sound of cracking and rending. Blood spurted forth.

Blindly, Einar swung blade. The edge smote but would not bite. A wave of grave-chill passed over him. He whirled and bounded back inside.

Thyra had seen. "Bar the door," she bade. The windows were already shuttered against frost. "Men, stand fast. Women, stoke up the fires."

They heard the lich groping about the yard. Walls creaked where Geirolf blundered into them. Thyra called through the door, "Why do you wish us ill, your own household?" But only those noises gave answer. The hounds cringed and whined.

"Lay iron at the doors and under every window," Thyra commanded. "If it will not cut him, it may keep him out."

All that night, then, folk huddled in the hall. Geirolf climbed onto the roof and rode the ridgepole, drumming his heels on the shakes till the whole building boomed. A little before sunrise, it stopped. Peering out by the first dull dawnlight, Thyra saw no mark of her husband but his deep-sunken footprints and the wrecked bodies he had left.

"He grew so horrible before he died," Unn wept. "Now he can't rest, can he?"

"We'll make him an offering," Thyra said through her weariness. "It may be we did not give him enough when we buried him."

Few would follow her to the howe. Those who dared, brought along the best horse on the farm. Einar, as the son of the house when Hauk was gone, himself cut its throat after a sturdy man had given the hammer-blow. Carls and

wenches butchered the carcass, which Thyra and Unn
cooked over a fire in whose wood was blent the charred
rest of the dragonship. Nobody cared to eat much of the
flesh or broth. Thyra poured what was left over the bones,
upon the grave.

Two ravens circled in sight, waiting for folk to go so they
could take the food. "Is that a good sign?" Thyra sighed.
"Will Odin fetch Geirolf home?"

That night everybody who had not fled to neighboring
steads gathered in the hall. Soon after the moon rose, they
heard the footfalls come nearer and nearer. They heard
Geirolf break into the storehouse and worry the laid-out
bodies of Atli and Kark. They heard him kill cows in the
barn. Again he rode the roof.

In the morning Leif Egilsson arrived, having gotten the
news. He found Thyra too tired and shaken to do anything
further. "The ghost did not take your offering," he said,
"but maybe the gods will."

In the oakenshaw, he led the giving of more beasts.
There was talk of a thrall for Odin, but he said that would
not help if this did not. Instead, he saw to the proper burial
of the slain, and of those kine which nobody would dare
eat. That night he abode there.

And Geirolf came back. Throughout the darkness, he
tormented the home which had been his.

"I will bide here one more day," Leif said next sunrise.
"We all need rest—though ill is it that we must sleep during
daylight when we've so much readying for winter to do."

By that time, some other neighborhood men were also
on hand. They spoke loudly of how they would hew the
lich asunder.

"You know not what you boast of," said aged Grim the
Wise. "Einar smote, and he strikes well for a lad, but the iron
would not bite. It never will. Ghost-strength is in Geirolf,
and all the wrath he could not set free during his life."

That night folk waited breathless for moonrise. But when
the gnawed shield climbed over the pines, nothing stirred.
The dogs, too, no longer seemed cowed. About midnight,
Grim murmured into the shadows, "Yes, I thought so.
Geirolf walks only when the moon is full."

"Then tomorrow we'll dig him up and burn him!" Leif
said.

"No," Grim told them. "That would spell the worst of luck for everybody here. Don't you see, the anger and un-peace which will not let him rest, those could be forever unslaked? They could not but bring doom on the burners."

"What then can we do?" Thyra asked dully.

"Leave this stead," Grim counselled, "at least when the moon is full."

"Hard will that be," Einar sighed. "Would that my brother Hauk were here."

"He should have returned erenow," Thyra said. "May we in our woe never know that he has come to grief himself."

In truth, Hauk had not. His wares proved welcome in Flanders, where he bartered for cloth that he took across to England. There Ottar greeted him, and he met the young King Alfred. At that time there was no war going on with the Danes, who were settling into the Danelaw and thus in need of household goods. Hauk and Ottar did a thriving business among them. This led them to think they might do as well in Iceland, whither Norse folk were moving who liked not King Harald Fairhair. They made a voyage to see. Foul winds hampered them on the way home. Hence fall was well along when Hauk's ship returned.

The day was still and cold. Low overcast turned sky and water the hue of iron. A few gulls cruised and mewed, while under them sounded creak and splash of oars, swear-ing of men, as the knorr was rowed. At the end of the fjord-branch, garth and leaves were tiny splashes of color, lost against rearing cliffs, brown fields, murky wildwood. Straining ahead from afar, Hauk saw that a bare handful of men came down to the shore, moving listlessly more than watchfully. When his craft was unmistakable, though, a few women—no youngsters—sped from the hall as if they could not wait. Their cries came to him more thin than the gulls'.

Hauk lay alongside the dock. Springing forth, he cried merrily, "Where is everybody? How fares Alfhild?" His words lost themselves in silence. Fear touched him. "What's wrong?"

Thyra trod forth. Years might have gone by during his summer abroad, so changed was she. "You are barely in time," she said in an unsteady tone. Taking his hands, she told him how things stood.

Hauk stared long into emptiness. At last, "Oh, no," he whispered. "What's to be done?"

"We hoped you might know that, my son," Thyra answered. "The moon will be full tomorrow night."

His voice stumbled. "I am no wizard. If the gods themselves would not lay this ghost, what can I do?"

Einar spoke, in the brashness of youth: "We thought you might deal with him as you did with the werewolf."

"But that was—No, I cannot!" Hauk croaked. "Never ask me."

"Then I fear we must leave," Thyra said. "For aye. You see how many had already fled, thrall and free alike, though nobody else has a place for them. We've not enough left to farm these acres. And who would buy them of us? Poor must we go, helpless as the poor ever are."

"Iceland—" Hauk wet his lips. "Well, you shall not want while I live." Yet he had counted on this homestead, whether to dwell on or sell.

"Tomorrow we move over to Leif's garth, for the next three days and nights," Thyra said.

Unn shuddered. "I know not if I can come back," she said. "This whole past month here, I could hardly ever sleep." Dulled skin and sunken eyes bore her out.

"What else would you do?" Hauk asked.

"Whatever I can," she stammered, and broke into tears. He knew: wedding herself too young to whoever would have her dowryless, poor though the match would be—or making her way to some town to turn whore, his little sister.

"Let me think on this," Hauk begged. "Maybe I can hit on something."

His crew were also daunted when they heard. At eventide they sat in the hall and gave only a few curt words about what they had done in foreign parts. Everyone lay down early on bed, bench, or floor, but none slept well.

Before sunset, Hauk had walked forth alone. First he sought the grave of Atli. "I'm sorry, dear old friend," he said. Afterward he went to Geirolf's howe. It loomed yellow-gray with withered grass wherein grinned the skull of the slaughtered horse. At its foot were strewn the charred bits of the ship, inside stones that outlined a greater but unreal hull. Around reached stubblefields and walls, hemmed in by woods on one side and water on the other, rock lifting sheer beyond. The chill and the quiet had deepened.

Hauk climbed to the top of the barrow and stood there a while, head bent downward. "Oh, father," he said, "I learned doubt in Christian lands. What's right for me to do?" There was no answer. He made a slow way back to the dwelling.

All were up betimes next day. It went slowly over the woodland path to Leif's, for animals must be herded along. The swine gave more trouble than most. Hauk chuckled once, not very merrily, and remarked that at least this took folk's minds off their sorrows. He raised no mirth.

But he had Alfhild ahead of him. At the end of the way, he sprinted into the yard. Leif owned less land than Geirolf, his buildings were smaller and fewer, most of his guests must house outdoors in sleeping bags. Hauk paid no heed. "Alfhild!" he called. "I'm here!"

She left the dough she was kneading and sped to him. They hugged each other hard and long, in sight of the whole world. None thought that shame, as things were. At last she said, striving not to weep. "How we've longed for you! Now the nightmare can end."

He stepped back. "What mean you?" he uttered slowly, knowing full well.

"Why—" She was bewildered. "Won't you give him his second death?"

Hauk gazed past her for some heartbeats before he said: "Come aside with me."

Hand in hand, they wandered off. A meadow lay hidden from the garth by a stand of aspen. Elsewhere around, pines speared into a sky that today was bright. Clouds drifted on a nipping breeze. Far off, a stag bugled.

Hauk spread feet apart, hooked thumbs in belt, and made himself meet her eyes. "You think over-highly of my strength," he said.

"Who has more?" she asked. "We kept ourselves going by saying you would come home and make things good again."

"What if the drow is too much for me?" His words sounded raw through the hush. Leaves dropped yellow from their boughs.

She flushed. "Then your name will live."

"Yes—" Softly he spoke the words of the High One:
"Kine die, kinfolk die,
and so at last oneself.
This I know that never dies:
how dead men's deeds are deemed."

"You will do it!" she cried gladly.

His head shook before it drooped. "No. I will not. I dare not."

She stood as if he had clubbed her.

"Won't you understand?" he began.

The wound he had dealt her hopes went too deep. "So you show yourself a nithing!"

"Hear me," he said, shaken. "Were the lich anybody else's—"

Overwrought beyond reason, she slapped him and choked. "The gods bear witness, I give them my holiest oath, never will I wed you unless you do this thing. See, by my blood I swear." She whipped out her dagger and gashed her wrists. Red rills coursed out and fell in drops on the fallen leaves.

He was aghast. "You know not what you say. You're too young, you've been too sheltered. *Listen.*"

She would have fled from him, but he gripped her shoulders and made her stand. "Listen," went between his teeth. "Geirolf is still my father—my father who begot me, reared me, named the stars for me, weaponed me to make my way in the world. How can I fight him? Did I slay him, what horror would come upon me and mine?"

"O-o-oh," broke from Alfhild. She sank to the ground and wept as if to tear loose her ribs.

He knelt, held her, gave what soothing he could. "Now I know," she mourned. "Too late."

"Never," he murmured. "We'll fare abroad if we must, take new land, make new lives together."

"No," she gasped. "Did I not swear? What doom awaits an oathbreaker?"

Then he was long still. Heedlessly though she had spoken, her blood lay in the earth, which would remember.

He too was young. He straightened. "I will fight," he said.

Now she clung to him and pleaded that he must not. But

an iron calm had come over him. "Maybe I will not be cursed," he said. "Or maybe the curse will be no more than I can bear."

"It will be mine too, I who brought it on you," she plighted herself.

Hand in hand again, they went back to the garth. Leif spied the haggard look on them and half guessed what had happened. "Will you fare to meet the drow, Hauk?" he asked. "Wait till I can have Grim the Wise brought here. His knowledge may help you."

"No," said Hauk. "Waiting would weaken me. I go this night."

Wide eyes stared at him—all but Thyra's; she was too torn.

Toward evening he busked himself. He took no helm, shield, or byrnie, for the dead man bore no weapons. Some said they would come along, armored themselves well, and offered to be at his side. He told them to follow him, but no farther than to watch what happened. Their iron would be of no help, and he thought they would only get in each other's way, and his, when he met the overhuman might of the drow. He kissed Alfhild, his mother, and his sister, and clasped hands with his brother, bidding them stay behind if they loved him.

Long did the few miles of path seem, and gloomy under the pines. The sun was on the world's rim when men came out in the open. They looked past fields and barrow down to the empty garth, the fjordside cliffs, the water where the sun lay as half an ember behind a trail of blood. Clouds hurried on a wailing wind through a greenish sky. Cold struck deep. A wolf howled.

"Wait here," Hauk said.

"The gods be with you," Leif breathed.

"I've naught tonight but my own strength," Hauk said. "Belike none of us ever had more."

His tall form, clad in leather and wadmal, showed black athwart the sunset as he walked from the edge of the woods, out across plowland toward the crouching howe. The wind fluttered his locks, a last brightness until the sun went below. Then for a while the evenstar alone had light.

Hauk reached the mound. He drew sword and leaned on it, waiting. Dusk deepened. Star after star came forth, small

and strange. Clouds blowing across them picked up a glow
from the still unseen moon.

It rose at last above the treetops. Its ashen sheen
stretched gashes of shadow across earth. The wind
loudened.

The grave groaned. Turfs, stones, timbers swung aside.
Geirolf shambled out beneath the sky. Hauk felt the
ground shudder under his weight. There came a carrion
stench, though the only sign of rotting was on the dead
man's clothes. His eyes peered dim, his teeth gnashed dry
in a face at once well remembered and hideously changed.
When he saw the living one who waited, he veered and
lumbered thitherward.

"Father," Hauk called. "It's I, your eldest son."

The drow drew nearer.

"Halt, I beg you," Hauk said unsteadily. "What can I do
to bring you peace?"

A cloud passed over the moon. It seemed to be hurtling
through heaven. Geirolf reached for his son with fingers
that were ready to clutch and tear. "Hold," Hauk shrilled.
"No step farther."

He could not see if the gaping mouth grinned. In another
stride, the great shape came well-nigh upon him. He lifted
his sword and brought it singing down. The edge struck
truly, but slid aside. Geirolf's skin heaved, as if to push the
blade away. In one more step, he laid grave-cold hands
around Hauk's neck.

Before that grip could close, Hauk dropped his useless
weapon, brought his wrists up between Geirolf's, and
mightily snapped them apart. Nails left furrows, but he was
free. He sprang back, into a wrestler's stance.

Geirolf moved in, reaching. Hauk hunched under those
arms and himself grabbed waist and thigh. He threw his
shoulder against a belly like rock. Any live man would have
gone over, but the lich was too heavy.

Geirolf smote Hauk on the side. The blows drove him
to his knees and thundered on his back. A foot lifted to
crush him. He rolled off and found his own feet again.
Geirolf lurched after him. The hastening moon linked their
shadows. The wolf howled anew, but in fear. Watching men
gripped spearshafts till their knuckles stood bloodless.

Hauk braced his legs and snatched for the first hold, around both of Geirolf's wrists. The drow strained to break loose and could not; but neither could Hauk bring him down. Sweat ran moon-bright over the son's cheeks and darkened his shirt. The reek of it was at least a living smell in his nostrils. Breath tore at his gullet. Suddenly Geirolf wrenched so hard that his right arm tore from between his foe's fingers. He brought that hand against Hauk's throat. Hauk let go and slammed himself backward before he was throttled.

Geirolf stalked after him. The drow did not move fast. Hauk sped behind and pounced on the broad back. He seized an arm of Geirolf's and twisted it around. But the dead cannot feel pain. Geirolf stood fast. His other hand groped about, got Hauk by the hair, and yanked. Live men can hurt. Hauk stumbled away. Blood ran from his scalp into his eyes and mouth, hot and salt.

Geirolf turned and followed. He would not tire. Hauk had no long while before strength ebbed. Almost, he fled. Then the moon broke through to shine full on his father.

"You . . . shall not . . . go on . . . like that," Hauk mumbled while he snapped after air.

The drow reached him. They closed, grappled, swayed, stamped to and fro, in wind and flickery moonlight. Then Hauk hooked an ankle behind Geirolf's and pushed. With a huge thud, the drow crashed to earth. He dragged Hauk along.

Hauk's bones felt how terrible was the grip upon him. He let go his own hold. Instead, he arched his back and pushed himself away. His clothes ripped. But he burst free and reeled to his feet.

Geirolf turned over and began to crawl up. His back was once more to Hauk. The young man sprang. He got a knee hard in between the shoulderblades, while both his arms closed on the frosty head before him.

He hauled. With the last and greatest might that was in him, he hauled. Blackness went in tatters before his eyes.

There came a loud snapping sound. Geirolf ceased pawing behind him. He sprawled limp. His neck was broken, his jawbone wrenched from the skull. Hauk climbed slowly off him, shuddering. Geirolf stirred, rolled, half rose. He lifted a hand toward Hauk. It traced a line through the air and a line growing from beneath that. Then he slumped and lay still.

Hauk crumpled too.

"Follow me who dare!" Leif roared, and went forth across the field. One by one, as they saw nothing move ahead of them, the men came after. At last they stood hushed around Geirolf—who was only a harmless dead man now, though the moon shone bright in his eyes—and on Hauk, who had begun to stir.

"Bear him carefully down to the hall," Leif said. "Start a fire and tend him well. Most of you, take from the wood-pile and come back here. I'll stand guard meanwhile . . . though I think there is no need."

And so they burned Geirolf there in the field. He walked no more.

In the morning, they brought Hauk back to Leif's garth. He moved as if in dreams. The others were too awestruck to speak much. Even when Alfhild ran to meet him, he could only say, "Hold clear of me. I may be under a doom."

"Did the drow lay a weird on you?" she asked, spear-stricken.

"I know not," he answered. "I think I fell into the dark before he was wholly dead."

"What?" Leif well-nigh shouted. "You did not see the sign he drew?"

"Why, no," Hauk said. "How did it go?"

"Thus. Even afar and by moonlight, I knew." Leif drew it.

"That is no ill-wishing!" Grim cried. "That's naught but the Hammer."

Life rushed back into Hauk. "Do you mean what I hope?"

"He blessed you," Grim said. "You freed him from what he had most dreaded and hated—his strawdeath. The mad-ness in him is gone, and he has wended hence to the world beyond."

Then Hauk was glad again. He led them all in heaping earth over the ashes of his father, and in setting things right on the farm. That winter, at the feast of Thor, he and Alfhild were wedded. Afterward he became well thought of by King Harald, and rose to great wealth. From him and Alfhild stem many men whose names are still remembered. Here ends the tale of Hauk the Ghost Slayer.

In a typically quirky piece, accompanying the photo of himself in
Patti Perret's book *The Faces of Science Fiction*, R. A. Lafferty said,
of himself, "When I was forty-five years old, I tried to be a writer . . .
I became the best short-story writer in the world. I've been telling
people that for twenty years, but some of them don't believe me."

He was right. For a while in there, he was the best.

His stories brimmed with ideas that no one had ever thought
before. The use of language was uniquely his own—a Lafferty
sentence is instantly utterly recognizable. The cockeyed, strange,
and wonderful world he painted in his tales often seems nearer
to our own, more joyful and more recognizable than many a more
worthy or more literal account by other authors the world stopped
to notice. "This is how it is!" you tell yourself on discovering
Lafferty, delighted, awed, changed.

His science fiction story "Slow Tuesday Night" (which, like "In
Our Block" can be found in *Nine Hundred Grandmothers,* Lafferty's finest collection) seems more and more relevant as the rate
of change in the world out there grows ever-faster, ever-weirder.
But some things don't change—and that's what this story is about.
Here Lafferty paints a blue-collar portrait of aliens (if that is what
they are) in an American city. It's a tale of immigration and inte-
gration, and it has a measure of sly humor and wonder in there
with which to be getting by.

—Neil Gaiman

IN OUR BLOCK
by R. A. Lafferty

There were a lot of funny people in that block.

"You ever walk down that street?" Art Slick asked
Jim Boomer, who had just come onto him there.

"Not since I was a boy. After the overall factory burned
down, there was a faith healer had his tent pitched there
one summer. The street's just one block long and it dead-
ends on the railroad embankment. Nothing but a bunch of
shanties and weed-filled lots. The shanties looked different

today, though, and there seem to be more of them. I thought they pulled them all down a few months ago."

"Jim, I've been watching that first little building for two hours. There was a tractor-truck there this morning with a forty-foot trailer, and it loaded out of that little shanty. Cartons about eight inches by eight inches by three feet came down that chute. They weighed about thirty-five pounds each from the way the men handled them. Jim, they filled that trailer up with them, and then pulled it off."

"What's wrong with that, Art?"

"Jim, I said they filled that trailer up. From the drag on it it had about a sixty-thousand-pound load when it pulled out. They loaded a carton every three and a half seconds for two hours; that's two thousand cartons."

"Sure, lots of trailers run over the load limit nowdays. They don't enforce it very well."

"Jim, that shack's no more than a cracker box seven feet on a side. Half of it is taken up by a door, and inside a man in a chair behind a small table. You couldn't get anything else in that half. The other half is taken up by whatever that chute comes out of. You could pack six of those little shacks on that trailer."

"Let's measure it," Jim Boomer said. "Maybe it's bigger than it looks." The shack had a sign on it: *Make Sell Ship Anything Cut Price*. Jim Boomer measured the building with an old steel tape. The shack was a seven-foot cube, and there were no hidden places. It was set up on a few piers of broken bricks, and you could see under it.

"Sell you a new fifty-foot steel tape for a dollar," said the man in the chair in the little shack. "Throw that old one away." The man pulled a steel tape out of a drawer of his table-desk, though Art Slick was sure it had been a plain flat-top table with no place for a drawer.

"Fully retractable, rhodium-plated, Dort glide, Ramsey swivel, and it forms its own carrying case. One dollar," the man said.

Jim Boomer paid him a dollar for it. "How many of them you got?"

"I can have a hundred thousand ready to load out in ten minutes," the man said. "Eighty-eight cents each in hundred-thousand lots."

"Was that a trailer-load of steel tapes you shipped out this morning?" Art asked the man.

"No, that must have been something else. This is the first steel tape I ever made. Just got the idea when I saw you measuring my shack with that old beat-up one."

Art Slick and Jim Boomer went to the rundown building next door. It was smaller, about a six-foot cube, and the sign said *Public Stenographer*. The clatter of a typewriter was coming from it, but the noise stopped when they opened the door.

A dark, pretty girl was sitting in a chair before a small table. There was nothing else in the room, and no typewriter.

"I thought I heard a typewriter in here," Art said.

"Oh, that is me." The girl smiled. "Sometimes I amuse myself make typewriter noises like a public stenographer is supposed to."

"What would you do if someone came in to have some typing done?"

"What are you think? I do it of course."

"Could you type a letter for me?"

"Sure I can, man friend, two bits a page, good work, carbon copy, envelope and stamp."

"Ah, let's see how you do it. I will dictate to you while you type."

"You dictate first. Then I write. No sense mix up two things at one time."

Art dictated a long and involved letter that he had been meaning to write for several days. He felt like a fool droning it to the girl as she filed her nails. "Why is public stenographer always sit filing her nails?" she asked as Art droned. "But I try to do it right, file them down, grow them out again, then file them down some more. Been doing it all morning. It seems silly."

"Ah—that is all," Art said when he had finished dictating.

"Not P.S. Love and Kisses?" the girl asked.

"Hardly. It's a business letter to a person I barely know."

"I always say P.S. Love and Kisses to persons I barely know," the girl said. "Your letter will make three pages, six bits. Please you both step outside about ten seconds and

I write it. Can't do it when you watch." She pushed them out and closed the door.

Then there was silence.

"What are you doing in there, girl?" Art called.

"Want I sell you a memory course too? You forget already? I type a letter," the girl called.

"But I don't hear a typewriter going."

"What is? You want verisimilitude too? I should charge extra." There as a giggle, and then the sound of very rapid typing for about five seconds.

The girl opened the door and handed Art the three-page letter. It was typed perfectly, of course.

"There is something a little odd about this," Art said.

"Oh? The ungrammar of the letter is your own, sir. Should I have correct?"

"No. It is something else. Tell me the truth, girl: how does the man next door ship out trailer-loads of material from a building ten times too small to hold the stuff?"

"He cuts prices."

"Well, what are you people? The man next door resembles you."

"My brother-uncle. We tell everybody we are Innominee Indians."

"There is no such tribe," Jim Boomer said flatly.

"Is there not? Then we will have to tell people we are something else. You got to admit it sounds like Indian. What's the best Indian to be?"

"Shawnee," said Jim Boomer.

"Okay then we be Shawnee Indians. See how easy it is."

"We're already taken," Boomer said. "I'm a Shawnee and I know every Shawnee in town."

"Hi cousin!" the girl cried, and winked. "That's from a joke I learn, only the begin was different. See how foxy I turn all your questions."

"I have two-bits coming out of my dollar," Art said.

"I know," the girl said. "I forgot for a minute what design is on the back of the two-bitser piece, so I stall while I remember it. Yes, the funny bird standing on the bundle of firewood. One moment till I finish it. Here." She handed the quarter to Art Slick. "And you tell everybody there's a smoothie public stenographer here who types letters good."

"Without a typewriter," said Art Slick. "Let's go, Jim."

"P.S. Love and Kisses," the girl called after them.

The Cool Man Club was next door, a small and shabby beer bar. The bar girl could have been a sister of the public stenographer.

"We'd like a couple of Buds, but you don't seem to have a stock of anything," Art said.

"Who needs stock?" the girl asked. "Here is beers." Art would have believed that she brought them out of her sleeves, but she had no sleeves. The beers were cold and good.

"Girl, do you know how the fellow on the corner can ship a whole trailer-load of material out of a space that wouldn't hold a tenth of it?" Art asked the girl.

"Sure. He makes it and loads it out at the same time. That way it doesn't take up space, like if he made it before time."

"But he has to make it out of something," Jim Boomer cut in.

"No, no," the girl said. "I study your language. I know words. Out of something is to assemble, not to make. He makes."

"This is funny." Slick gaped. "Budweiser is misspelled on this bottle, the *i* before the *e*."

"Oh, I goof," the bar girl said. "I couldn't remember which way it goes so I make it one way on one bottle and the other way on the other. Yesterday a man ordered a bottle of Progress beer, and I spelled it Progers on the bottle. Sometimes I get things wrong. Here, I fix yours."

She ran her hand over the label, and then it was spelled correctly.

"But that thing is engraved and then reproduced," Slick protested.

"Oh, sure, all fancy stuff like that," the girl said. "I got to be more careful. One time I forget and make Jax-taste beer in Schlitz bottle and the man didn't like it. I had to swish swish change the taste while I pretended to give him a different bottle. One time I forgot and produced a green-bottle beer in a brown bottle. 'It is the light in here, it just makes it look brown,' I told the man. Hell, we don't even have a light in here. I go swish fast and make the bottle green. It's hard to keep from making mistake when you're stupid."

"No, you don't have a light or a window in here, and it's light," Slick said. "You don't have refrigeration. There are no power lines to any of the shanties in this block. How do you keep the beer cold?"

"Yes, is the beer not nice and cold? Notice how tricky I evade your question. Will you good men have two more beers?"

"Yes, we will. And I'm interested in seeing where you get them," Slick said.

"Oh look, is snakes behind you!" the girl cried.

"Oh how you startle and jump!" she laughed. "It's all joke. Do you think I will have snakes in my nice bar?"

But she had produced two more beers, and the place was as bare as before.

"How long have you tumble-bugs been in this block?" Boomer asked.

"Who keep track?" the girl said. "People come and go."

"You're not from around here," Slick said. "You're not from anywhere I know. Where do you come from? Jupiter?"

"Who wants Jupiter?" the girl seemed indignant. "Do business with a bunch of insects there, is all! Freeze your tail too."

"You wouldn't be a kidder, would you, girl?" Slick asked.

"I sure do try hard. I learn a lot of jokes but I tell them all wrong yet. I get better, though. I try to be the witty bar girl so people will come back."

"What's in the shanty next door toward the tracks?"

"My cousin-sister," said the girl. "She set up shop just today. She grow any color hair on bald-headed men. I tell her she's crazy. No business. If they wanted hair they wouldn't be bald-headed in the first place."

"Well, *can* she grow hair on bald-headed men?" Slick asked.

"Oh sure. Can't you?"

There were three or four more shanty shops in the block. It didn't seem that there had been that many when the men went into the Cool Man Club.

"I don't remember seeing this shack a few minutes ago," Boomer said to the man standing in front of the last shanty on the line.

"Oh, I just made it," the man said.

Weathered boards, rusty nails . . . and he had just made it.

"Why didn't you—ah—make a decent building while you were at it?" Slick asked.

"This is more inconspicuous," the man said. "Who notices when an *old* building appears suddenly? We're new here and want to feel our way in before we attract attention. Now I'm trying to figure out what to make. Do you think there *is* a market for a luxury automobile to sell for a hundred dollars? I suspect I would have to respect the local religious feeling when I make them though."

"What is that?" Slick asked.

"Ancestor worship. The old gas tank and fuel system still carried as vestiges after natural power is available. Oh, well, I'll put them in. I'll have one done in about three minutes if you want to wait."

"No, I've already got a car," Slick said. "Let's go, Jim."

That was the last shanty in the block, so they turned back.

"I was just wondering what was down in this block where nobody ever goes," Slick said. "There's a lot of odd corners in our town if you look them out."

"There are some queer guys in the shanties that were here before this bunch," Boomer said. "Some of them used to come up to the Red Rooster to drink. One of them could gobble like a turkey. One of them could roll one eye in one direction and the other eye the other way. They shoveled hulls at the cottonseed oil float before it burned down."

They went by the public stenographer shack again.

"No kidding, honey, how do you type without a typewriter?" Slick asked.

"Typewriter is too slow," the girl said.

"I asked *how,* not *why,*" Slick said.

"I know. Is it not nifty the way I turn away a phrase? I think I will have a big oak tree growing in front of my shop tomorrow for shade. Either of you nice men have an acorn in your pocket?"

"Ah—no. How do you really do the typing, girl?"

"You promise you won't tell anybody."

"I promise."

"I make the marks with my tongue," the girl said.

They started slowly on up the block.

"Hey, how do you make the carbon copies?" Jim Boomer called back.

"With my other tongue," the girl said.

There was another forty-foot trailer loading out of the first shanty in the block. It was bundles of half-inch plumbers' pipe coming out of the chute—in twenty-foot lengths. Twenty-foot rigid pipe out of a seven-foot shed.

"I wonder how he can sell trailer-loads of such stuff out of a little shack like that," Slick puzzled, still not satisfied.

"Like the girl says, he cuts prices," Boomer said. "Let's go over to the Red Rooster and see if there's anything going on. There always were a lot of funny people in that block."

I came across this in a second-hand anthology of stories from the late (and not sufficiently lamented) *Unknown* fantasy magazine, which was written by demigods. Thirty-five years later, I can practically quote it by heart.

It belongs to the ancient category of "a story told by a mysterious stranger." It's a simple narrative, not big on suspense, but it left white-hot lines across my brain. It made me *think*.

This immortal isn't planning to conquer the world by chopping off heads. He invents soup when his teeth fall out, he gets into armor making (because who would kill a good armorer?), and he keeps out of the way of important people because they're dangerous to know. Don't ask him about history. You don't *know* it's history until later. If he was around, he was the man at the back of the crowd, wondering what the all excitement was about and planning to move on.

The image has remained with me for years—the patient, skilled immortal, the template of ancient smithy gods and ugly story tellers, forever avoiding dogs and taking the late-night bus out of town and *surviving*. You think: this is how it could have been, this is how it would have to be. When an author spins your head like that, you're in the presence of genius.

—Terry Pratchett

THE GNARLY MAN
by L. Sprague de Camp

Dr. Matilda Saddler first saw the gnarly man on the evening of June 14, 1946, at Coney Island.

The spring meeting of the Eastern Section of the American Anthropological Association had broken up, and Dr. Saddler had had dinner with two of her professional colleagues, Blue of Columbia and Jeffcott of Yale. She mentioned that she had never visited Coney, and meant to go there that evening. She urged Blue and Jeffcott to come along, but they begged off.

Watching Dr. Saddler's retreating back, Blue of Columbia cackled: "The Wild Woman from Wichita. Wonder if she's hunting another husband?" He was a thin man with a small gray beard and a who-the-hell-are-you-sir expression.

"How many has she had?" asked Jeffcott of Yale.

"Two to date. Don't know why anthropologists lead the most disorderly private lives of any scientists. Must be that they study the customs and morals of all these different peoples, and ask themselves, 'If the Eskimos can do it, why can't we?' I'm old enough to be safe, thank God."

"I'm not afraid of her," said Jeffcott. He was in his early forties and looked like a farmer uneasy in store clothes. "I'm so very thoroughly married."

"Yeah? Ought to have been at Stanford a few years ago, when she was there. Wasn't safe to walk across the campus, with Tuthill chasing all the females and Saddler all the males."

Dr. Saddler had to fight her way off the subway train, as the adolescents who infest the platform of the B.M.T.'s Stillwell Avenue station are probably the worst-mannered people on earth, possibly excepting the Dobu Islanders, of the western Pacific. She didn't much mind. She was a tall, strongly built woman in her late thirties, who had been kept in trim by the outdoor rigors of her profession. Besides, some of the inane remarks in Swift's paper on acculturation among the Arapaho Indians had gotten her fighting blood up.

Walking down Surf Avenue toward Brighton Beach, she looked at the concessions without trying them, preferring to watch the human types that did and the other human types that took their money. She did try a shooting gallery, but found knocking tin owls off their perch with a .22 too easy to be much fun. Long-range work with an army rifle was her idea of shooting.

The concession next to the shooting gallery would have been called a side show if there had been a main show for it to be a side show to. The usual lurid banner proclaimed the uniqueness of the two-headed calf, the bearded woman, Arachne the spider girl, and other marvels. The pièce de résistance was Ungo-Bungo, the ferocious ape-man, captured in the Congo at a cost of twenty-seven lives. The picture showed an enormous Ungo-Bungo squeezing a hapless Negro in each hand, while others sought to throw a net over him.

Dr. Saddler knew perfectly well that the ferocious ape-man would turn out to be an ordinary Caucasian with false hair on his chest. But a streak of whimsicality impelled her to go in. Perhaps, she thought, she could have some fun with her colleagues about it.

The spieler went through his leather-lunged harangue. Dr. Saddler guessed from his expression that his feet hurt. The tattooed lady didn't interest her, as her decorations obviously had no cultural significance, as they have among the Polynesians. As for the ancient Mayan, Dr. Saddler thought it in questionable taste to exhibit a poor microcephalic idiot that way. Professor Yoki's legerdemain and fire eating weren't bad.

There was a curtain in front of Ungo-Bungo's cage. At the appropriate moment there were growls and the sound of a length of chain being slapped against a metal plate. The spieler wound up on a high note: "—ladies and gentlemen, the one and only UNGO-BUNGO!" The curtain dropped.

The ape-man was squatting at the back of his cage. He dropped his chain, got up, and shuffled forward. He grasped two of the bars and shook them. They were appropriately loose and rattled alarmingly. Ungo-Bungo snarled at the patrons, showing his even, yellow teeth.

Dr. Saddler stared hard. This was something new in the ape-man line. Ungo-Bungo was about five feet three, but very massive, with enormous hunched shoulders. Above and below his blue swimming trunks thick, grizzled hair covered him from crown to ankle. His short, stout-muscled arms ended in big hands with thick, gnarled fingers. His neck projected slightly forward, so that from the front he seemed to have but little neck at all.

His face—well, thought Dr. Saddler, she knew all the living races of men, and all the types of freak brought about by glandular maladjustment, and none of them had a face like *that*. It was deeply lined. The forehead between the short scalp hair and the brows on the huge supraorbital ridges receded sharply. The nose, although wide, was not apelike; it was a shortened version of the thick, hooked Armenoid nose, so often miscalled Jewish. The face ended in a long upper lip and a retreating chin. And the yellowish skin apparently belonged to Ungo-Bungo.

The curtain was whisked up again.

Dr. Saddler went out with the others, but paid another dime, and soon was back inside. She paid no attention to the spieler, but got a good position in front of Ungo-Bungo's cage before the rest of the crowd arrived.

Ungo-Bungo repeated his performance with mechanical precision. Dr. Saddler noticed that he limped a little as he came forward to rattle the bars, and that the skin under his mat of hair bore several big whitish scars. The last joint of his left ring finger was missing. She noted certain things about the proportions of his shin and thigh, of his forearm and upper arm, and his big splay feet.

Dr. Saddler paid a third dime. An idea was knocking at her mind somewhere. If she let it in, either she was crazy or physical anthropology was haywire or—something. But she knew that if she did the sensible thing, which was to go home, the idea would plague her from now on.

After the third performance she spoke to the spieler. "I think your Mr. Ungo-Bungo used to be a friend of mine. Could you arrange for me to see him after he finishes?"

The spieler checked his sarcasm. His questioner was so obviously not a—not the sort of dame who asks to see guys after they finish.

"Oh, him," he said. "Calls himself Gaffney—Clarence Aloysius Gaffney. That the guy you want?"

"Why, yes."

"I guess you can." He looked at his watch. "He's got four more turns to do before we close. I'll have to ask the boss." He popped through a curtain and called, "Hey, Morrie!" Then he was back. "It's okay. Morrie says you can wait in his office. Foist door to the right."

Morrie was stout, bald, and hospitable. "Sure, sure," he said, waving his cigar. "Glad to be of soivace, Miss Saddler. Chust a min while I talk to Gaffney's manager." He stuck his head out. "Hey, Pappas! Lady wants to talk to your ape-man later. I meant *lady,* O.K." He returned to orate on the difficulties besetting the freak business. "You take this Gaffney, now. He's the best damn ape-man in the business; all that hair rilly grows outa him. And the poor guy rilly has a face like that. But do people believe it? No! I hear 'em going out, saying about how the hair is pasted on, and the whole thing is a fake. It's mawtifying." He cocked his head, listening. "That rumble wasn't no rolly-coaster;

it's gonna rain. Hope it's over by tomorrow. You wouldn't believe the way a rain can knock ya receipts off. If you drew a coive, it would be like this." He drew his finger horizontally through space, jerking it down sharply to indicate the effect of rain. "But as I said, people don't appreciate what you try to do for 'em. It's not just the money; I think of myself as an ottist. A creative ottist. A show like this got to have balance and propawtion, like any other ott—"

It must have been an hour later when a slow, deep voice at the door said: "Did somebody want to see me?"

The gnarly man was in the doorway. In street clothes, with the collar of his raincoat turned up and his hat brim pulled down, he looked more or less human, though the coat fitted his great, sloping shoulders badly. He had a thick, knobby walking stick with a leather loop near the top end. A small, dark man fidgeted behind him.

"Yeah," said Morrie, interrupting his lecture. "Clarence, this is Miss Saddler. Miss Saddler, this is Mr. Gaffney, one of our outstanding creative ottists."

"Pleased to meetcha," said the gnarly man. "This is my manager, Mr. Pappas."

Dr. Saddler explained, and said she'd like to talk to Mr. Gaffney if she might. She was tactful; you had to be to pry into the private affairs of Naga headhunters, for instance. The gnarly man said he'd be glad to have a cup of coffee with Miss Saddler; there was a place around the corner that they could reach without getting wet.

As they started out, Pappas followed, fidgeting more and more. The gnarly man said: "Oh, go home to bed, John. Don't worry about me." He grinned at Dr. Saddler. The effect would have been unnerving to anyone but an anthropologist. "Every time he sees me talking to anybody, he thinks it's some other manager trying to steal me." He spoke general American, with a suggestion of Irish brogue in the lowering of the vowels in words like "man" and "talk." "I made the lawyer who drew up our contract fix it so it can be ended on short notice."

Pappas departed, still looking suspicious. The rain had practically ceased. The gnarly man stepped along smartly despite his limp.

A woman passed with a fox terrier on a leash. The dog sniffed in the direction of the gnarly man, and then to all appearances went crazy, yelping and slavering. The gnarly man shifted his grip on the massive stick and said quietly, "Better hang onto him, ma'am." The woman departed hastily. "They just don't like me," commented Gaffney. "Dogs, that is."

They found a table and ordered their coffee. When the gnarly man took off his raincoat, Dr. Saddler became aware of a strong smell of cheap perfume. He got out a pipe with a big knobby bowl. It suited him, just as the walking stick did. Dr. Saddler noticed that the deep-sunk eyes under the beetling arches were light hazel.

"Well?" he said in his rumbling drawl.

She began her questions.

"My parents were Irish," he answered. "But I was born in South Boston . . . let's see . . . forty-six years ago. I can get you a copy of my birth certificate. Clarence Aloysius Gaffney, May 2, 1900." He seemed to get some secret amusement out of that statement.

"Were either of your parents of your somewhat unusual physical type?"

He paused before answering. He always did, it seemed. "Uh-huh. Both of 'em. Glands, I suppose."

"Were they both born in Ireland?"

"Yep. County Sligo." Again that mysterious twinkle.

She thought. "Mr. Gaffney, you wouldn't mind having some photographs and measurements made, would you? You could use the photographs in your business."

"Maybe." He took a sip. "Ouch! Gazooks, that's hot!"

"What?"

"I said the coffee's hot."

"I mean, before that."

The gnarly man looked a little embarrassed. "Oh, you mean the 'gazooks'? Well, I . . . uh . . . once knew a man who used to say that."

"Mr. Gaffney, I'm a scientist, and I'm not trying to get anything out of you for my own sake. You can be frank with me."

There was something remote and impersonal in his stare that gave her a slight spinal chill. "Meaning that I haven't been so far?"

"Yes. When I saw you I decided that there was something extraordinary in your background. I still think there is. Now, if you think I'm crazy, say so and we'll drop the subject. But I want to get to the bottom of this."

He took his time about answering. "That would depend." There was another pause. Then he said: "With your connections, do you know any really first-class surgeons?"

"But . . . yes, I know Dunbar."

"The guy who wears a purple gown when he operates? The guy who wrote a book on 'God, Man, and the Universe'?"

"Yes. He's a good man, in spite of his theatrical mannerisms. Why? What would you want of him?"

"Not what you're thinking. I'm satisfied with my . . . uh . . . unusual physical type. But I have some old injuries—broken bones that didn't knit properly—that I want fixed up. He'd have to be a good man, though. I have a couple of thousand dollars in the savings bank, but I know the sort of fees those guys charge. If you could make the necessary arrangements—"

"Why, yes, I'm sure I could. In fact, I could guarantee it. Then I *was* right? And you'll—" She hesitated.

"Come clean? Uh-huh. But remember, I can still prove I'm Clarence Aloysius if I have to."

"Who *are* you, then?"

Again there was a long pause. Then the gnarly man said: "Might as well tell you. As soon as you repeat any of it, you'll have put your professional reputation in my hands, remember.

"First off, I wasn't born in Massachusetts. I was born on the upper Rhine, near Mommenheim. And I was born, as nearly as I can figure out, about the year 50,000 B.C."

Matilda Saddler wondered whether she'd stumbled on the biggest thing in anthropology, or whether this bizarre personality was making Baron Munchausen look like a piker.

He seemed to guess her thoughts. "I can't prove that, of course. But so long as you arrange about that operation, I don't care whether you believe me or not."

"But . . . but . . . *how?*"

"I think the lightning did it. We were out trying to drive some bison into a pit. Well, this big thunderstorm came up, and the bison bolted in the wrong direction. So we gave up and tried to find shelter. And the next thing I knew I was lying on the ground with the rain running over me, and the rest of the clan standing around wailing about what had they done to get the storm god sore at them, so he made a bull's-eye on one of their best hunters. They'd never said *that* about me before. It's funny how you're never appreciated while you're alive.

"But I was alive, all right. My nerves were pretty well shot for a few weeks, but otherwise I was okay, except for some burns on the soles of my feet. I don't know just what happened, except I was reading a couple of years ago that scientists had located the machinery that controls the replacement of tissue in the medulla oblongata. I think maybe the lightning did something to my medulla to speed it up. Anyway, I never got any older after that. Physically, that is. I was thirty-three at the time, more or less. We didn't keep track of ages. I look older now, because the lines in your face are bound to get sort of set after a few thousand years, and because our hair was always gray at the ends. But I can still tie an ordinary *Homo sapiens* in a knot if I want to."

"Then you're . . . you mean to say you're . . you're trying to tell me you're—"

"A Neanderthal man? *Homo neanderthalensis?* That's right."

* * *

Matilda Saddler's hotel room was a bit crowded, with the gnarly man, the frosty Blue, the rustic Jeffcott, Dr. Saddler herself, and Harold McGannon, the historian. This McGannon was a small man, very neat and pink-skinned. He looked more like a New York Central director than a professor. Just now his expression was one of fascination. Dr. Saddler looked full of pride; Professor Jeffcott looked interested but puzzled; Dr. Blue looked bored—he hadn't wanted to come in the first place. The gnarly man, stretched out in the most comfortable chair and puffing his overgrown pipe, seemed to be enjoying himself.

McGannon was formulating a question. "Well, Mr.— Gaffney? I suppose that's your name as much as any."

"You might say so," said the gnarly man. "My original name meant something like Shining Hawk. But I've gone under hundreds of names since then. If you register in a hotel as 'Shining Hawk,' it's apt to attract attention. And I try to avoid that."

"Why?" asked McGannon.

The gnarly man looked at his audience as one might look at willfully stupid children. "I don't like trouble. The best way to keep out of trouble is not to attract attention. That's why I have to pull up stakes and move every ten or fifteen years. People might get curious as to why I never get any older."

"Pathological liar," murmured Blue. The words were barely audible, but the gnarly man heard them.

"You're entitled to your opinion, Dr. Blue," he said affably. "Dr. Saddler's doing me a favor, so in return I'm letting you all shoot questions at me. And I'm answering. I don't give a damn whether you believe me or not."

McGannon hastily threw in another question. "How is it that you have a birth certificate, as you say you have?"

"Oh, I knew a man named Clarence Gaffney once. He got killed by an automobile, and I took his name."

"Was there any reason for picking this Irish background?"

"Are you Irish, Dr. McGannon?"

"Not enough to matter."

"Okay I didn't want to hurt any feelings. It's my best bet. There are real Irishmen with upper lips like mine."

Dr. Saddler broke in. "I meant to ask you, Clarence." She put a lot of warmth into his name. "There's an argument as to whether your people interbred with mine, when mine overran Europe at the end of the Mousterian. Some scientists have thought that some modern Europeans, especially along the west coast of Ireland, might have a little Neanderthal blood."

He grinned slightly. "Well—yes and no. There never was any back in the stone age, as far as I know. But these long-lipped Irish are my fault."

"How?"

"Believe it or not, but in the last fifty centuries there have been some women of your species that didn't find me too repulsive. Usually there was no offspring. But in the sixteenth century I went to Ireland to live. They were burning too many people for witchcraft in the rest of Europe to suit me at that time. And there was a woman. The result this time was a flock of hybrids—cute little devils, they were. So the Irishmen who look like me are my descendants."

"What did happen to your people?" asked McGannon. "Were they killed off?"

The gnarly man shrugged. "Some of them. We weren't at all warlike. But then the tall ones, as we called them, weren't either. Some of the tribes of the tall ones looked on us as legitimate prey, but most of them let us severely alone. I guess they were almost as scared of us as we were of them. Savages as primitive as that are really pretty peaceable people. You have to work so hard to keep fed, and there are so few of you, that there's no object in fighting wars. That comes later, when you get agriculture and livestock, so you have something worth stealing.

"I remember that a hundred years after the tall ones had come, there were still Neanderthalers living in my part of the country. But they died out. I think it was that they lost their ambition. The tall ones were pretty crude, but they were so far ahead of us that our things and our customs seemed silly. Finally we just sat around and lived on the scraps we could beg from the tall ones' camps. You might say we died of an inferiority complex."

"What happened to you?" asked McGannon.

"Oh, I was a god among my own people by then, and naturally I represented them in their dealings with the tall ones. I got to know the tall ones pretty well, and they were willing to put up with me after all my own clan were dead. Then in a couple of hundred years they'd forgotten all about my people, and took me for a hunchback or something. I got to be pretty good at flint working, so I could earn my keep. When metal came in, I went into that, and finally into blacksmithing. If you'd put all the horseshoes I've made in a pile, they'd—well, you'd have a damn big pile of horseshoes, anyway."

"Did you . . . ah . . . limp at that time?" asked McGannon.

"Uh-huh. I busted my leg back in the Neolithic. Fell out

of a tree, and had to set it myself, because there wasn't anybody around. Why?"

"Vulcan," said McGannon softly.

"Vulcan?" repeated the gnarly man. "Wasn't he a Greek god or something?"

"Yes. He was the lame blacksmith of the gods."

"You mean you think that maybe somebody got the idea from me? That's an interesting theory. Little late to check up on it, though."

Blue leaned forward and said crisply: "Mr. Gaffney, no real Neanderthal man could talk so fluently and entertainingly as you do. That's shown by the poor development of the frontal lobes of the brain and the attachments of the tongue muscles."

The gnarly man shrugged again. "You can believe what you like. My own clan considered me pretty smart, and then you're bound to learn something in fifty thousand years."

Dr. Saddler beamed. "Tell them about your teeth, Clarence."

The gnarly man grinned. "They're false, of course. My own lasted a long time, but they still wore out somewhere back in the Paleolithic. I grew a third set, and they wore out, too. So I had to invent soup."

"You *what?*" It was the usually taciturn Jeffcott.

"I had to invent soup, to keep alive. You know, the bark-dish-and-hot-stones method. My gums got pretty tough after a while, but they still weren't much good for chewing hard stuff. So after a few thousand years I got pretty sick of soup and mushy foods generally. And when metal came in I began experimenting with false teeth. Bone teeth in copper plates. You might say I invented them, too. I tried often to sell them, but they never really caught on until around 1750 A.D. I was living in Paris then, and I built up quite a little business before I moved on." He pulled the handkerchief out of his breast pocket to wipe his forehead; Blue made a face as the wave of perfume reached him.

"Well, Mr. Shining Hawk," snapped Blue with a trace of sarcasm, "how do you like our machine age?"

The gnarly man ignored the tone of the question. "It's not bad. Lots of interesting things happen. The main trouble is the shirts."

"Shirts?"

"Uh-huh. Just try to buy a shirt with a twenty neck and a twenty-nine sleeve. I have to order 'em special. It's almost as bad with hats and shoes. I wear an eight and one half hat and a thirteen shoe." He looked at his watch. "I've got to get back to Coney to work."

McGannon jumped up. "Where can I get in touch with you again, Mr. Gaffney? There's lots of things I'd like to ask you."

The gnarly man told him. "I'm free mornings. My working hours are two to midnight on weekdays, with a couple of hours off for dinner. Union rules, you know."

"You mean there's a union for you show people?"

"Sure. Only they call it a guild. They think they're artists, you know. Artists don't have unions; they have guilds. But it amounts to the same thing."

* * *

Blue and Jeffcott saw the gnarly man and the historian walking slowly toward the subway together. Blue said: "Poor old Mac! Always thought he had sense. Looks like he's swallowed this Gaffney's ravings, hook, line, and sinker."

"I'm not so sure," said Jeffcott, frowning. "There's something funny about the business."

"What?" barked Blue. "Don't tell me that *you* believe this story of being alive fifty thousand years? A caveman who uses perfume! Good God!"

"N–no," said Jeffcott. "Not the fifty thousand part. But I don't think it's a simple case of paranoia or plain lying, either. And the perfume's quite logical, if he were telling the truth."

"Huh?"

"Body odor. Saddler told us how dogs hate him. He'd have a smell different from ours. We're so used to ours that we don't even know we have one, unless somebody goes without a bath for a month. But we might notice his if he didn't disguise it."

Blue snorted. "You'll be believing him yourself in a minute. It's an obvious glandular case, and he's made up this story to fit. All that talk about not caring whether we believe him or not is just bluff. Come on, let's get some lunch. Say, see the way Saddler looked at him every time she said 'Clarence'? Like a hungry wolf. Wonder what she thinks she's going to do with him?"

Jeffcott thought. "I can guess. And if he *is* telling the truth, I think there's something in Deuteronomy against it."

* * *

The great surgeon made a point of looking like a great surgeon, to pince-nez and Vandyke. He waved the X-ray negatives at the gnarly man, pointing out this and that.

"We'd better take the leg first," he said. "Suppose we do that next Thursday. When you've recovered from that we can tackle the shoulder. It'll all take time, you know."

The gnarly man agreed, and shuffled out of the little private hospital to where McGannon awaited him in his car. The gnarly man described the tentative schedule of operations, and mentioned that he had made arrangements to quit his job. "Those two are the main thing," he said. "I'd like to try professional wrestling again some day, and I can't unless I get this shoulder fixed so I can raise my left arm over my heard."

"What happened to it?" asked McGannon.

The gnarly man closed his eyes, thinking. "Let me see. I get things mixed up sometimes. People do when they're only fifty years old, so you can imagine what it's like for me.

"In 42 B.C. I was living with the Bituriges in Gaul. You remember that Cæsar shut up Werkinghetorich—Vercingetorix to you—in Alesia, and the confederacy raised an army of relief under Coswollon."

"Coswollon?"

The gnarly man laughed shortly. "I meant Warcaswollon. Coswollon was a Briton, wasn't he? I'm always getting those two mixed up.

"Anyhow, I got drafted. That's all you can call it; I didn't want to go. It wasn't exactly *my* war. But they wanted me because I could pull twice as heavy a bow as anybody else.

"When the final attack on Cæsar's ring fortifications came, they sent me forward with some other archers to provide a covering fire for their infantry. At least, that was the plan. Actually, I never saw such a hopeless muddle in my life. And before I even got within bowshot, I fell into one of the Romans' covered pits. I didn't land on the point of the stake, but I fetched up against the side of it and busted my shoulder. There wasn't any help, because the Gauls were too busy running away from Cæsar's German cavalry to bother about wounded men."

* * *

The author of "God, Man, and the Universe" gazed after his departing patient. He spoke to his head assistant: "What do you think of him?"

"I think it's so," said the assistant. "I looked over those X rays pretty closely. That skeleton never belonged to a human being. And it has more healed fractures than you'd think possible."

"Hm-m-m," said Dunbar. "That's right, he wouldn't be human, would he? Hm-m-m. You know, if anything happened to him—"

The assistant grinned understandingly. "Of course, there's the S.P.C.A."

"We needn't worry about *them*. Hm-m-m." He thought, you've been slipping; nothing big in the papers for a year. But if you published a complete anatomical description of a Neanderthal man—or if you found out why his medulla functions the way it does—Hm-m-m. Of course, it would have to be managed properly—

* * *

"Let's have lunch at the Natural History Museum," said McGannon. "Some of the people there ought to know you."

"Okay," drawled the gnarly man. "Only I've still got to get back to Coney afterward. This is my last day. Tomorrow, Pappas and I are going up to see our lawyer about ending our contract. Guy named Robinette. It's a dirty trick on poor old John, but I warned him at the start that this might happen."

"I suppose we can come up to interview you while you're . . . ah . . . convalescing? Fine. Have you ever been to the museum, by the way?"

"Sure," said the gnarly man. "I get around."

"What did you . . . ah . . . think of their stuff in the Hall of the Age of Man?"

"Pretty good. There's a little mistake in one of those big wall paintings. The second horn on the woolly rhinoceros ought to slant forward more. I thought of writing them a letter. But you know how it is. They'd say: 'Were you there?' and I'd say, 'Uh-huh,' and they'd say, 'Another nut.' "

"How about the pictures and busts of Paleolithic men?"

"Pretty good. But they have some funny ideas. They always show us with skins wrapped around our middles. In summer we didn't wear skins, and in winter we hung them around our shoulders, where they'd do some good.

"And then they show those tall ones that you call Cro-Magnon men clean-shaven. As I remember, they all had whiskers. What would they shave with?"

"I think," said McGannon, "that they leave the beards off the busts to . . . ah . . . show the shape of the chins. With the beards they'd all look too much alike."

"Is that the reason? They might say so on the labels." The gnarly man rubbed his own chin, such as it was. "I wish beards would come back into style. I look much more human with a beard. I got along fine in the sixteenth century when everybody had whiskers.

"That's one of the ways I remember when things happened, by the haircuts and whiskers that people had. I remember when a wagon I was driving in Milan lost a wheel and spilled flour bags from hell to breakfast. That must have been in the sixteenth century, before I went to Ireland, because I remember that most of the men in the crowd that collected had beards. Now—wait a minute— maybe that was the fourteenth. There were a lot of beards, then, too."

"Why, why didn't you keep a diary?" asked McGannon with a groan of exasperation.

The gnarly man shrugged characteristically. "And pack around six trunks full of paper every time I moved? No, thanks."

"I . . . ah . . . don't suppose you could give me the real story of Richard III and the princes in the tower?"

"Why should I? I was just a poor blacksmith, or farmer, or something most of the time. I didn't go around with the big shots. I gave up all my ideas of ambition a long time before that. I had to, being so different from other people. As far as I can remember, the only real king I ever got a good look at was Charlemagne, when he made a speech in Paris one day. He was just a big, tall man with Santa Claus whiskers and a squeaky voice."

* * *

Next morning McGannon and the gnarly man had a session with Svedberg at the museum. Then McGannon drove Gaffney around to the lawyer's office, on the third floor of a seedy office building in the West Fifties. James Robinette looked something like a movie actor and something like a chipmunk. He looked at his watch and said to McGannon: "This won't take long. If you'd like to stick around, I'd be glad to have lunch with you." The fact was that he was feeling just a trifle queasy about being left with this damn queer client, this circus freak or whatever he was, with his barrel body and his funny slow drawl.

When the business had been completed, and the gnarly man had gone off with his manager to wind up his affairs at Coney, Robinette said: "Whew! I thought he was a half-wit, from his looks. But there was nothing half-witted about the way he went over those clauses. You'd have thought the damn contract was for building a subway system. What is he, anyhow?"

McGannon told him what he knew.

The lawyer's eyebrows went up. "Do you *believe* his yarn? Oh, I'll take tomato juice and filet of sole with tartar sauce—only without the tartar sauce—on the lunch, please."

"The same for me. Answering your question, Robinette, I do. So does Saddler. So does Svedberg up at the museum. They're both topnotchers in their respective fields. Saddler and I have interviewed him, and Svedberg's examined him physically. But it's just opinion. Fred Blue still swears it's a hoax or . . . ah . . . some sort of dementia. Neither of us can prove anything."

"Why not?"

"Well . . . ah . . . how are you going to prove that he was, or was not, alive a hundred years ago?" Take one case: Clarence says he ran a sawmill in Fairbanks, Alaska, in 1906 and '07, under the name of Michael Shawn. How are you going to find out whether there was a sawmill operator in Fairbanks at that time? And if you did stumble on a record of a Michael Shawn, how would you know whether he and Clarence were the same? There's not a chance in a thousand that there'd be a photograph or a detailed description that you could check with. And you'd have an awful time trying to find anybody who remembered him at this late date.

"Then, Svedberg poked around Clarence's face, yesterday, and said that no *Homo sapiens* ever had a pair of zygomatic arches like that. But when I told Blue that, he offered to produce photographs of a human skull that did. I know what'll happen. Blue will say that they're obviously different. So there we'll be."

Robinette mused, "He does seem damned intelligent for an ape-man."

"He's not an ape-man, really. The Neanderthal race was a separate branch of the human stock: they were more primitive in some ways and more advanced in others than we are. Clarence may be slow, but he usually grinds out the right answer. I imagine that he was . . . ah . . . brilliant, for one of his kind, to begin with. And he's had the benefit of so much experience. He knows an incredible lot. He knows us; he sees through us and our motives."

The little pink man puckered up his forehead. "I do hope nothing happens to him. He's carrying around a lot of priceless information in that big head of his. Simply priceless. Not much about war and politics; he kept clear of those as a matter of self-preservation. But little things, about how people lived and how they thought thousands of years ago. He gets his periods mixed up sometimes, but he gets them straightened out if you give him time.

"I'll have to get hold of Pell, the linguist. Clarence knows dozens of ancient languages, such as Gothic and Gaulish. I was able to check him on one of them, like vulgar Latin; that was one of the things that convinced me. And there are archeologists and psychologists—

"If only something doesn't happen to scare him off. We'd never find him. I don't know. Between a man-crazy female scientist and a publicity-mad surgeon—I wonder how it'll work out—"

* * *

The gnarly man innocently entered the waiting room of Dunbar's hospital. He, as usual, spotted the most comfortable chair and settled luxuriously into it.

Dunbar stood before him. His keen eyes gleamed with anticipation behind their pince-nez. "There'll be a wait of about half an hour, Mr. Gaffney," he said. "We're all tied up now, you know. I'll send Mahler in; he'll see that you have anything you want." Dunbar's eyes ran lovingly over the gnarly man's stumpy frame. What fascinating secrets mightn't he discover once he got inside it?

Mahler appeared, a healthy-looking youngster. Was there anything Mr. Gaffney would like? The gnarly man paused as usual to let his massive mental machinery grind. A vagrant impulse moved him to ask to see the instruments that were to be used on him.

Mahler had his orders, but this seemed a harmless enough request. He went and returned with a tray full of gleaming steel. "You see," he said, "these are called scalpels."

Presently the gnarly man asked: "What's this?" He picked up a peculiar-looking instrument.

"Oh, that's the boss's own invention. For getting at the mid-brain."

"Mid-brain? What's that doing here?"

"Why, that's for getting at your— That must be there by mistake—"

Little lines tightened around the queer hazel eyes. "Yeah?" He remembered the look Dunbar had given him, and Dunbar's general reputation. "Say, could I use your phone a minute?"

"Why . . . I suppose . . . what do you want to phone for?"

"I want to call my lawyer. Any objections?"

"No, of course not. But there isn't any phone here."

"What do you call that?" The gnarly man got up and walked toward the instrument in plain sight on a table. But Mahler was there before him, standing in front of it.

"This one doesn't work. It's being fixed."

"Can't I try it?"

"No, not till it's fixed. It doesn't work, I tell you."

The gnarly man studied the young physician for a few

seconds. "Okay, then I'll find one that does." He started for the door.

"Hey, you can't go out now!" cried Mahler.

"Can't I? Just watch me!"

"Hey!" It was a full-throated yell. Like magic more men in white coats appeared.

Behind them was the great surgeon. "Be reasonable, Mr. Gaffney," he said. "There's no reason why you should go out now, you know. We'll be ready for you in a little while."

"Any reason why I shouldn't?" The gnarly man's big face swung on his thick neck, and his hazel eyes swiveled. All the exits were blocked. "I'm going."

"Grab him!" said Dunbar.

The white coats moved. The gnarly man got his hands on the back of a chair. The chair whirled, and became a dissolving blur as the men closed on him. Pieces of chair flew about the room, to fall with the dry, sharp *ping* of short lengths of wood. When the gnarly man stopped swinging, having only a short piece of the chair back left in each fist, one assistant was out cold. Another leaned whitely against the wall and nursed a broken arm.

"Go on!" shouted Dunbar when he could make himself heard. The white wave closed over the gnarly man, then broke. The gnarly man was on his feet, and held young Mahler by the ankles. He spread his feet and swung the shrieking Mahler like a club, clearing the way to the door. He turned, whirled Mahler around his head like a hammer thrower, and let the now mercifully unconscious body fly. His assailants went down in a yammering tangle.

One was still up. Under Dunbar's urging he sprang after the gnarly man. The latter had gotten his stick out of the umbrella stand in the vestibule. The knobby upper end went *whoosh* past the assistant's nose. The assistant jumped back and fell over one of the casualties. The front door slammed, and there was a deep roar of "Taxi!"

"Come on!" shrieked Dunbar. "Get the ambulance out!"

* * *

James Robinette was sitting in his office, thinking the thoughts that lawyers do in moments of relaxation, when there was a pounding of large feet in the corridor, a startled protest from Miss Spevak in the outer office, and the strange client of the day before was at Robinette's desk, breathing hard.

"I'm Gaffney," he growled between gasps. "Remember me? I think they followed me down here. They'll be up any minute. I want your help."

"They? Who's they?" Robinette winced at the impact of that damn perfume.

The gnarly man launched into his misfortunes, He was going well when there were more protests from Miss Spevak, and Dr. Dunbar and four assistants burst into the office.

"He's ours," said Dunbar, his glasses agleam.

"He's an ape-man," said the assistant with the black eye.

"He's a dangerous lunatic," said the assistant with the cut lip.

"We've come to take him away," said the assistant with the torn coat.

The gnarly man spread his feet and gripped his stick like a baseball bat by the small end.

Robinette opened a desk drawer and got out a large pistol. "One move toward him and I'll use this. The use of extreme violence is justified to prevent commission of a felony, to wit: kidnapping."

The five men backed up a little. Dunbar said: "This isn't kidnapping. You can only kidnap a person, you know. He isn't a human being, and I can prove it."

The assistant with the black eye snickered. "If he wants protection, he better see a game warden instead of a lawyer."

"Maybe that's what *you* think," said Robinette. "You aren't a lawyer. According to the law, he's human. Even corporations, idiots, and unborn children are legally persons, and he's a damned sight more human they they are."

"Then he's a dangerous lunatic," said Dunbar.

"Yeah? Where's your commitment order? The only persons who can apply for one are: (a) close relatives and (b) public officials charged with the maintenance of order. You're neither."

Dunbar continued stubbornly: "He ran amuck in my hospital and nearly killed a couple of my men, you know. I guess that gives us some rights."

"Sure," said Robinette. "You can step down to the nearest station and swear out a warrant." He turned to the gnarly man. "Shall we throw the book at 'em. Gaffney?"

"I'm all right," said that individual, his speech returning to its normal slowness. "I just want to make sure these guys don't pester me any more."

"Okay Now listen, Dunbar. One hostile move out of you and we'll have a warrant out for you for false arrest, assault and battery, attempted kidnapping, criminal conspiracy, and disorderly conduct. *And* we'll slap on a civil suit for damages for sundry torts, to wit: assault, deprivation of civil rights, placing in jeopardy of life and limb, menace, and a few more I may think of later."

"You'll never make that stick," snarled Dunbar. "We have all the witnesses."

"Yeah? And wouldn't the great Evan Dunbar look sweet defending such actions? Some of the ladies who gush over your books might suspect that maybe you weren't such a damn knight in shining armor. We can make a prize monkey of you, and you know it."

"You're destroying the possibility of a great scientific discovery, you know, Robinette."

"To hell with that. My duty is to protect my client. Now beat it, all of you, before I call a cop." His left hand moved suggestively to the telephone.

Dunbar grasped at a last straw. "Hm-m-m. Have you got a permit for that gun?"

"Damn right. Want to see it?"

Dunbar sighed. "Never mind. You *would* have." His greatest opportunity for fame was slipping out of his fingers. He drooped toward the door.

The gnarly man spoke up. "If you don't mind, Dr. Dunbar, I left my hat at your place. I wish you'd send it to Mr. Robinette here. I have a hard time getting hats to fit me."

Dunbar looked at him silently and left with his cohorts.

The gnarly man was giving the lawyer further details when the telephone rang. Robinette answered: "Yes. . . . Saddler? Yes, he's here. . . . Your Dr. Dunbar was going to murder him so he could dissect him. . . . okay." He turned to the gnarly man. "Your friend Dr. Saddler is looking for you. She's on her way up here."

"Zounds!" said Gaffney. "I'm going."

"Don't you want to see her? She was phoning from around the corner. If you go out now you'll run into her. How did she knew where to call?"

"I gave her your number. I suppose she called the hospital and my boardinghouse, and tried you as a last resort. This door goes into the hall, doesn't it? Well, when she comes in the regular door I'm going out this one. And I don't want you saying where I've gone. It's nice to have known you, Mr. Robinette."

"Why? What's the matter? You're not going to run out now, are you? Dunbar's harmless, and you've got friends. I'm your friend."

"You're durn tootin' I'm going to run out. There's too much trouble. I've kept alive all these centuries by staying away from trouble. I let down my guard with Dr. Saddler, and went to the surgeon she recommended. First he plots to take me apart to see what makes me tick. If that brain instrument hadn't made me suspicious, I'd have been on my way to the alcohol jars by now. Then there's a fight, and it's just pure luck I didn't kill a couple of those interns, or whatever they are, and get sent up for manslaughter. Now Matilda's after me with a more-than-friendly interest. I know what it means when a woman looks at you that way and calls you 'dear.' I wouldn't mind if she weren't a prominent person of the kind that's always in some sort of garboil. That would mean more trouble, sooner or later. You don't suppose I *like* trouble, do you?"

"But look here, Gaffney, you're getting steamed up over a lot of damn—"

"*Ssst!*" The gnarly man took his stick and tiptoed over to the private entrance. As Dr. Saddler's clear voice sounded in the outer office, he sneaked out. He was closing the door behind him when the scientist entered the inner office.

Matilda Saddler was a quick thinker. Robinette hardly had time to open his mouth when she flung herself at and through the private door with a cry of "Clarence!"

Robinette heard the clatter of feet on the stairs. Neither the pursued nor the pursuer had waited for the creaky elevator. Looking out the window, he saw Gaffney leap into a taxi. Matilda Saddler sprinted after the cab, calling: "Clarence! Come back!" But the traffic was light and the chase correspondingly hopeless.

* * *

They did hear from the gnarly man once more. Three months later Robinette got a letter whose envelope contained, to his vast astonishment, ten ten-dollar bills. The single sheet was typed, even to the signature.

DEAR MR. ROBINETTE:

I do not know what your regular fees are, but I hope that the inclosed will cover your services to me of last June.

Since leaving New York I have had several jobs. I pushed a hack—as we say—in Chicago, and I tried out as pitcher on a bush league baseball team. Once I made my living by knocking over rabbits and things with stones, and I can still throw fairly well. Nor am I bad at swinging a club, such as a baseball bat. But my lameness makes me too slow for a baseball career, and it will be some time before I try any remedial operations again.

I now have a job whose nature I cannot disclose because I do not wish to be traced. You need pay no attention to the postmark; I am not living in Kansas City, but had a friend post this letter there.

Ambition would be foolish for one in my peculiar position. I am satisfied with a job that furnishes me with the essentials, and allows me to go to an occasional movie, and a few friends with whom I can drink beer and talk.

I was sorry to leave New York without saying goodby to Dr. Harold McGannon, who treated me very nicely. I wish you would explain to him why I had to leave as I did. You can get in touch with him through Columbia University.

If Dunbar sent you my hat as I requested, pleased mail it to me: General Delivery, Kansas City, Mo. My friend will pick it up. There is not a hat store in this town where I live that can fit me. With best wishes, I remain,

Yours sincerely,
SHINING HAWK
Alias CLARENCE ALOYSIUS GAFFNEY

Montague Rhodes James was a true master of the supernatural. The term is thrown about all too casually these days, but he earned it in full measure. His language was that of the nineteenth century, elegant and erudite, which enhances the authenticity of his tales. James did not rely upon gore and ghoulishness for his effects. He piled one commonplace detail upon another to bring his characters and their world to life, while at the same time, and with great subtlety, developing a claustrophobic, almost over-whelming atmosphere of dread. His ghosts were neither friendly nor whimsical, but mysterious, vindictive, and terrible in the literal meaning of the word.

The work included here is a perfect example. A single image from this story has haunted my worst nightmares since I first read it as a teenager. Over the years, tales of terror have grown progressively more violent and thus supposedly more frightening. Yet nothing has ever put such a chill up my spine as "Oh, Whistle, and I'll Come to You, My Lad."

—Morgan Llywelyn

OH, WHISTLE, AND I'LL COME TO YOU, MY LAD
by M. R. James

"I suppose you will be getting away pretty soon, now full term is over, professor," said a person not in the story to the professor of ontography, soon after they had sat down next to each other at a feast in the hospitable hall of St. James's College.

The professor was young, neat, and precise in speech.

"Yes," he said; "my friends have been making me take up golf this term, and I mean to go to the east coast—in point of fact to Burnstow—(I daresay you know it) for a week or ten days, to improve my game. I hope to get off tomorrow."

"Oh, Parkins," said his neighbor on the other side, "if you are going to Burnstow, I wish you would look at the site of the Templars' preceptory, and let me know if you think it would be any good to have a dig there in the summer."

It was, as you might suppose, a person of antiquarian pursuits who said this, but, since he merely appears in this prologue, there is no need to give his entitlements.

"Certainly," said Parkins, the professor: "if you will describe to me whereabouts the site is, I will do my best to give you an idea of the lie of the land when I get back; or I could write to you about it, if you would tell me where you are likely to be."

"Don't trouble to do that, thanks. It's only that I'm thinking of taking my family in that direction in the Long, and it occurred to me that, as very few of the English preceptories have ever been properly planned, I might have an opportunity of doing something useful on off-days."

The professor rather sniffed at the idea that planning out a preceptory could be described as useful. His neighbor continued: "The site—I doubt if there is anything showing above ground—must be down quite close to the beach now. The sea has encroached tremendously, as you know, all along that bit of coast. I should think, from the map, that it must be about three-quarters of a mile from the Globe Inn, at the north end of the town. Where are you going to stay?"

"Well, *at* the Globe Inn, as a matter of fact," said Parkins; "I have engaged a room there. I couldn't get in anywhere else; most of the lodging houses are shut up in winter, it seems; and, as it is, they tell me that the only room of any size I can have is really a double-bedded one, and that they haven't a corner in which to store the other bed, and so on. But I must have a fairly large room, for I am taking some books down, and mean to do a bit of work; and though I don't quite fancy having an empty bed—not to speak of two—in what I may call for the time being my study, I suppose I can manage to rough it for the short time I shall be there."

"Do you call having an extra bed in your room roughing it, Parkins?" said a bluff person opposite. "Look here, I shall come down and occupy it for a bit; it'll be company for you."

The professor quivered, but managed to laugh in a courteous manner.

"By all means, Rogers; there's nothing I should like better. But I'm afraid you would find it rather dull; you don't play golf, do you?"

"No, thank heaven!" said rude Mr. Rogers.

"Well, you see, when I'm not writing I shall most likely be out on the links, and that, as I say, would be rather dull for you, I'm afraid."

"Oh, I don't know! There's certain to be somebody I know in the place; but, of course, if you don't want me, speak the word, Parkins; I shan't be offended. Truth, as you always tell us, is never offensive."

Parkins was, indeed, scrupulously polite and strictly truthful. It is to be feared that Mr. Rogers sometimes practiced upon his knowledge of these characteristics. In Parkins's breast there was a conflict now raging, which for a moment or two did not allow him to answer. That interval being over, he said: "Well, if you want the exact truth, Rogers, I was considering whether the room I speak of would really be large enough to accommodate us both comfortably; and also whether (mind, I shouldn't have said this if you hadn't pressed me) you would not constitute something in the nature of a hindrance to my work."

Rogers laughed loudly.

"Well done, Parkins!" he said. "It's all right, I promise not to interrupt your work; don't you disturb yourself about that. No, I won't come if you don't want me; but I thought I should do so nicely to keep the ghosts off." Here he might have been seen to wink and to nudge his next neighbor. Parkins might also have been seen to become pink. "I beg pardon, Parkins," Rogers continued; "I oughtn't to have said that. I forgot you didn't like levity on these topics."

"Well," Parkins said, "as you have mentioned the matter, I freely own that I do *not* like careless talk about what you call ghosts. A man in my position," he went on, raising his voice a little, "cannot, I find, be too careful about appearing to sanction the current beliefs on such subjects. As you know, Rogers, or as you ought to know; for I think I have never concealed my views—"

"No, you certainly have not, old man," put in Rogers *sotto voce*.

"—I hold that any semblance, any appearance of concession to the view that such things might exist is equivalent to a renunciation of all that I hold most sacred. But I'm afraid I have not succeeded in securing your attention."

"Your *undivided* attention, was what Dr. Blimber actually *said*," Rogers interrupted, with every appearance of an earnest desire for accuracy. "But I beg your pardon, Parkins: I'm stopping you."

"No, not at all," said Parkins. "I don't remember Blimber; perhaps he was before my time. But I needn't go on. I'm sure you know what I mean."

"Yes, yes," said Rogers, rather hastily—"just so. We'll go into it fully at Burnstow, or somewhere."

In repeating the above dialogue I have tried to give the impression which it made on me, that Parkins was something of an old woman—rather henlike, perhaps, in his little ways; totally destitute, alas! of the sense of humor, but at the same time dauntless and sincere in his convictions, and a man deserving of the greatest respect. Whether or not the reader has gathered so much, that was the character which Parkins had.

* * *

On the following day Parkins did, as he had hoped, succeed in getting away from his college, and in arriving at Burnstow. He was made welcome at the Globe Inn, was safely installed in the large double-bedded room of which we have heard, and was able before retiring to rest to arrange his materials for work in apple-pie order upon a commodious table which occupied the outer end of the room, and was surrounded on three sides by windows looking out seaward; that is to say, the central window looked straight out to sea, and those on the left and right commanded prospects along the shore to the north and south respectively. On the south you saw the village of Burnstow. On the north no houses were to be seen, but only the beach and the low cliff backing it. Immediately in front was a strip—not considerable—of rough grass, dotted with old anchors, capstans and so forth; then a broad path; then the beach. Whatever may have been the original distance between the Globe Inn and the sea, not more than sixty yards now separated them.

The rest of the population of the inn was, of course, a golfing one, and included few elements that call for a special description. The most conspicuous figure was, perhaps, that of an *ancien militaire,* secretary of a London club, and possessed of a voice of incredible strength, and of views of a pronouncedly Protestant type. These were apt to find utterance after his attendance upon the ministrations of the vicar, an estimable man with inclinations towards a picturesque ritual, which he gallantly kept down as far as he could out of deference to East Anglian tradition.

Professor Parkins, one of whose principal characteristics was pluck, spent the greater part of the day following his arrival at Burnstow in what he had called improving his game, in company with this Colonel Wilson: and during the afternoon—whether the process of improvement were to blame or not, I am not sure—the colonel's demeanor assumed a coloring so lurid that even Parkins jibbed at the thought of walking home with him from the links. He determined, after a short and furtive look at that bristling mustache and those incarnadined features, that it would be wiser to allow the influences of tea and tobacco to do what they could with the colonel before the dinner hour should render a meeting inevitable.

"I might walk home tonight along the beach," he reflected—"yes, and take a look—there will be light enough for that—at the ruins of which Disney was talking. I don't exactly know where they are, by the way; but I expect I can hardly help stumbling on them."

This he accomplished, I may say, in the most literal sense, for in picking his way from the links to the shingle beach his foot caught, partly in a gorse root and partly in a biggish stone, and over he went. When he got up and surveyed his surroundings, he found himself in a patch of somewhat broken ground covered with small depressions and mounds. These latter, when he came to examine them, proved to be simply masses of flints embedded in mortar and grown over with turf. He must, he quite rightly concluded, be on the site of the preceptory he had promised to look at. It seemed not unlikely to reward the spade of the explorer; enough

of the foundations was probably left at no great depth to
throw a good deal of light on the general plan. He remembered vaguely that the Templars, to whom this site had
belonged, were in the habit of building round churches, and
he thought a particular series of the humps or mounds near
him did appear to be arranged in something of a circular
form. Few people can resist the temptation to try a little
amateur research in a department quite outside their own,
if only for the satisfaction of showing how successful they
would have been had they only taken it up seriously. Our
professor, however, if he felt something of this mean desire,
was also truly anxious to oblige Mr. Disney. So he paced
with care the circular area he had noticed, and wrote down
its rough dimensions in his pocketbook. Then he proceeded
to examine an oblong eminence which lay east of the center
of the circle, and seemed to his thinking likely to be the
base of a platform or altar. At one end of it, the northern,
a patch of the turf was gone—removed by some boy or
other creature *ferae naturae*. It might, he thought, be as
well to probe the soil for evidences of masonry, and he
took out his knife and began scraping away the earth. And
now followed another little discovery: a portion of soil fell
inward as he scraped, and disclosed a small cavity. He
lighted one match after another to help him to see of what
nature the hole was, but the wind was too strong for them
all. By tapping and scratching the sides with his knife, however, he was able to make out that it must be an artificial
hole in masonry. It was rectangular, and the sides, top and
bottom, if not actually plastered, were smooth and regular.
Of course it was empty. No! As he withdrew the knife he
heard a metallic clink, and when he introduced his hand it
met with a cylindrical object lying on the floor of the hole.
Naturally enough, he picked it up, and when he brought it
into the light, now fast fading, he could see that it, too, was
of man's making—a metal tube about four inches long, and
evidently of some considerable age.

By the time Parkins had made sure that there was nothing else in this odd receptacle, it was too late and too dark
for him to think of undertaking any further search. What
he had done had proved so unexpectedly interesting that
he determined to sacrifice a little more of the daylight on
the morrow to archaeology. The object which he now had

safe in his pocket was bound to be of some slight value at least, he felt sure.

Bleak and solemn was the view on which he took a last look before starting homeward. A faint yellow light in the west showed the links, on which a few figures moving towards the clubhouse were still visible, the squat martello tower, the lights of Aldsey village, the pale ribbon of sands intersected at intervals by black wooden groinings, the dim and murmuring sea. The wind was bitter from the north, but was at his back when he set out for the Globe. He quickly rattled and clashed through the shingle and gained the sand, upon which, but for the groinings which had to be got over every few yards, the going was both good and quiet. One last look behind, to measure the distance he had made since leaving the ruined Templars' church, showed him a prospect of company on his walk, in the shape of a rather indistinct personage, who seemed to be making great efforts to catch up with him, but made little, if any, progress. I mean that there was an appearance of running about his movements, but that the distance between him and Parkins did not seem materially to lessen. So, at least, Parkins thought, and decided that he almost certainly did not know him, and that it would be absurd to wait until he came up. For all that, company, he began to think, would really be very welcome on that lonely shore, if only you could choose your companion. In his unenlightened days he had read of meetings in such places which even now would hardly bear thinking of. He went on thinking of them, however, until he reached home, and particularly of one which catches most people's fancy at some time of their childhood. "Now I saw in my dream that Christian had gone but a very little way when he saw a foul fiend coming over the field to meet him." "What should I do now," he thought, "if I looked back and caught sight of a black figure sharply defined against the yellow sky, and saw that it had horns and wings? I wonder whether I should stand or run for it. Luckily, the gentleman behind is not of that kind, and he seems to be about as far off now as when I saw him first. Well, at this rate, he won't get his dinner as soon as I shall; and, dear me! It's within a quarter of an hour of the time now. I must run!"

Parkins had, in fact, very little time for dressing. When he met the colonel at dinner, peace—or as much of her as that gentleman could manage—reigned once more in the military bosom; nor was she put to flight in the hours of bridge that followed dinner, for Parkins was a more than respectable player. When, therefore, he retired towards twelve o'clock, he felt that he had spent his evening in quite a satisfactory way, and that, even for so long as a fortnight or three weeks, life at the Globe would be supportable under similar conditions—"especially," thought he, "if I go on improving my game."

As he went along the passages he met the boots of the Globe, who stopped and said: "Beg your pardon, sir, but as I was a-brushing your coat just now there was something fell out of the pocket. I put it on your chest of drawers, sir, in your room, sir—a piece of a pipe or something of that, sir. Thank you, sir. You'll find it on your chest of drawers, sir—yes, sir. Good night, sir."

The speech served to remind Parkins of his little discovery of that afternoon. It was with some considerable curiosity that he turned it over by the light of his candles. It was of bronze, he now saw, and was shaped very much after the manner of the modern dog whistle; in fact it was—yes, certainly it was—actually no more nor less than a whistle. He put it to his lips, but it was quite full of a fine, caked-up sand or earth, which would not yield to knocking, but must be loosened with a knife. Tidy as ever in his habits, Parkins cleared out the earth onto a piece of paper, and took the latter to the window to empty it out. The night was clear and bright, as he saw when he had opened the casement, and he stopped for an instant to look at the sea and not a belated wanderer stationed on the shore in front of the inn. Then he shut the window, a little surprised at the late hours people kept at Burnstow, and took his whistled to the light again. Why, surely there were marks on it, and not merely marks, but letters! A very little rubbing rendered the deeply cut inscription quite legible, but the professor had to confess, after some earnest thought, that the meaning of it was as obscure to him as the writing on the wall to Belshazzar. There were legends both on the front and on the back of the whistle. The one read thus:

FLA

FUR   BIS

FLE

The other:

QUIS EST ISTE QUI VENIT

"I ought to be able to make it out," he thought; "but I suppose I am a little rusty in my Latin. When I come to think of it, I don't believe I even know the word for a whistle. The long one does seem simple enough. It ought to mean: Who is this who is coming? Well the best way to find out is evidently to whistle for him."

He blew tentatively and stopped suddenly, startled and yet pleased at the note he had elicited. It had a quality of infinite distance in it, and, soft as it was, he somehow felt it must be audible for miles round. It was a sound, too, that seemed to have the power (which many scents possess) of forming pictures in the brain. He saw quite clearly for a moment a vision of a wide, dark expanse at night, with a fresh wind blowing, and in the midst a lonely figure—how employed, he could not tell. Perhaps he would have seen more had not the picture been broken by the sudden surge of a gust of wind against his casement, so sudden that it made him look up, just in time to see the white glint of a seabird's wing somewhere outside the dark panes.

The sound of the whistle had so fascinated him that he could not help trying it once more, this time more boldly. The note was little, if at all, louder than before, and repetition broke the illusion—no picture followed, as he had half-hoped it might. "But what is this? Goodness! What force the wind can get up in a few minutes! What a tremendous gust! There! I knew that window fastening was no use! Ah! I thought so—both candles out. It is enough to tear the room to pieces."

The first thing was to get the window shut. While you might count twenty, Parkins was struggling with the small casement and felt almost as if he were pushing back a sturdy burglar, so strong was the pressure. It slackened all at once, and the window banged to and latched itself. Now to relight the candles and see what damage, if any, had been done. No, nothing seemed amiss; no glass even was broken in the casement. But the noise had evidently roused at least one member of the household: the colonel was to be heard stumping in his stockinged feet on the floor above, and growling.

Quickly as it had risen, the wind did not fall at once. On it went, moaning and rushing past the house, at times rising to a cry so desolate that, as Parkins disinterestedly said, it might have made fanciful people feel quite uncomfortable; even the unimaginative, he thought after a quarter of an hour, might be happier without it.

Whether it was the wind, or the excitement of golf or of the researches in the preceptory that kept Parkins awake, he was not sure. Awake he remained, in any case, long enough to fancy (as I am afraid I often do myself under such conditions) that he was the victim of all manner of fatal disorders: he would lie counting the beats of his heart, convinced that it was going to stop work every moment, and would entertain grave suspicions of his lungs, brain, liver, etc.—suspicions which he was sure would be dispelled by the return of daylight, but which until then refused to be put aside. He found a little vicarious comfort in the idea that someone else was in the same boat. A near neighbor (in the darkness it was not easy to tell his direction) was tossing and rustling in his bed, too.

The next stage was that Parkins shut his eyes and determined to give sleep every chance. Here again overexcitement asserted itself in another form—that of making pictures. *Experto crede,* pictures do come to the closed eyes of one trying to sleep, and are often so little to his taste that he must open his eyes and disperse them.

Parkins's experience on this occasion was a very distressing one. He found that the picture which presented itself to him was continuous. When he opened his eyes, of course, it went; but when he shut them once more it framed itself afresh, and acted itself out again, neither quicker nor slower than before. What he saw was this: a long stretch of shore—shingle-edged by sand, and intersected at short intervals with black groins running down to the water—a scene, in fact, so like that of his afternoon's walk that, in the absence of any landmark, it could not be distinguished therefrom. The light was obscure, conveying an impression of gathering storm, late winter evening and slight cold rain. On this bleak stage at first no actor was visible. Then, in the distance, a bobbing black object appeared; a moment more, and it was a man running, jumping, clambering over the groins, and every few seconds looking eagerly back. The nearer he came the more obvious it was that he was not only anxious, but even terribly frightened, though his face was not to be distinguished. He was, moreover, almost at the end of his strength. On he came; each successive obstacle seemed to cause him more difficulty than the last. "Will he get over this next one?" thought Parkins; "it seems a little higher than the others." Yes; half-climbing, half-throwing himself, he did get over, and fell all in a heap on the other side (the side nearest to the spectator). There, as if really unable to get up again, he remained crouching under the groin, looking up in an attitude of painful anxiety.

So far no cause whatever for the fear of the runner had been shown; but now there began to be seen, far up the shore, a little flicker of something light colored moving to and fro with great swiftness and irregularity. Rapidly growing larger, it, too, declared itself as a figure in pale, fluttering draperies, ill defined. There was something about its motion which made Parkins very unwilling to see it at close quarters. It would stop, raise arms, bow itself toward the sand, then run stooping across the beach to the water's edge and back again; and then, rising upright, once more continue its course forward at a speed that was startling and terrifying. The moment came when the pursuer was hovering about from left to right only a few yards beyond the groin where the runner lay in hiding. After two or three ineffectual castings hither and thither it came to a stop, stood upright, with arms raised high, and then darted straight forward toward the groin.

It was at this point that Parkins always failed in his resolution to keep his eyes shut. With many misgivings as to incipient failure of eyesight, overworked brain, excessive smoking and so on, he finally resigned himself to light his candle, get out a book and pass the night waking, rather than be tormented by this persistent panorama, which he saw clearly enough could only be a morbid reflection of his walk and this thoughts on that very day.

The scraping of the match on box and the glare of light must have startled some creatures of the night—rats or what not—which he heard scurry across the floor from the side of his bed with much rustling. Dear, dear! the match is out! Fool that it is! But the second one burned better, and a candle and book were duly procured, over which Parkins pored till sleep of a wholesome kind came upon him, and that in no long space. For about the first time in his orderly and prudent life he forgot to blow out the candle, and when he was called next morning at eight there was still a flicker in the socket and a sad mess of guttered grease on the top of the little table.

After breakfast he was in his room, putting the finishing touches to his golfing costume—fortune had again allotted the colonel to him for a partner—when one of the maids came in.

"Oh, if you please," she said, "would you like any extra blankets on your bed, sir?"

"Ah! Thank you," said Parkins. "Yes, I think I should like one. It seems likely to turn rather colder."

In a very short time the maid was back with the blanket.

"Which bed should I put it on, sir?" she asked.

"What? Why, that one—the one I slept in last night," he said, pointing to it.

"Oh yes! I beg your pardon, sir, but you seemed to have tried both of 'em; leastways, we had to make 'em both up this morning."

"Really? How very absurd!" said Parkins. "I certainly never touched the other, except to lay some things on it. Did it actually seem to have been slept in?"

"Oh yes, sir!" said the maid. "Why, all the things was crumpled and throwed about all ways, if you'll excuse me, sir—quite as if anyone 'adn't passed but a very poor night, sir."

"Dear me," said Parkins. "Well, I may have disordered it more than I thought when I unpacked my things. I'm very sorry to have given you the extra trouble, I'm sure. I expect a friend of mine soon, by the way—a gentleman from Cambridge—to come and occupy it for a night or two. That will be all right, I suppose, won't it?"

"Oh yes, to be sure, sir. Thank you, sir. It's no trouble,

sir, I'm sure," said the maid, and departed to giggle with her colleagues.

Parkins set forth, with a stern determination to improve his game.

I am glad to be able to report that he succeeded so far in this enterprise that the colonel, who had been rather repining at the prospect of a second day's play in his company, became quite chatty as the morning advanced; and his voice boomed out over the flats, as certain also of our own minor poets have said, "like some great bourdon in a minster tower."

"Extraordinary wind, that, we had last night," he said. "In my old home we should have said someone had been whistling for it."

"Should you, indeed!" said Parkins. "Is there a superstition of that kind still current in your part of the country?"

"I don't know about superstition," said the colonel. "They believe in it all over Denmark and Norway, as well as on the Yorkshire coast; and my experience is, mind you, that there's generally something at the bottom of what these countryfolk hold to, and have held to for generations. But it's your drive" (or whatever it might have been: the golfing reader will have to imagine appropriate disgressions at the proper intervals).

When conversation was resumed, Parkins said, with a slight hesitancy: "Apropos of what you were saying just now, colonel, I think I ought to tell you that my own views on such subjects are very strong. I am, in fact, a convinced disbeliever in what is called the supernatural."

"What!" said the colonel, "do you mean to tell me you don't believe in second sight, or ghosts or anything of that kind?"

"In nothing whatever of that kind," returned Parkins firmly.

"Well," said the colonel, "but it appears to me at that rate, sir, that you must be little better than a Sadducee."

Parkins was on the point of answering that, in his opinion, the Sadducees were the most sensible persons he had ever read of in the Old Testament; but, feeling some doubt as to whether such mention of them was to be found in that work, he preferred to laugh the accusation off.

"Perhaps I am," he said; "but—Here, give me my cleek,

boy!—Excuse me one moment, colonel." A short interval.
"Now, as to whistling for the wind, let me give you my
theory about it. The laws which govern winds are really not
at all perfectly known—to fisherfolk and such, of course,
not known at all. A man or woman of eccentric habits,
perhaps, or a stranger, is seen repeatedly on the beach at
some unusual hour, and is heard whistling. Soon afterwards
a violent wind rises; a man who could read the sky perfectly
or who possessed a barometer could have foretold that it
would. The simple people of a fishing village have no ba-
rometers, and only a few rough rules for prophesying
weather. What more natural than that the eccentric personage I postulated should be regarded as having raised the
wind, or that he or she should clutch eagerly at the reputation of being able to do so? Now, take last night's wind: as
it happens, I myself was whistling. I blew a whistle twice,
and the wind seemed to come absolutely in answer to my
call. If anyone had seen me—"

The audience had been a little restive under this harangue, and Parkins had, I fear, fallen somewhat into the
tone of a lecturer; but at the last sentence the colonel
stopped.

"Whistling, were you?" he said. "And what sort of whistle did you use? Play this stroke first." Interval.

"About that whistle you were asking, colonel. It's rather
a curious one. I have it in my—No; I see I've left it in my
room. As a matter of fact, I found it yesterday."

And then Parkins narrated the manner of his discovery
of the whistle, upon hearing which the colonel grunted, and
opined that, in Parkins's place, he should himself be careful
about using a thing that had belonged to a set of Papists,
of whom, speaking generally, it might be affirmed that you
never knew what they might not have been up to. From
this topic he diverged to the enormities of the vicar, who
had given notice on the previous Sunday that Friday would
be the Feast of St. Thomas the Apostle, and that there
would be service at eleven o'clock in the church. This and
other similar proceedings constituted in the colonel's view
a strong presumption that the vicar was a concealed Papist,
if not a Jesuit; and Parkins, who could not very readily
follow the colonel in this region, did not disagree with him.
In fact, they got on so well together in the morning that

there was no talk on either side of their separating after lunch.

Both continued to play well during the afternoon, or at least, well enough to make them forget everything else until the light began to fail them. Not until then did Parkins remember that he had meant to do some more investigating at the preceptory; but it was of no great importance, he reflected. One day was as good as another; he might as well go home with the colonel.

As they turned the corner of the house, the colonel was almost knocked down by a boy who rushed into him at the very top of his speed, and then, instead of running away, remained hanging onto him and panting. The first words of the warrior were naturally those of reproof and objurgation, but he very quickly discerned that the boy was almost speechless with fright. Inquiries were useless at first. When the boy got his breath he began to howl, and still clung to the colonel's legs. He was at last detached, but continued to howl.

"What in the world *is* the matter with you? What have you been up to? What have you seen?" said the two men.

"Ow, I seen it wive at me out of the winder," wailed the boy, "and I don't like it."

"What window?" said the irritated colonel. "Come pull yourself together, my boy."

"The front winder it was, at the 'otel," said the boy.

At this point Parkins was in favor of sending the boy home, but the colonel refused; he wanted to get to the bottom of it, he said; it was most dangerous to give a boy such a fright as this one had had, and if it turned out that people had been playing jokes, they should suffer for it in some way. And by a series of questions he made out this story: The boy had been playing about on the grass in front of the Globe with some others; then they had gone home to their teas, and he was just going, when he happened to look up at the front winder and see it a-wiving at him. *It* seemed to be a figure of some sort, in white as far as he knew—couldn't see its face; but it wived at him, and it warn't a right thing—not to say not a right person. Was there a light in the room? No, he didn't think to look if there was a light. Which was the window? Was it the top

one or the second one? The seckind one it was—the big
winder what got two little uns at the sides.

"Very well, my boy," said the colonel, after a few more
questions. "You run away home now. I expect it was some
person trying to give you a start. Another time, like a brave
English boy, you just throw a stone—well, no, not that exactly, but you go and speak to the waiter, or to Mr. Simpson, the landlord, and—yes—and say that I advised you to
do so."

The boy's face expressed some of the doubt he felt as to
the likelihood of Mr. Simpson's lending a favorable ear to his
complaint, but the colonel did not appear to perceive this,
and went on:

"And here's a sixpence—no, I see it's a shilling—and you
be off home, and don't think any more about it."

The youth hurried off with agitated thanks, and the colonel and Parkins went round to the front of the Globe and
reconnoitered. There was only one window answering to
the description they had been hearing.

"Well, that's curious," said Parkins; "it's evidently my
window the lad was talking about. Will you come up for a
moment, Colonel Wilson? We ought to be able to see if
anyone has been taking liberties in my room."

They were soon in the passage, and Parkins made as if
to open the door. Then he stopped and felt in his pockets.

"This is more serious than I thought," was his next remark. "I remember now that before I started this morning
I locked the door. It is locked now, and, what is more, here
is the key." And he held it up. "Now," he went on, "if the
servants are in the habit of going into one's room during
the day when one is away, I can only say that—well, that
I don't approve of it at all." Conscious of a somewhat weak
climax, he busied himself in opening the door (which was
indeed locked) and in lighting candles. "No," he said,
"nothing seems disturbed."

"Except your bed," put in the colonel.

"Excuse me, that isn't my bed," said Parkins. "I don't
use that one. But it does look as if someone had been
playing tricks with it."

It certainly did: the clothes were bundled up and twisted
together in a most tortuous confusion. Parkins pondered.

"That must be it," he said at last. "I disordered the

clothes last night in unpacking, and they haven't made it since. Perhaps they came in to make it, and that boy saw them through the window; and then they were called away and locked the door after them. Yes, I think that must be it."

"Well, ring and ask," said the colonel, and this appealed to Parkins as practical.

The maid appeared, and, to make a long story short, deposed that she had made the bed in the morning when the gentleman was in the room, and hadn't been there since. No, she hadn't no other key. Mr. Simpson, he kep' the keys; he'd be able to tell the gentleman if anyone had been up.

This was a puzzle. Investigation showed that nothing of value had been taken, and Parkins remembered the disposition of the small objects on tables and so forth well enough to be pretty sure that no pranks had been played with them. Mr. and Mrs. Simpson furthermore agreed that neither of them had given the duplicate key of the room to any person whatever during the day. Nor could Parkins, fair-minded man as he was, detect anything in the demeanor of master, mistress or maid that indicated guilt. He was much more inclined to think that the boy had been imposing on the colonel.

The latter was unwontedly silent and pensive at dinner and throughout the evening. When he bade good night to Parkins, he murmured in a gruff undertone:

"You know where I am if you want me during the night."

"Why, yes, thank you, Colonel Wilson, I think I do; but there isn't much prospect of my disturbing you, I hope. By the way," he added, "did I show you that old whistle I spoke of? I think not. Well, here it is."

The colonel turned it over gingerly in the light of the candle.

"Can you make anything of the inscription?" asked Parkins, as he took it back.

"No, not in this light. What do you mean to do with it?"

"Oh, well, when I get back to Cambridge I shall submit it to some of the archaeologists there, and see what they think of it; and very likely, if they consider it worth having, I may present it to one of the museums."

"Hmm," said the colonel. "Well, you may be right. All

I know is that, if it were mine, I should chuck it straight
into the sea. It's no use talking, I'm well aware, but I expect
that with you it's a case of live and learn. I hope so, I'm
sure, and I wish you a good night.''

He turned away, leaving Parkins in act to speak at the
bottom of the stair, and soon each was in his own bedroom.

By some unfortunate accident, there were neither blinds
nor curtains to the windows of the professor's room. The
previous night he had thought little of this, but tonight
there seemed every prospect of a bright moon rising to
shine directly on his bed, and probably wake him later on.
When he noticed this he was a good deal annoyed, but,
with an ingenuity which I can only envy, he succeeded in
rigging up, with the help of a railway rug, some safety pins,
and a stick and umbrella, a screen which, if it only held
together, would completely keep the moonlight off his bed.
And shortly afterwards he was comfortably in that bed.
When he had read a somewhat solid work long enough to
produce a decided wish for sleep, he cast a drowsy glance
round the room, blew out the candle and fell back upon
the pillow.

He must have slept soundly for an hour or more, when
a sudden clatter shook him up in a most unwelcome manner. In a moment he realized what had happened: his carefully constructed screen had given way, and a very bright
frosty moon was shining directly on his face. This was
highly annoying. Could he possibly get up and reconstruct
the screen? or could he manage to sleep if he did not?

For some minutes he lay and pondered over the possibili-
ties; then he turned over sharply, and with all his eyes open
lay breathlessly listening. There had been a movement, he
was sure, in the empty bed on the opposite side of the
room. Tomorrow he would have it moved, for there must
be rats or something playing about in it. It was quiet now.
No! the commotion began again. There was a rustling and
shaking: surely more than any rat could cause.

I can figure to myself something of the professor's bewilderment and horror, for I have in a dream thirty years back
seen the same thing happen; but the reader will hardly,
perhaps, imagine how dreadful it was to him to see a figure
suddenly sit up in what he had known was an empty bed.
He was out of his own bed in one bound, and made a dash

towards the window, where lay his only weapon, the stick
with which he had propped his screen. This was, as it
turned out, the worst thing he could have done, because
the personage in the empty bed, with a sudden smooth
motion, slipped from the bed and took up a position, with
outspread arms, between the two beds, and in front of the
door. Parkins watched it in a horrid perplexity. Somehow,
the idea of getting past it and escaping through the door
was intolerable to him; he could not have borne—he didn't
know why—to touch it; and as for its touching him, he
would sooner dash himself through the window than have
that happen. It stood for the moment in a band of dark
shadow, and he had not seen what its face was like. Now
it began to move, in a stooping posture, and all at once the
spectator realized, with some horror and some relief, that
it must be blind, for it seemed to feel about it with its
muffled arms in a groping and random fashion. Turning
half-away from him, it became suddenly conscious of the
bed he had just left, and darted towards it, and bent and
felt over the pillows in a way which made Parkins shudder
as he had never in his life thought it possible. In a very
few moments it seemed to know that the bed was empty,
and then, moving forward into the area of light and facing
the window, it showed for the first time what manner of
thing it was.

Parkins, who very much dislikes being questioned about
it, did once describe something of it in my hearing, and I
gathered that what he chiefly remembers about it is a horrible, an intensely horrible, face *of crumpled linen*. What expression he read upon it he could not or would not tell, but
that the fear of it went nigh to maddening him is certain.

But he was not at leisure to watch it for long. With formidable quickness it moved into the middle of the room, and,
as it groped and waved, one corner of its draperies swept
across Parkins's face. He could not, though he knew how
perilous a sound was—he could not keep back a cry of
disgust, and this gave the searcher an instant clue. It leaped
towards him upon the instant, and the next moment he was
halfway through the window backwards, uttering cry upon
cry at the utmost pitch of his voice, and the linen face was
thrust close into his own. At this, almost the last possible
second, deliverance came, as you will have guessed: the

colonel burst the door open, and was just in time to see the dreadful group at the window. When he reached the figures only one was left. Parkins sank forward into the room in a faint, and before him on the floor lay a tumbled heap of bedclothes.

Colonel Wilson asked no questions, but busied himself in keeping everyone else out of the room and in getting Parkins back to his bed; and himself, wrapped in a rug, occupied the other bed for the rest of the night. Early on the next day Rogers arrived, more welcome than he would have been a day before, and the three of them held a very long consultation in the professor's room. At the end of it the colonel left the hotel door carrying a small object between his finger and thumb, which he cast as far into the sea as a very brawny arm could send it. Later on the smoke of a burning ascended from the back premises of the Globe.

Exactly what explanation was patched up for the staff and visitors at the hotel I must confess I do not recollect. The professor was somehow cleared of the ready suspicion of delirium tremens, and the hotel of the reputation of a troubled house.

There is not much question as to what would have happened to Parkins if the colonel had not intervened when he did. He would either have fallen out of the window or else lost his wits. But it is not so evident what more the creature that came in answer to the whistle could have done than frighten. There seemed to be absolutely nothing material about it save the bedclothes of which it had made itself a body. The colonel, who remembered a not very dissimilar occurrence in India, was of opinion that if Parkins had closed with it, it could really have done very little, and that its one power was that of frightening. The whole thing, he said, served to confirm his opinion of the Church of Rome.

There is really nothing more to tell, but, as you may imagine, the professor's views on certain points are less clear-cut than they used to be. His nerves, too, have suffered: he cannot even now see a surplice hanging on a door quite unmoved, and the spectacle of a scarecrow in a field late on a winter afternoon has cost him more than one sleepless night.

There are those who hold to the idea that fantasy should offer an escape from the troubles and trials of the real world. Nothing wrong with that, of course, except all fiction is an escape of one kind or another, and usually, given a choice, I'd rather escape into a fictional world that reveals and expands upon the magic and wonder of our own, than one wherein all the fantastical elements are exaggerated, or presented as so common that they wake no sense of wonder.

What strikes me so much when I read and reread "Homeland" is the same thing that first captured me with Kingsolver's fiction when I discovered her novel *Animal Dreams*. It's this gift she has of creating characters and stories in which myth and folklore and the spirit world are inextricably entwined with the events of the story as it plays out, yet don't have to actually appear on stage.

The wonderful relationship between Waterbug and her Native American great-grandmother doesn't need the small people and creation myths, the little animal and flower cousins, to be poignant and memorable; their addition, however, lays a great, humming resonance under the events and locks them forever in one's mind.

I could go on and on about how much I love Kingsolver's prose, the voices of her characters, the questions she asks in her stories that she lets us answer for ourselves, but in the end, trying to explain exactly why a particular writer or artist or musician moves us so much becomes an impossible task. I find myself reduced to what St. Augustine had to say about the nature of time: "If no one asks me, I know; but if any person should require me to tell him, I cannot."

I do know that "Homeland" is about many things. I know as well that the reason it's one of my all-time favorite stories is for how lyrically Kingsolver shows us, in just a few pages, the importance of story, and memories, and the interconnectedness of all things without once stumbling into lecture. This is a simple, heartfelt tale that will disappoint those looking for flashy marvels and the big bang, but will linger for a very long time in the hearts of those who understand that great and marvelous wonders can, indeed, come in small and subtle packages.

—Charles de Lint

HOMELAND
by Barbara Kingsolver

I

My great-grandmother belonged to the Bird Clan. Hers was one of the fugitive bands of Cherokee who resisted capture in the year that General Winfield Scott was in charge of prodding the forest people from their beds and removing them westward. Those few who escaped his notice moved like wildcat families through the Carolina mountains, leaving the ferns unbroken where they passed, eating wild grapes and chestnuts, drinking when they found streams. The ones who could not travel, the aged and the infirm and the very young, were hidden in deep cane thickets where they would remain undiscovered until they were bones. When the people's hearts could not bear any more, they laid their deerskin packs on the ground and settled again.

General Scott had moved on to other endeavors by this time, and he allowed them to thrive or perish as they would. They build clay houses with thin, bent poles for spines, and in autumn they went down to the streams where the sycamore trees had let their year's work fall, the water steeped brown as leaf tea, and the people cleansed themselves of the sins of the scattered-bone time. They called their refugee years The Time When We Were Not, and they were forgiven, because they had carried the truth of themselves in a sheltered place inside the flesh, exactly the way a fruit that has gone soft still carries inside itself the clean, hard stone of its future.

II

My name is Gloria St. Claire, but like most people I've been called many things. My maiden name was Murray. My grown children have at one time or another hailed me by nearly anything pronounceable. When I was a child my-

self, my great-grandmother called me by the odd name of
Waterbug. I asked her many times why this was, until she
said once, to quiet me, "I'll tell you that story."

We were on the front-porch swing, in summer, in darkness. I waited while she drew tobacco smoke in and out of
her mouth, but she said nothing. "Well," I said.

Moonlight caught the fronts of her steel-framed spectacles and she looked at me from her invisible place in the
dark. "I said I'd tell you that story. I didn't say I would
tell it right now."

We lived in Morning Glory, a coal town hacked with
sharp blades out of a forest that threatened always to take
it back. The hickories encroached on the town, springing
up unbidden in the middle of dog pens and front yards and
the cemetery. The creeping vines for which the town was
named drew themselves along wire fences and up the sides
of houses with the persistence of the displaced. I have
heard it said that if a man stood still in Morning Glory, he
would be tied down by vines and not found until first frost.
Even the earth underneath us sometimes moved to repos-
sess its losses: the long, deep shafts that men opened to
rob the coal veins would close themselves up again, as quietly as flesh wounds.

My great-grandmother lived with us for her last two
years. When she came to us we were instructed to call her
Great Grandmother, but that proved impossible and so we
called her Great Mam. My knowledge of her life follows
an oddly obscured pattern, like a mountain road where
much of the scenery is blocked by high laurel bushes, not
because they were planted there, but because no one
thought to cut them down.

I know that her maternal lineage was distinguished. Her
mother's mother's father was said to have gone to England,
where he dined with King George and contracted smallpox.
When he returned home his family plunged him into an icy
stream, which was the curative custom, and he died. Also,
her mother was one of the Bird Clan's Beloved Women.
When I asked what made her a Beloved Woman, Great
Mam said that it was because she kept track of things.

But of Great Mam's own life, before she came to us, I
know only a little. She rarely spoke of personal things, fa-
voring instead the legendary and the historic, and so what

I did discover came from my mother, who exercised over all matters a form of reverse censorship: she spoke loudly and often of events of which she disapproved, and rarely of those that might have been ordinary or redemptive. She told us, for instance, that Great-Grandfather Murray brought Great Mam from her tribal home in the Hiwassee Valley to live in Kentucky, without Christian sanction, as his common-law wife. According to Mother, he accomplished all of this on a stolen horse. From that time forward Great Mam went by the name of Ruth.

It was my mother's opinion that Great-Grandfather Murray was unfit for respectable work. He died after taking up the honest vocation of coal mining, which also killed their four sons, all on the same day, in a collapsed shaft. Their daughter perished of fever after producing a single illegitimate boy, who turned out to be my father, John Murray. Great Mam was thus returned to refugee ways, raising her grandson alone in hard circumstances, moving from place to place where she could find the odd bit of work. She was quite remarkably old when she came to us.

I know, also, that her true name was Green Leaf, although there is no earthly record of this. The gravesite is marked Ruth. Mother felt we ought to bury her under her Christian name in the hope that God in His infinite mercy would forget about the heathen marriage and stolen horses and call her home. It is likely, however, that He might have passed over the headstone altogether in his search for her, since virtually all the information written there is counterfeit. We even had to invent a date and year of birth for her since these things were unknown. This, especially, was unthinkable to my brothers and me. But we were children, of course, and believed our own birthdays began and ended the calendar.

* * *

To look at her, you would not have thought her an Indian. She wore blue and lavender flowered dresses with hand-tatted collars, and brown lace-up shoes with sturdy high heels, and she smoked a regular pipe. She was tall, with bowed calves and a faintly bent-forward posture, spine straight and elbows out and palms forward, giving the impression that she was at any moment prepared to stoop and lift a burden of great bulk or weight. She spoke with a soft hill accent, and spoke properly. My great-grandfather had been an educated man, more prone in his lifetime to errors of judgment than errors of grammar.

Great Mam smoked her pipe mainly in the evenings, and always on the front porch. For a time I believed this was because my mother so vigorously objected to the smell, but Great Mam told me otherwise. A pipe had to be smoked outdoors, she said, where the smoke could return to the Beloved Old Father who gave us tobacco. When I asked her what she meant, she said she meant nothing special at all. It was just the simplest thing, like a bread-and-butter note you send to an aunt after she has fed you a meal.

I often sat with Great Mam in the evenings on our porch swing, which was suspended by four thin, painted chains that squeaked. The air at night smelled of oil and dust, and faintly of livestock, for the man at the end of our lane kept hogs. Great Mam would strike a match and suck the flame into her pipe, lighting her creased face in brief orange bursts.

"The small people are not very bright tonight," she would say, meaning the stars. She held surprising convictions, such as that in the daytime the small people walked among us. I could not begin to picture it.

"You mean down here in the world, or do you mean right here in Morning Glory?" I asked repeatedly. "Would they walk along with Jack and Nathan and me to school?"

She nodded. "They would."

"But why would they come *here?*" I asked.

"Well, why wouldn't they?" she said.

I thought about this for a while, entirely unconvinced.

"You don't ever have to be lonesome," she said. "That's one thing you never need be."

"But mightn't I step on one of them, if it got in my way and I didn't see it?"

Great Mam said, "No. They aren't that small."

She had particular names for many things, including the months. February she called "Hungry Month." She spoke of certain animals as if they were relatives our parents had neglected to tell us about. The cowering white dog that begged at our kitchen door she called "the sad little cousin." If she felt like it, on these evenings, she would tell me stories about the animals, their personalities and kindnesses and trickery, and the permanent physical markings they invariably earned by doing something they ought not to have done. "Remember that story," she often commanded at the end, and I would be stunned with guilt because my mind had wandered onto crickets and pencil erasers and Black Beauty.

"I might not remember," I told her. "It's too hard."

Great Mam allowed that I might *think* I had forgotten. "But you haven't. You'll keep it stored away," she said. "If it's important, your heart remembers."

I had known that hearts could break and sometimes even be attacked, with disastrous result, but I had not heard of hearts remembering. I was eleven years old. I did not trust any of my internal parts with the capacity of memory.

* * *

When the seasons changed, it never occurred to us to think to ourselves, "This will be Great Mam's last spring. Her last June apples. Her last fresh roasting ears from the garden." She was like an old pine, whose accumulated years cause one to ponder how long it has stood, not how soon it will fall. Of all of us, I think Papa was the only one who believed she could die. He planned the trip to Tennessee. We children simply thought it was a great lark.

This was in June, following a bad spring during which the whole southern spine of the Appalachians had broken out in a rash of wildcat strikes. Papa was back to work at last, no longer home taking up kitchen-table space, but still Mother complained of having to make soups of neckbones and cut our school shoes open to bare our too-long toes to summer's dust, for the whole darn town to see. Papa pointed out that the whole darn town had been on the picket lines, and wouldn't pass judgment on the Murray kids if they ran their bare bottoms down Main Street. And what's more, he said, it wasn't his fault if John L. Lewis had sold him down the river.

My brothers and I thrilled to imagine ourselves racing naked past the Post Office and the women shopping at Herman Ritchie's Market, but we did not laugh out loud.

We didn't know exactly who Mr. John L. Lewis was, or what river Papa meant, but we knew not to expect much. The last thing we expected was a trip.

My brother Jack, because of his nature and superior age, was suspicious from the outset. While Papa explained his plan, Jack made a point of pushing lima beans around his plate in single file to illustrate his boredom. It was 1955. Patti Page and Elvis were on the radio and high school boys were fighting their mothers over ducktails. Jack had a year to go before high school, but already the future was plainly evident.

He asked where in Tennessee we would be going, if we did go. The three of us had not seen the far side of a county line.

"The Hiwassee Valley, where Great Mam was born," Papa said.

My brother Nathan grew interested when Jack laid down his fork. Nathan was only eight, but he watched grownups. If there were no men around, he watched Jack.

"Eat your beans, Jack," Mother said. "I didn't put up these limas last fall so you could torment them."

Jack stated, "I'm not eating no beans with guts in them."

Mother took a swat at Jack's arm. "Young man, you watch your mouth. That's the insides of a hog, and a hog's a perfectly respectable animal to eat." Nathan was making noises with his throat. I tried not to make any face one way or the other.

Great Mam told Mother it would have been enough just to have the limas, without the meat. "A person can live on green corn and beans, Florence Ann," she said. "There's no shame in vegetables."

We knew what would happen next, and watched with interest. "If I have to go out myself and throw a rock at a songbird," Mother said, having deepened to the color of beetroot, "nobody is going to say this family goes without meat!"

Mother was a tiny woman who wore stockings and shirt-waists even to hoe the garden. She had yellow hair pinned in a tight bun, with curly bangs in front. We waited with our chins cupped in our palms for Papa's opinion of her plan to make a soup of Robin Redbreast, but he got up from the table and rummaged in the bureau drawer for the gas-station map. Great Mam ate her beans in a careful way, as though each one had its own private importance.

"Are we going to see Injuns?" Nathan asked, but no one answered. Mother began making a great deal of noise clearing up the dishes. We could hear her out in the kitchen, scrubbing.

Papa unfolded the Texaco map on the table and found where Tennessee and North Carolina and Georgia came together in three different pastel colors. Great Mam looked down at the colored lines and squinted, holding the sides of her glasses. "Is this the Hiwassee River?" she wanted to know.

"No, now those lines are highways," he said. "Red is interstate. Blue is river."

"Well, what's this?"

He looked. "That's the state line."

"Now why would they put that on the map? You can't see it."

Papa flattened the creases of the map with his broad hands, which were crisscrossed with fine black lines of coal dust, like a map themselves, no matter how clean. "The Hiwassee Valley's got a town in it now, it says 'Cherokee.' Right here."

"Well, those lines make my eyes smart," Great Mam said, "I'm not going to look anymore."

The boys started to snicker, but Papa gave us a look that said he meant business and sent us off to bed before it went any farther.

"Great Mam's blind as a post hole," Jack said once we were in bed. "She don't know a road from a river."

"She don't know beans from taters," said Nathan.

"You boys hush up, I'm tired," I said. Jack and Nathan slept lengthwise in the bed, and I slept across the top with my own blanket.

"Here's Great Mam," Nathan said. He sucked in his cheeks and crossed his eyes and keeled over backward, bouncing us all on the bedsprings. Jack punched him in the ribs, and Nathan started to cry louder than he had to. I got up and sat by the bedroom door hugging my knees, listening to Papa and Mother. I could hear them in the kitchen.

"As if I hadn't put up with enough, John. It's not enough that Murrays have populated God's earth without the benefit of marriage," Mother said. This was her usual starting point. She was legally married to my father in a Baptist Church, a fact she could work into any conversation.

"Well, I don't see why," she said, "if we never had the money to take the kids anyplace before."

Papa's voice was quieter, and I couldn't hear his answers.

"Was this her idea, John, or yours?"

When Nathan and Jack were asleep I went to the window and slipped over the sill. My feet landed where they always did, in the cool mud of Mother's gladiolus patch alongside the house. Great Mam did not believe in flower patches. Why take a hoe and kill all the growing things in a piece of ground, and then plant others that have been uprooted from somewhere else? This was what she asked me. She thought Mother spent a fearful amount of time moving things needlessly from one place to another.

"I see you, Waterbug," said Great Mam in the darkness, though what she probably meant was that she heard me. All I could see was the glow of her pipe bowl moving above the porch swing.

"Tell me the waterbug story tonight," I said, settling onto the swing. The fireflies were blinking on and off in the black air above the front yard.

"No, I won't," she said. The orange glow moved to her lap, and faded from bright to dim. "I'll tell you another time."

The swing squeaked its sad song, and I thought about Tennessee. It had never occurred to me that the place where Great Mam had been a child was still on this earth. "Why'd you go away from home?" I asked her.

"You have to marry outside your clan," she said. "That's law. And all the people we knew were Bird Clan. All the others were gone. So when Steward Murray came and made baby eyes at me, I had to go with him." She laughed. "I liked his horse."

I imagined the two of them on a frisking, strong horse, crossing the mountains to Kentucky. Great Mam with black hair. "Weren't you afraid to go?" I asked.

"Oh, yes I was. The canebrakes were high as a house. I was afraid we'd get lost."

* * *

We were to leave on Saturday after Papa got off work. He worked days then, after many graveyard-shift years during which we rarely saw him except asleep, snoring and waking throughout the afternoon, with Mother forever forced to shush us; it was too easy to forget someone was trying to sleep in daylight. My father was a soft-spoken man who sometimes drank but was never mean. He had thick black hair, no beard stubble at all nor hair on his chest, and a nose he called his Cherokee nose. Mother said she thanked the Lord that at least He had seen fit not to put that nose on her children. She also claimed he wore his hair long to flout her, although it wasn't truly long, in our opinion. His nickname in the mine was "Indian John."

There wasn't much to get ready for the trip. All we had to do in the morning was wait for afternoon. Mother was in the house scrubbing so it would be clean when we came back. The primary business of Mother's life was scrubbing things, and she herself looked scrubbed. Her skin was the color of a clean boiled potato. We didn't get in her way.

My brothers were playing a ferocious game of cowboys and Indians in the backyard, but I soon defected to my own amusements along the yard's weedy borders, picking morning glories, pretending to be a June bride. I grew tired of trying to weave the flowers into my coarse hair and decided to give them to Great Mam. I went around to the front and came up the three porch steps in one jump, just exactly the way Mother said a lady wouldn't do.

"Surprise," I announced. "These are for you." The flowers were already wilting in my hand.

"You shouldn't have picked those," she said.

"They were a present." I sat down, feeling stung.

"Those are not mine to have and not yours to pick," she said, looking at me, not with anger but with intensity. Her brown pupils were as dark as two pits in the earth. "A flower is alive, just as much as you are. A flower is your cousin. Didn't you know that?"

I said, No ma'am, that I didn't.

"Well, I'm telling you now, so you will know. Sometimes a person has got to take a life, like a chicken's or a hog's when you need it. If you're hungry, then they're happy to give their flesh up to you because they're your relatives. But nobody is so hungry they need to kill a flower."

I said nothing.

"They ought to be left where they stand, Waterbug. You need to leave them for the small people to see. When they die they'll fall where they are, and make a seed for next year."

"Nobody cared about these," I contended. "They weren't but just weeds."

"It doesn't matter what they were or were not. It's a bad thing to take for yourself something beautiful that belongs to everybody. Do you understand? To take it is a sin."

"I didn't, and I did. I could sense something of wasted life in the sticky leaves, translucent with death, and the purple flowers turning wrinkled and limp. I'd once brought home a balloon from a Ritchie child's birthday party, and it had shriveled and shrunk with just such a slow blue agony.

"I'm sorry," I said.

"It's all right." She patted my hands. "Just throw them over the porch rail there, give them back to the ground. The small people will come and take them back."

I threw the flowers over the railing in a clump, and came back, trying to rub the purple and green juices off my hands onto my dress. In my mother's eyes, this would have been the first sin of my afternoon. I understood the difference between Great Mam's rules and the Sunday-school variety, and that you could read Mother's Bible forward and backward and never find where it said it's a sin to pick flowers because they are our cousins.

"I'll try to remember," I said.

"I want you to," said Great Mam. "I want you to tell your children."

"I'm not going to have any children," I said. "No boy's going to marry me. I'm too tall. I've got knob knees."

"Don't ever say you hate what you are." She tucked a loose sheaf of black hair behind my ear. "It's an unkindness to those that made you. That's like a red flower saying it's too red, do you see what I mean?"

"I guess," I said.

"You will have children. And you'll remember about the flowers," she said, and I felt the weight of those promises fall like a deerskin pack between my shoulder blades.

* * *

By four o'clock we were waiting so hard we heard the truck crackle up the gravel road. Papa's truck was a rust-colored Ford with complicated cracks hanging like spiderwebs in the corners of the windshield. He jumped out with his long, blue-jean strides and patted the round front fender.

"Old Paint's had her oats," he said. "She's raring to go." This was a game he played with Great Mam. Sometimes she would say, "John Murray, you couldn't ride a mule with a saddle on it," and she'd laugh, and we would for a moment see the woman who raised Papa. Her bewilderment and pleasure, to have ended up with this broad-shouldered boy.

Today she said nothing, and Papa went in for Mother. There was only room for three in the cab, so Jack and Nathan and I climbed into the back with the old quilt Mother gave us and a tarpaulin in case of rain.

"What's she waiting for, her own funeral?" Jack asked me.

I looked at Great Mam, sitting still on the porch like a funny old doll. The whole house was crooked, the stoop sagged almost to the ground, and there sat Great Mam as straight as a schoolteacher's ruler. Seeing her there, I fiercely wished to defend my feeling that I knew her better than others did.

"She doesn't want to go," I said. I knew as soon as I'd spoken that it was the absolute truth.

"That's stupid. She's the whole reason we're going. Why wouldn't she want to go see her people?"

"I don't know, Jack," I said.

Papa and Mother eventually came out of the house, Papa in a clean shirt already darkening under the arms, and Mother with her Sunday purse, the scuff marks freshly covered with white shoe polish. She came down the front steps in the bent-over way she walked when she wore high heels. Papa put his hand under Great Mam's elbow and she silently climbed into the cab.

When he came around to the other side I asked him, "Are you sure Great Mam wants to go?"

"Sure she does," he said. "She wants to see the place where she grew up. Like what Morning Glory is to you."

"When I grow up I'm not never coming back to Morning Glory," Jack said.

"Me neither." Nathan spat over the side of the truck, the way he'd seen men do.

"Don't spit, Nathan," Papa said.

"Shut up," Nathan said, after Papa had gotten in the truck and shut the door.

The houses we passed had peeled paint and slumped porches like our own, and they all wore coats of morning-glory vines, deliciously textured and fat as fur coats. We pointed out to each other the company men's houses, which had bright white paint and were known to have indoor bathrooms. The deep ditches along the road, filled with blackberry brambles and early goldenrod, ran past us like rivers. On our walks to school we put these ditches to daily use practicing Duck and Cover, which was what our teachers felt we ought to do when the Communists dropped the H-bomb.

"We'll see Indians in Tennessee," Jack said. I knew we would. Great Mam had told me how it was.

"Great Mam don't look like an Indian, Nathan said.

"Shut up, Nathan," Jack said. "How do you know what an Indian looks like? You ever seen one?"

"She does so look like an Indian," I informed my brothers. "She is one."

According to Papa we all looked like little Indians, I especially. Mother hounded me continually to stay out of the sun, but by each summer's end I was so dark-skinned my schoolmates teased me, saying I ought to be sent over to the Negro school.

"Are we going to be Indians when we grow up?" Nathan asked.

"No, stupid," said Jack. "We'll just be the same as we are now."

* * *

We soon ran out of anything productive to do. We played White Horse Zit many times over, until Nathan won, and we tried to play Alphabet but there weren't enough signs. The only public evidence of literacy in that part of the country was the Beech Nut Tobacco signs on barn roofs, and every so often, nailed to a tree trunk, a clapboard on which someone had painted "PREPARE TO MEET GOD."

Papa's old truck didn't go as fast as other cars. Jack and Nathan slapped the fenders like jockeys as we were passed on the uphill slopes, but their coaxing amounted to nought. By the time we went over Jellico Mountain, it was dark.

An enormous amount of sky glittered down at us on the mountain pass, and even though it was June we were cold. Nathan had taken the quilt for himself and gone to sleep. Jack said he ought to punch him one to teach him to be nice, but truthfully, nothing in this world could have taught Nathan to share. Jack and I huddled together under the tarp, which stank of coal oil, and sat against the back of the cab where the engine rendered up through the truck's metal body a faint warmth.

"Jack?" I said.

"What."

"Do you reckon Great Mam's asleep?"

He turned around and cupped his hands to see into the cab. "Nope," he said. "She's sitting up there in between 'em, stiff as a broom handle."

"I'm worried about her," I said.

"Why? If we were home she'd be sitting up just the same, only out front on the porch."

"I know."

"Glorie, you know what?" he asked me.

"What?"

A trailer truck loomed up behind us, decked with rows of red and amber lights like a Christmas tree. We could see the driver inside the cab. A faint blue light on his face made him seem ghostly and entirely alone. He passed us by, staring ahead, as though only he were real on this cold night and we were among all the many things that were not. I shivered, and felt an identical chill run across Jack's shoulders

"What?" I asked again.

"What, what?"

"You were going to tell me something."

"Oh. I forgot what it was."

"Great Mam says the way to remember something you forgot is to turn your back on it. Say, 'The small people came dancing. They ran through the woods today.' Talk about what they did, and then whatever it was you forgot, they'll bring it back to you."

"That's dumb," Jack said. "That's Great Mam's hobbledy-gobbledy."

For a while we played See Who Can Go to Sleep First, which we knew to be a game that can't consciously be won. He never remembered what he'd meant to say.

* * *

When Papa woke us the next morning we were at a truck stop in Knoxville. He took a nap in the truck with his boots sticking out the door while the rest of us went in for breakfast. Inside the restaurant was a long glass counter containing packs of Kools and Mars Bars lined up on cotton batting, objects of great value to be protected from dust and children. The waitress who brought us our eggs had a red wig perched like a bird on her head, and red eyebrows painted on over the real ones.

When it was time get back in the truck we dragged and pulled on Mother's tired, bread-dough arms, like little babies, asking her how much farther.

"Oh, it's not far. I expect we'll be in Cherokee by lunchtime," she said, but her mouth was set and we knew she was as tired of this trip as any of us.

It was high noon before we saw a sign that indicated we were approaching Cherokee. Jack pummeled the cab window with his fists to make sure they all saw it, but Papa and Mother were absorbed in some kind of argument. There were more signs after that, with pictures of cartoon Indian boys urging us to buy souvenirs or stay in so-and-so's motor lodge. The signs were shaped like log cabins and teepees. Then we saw a real teepee. It was made of aluminum and taller than a house. Inside, it was a souvenir store.

We drove around the streets of Cherokee and saw that the town was all the same, as single-minded in its offerings as a corn patch or an orchard, so that it made no difference where we stopped. We parked in front of Sitting Bull's Genuine Indian Made Souvenirs, and Mother crossed the street to get groceries for our lunch. I had a sense of something gone badly wrong, like a lie told in my past and then forgotten, and now about to catch up with me.

A man in a feather war bonnet danced across from us in the parking lot. His outfit was bright orange, with white

fringe trembling along the seams of the pants and sleeves,
and a woman in the same clothes sat cross-legged on the
pavement playing a tom-tom while he danced. People with
cameras gathered and side-stepped around one another to
snap their shots. The woman told them that she and her
husband Chief Many Feathers were genuine Cherokees,
and that this was their welcoming dance. Papa sat with his
hands frozen on the steering wheel for a very long time.
Then suddenly, without saying anything, he got out of the
truck and took Jack and Nathan and me into Sitting Bull's.
Nathan wanted a tomahawk.

The store was full of items crowded on shelves, so bright-
colored it hurt my eyes to look at them all. I lagged behind
the boys. There were some Indian dolls with real feathers
on them, red and green, and I would like to have stroked
the soft feathers but the dolls were wrapped in cellophane.
Among all those bright things, I grew fearfully uncertain
about what I ought to want. I went back out to the truck
and found Great Mam still sitting in the cab.

"Don't you want to get out?" I asked.

The man in the parking lot was dancing again, and she
was watching. "I don't know what they think they're doing.
Cherokee don't wear feather bonnets like that," she said.

They looked like Indians to me. I couldn't imagine Indians without feathers. I climbed up onto the seat and closed
the door and we sat for a while. I felt a great sadness and
embarrassment, as though it were I who had forced her to
come here, and I tried to cover it up by pretending to be
foolishly cheerful.

"Where's the pole houses, where everybody lives, I wonder," I said. "Do you think maybe they're out of town
a ways?"

She didn't answer. Chief Many Feathers hopped around
his circle, forward on one leg and backward on the other.
Then the dance was over. The woman beating the tom-tom
turned it upside down and passed it around for money.

"I guess things have changed pretty much since you
moved away, huh, Great Mam?" I asked.

She said, "I've never been here before."

* * *

Mother made bologna sandwiches and we ate lunch in a place called Cherokee Park. It was a shaded spot along the river, where the dry banks were worn bald of their grass. Sycamore trees grew at the water's edge, with colorful, waterlogged trash floating in circles in the eddies around their roots. The park's principal attraction was an old buffalo in a pen, identified by a sign as the Last Remaining Buffalo East of the Mississippi. I pitied the beast, thinking it must be lonely without a buffalo wife or buffalo husband, whichever it needed. One of its eyes was put out.

I tried to feed it some dead grass through the cage, while Nathan pelted it with gravel. He said he wanted to see it get mad and charge the fence down, but naturally it did not do that. It simply stood and stared and blinked with its one good eye, and flicked its tail. There were flies all over it, and shiny bald patches on its back, which Papa said were caused by the mange. Mother said we'd better get away from it or we would have the mange too. Great Mam sat at the picnic table with her shoes together, and looked at her sandwich.

We had to go back that same night. It seemed an impossible thing, to come such a distance only to turn right around, but Mother reminded us all that Papa had laid off from work without pay. Where money was concerned we did not argue. The trip home was quiet except for Nathan, who pretended at great length to scalp me with his tomahawk, until the rubber head came loose from its painted stick and fell with a clunk.

III

Before there was a world, there was only the sea, and the high, bright sky arched above it like an overturned bowl.

For as many years as anyone can imagine, the people in the stars looked down at the ocean's glittering face without giving a thought to what it was, or what might lie beneath it. They had their own concerns. But as more time passed, as is natural, they began to grow curious. Eventually it was the waterbug who volunteered to go exploring. She flew down and landed on top of the water, which was beautiful, but not firm as it had appeared. She skated in every direction but could not find a place to stop and rest, so she dived underneath.

She was gone for days and the star people thought she must have drowned, but she hadn't. When she joyfully broke the surface again she had the answer: on the bottom of the sea, there was mud. She had brought a piece of it back with her, and she held up her sodden bit of proof to the bright light.

There, before the crowd of skeptical star eyes, the ball of mud began to grow, and dry up, and grow some more, and out of it came all the voices and life that now dwell on this island that is the earth. The star people fastened it to the sky with four long grape vines so it wouldn't be lost again.

* * *

"In school," I told Great Mam, "they said the world's round."

"I didn't say it wasn't round," she said. "It's whatever shape they say it is. But that's how it started. Remember that."

These last words terrified me, always, with their impossible weight. I have had dreams of trying to hold a mountain of water in my arms. "What if I forget?" I asked.

"We already talked about that. I told you how to remember."

"Well, all right," I said. "But if that's how the world started, then what about Adam and Eve?"

She thought about that. "They were the waterbug's children," she said. "Adam and Eve, and the others."

"But they started all the trouble," I pointed out." Adam and Eve started sin."

"Sometimes that happens. Children can be your heartache. But that doesn't matter, you have to go on and have them," she said. "It works out."

IV

Morning Glory looked no different after we had seen the world and returned to it. Summer settled in, with heat in the air and coal dust thick on the vines. Nearly every night

I slipped out and sat with Great Mam where there was the tangible hope of a cool breeze. I felt pleased to be up while my brothers breathed and tossed without consciousness on the hot mattress. During those secret hours, Great Mam and I lived in our own place, a world apart from the arguments and the tired, yellowish light bulbs burning away inside, seeping faintly out the windows, getting used up. Mother's voice in the kitchen was as distant as heat lightning, and as unthreatening. But we could make out words, and I realized once, with a shock, that they were discussing Great Mam's burial.

"Well, it surely can't do her any harm once she's dead and gone, John, for heaven's sakes," Mother said.

Papa spoke more softly and we could never make out his answer.

Great Mam seemed untroubled. "In the old days," she said, "whoever spoke the quietest would win the argument."

* * *

She died in October, the Harvest Month. It was my mother who organized the burial and the Bible verses and had her say even about the name that went on the gravestone, but Great Mam secretly prevailed in the question of flowers. Very few would ever have their beauty wasted upon her grave. Only one time for the burial service, and never again after that, did Mother trouble herself to bring up flowers. It was half a dozen white gladioli cut hastily from her garden with a bread knife, and she carried them from home in a jar of water, attempting to trick them into believing they were still alive.

My father's shoes were restless in the grass and hickory saplings at the edge of the cemetery. Mother knelt down in her navy dress and nylon stockings and with her white-gloved hands thumped the flower stems impatiently against the jar bottom to get them to stand up straight. Already the petals were shriveling from thirst.

As soon as we turned our backs, the small people would come dancing and pick up the flowers. They would kick over the jar and run through the forest, swinging the hollow stems above their heads, scattering them like bones.

A great many readers of science fiction and fantasy are also fans of thrillers, mystery novels, and conspiracy theories. "Stealing God" combines some of the best elements of all these genres and then gives them its own unique twist, the while keeping tongue very firmly in cheek. (Imagine, if you will, *Illuminatus* meets *Holy Blood, Holy Grail*, in an idiom reminiscent of Raymond Chandler or one of the other classic detective writers.) It all begins with the theft of the Holy Grail. (Bet you didn't know that the Grail currently lives in New York, did you?)

The characters and premise are so much fun that I urged Doyle and Macdonald to expand the concept and consider doing a full novel (or two, or three!) about modern-day Templar operative Peter Crossman and his spunky sidekick, Sister Mary Magdalene of the Special Action Executive of the Poor Clares. The first book, they tell me, is already in the works.

In the meantime, however, "Stealing God" will have to serve as a tasty introduction to a most adroit partnership, whether it's Crossman and the delectable Sister MM or Doyle and Macdonald themselves. I, for one, can hardly wait for the next installment, whatever form it may take!

—Katherine Kurtz

STEALING GOD
by Debra Doyle and James D. Macdonald

I was working the security leak at Rennes-le-Château when the word came down. The Rennes flub was over a hundred years old, but the situation needed constant tending to keep people off the scent. That's the thing about botches. They never go away.

Now I had new orders. Drop whatever I was doing and get my young ass over to New York mosh-gosh. Roger that, color me gone. I was on the Concorde out of Paris before the hole in the air finished closing behind me in Languedoc.

With the Temple paying my way, cost wasn't a worry. I had enough other things to think about. The masters weren't bringing me across the Atlantic just to chew the fat. We had plenty of secure links. Whatever this was, it required my presence.

Sherlock Holmes said that it was a capital mistake to theorize before one had information. My old sergeant, back when I was learning the trade, told me to catch some sleep whenever I could. I dozed my way over the Atlantic and didn't wake up until we hit JFK.

Customs inspection was smooth and uneventful—I had only one piece of carry-on luggage, with nothing in it that the customs people might recognize as a weapon. I took the third cab in the rank outside the terminal and was on my way. First stop was at The Cloisters in Fort Tryon Park, to pay my respects to the Magdalene Chalice. My arrival would be noted there, and the contact would come soon.

Outside the museum I got another cab to Central Park West. I made my way to the Rambles, that part of the park where the city can't be seen and you can almost imagine yourself in the wilderness.

Sure enough, a man was waiting. He wore the signs, the air, and the majesty. I made a quiet obeisance, just to go by the book, and he responded. But I didn't need any of the signals in order to recognize one of the two masters.

There are only three and thirty of us in the inner Temple, plus the masters. We're the part of the Temple that's hidden from all the other Knights Templar: the secret from the holders of the secrets, the ace up the sleeve. All of us warriors, all of us priests. We serve, we obey. When needed, we kick ass.

"Hello," he said. "It's been years."

"Sure has, John," I replied. "What's up?"

We spoke in Latin, for the same reason the Church does. No matter where you are or where you're from, you can communicate.

"There's a problem," he said. "Over on the East Side."

The Grail. It had to be. "Instructions?"

"Go in, check it out, report back"

"Anything special I'm looking for?"

"No," he said. "Just be aware that the last three people who got those same orders haven't reported in yet."

We nodded to each other and parted. I walked south. There are a bunch of hotels along Central Park South, and I wanted to hit the bar in one of them and do some thinking. For Prester John to be away from Chatillon meant that things were more serious than I'd suspected.

I sat in the bar at the Saint Moritz, drinking Laphroaig neat the way God and Scotland made it, while I wondered what in the name of King Anfortas could be going on over at the UN, and how I was going to check. Halfway down the bar another man sat playing with the little puddle of water that had collected around the base of his frosty mug of beer. He was drinking one of those watery American brews with no flavor, no body, and no strength to recommend it, though it had apparently gotten him half plowed regardless. After a minute or two I realized what had drawn my attention: He was tracing designs in the water on the bar.

Designs I recognized. Runes.

Did they think I was blind, I wondered, or so ignorant that I wouldn't notice? But I didn't perceive any immediate danger, and a sudden departure would tip my hand to whoever was watching. Maybe this guy was just a random drunk who happened to know his mystic symbols.

Sure, and maybe random drunks had nailed three other knights.

No, more likely he was a Golden Dawner or a Luciferian. Probably a Luciferian. Lucies have a special relationship with the Grail, or they think they do. I tipped up the last drops of Laphroaig, harsh on my tongue like a slurry of ground glass and peat moss, called for another shot, and drank half of it. The money lying by the shot glass would pay for my drink. I left the bar, left the hotel, turned east, and started walking. Leaving good booze unfinished is a venial sin, but that way it'd look like I'd just stepped over to the men's room and was coming back soon—good for a head start.

Halfway down the block I spotted a convenient bunch of construction barriers. I ducked behind them, and as soon as I was out of sight from the street, my left hand darted into my bag. A couple of seconds to work the charm and I stepped out onto the sidewalk, Tarnkappe fully charged and ready in my hand. My bag remained behind, looking for anyone without True Sight like a rotting sack of garbage.

There are only three Tarnkappen in the world, and I had one of them. Something like that can come in handy in my line of work, and it was about to come in handy again. I walked slowly until I was sure that anyone following me from the Saint Moritz was on my tail. Then I cruised eastward, window-shopping. Windows make great mirrors to show what's behind you—and sure enough, here came my runic friend, Mr. Beer.

I turned a few random corners to make certain he was following, then got into a crowd and slipped on the Kappe. A few seconds later, after a bit of fancy footwork to make sure that my location and method weren't revealed by a trail of people tripping over nothing, I leaned against the side of a building and watched to see what would happen next.

Mr. Beer was confused, all right. He cast up and down the street a bit, but pretty soon he figured out that he'd botched the job. He stepped into a phone booth, then punched in a string and spoke a couple of words. His face was at the wrong angle for lipreading, but I could guess what he was saying: "I lost him."

Maybe I couldn't see what he was saying, but I'd managed to get the number he'd dialed. The whole time he was on the phone, I was on the other side of the street with a small pair of binoculars. He hadn't shielded the button pad with his hand. Half trained—a Lucie, for sure.

I trailed him until he went into a hotel and up to a room. Then I slipped the Kappe into my back pocket and followed that up by slipping a few quick questions to people who didn't even know afterward that they'd been questioned. Before long I knew that Beer's name was Max Lang, that he spoke with a foreign accent, that he'd been there for one week and planned to stay for another, and that he tipped well.

I left him in the hotel. The trail had taken me to the Waldorf-Astoria in midtown. Might as well head over to the United Nations building. It was still early, with lots of light in the sky and lots of people on the sidewalk. I kept my eyes open, but I didn't pick up a tail.

I turned the problem over in my mind. Max Lang couldn't have found his way out of a paper bag if you gave him a map and printed instructions. So how did he find me in the bar? And how did he come to know the Therion rune sequence?

The UN building stands towering over FDR Drive, along the East River. Security there is tight by American standards, which means laughable for any place else in the world. Inside the building I knew which way to go, and I had passes that were as good as genuine to get me anywhere I needed.

I stood for a moment just inside the metal detectors at the front doors, feeling with my senses. Was there something wrong in the building? Nothing big enough to show up without a divination, and I doubted that the guards would let me get away with performing one here, even if they weren't bent to the left—and with three knights missing already, only a fool wouldn't assume that the guards were bent. Prester John doesn't use fools. I headed for the Meditation Room.

The Meditation Room was right where I'd left it last time I'd been in town. No obvious problems. I went in. Everything was still in place. There was the mural in the front of the room, with its abstract picture of the sun, half dark, and half light. Cathar symbolism, and Manichean before that. We kept the picture up there to remind the Cathars how wrong they'd been. And there was the Grail—a natural lodestone, cut and polished into a gleaming rectangular block.

Wolfram von Eschenbach let the cat out of the bag when he wrote *Parzival*, back in the twelve hundreds. Somehow he'd gotten the straight word on what the grail looked like. According to the Luciferians, who claim to know the inside story, the Grail had been the central stone in Lucifer's crown, back before he had a couple of really bad days and got his dumb ass tossed out of Heaven. When Lucifer landed in Hell, they say, the Grail landed on Earth.

What *was* true was that the Grail had banged around the Middle East for quite a while—capstone of the Great Pyramid, cornerstone of the Temple of Solomon, that sort of thing. Back during the Crusades we'd been given the keeping of it. We never could hide the fact that there was a Grail, or that it was holy, but for a long time we tried to get people to go looking for dinnerware. Then someone talked. Somewhere, somehow, there was a leak. And blunders, like I said, never go away.

So far, though, everything looked all peachy-keen and

peaceful at the United Nations. The room, the mural, the big chunk of polished rock. I pulled out a little pocket compass. Yep, that was still a lodestone over there.

One more test. I opened the little gold case in my pants pocket and slipped out a consecrated Host. I palmed it, then walked past the Grail on my way out of the room. My hand brushed the polished stone as I went by. Then I was out of the room, heading for the main doors and the street.

I raised my hand to straighten my hair, and as my hand passed my lips, I took the Host. Then I knew there was something really, desperately wrong. No taste of blood.

Hosts bleed when they touch the Holy Grail. Don't ask me how; I'm not enough of a mystic to answer. But I do know why—Godhood in the presence of Itself makes for interesting physical manifestations.

There was a stone back there in the meditation room. But either it wasn't the real Grail, or it wasn't holy anymore.

Whoever did this was far more powerful than I'd imagined. They either had to smuggle a six-and-a-half-ton block of rock into the UN, and smuggle another six-and-a-half-ton block of rock out of there without anyone noticing, or they had to defile something that had never been defiled—not even on Friday the 13th, when some men with real power and knowledge had given it their best shot and come away with nothing but their own sins to show for the effort.

I had to report back. Prester John needed to know about this as soon as possible.

That was when they hit me, just as I stepped out onto the street. I felt a light impact on the side of my neck, like a mosquito. I slapped at it by reflex, but before my hand got there, my knees were already buckling. Two men moved in on either side of me, supporting me. My eyes were open, and I could see and remember, but my arms and legs weren't responding anymore.

"Come on," the man on my right said. "You're going for a little ride."

They walked me across the plaza, three men holding hands. No one looked twice. You see some funny things in New York.

They put me in the back of a limo. Another man was

behind the wheel, waiting for them. The door shut and we pulled away from the curb. The guy on my right pushed my head down so I wasn't visible from outside, which meant I couldn't see where they were taking me, either.

We crossed a bridge—I could hear it humming in the tires—the slowed to join other traffic. I pulled inside myself and looked for where the poison was in my body. It was potent, but there couldn't be much of it. I could handle not-much.

With enough concentration some people can slow their heartbeat down to where doctors can't detect it. Other people can slow their breathing to where they can make a coffinful of air last a week. I concentrated on finding all the molecules of poison in my bloodstream and making Maxwell's Demon shunt them off to somewhere harmless.

Little finger of my left hand, say. Let it concentrate there and not get out.

The car was slowing again. Stopping. Too soon. I hadn't gotten all the poison localized yet.

They pulled me out of the backseat. We were on a dock, probably on Long Island. No one else was in sight. I could see now what was going to happen: Into the water, the current carries me away, I'm too weak to swim, I drown. The poison is too dilute, or it breaks down, or its masked by the by-products of decomposition and the toxicological examination doesn't find it at the autopsy.

They weren't asking any questions. Instead, we went out to the end of the pier, them walking and me being walked. Two of them held me out over the water while the third— the one who'd been the driver—spoke.

"We do not slay thee. Thy blood is not on us. We desire no earthly thing: Go to God with all ye possess. Sink ye or swim ye, thou art nothing more to us."

A roaring sounded in my ears, and I was falling forward. Water, cold and salt, rushed into my nose and mouth.

Human bodies float in salt water. *Concentrate on moving the poison. Give me enough control that I can float on my back . . .* I was sinking. The light was growing dim. I concentrated on lowering my need for oxygen, lowering my heartbeat, lowering everything.

Move the poison. Don't use air. Float.

Then it was working. I could feel strength and control

return to my arms and legs. I was deep underwater. I opened my eyes and looked around. I saw shadow and pilings not too far away: the bottom of the pier.

Swim that way—slowly—keep the poison in the left little finger. Don't use air. Then float up.

I didn't dare gasp for breath when I got to the surface. For all I knew, my assailants were still up there waiting. Slowly, quietly, I allowed my lungs to empty, then fill again. I hooked my left arm around the nearest piling, then reached down with my right hand and undid a shoelace. I hoped I wouldn't lose the shoe.

Using the lace, I tied a tourniquet around my left little finger—now the drug couldn't get out—and reached down again to my belt. The buckle hid a small push-dagger, made of carbonite so metal detectors wouldn't pick it up. Don't let the material fool you; it's hard and sharp. I cut the end of my little finger, held the knife between my teeth, and squeezed out the poisoned blood. The blood came out thick and dark, trailing away in the water like a streamer of red. Then I unloosed the tourniquet and it was time to go.

The foot of the pier was set in a cement wall about seven feet high, but the wall was old and crumbling. I got a fingerhold, then a foothold. At last I was out of the water. I crawled up until I was lying on top of the wall, under the decking of the pier. Anyone looking for me would have to be in the water to see me. I stayed there, waiting and listening, for a hundred heartbeats, then two hundred, and heard nothing but waves lapping up against the wall.

A sound. A board creaked on the dock. They'd left someone behind, all right—someone waiting like I was, only not so quietly.

But those cowboys had been a little slack. Either they'd trusted their drug too much, or else it was really important to their ritual that I keep all my possessions. The end result was the same; I hadn't been searched. When I reached a hand down to my pocket, the Tarnkappe was still where I'd stuffed it when I'd gotten done with Max Lang.

A visit to Lang looked like it was in the cards. Later. There were other things to do first.

I put on the Kappe, then crawled out of my hiding place and up onto the shore. There he was, out on the pier: a man in a business suit, carrying a Ruger mini-14 at high port. I sat on the shore, hoping I'd dry out enough so that water drops splashing on the pavement wouldn't give me away. Or chattering teeth—the sun was heading down and it was going to get cold pretty soon for a man in wet clothes.

Whatever those lads had hit me with, it'd left me with the beginning of a king-of-hell headache. I ignored the discomfort and concentrated on the man on the pier. Who was he? I'd never seen him before.

I heard the second man coming before I saw him, tramping heavy-footed down the road to the pier. He walked out and greeted the first. This time I could read their lips: "Time to go . . . there's a meeting . . . yes, we both have to be there . . . forget him, he's gone."

They walked back off the pier and I swung in behind them, letting the sound of their footfalls cover mine.

They had a car parked up the way—not the one that had brought me here. This one had two bucket seats up in front and nothing behind. They got inside; I got up on the back bumper and leaned forward across the trunk, holding on with arms spread wide. The car pulled away. All I had to do now was stay on board until they got to wherever they were going. That, and hope the Tarnkappe didn't come off at highway speeds.

The first sign we came to told me that I was NOW LEAVING BABYLON, NEW YORK. Babylon. Figures. Nothing happens by chance, not when you have the Grail involved. It all means something. The trick is finding out what.

This pair wasn't real gabby. I'd hoped to do some more lipreading in the rearview mirror, but as far as I could tell they drove back to the Big Apple in stony silence. They took the Midtown Tunnel back in, then local streets to somewhere on the East Side around 70th street. That was where I had my next bit of bad luck.

Out on the highway, the Tarnkappe had stuck on my head like glue. But here in the concrete canyons, a side gust took it away and there I was in plain view on the back deck. All I could do was roll off and scuttle for safety between the rushing cars, while taxis screamed at me and bicycle messengers tried to leave tire stripes up my back.

I made it to the other side of the street. The Tarnkappe was gone, blown who-knows-where by the wind, and I

couldn't make myself conspicuous by doubling back to look
for it. A quick stroll around the corner, down one subway
entrance and up another, and I was as safe as I could hope
to be with my shoes squishing seawater.

I started out at a New Yorker's street pace for the spot
where I'd ditched my bag. By now the sun was down for
real and the neon darkness was coming up: a bad time of
day for strangers to go wandering around Central Park.
Me, I kind of hoped someone would try for a mugging. I
had a foul mood to work off, and smashing someone's face
in the name of righteousness would just about to the trick.

Nobody tried anything, and my bag was waiting where
I'd left it. I changed clothes right there in the alley, and
debated reporting in. But someone had gone to a lot of
trouble to make me vanish, and I wanted the secret of my
survival to be shared by the minimum number.

Sure, I had my orders. But blind obedience isn't what
the Temple needs from the thirty and three. Distasteful as
I found the possibility, I had to consider whether I'd been
sold out from inside. If so, then reporting in would be a
very bad idea.

Maybe those other three knights had figured things out
the same way. They could be lying low and saying nothing
until the situation clarified. But I didn't think it was likely.
Odds were that they were sweating it out in Purgatory right
now—like I'd be, if I didn't start taking precautions.

I began by using the kit in my bag to make a few changes
to my appearance. No sense having everyone who's already
seen me recognize me the next time I showed up. Meanwhile, it was dinner time, which meant there was a good
chance that my Mr. Lang would be away from his room.
A search might show me something useful. And when he
got back from dinner, I wanted to ask him some questions.

The rooms at his hotel had those new-style keycards with
the magnetic strip. Some people think the keycards are secure, and they'll probably stop the teenagers who bought a
Teach Yourself Locksmithing course out of the back of
a comic book. The one on Lang's room didn't even slow
me down.

Lang wasn't out, after all. He was in the room, but I
wasn't going to get any answers out of him without a Ouija
board. He was naked, lying on his back in the bathtub.

Someone had been there before me—someone with a sharp knife and a sick imagination.

I dipped my finger in the little bottle of chrism I carry in my tote and made a quick cross on his forehead.

"For thy sins I grant thee absolution," I muttered—wherever he'd gone, he needed all the help he could get. Lucies aren't famed for their high salvation rate.

Then I searched the room, even though whoever had taken care of Lang would have done that job once already. Aside from the mess in the bathtub, the contents of the hotel room didn't have much to say about anything, except maybe the banality of evil: no address books; no letters or memos; no telltale impressions on the memo pad. Nothing of any interest at all.

Then I found something, taped to the back of a drawer. My unknown searcher had missed it. Or maybe he'd left it behind, having no use for it—he hadn't used bullets on Lang, only the knife. But there it was, a Colt Commander, a big mean .45 automatic.

I checked it over. Five rounds in the magazine, one up the spout. Weapon cocked, safety off. I lowered the hammer to half-cock and took the Colt with me, stuffing it in my waistband in the back, under the sport coat I was wearing. That lump of cold metal made me feel a lot better about the rest of the evening.

One more thing to do: I picked up the room phone, got an outside line, and punched in the number Lang had called that afternoon. After two rings, someone picked it up.

"International Research," said a female voice.

"This is Max," I said, my voice as muffled as I could make it. "I'm in trouble."

Then I hung up.

Before I left the room, I opened the curtains all the way. Then I eased myself out of the hotel and over to a vantage point across the street, where a water tower on a lower building gave me a view of the room I'd just left. The bad guys who'd tried to drown me hadn't taken my pocket binoculars, either. Those were good optics—when I used the binocs to look across the street, it was like I was standing in the hotel room.

I waited. The wind was cold, and a little after one in the morning it started to rain. It was just past 4 AM, at that hour before dawn when sick men die, when I spotted something happening.

Across the street the door eased open, then drifted shut. A woman walked into the room. She was tall, slender, and stacked. Black lace-up boots, tight black jeans, tight black sweater. Single strand of pearls. Red hair, long enough to sit on, loose down her back. A black raincoat hung over her right arm. She was wearing black leather gloves. In he left hand she had a H&K nine-millimeter. Color coordinated: The artillery was black, too.

She did a walk-through of the room. Nothing hurried. I watched her long enough that I could recognize her again, and then I was sliding down from my perch. The lady had carried a raincoat. If she planned to go out into the weather, I was going to find out where she was headed. My guess was that she was from International Research, whoever they really were.

I was betting that she'd come out the main door. So I did a slow walk up and down the street, one sidewalk and then the other, before I spotted her through the glass in the lobby, putting on that coat. Then she was out the revolving door and away.

One nice thing about New York is that it's possible to follow someone on foot. The car situation is so crazy that no one brings a private vehicle onto the island if they can help it. She might still call a cab, but if she did, so could I. I've never yet in my career told a cabbie to "Follow that car," but there's a first time for everything.

I wasn't going to get the chance tonight. A limo was cruising up the street at walking speed, coming up behind the lady in black. I recognized it. The boys who grabbed me yesterday had used that car or one just like it to carry me out to Babylon for sacrifice.

The car stopped and the two clowns in the back got out. They looked like the same pair of devout souls who'd invited me to a total-immersion baptism. It was time for me to join the fun. I angled across the rain-soaked street, pulling that big-ass Colt into my hand as I went.

The two goons had caught up with the lady, but she wasn't going as quietly as I had the day before. Maybe they'd missed with their drugged dart—she was muffled to the nose in her raincoat, with the collar turned up. Or maybe they wanted her talkative when they got wherever they were going. No matter. They were distracted, and the driver was watching the show.

I came up beside the window out of his blind spot. Using the .45 as a pair of knucks, I punched right through the glass into the back of his head. Then I pulled the door open and him out with it, spilling him onto his back in the street. I kicked him once on the point of the chin while he lay there.

"For these and all thy sins I absolve thee," I muttered, making a cross over him with the Colt.

The whole thing hadn't taken more than a couple of seconds, and now it was time to go help the lady. Generally speaking I'm not the kind of knight who goes around rescuing damsels in distress—but I wanted to talk with this one, and keeping her alive was the only way to go.

I used the roof of the car as a vaulting horse and landed feet first on top of one of the goons, bringing him down with me in a tangle of arms and legs. It took me a second to extricate myself, with elbows, knees, and the heavy automatic smashing into my man along the way. He got in a couple of good licks, then gave up all interest and started holding what was left of his nuts.

Meanwhile the lady in black was doing the best she could. But her little nine-millimeter was caught under the raincoat, and the man who had her was too strong. He'd thrown an arm around her neck in the classic choke come-along and was dragging her into the backseat. Maybe he hadn't noticed that the driver wasn't there anymore.

I took him in the back of the skull with the butt of the Colt Commander. He slipped to the ground to join his moaning pal.

"Come on!" I yelled at the lady. "Let's get out of here!"

"Where to?" she gasped.

"Into the car."

I slid behind the wheel—the keys were still in the ignition and the engine was turning over—and slammed the driver's-side door. The lady didn't argue. She got in beside me and closed the other door, and I took off from the curb.

I made a left turn across traffic into a side street, and said, "Where to, sister?"

"Who are you?"

Rather than give her an answer, I said, "The cops are gonna be all over this block in a couple of minutes—I saw the doorman go running inside like a man with 911 on his mind. You got a safe place to go?"

She gave an address down in SoHo. I drove to the address, ditched the car, and went with her up to an apartment: third floor of a brownstone, three rooms and a kitchen. I hoped she was in a rent-controlled building, or this place would be costing her a pretty penny.

The apartment was almost empty: nothing but a coffeemaker in the kitchen, a couple of sofas, and a bed, all visible from right inside the front door.

"Take a seat," she said. "I'll make coffee."

She stripped off her coat and turned to hang it on a peg by the door. When she turned back, the little nine-millimeter was pointing right between my eyes. I'd stuffed the .45 into my waistband in back again, to keep her from getting nervous. Her get nervous? That was a laugh.

"You've missed three recognition signals," she said. "You aren't from Section. So how's about you tell me who you are?"

"People call me Crossman," I said. "Peter Crossman."

"Is that your real name?"

"No, but it'll do. I'm the connection for midtown. You want coke, you call me."

"Your kind isn't known for making citizen arrests," she said. The muzzle of the nine-millimeter never wavered, even though from the way her chest was going up and down she had to be nervous about something. "What did you think you were up to tonight?"

"Someone who doesn't work for me using muscle in my territory, that interests me. Let one bunch get away with it, pretty soon it's all over town that Crossman's gone soft, and they're all trying to move in. Can't let that happen."

"So—" she started, but never finished. A knock sounded on the door.

"Maggie," came a voice from outside. "Maggie, I know you're in there. Open up."

She made the little pistol vanish. "Come on in—it isn't locked."

The door swung open, and I got a sinking feeling in my guts. The Mutt and Jeff act waiting on the landing were the same pair who'd given me the ride back to town the day before. The watchers from the dock in Babylon. I didn't think they recognized me—the Tarnkappe had kept me invisible at first, and then I'd changed my face. I was glad now that I'd taken the precaution.

They came in. They were wrapped in dripping rain-coats—no way of telling what kind of firepower they were carrying underneath, but it would take 'em a while to pull anything clear. The first guy, the short one, nodded over at me. "Who's the meat?"

"A guy named Crossman," Maggie said. "He's some kind of drug lord. Showed up tonight and pulled my buns out of a bad situation while you two were sucking down cold ones in some bar."

"Get rid of him," the second guy said.

"No, I think I want him to stay." She looked at me. "You do want to stay, don't you? I'll let you buy me a drink after all this is over."

"Yeah," I said. "I want to stay."

That was the truth. This whole affair was getting more interesting by the minute. And as for buying that drink—I couldn't help wondering what sort of temptation she had in mind for me to resist.

She started to say something else, and that was when the door to the apartment flew open again. This time it was the two guys from the street—the ones who had tried to stuff Maggie into their car, the same ones who'd grabbed me outside the UN. One of them was carrying a Remington Model 870. The other was lugging a Stoner. They both looked pissed off.

They didn't bother with the formalities.

"One of you bastards," the guy with the Stoner said, "knows something we want to know. So we aren't going to kill you now. But we have other ways of finding out, so don't think we'll hesitate to shoot you if we have to. So. Who's going to tell me: Where's the Holy Grail?"

"It's in Logres, asshole," said Maggie's shorter guy.

The new arrival with the riot gun butt-stroked him across the room. He went down hard.

"I sure hope he wasn't the only guy who knew," Remington said, "or the rest of you are going to have a really rough time. Who wants to give us a serious answer?"

Maggie was standing beside and a little behind me. I felt something soft and warm pressing into my hand while everyone else was looking at the guy on the floor. It felt like a leather bag with marbles inside. I took it and made it vanish into my front pants pocket.

Stoner looked at me—maybe he'd seen me move. "Don't I know you from somewhere?"

I shook my head a fraction of an inch one way and then the other. "I don't think so."

I wasn't as scared as I hoped I looked, but things weren't shaping up too good. The new guys hadn't disarmed anyone yet, and neither weapon was pointing right at me, but with my piece tucked into my waistband in back, I wouldn't have put a lot of money on getting it clear before they could turn me into Swiss cheese with ketchup. Besides, I wanted these gents alive. Someone knew where the Grail was, and all of these jokers looked like they knew more than I did.

"Lay off," Maggie said. "This one's your basic crook I picked up. You don't want him, you want me."

Whatever they were after, odds were it was in that little sack—at least Maggie thought it was. But I knew better. You don't carry a six-point-five-ton block of lodestone around in a leather drawstring bag.

"Yeah, sister, we want you," Remington said. "What were you doing at the Waldorf tonight?"

"Visiting a friend. Got a problem with that?" She'd drifted a little away from me. Maybe no one remembered she'd ever gotten close.

"Do you have it?"

"No. It isn't here."

Even the guys with the long guns were treating Maggie with respect—she must rate in someone's organization, I thought. Meanwhile, she was getting close to the light switch. I kept watch out of the corner of my eye, ready to make my move when she made hers.

"Where is it?" Remington said again.

She drifted another step sideways. "Do you know the stoneyard for St. John the Divine?"

Then her elbow smashed backward against the switch and the lights went out. I leaped over the sofa in a flat dive, rolled, and came up crouching in the corner near the window, with my back to the wall and the .45 in a two-hand grip in front of me.

I heard a nine-millimeter go popping off where Maggie had been standing, and an answering roar from the Remington—both of them laid over the stitching sound of the Stoner firing full auto.

That about did it for my ears. Too much gunfire and you're hearing bells ring an hour later. Of course, now the bad guys couldn't hear me, either. But my eyes were adjusting to the dark, and anyone standing up in front of the windows would be silhouetted against the skyglow.

I started duckwalking in the direction of the door, keeping my head low. My foot hit something hard. I reached down with my right hand, my left holding the .45 steady in front of me. It was the Stoner. The barrel was warm, which was more than you could say about the hand that held it. No pulse in the radial artery. I mouthed an absolution and continued moving along the wall.

Over by the window, another shadow was moving—a male, standing, with the distinctive shape of a pump-action in his hands. The weapon was swinging in slow arcs across the room. It stopped—he'd seen something. He started raising the shotgun to his shoulder.

I drew a careful bead on him. "Go in peace to love and serve the Lord," I muttered, and pulled the trigger.

Then I was rolling away, because a scattergun like the Remington doesn't need much aiming. But I needn't have worried—I saw his shadow drop in that boneless way people get when they're shot. A .45 yields a 98 percent one-shot kill rate. If I hit him . . . well, I don't miss often.

I fetched up against someone very soft and very warm—Maggie, waiting in the shadows by the other corner. She reached up and flipped the lights back on.

I stood flattened against the wall and looked around. Stone and Remington had both bought their parts of the farm. Maggie's two prettyboys were hugging the carpet and playing possum—at least they'd been smart enough not to be targets.

The tall one got to his feet.

"You found it?" he said to Maggie. "Come on, let's get over there."

"It isn't so far," Maggie said. "In fact it's—"

"Shut up," I said. "These two jokers aren't on your team."

"What do you mean?"

She was bringing the nine-mike-mike to bear on me. I pointed my own weapon at the floor, so she wouldn't get the wrong idea and make a hasty move, and nodded at the pair of corpses.

"How do you think the Bobbsey Twins over there found this place?" I asked. "They sure didn't follow us. I bet these two guys brought 'em along, and were going to play good cop/bad cop with us."

"But—" Maggie began.

"He's right, you know," the shorter one said. He produced an Uzi and brought it up to cover us. "Put down your weapons."

There comes a time when you know you've lost. I dropped my piece. Maggie did the same. The guy with the Uzi nodded at his buddy.

"Fred, pick them up."

The tall one—Fred, I guess his name was—stepped forward and bent over to pick up the handguns.

Shorty was still talking to Maggie. "The Grail isn't at St. John the Divine. We already checked. So I'm afraid I'll have to search you—several times, in a variety of positions. Unless you tell me where the Grail is right now. The truth and no tricks."

Maggie shook her head. "I don't think so."

"A pity," said Shorty. "You'll still be a Bride of Christ— you just won't be a virgin Bride of Christ—and you'll wind up telling me anyway."

"I don't know where it is," Maggie said.

"Then all my work will be for nothing," Shorty said, but he was grinning as he said it.

"Please," I said, trying to make my voice sound like I was scared witless. "I don't know what any of this is about. Please let me go—"

"Shut him up," Shorty said.

At least I'd gotten his eyes on me instead of Maggie. And Fred was coming up, his pistol in one hand, mine in the other. That's when I kicked him, a reaping circular kick, taking him in the throat. It raised him to his feet and set him stumbling backward.

Shorty fired—but someone should have taught him how to shoot. His round missed me, thought I could feel the wind of it past my cheek and the answering spatter of plaster from the wall. I dove forward, spearing Fred in the belly with my head. Shorty's second shot took his partner between the shoulder blades as Fred was driven backward into him.

Then all three of us went down, and a moment later it was over. I rolled onto my back. Maggie was standing over me.

"You've been hit."

"I don't think so." But when I looked down at myself, sure enough here was blood pouring out, soaking the pocket where I'd put her bag—and where I kept my supply of Hosts. The Hosts were bleeding.

At that moment I knew. And looking into her eyes, I could tell she knew, too.

"It really was the Grail," she said.

"Looks like. Let's get out of here before the cops show up."

"Where to?"

"I'll introduce you to a man," I said. "You'll like him."

We left. The first police car arrived, lights flashing, when we were halfway down the block.

As dawn was breaking over a soggy New York morning, I was in the Rambles again. Prester John was waiting.

"Here it is," I said, tossing the sack to him. He opened the bag and rolled out the gemstones inside it.

"Yes," he said. "The substance is here, though the accidents have changed." The accidents. I should have thought of that back at the UN, when the Host that touched the meditation stone didn't bleed. A wafer, when its transubstantiated, still has the outward appearance—the accidents—of a flat bit of unleavened bread, while it's substance is the body of Christ. In the same way, the Grail's substance—whatever it is that makes it truly the Grail—now had the accidents of a handful of precious stones.

John looked back up at me, his hand clenching around the Grail. "Who's your friend?"

"Sister Mary Magdalene," she said. "From the Special Action Executive of the Poor Clares. I presume you're with the Temple?"

Prester John inclined his head.

"Pleased to meet you," she said. "We'd heard that there was some hanky-panky going on, especially when the Cathar Liberation Army started moving people into town."

"I can fill in the rest," I said. "Maggie's group was infiltrated by the Cathars, just before they got sold out themselves by the Luciferians. That's where Max Lang fits in. The Lucies had been contracted to grab the Grail because they were the only ones besides us who could handle it. Lang carried a bag of jewels in—swapped the substance of the jewels into the lodestone and the substance of the Grail into the jewels—and walked out. That gave them the Grail, but once the Lucies had it, they didn't want to turn it over, at least not to the Cathars. You remember what kind of mess there was last time *they* owned it."

"As if you can speak of anyone owning the Grail," Prester John said. "You're right: Lang must have transubstantiated the Grail into this little sack of jewels, and left the stone in the Meditation Room transubstantiated into a hunk of rock."

It all made sense. It also explained how the Lucies had smuggled six and a half tons of lodestone into and out of the UN—they hadn't. Nobody had carried anything through security that was bigger and heavier than a bag of marbles.

Prester John was shaking his head thoughtfully. "I wonder what made them think they could get away with it?"

"Maybe there's some truth to those stories about Lucifer's crown," I said. "The Lucies sure think so. And the Cathars knew they'd never get close working on their own, so they hired the Luciferians to do the dirty work for them. Then Lang got cold feet. Maybe he saw a vision or something. It's been known to happen. He was working up his nerve to return the Grail when he got hit."

"Lang had swallowed the stones," Maggie said. "I got 'em back. We'd been running electronic intelligence ops on the Lucies for a while. We intercepted one call yesterday afternoon that alerted us, and another call last evening from the hotel. That's when I got sent in. He was messed up enough when I got there that nobody's going to notice a few cuts more."

"Who was it who nailed him?" Prester John said.

"The Cathars," I said. "They'd figured out by then that he was trying to double-cross them."

"Any thoughts on how to get the Grail back to its rightful shape and rightful place?" John said. "We'll have to set new wards, too, so this won't happen again."

"That's your problem," I said. "Maybe you could hire the Lucies yourself. Me, I've got a social engagement. I promised Maggie a drink and I'm going to find her one."

"Hang on," Prester John said. "You're a priest. She's a nun. You can't go on a date."

"Don't worry," I said. "I won't get into the habit."

I've been an anthologist and writer for over forty years, yet my early favorites still impress me. But my all-time favorite is Elisabeth Waters' "Shadowlands"—with its perfect take on the Orpheus legend. I've never read anything in over forty years to top it.

—Marion Zimmer Bradley

SHADOWLANDS
by Elisabeth Waters

Oriana confronted the household priest over her husband's body, which lay on the bier in front of her. "No, I will not agree to hold the funeral at first light tomorrow! Why are you in such a hurry to put my husband underground?"

The priest sighed. He had been in the chapel with her and the body for several hours now, it was late, and he was tired. "My lady, why do you insist on delaying the funeral? This refusal to accept the situation avails you nothing."

Oriana simply stood there, a silent column of black. Her sole concession to her husband's death had been to put on mourning robes: a loose black gown, tied at the waist with a plain black cord, covered with layers of black veiling, enough to hide her pale face, her dark hair, and anything of the slender body the garments might conceivably have revealed. She felt like a walking shadow, and everything seemed distant and unreal.

The priest gathered what remained of his patience and tried again. "You are overwrought," he said gently, "and it's late. Please, my lady, go to your bed; sleep, and things won't seem as bad in the morning."

That argument she had heard before. "No," Oriana said firmly. "I did as you ask last night, and I assure you *nothing* was the slightest bit better this morning."

"Healing takes time—" the priest began weakly.

Oriana ignored him. "But, as you say, it is late, and I am sure you are tired. You have my leave to retire; I shall

181

stay with my husband. I'm not as ready as you to consign him to the lands of the dead.''

The priest opened his mouth to protest, decided it wouldn't help, and left, shaking his head.

Oriana knelt at her husband's side, the perfect picture of a devoted widow—no, wife; she absolutely refused to think of herself as a widow—and listened to the priest's footsteps fade away into the silence. It was nearing midnight, and the rest of the household had gone to bed long since.

Oriana looked steadily at the face before her. Quaren looked magnificent. He had always worn his age lightly, even in life. Oriana had never thought of him as old, even though he was twice her age. Now, with his body at rest and his face peaceful, he looked even less than his forty years. The few threads of gray in his dark hair seemed to be nothing but a trick of the flickering light cast by the candles about his bier reflecting off the silver embroidery of his dark green tunic. She still expected him to open his eyes and speak to her at any second.

He'd never been ill a single day in the six years of their marriage. It was totally inconceivable to Oriana that he could be gone so suddenly, in a single hour. The huntsmen who brought his body to her spoke of an accident, a bad fall with his horse, which had landed on him, but it made no sense to her. Her husband lay on the bier before her, but he just *couldn't* be dead.

And if he was, she was going to bring him back.

* * *

The house was still now; even the priest had gone to bed, and there was no one about to interrupt what she was about to do. Quaren might yet benefit from the things he had taught her. Of course, every minstrel knew the song of Orfeo, who had gone to the lands of death to bring back his wife, but very few people knew how to make the journey in truth. Such studies had been a hobby of Quaren's, and he had taught Oriana everything she could absorb. She rose silently to her feet and crossed the room to the door standing open between the chapel and the rest of the house. Quietly she closed the door and locked it. Then she returned to the bier.

From its hiding place in the long sleeve of her undertunic she pulled a small silver dagger, Quaren's ritual knife. The household priest didn't know about all of the rituals performed in the chapel. This would not be the first ritual she had done behind locked chapel doors, even if it was the first one she had tried to do alone. She could only hope that Quaren had taught her enough.

Using the dagger, she cut a lock of his hair and two locks of her own, braided them together and wound them around the hilt of the dagger. Now the dagger would tie her spirit to her husband's and help her to find him. She circled the bier, blowing out the candles, until the chapel was absolutely dark. Then she lay down on the bier, draping herself carefully across Quaren's body, and shifted into trance state.

* * *

She was in a narrow rock passageway, filled with billowing fog. Everything around her was a very dark gray, but as she went forward down the sloping tunnel, it widened and became lighter. Soon she could see quite well. She needed to be able to see here, for this was the place of the recently dead, the spirits not yet detached from the world and its concerns. Quaren should be here, if she was lucky.

The fog had slacked off to the occasional wisp by the time she reached the gates. There were two sets of them, made of round iron bars the size of her arm welded together into giant lattices. One could climb them easily, as many of the forms on the far side of them were doing, but since they went right up to the ceiling, they couldn't be climbed over.

Oriana walked up to the first gates, the ones that didn't have whoever they were crawling all over them. The gates were latched on the other side, but they didn't fit together snugly and it was easy enough for Oriana to slide the blade of the dagger through the crack and lift the latch. Opening the gates was much harder; she had to lean on one of them and push with all her might before it opened wide enough for her to slip through. It fell shut with a loud clang as soon as she released it, but by then she was safely through.

Holding the dagger tightly with both hands, she approached the second gates.

The forms on the other side proved to be people—more or less. They wore no clothes, and their bodies lacked the sharp detail of a human body, rather they were pale brown human-shaped manikins. But their faces were definitely human, as were their voices.

"Who are you to walk through the dark mists before Death has summoned you?" one of them demanded.

"This place will fill you with horror and drive you mad!" said another form. It was not a friendly warning; the voice sounded gleeful at the prospect.

"You will be trapped here forever—unless Death deigns to release you!"

Oriana looked from face to face. Their threats didn't terrify her; if she couldn't save Quaren, she didn't care what happened to her. But his face was not among the ones around her.

"Why have you come here?" one of the spirits challenged her, facing her through the gates.

"I am looking for my husband," Oriana replied steadily.

"Husband!" The spirit laughed. It was not a happy sound. "Do you see him here?"

"No," Oriana answered.

"Perhaps he is on the Isle of the Blessed," one of the others said sarcastically. Oriana started; the voice sounded very much like that of her eldest sister, who had almost invariably used that tone when talking to her. Well, she knew how to deal with sarcastic bullying.

"Perhaps he is," Oriana agreed quietly.

"And do you plan to go all the way there to look for him?" This spirit also seemed to have been female; its face reminded Oriana of the way her sisters used to look when they teased her.

"Yes," she said firmly, "I do."

This produced a great burst of hilarity, and the spirits pulled open the gates and bowed Oriana through—or perhaps they were simply doubled up with laughter. Oriana walked quickly past them, glad that Quaren wasn't there. Even for the sake of finding him easily, she wouldn't wish him condemned to such company. But it was odd that he

could have gone so far so quickly. Was he truly already on
the Isle of the Blessed?

* * *

The mocking laughter faded into the distance behind her
and was replaced by the sound of water lapping sluggishly
against the shore. Oriana knew this landmark well. The
river had many names, but everyone knew one had to cross
it to get to the Isle of the Blessed. Some people said there
was a ferry across it and buried their dead with coins for
passage money. Oriana had always thought that story
rather fanciful, and certainly she saw no sign of a boat or
a landing for one now.

She looked down at the dagger in her hands; it was glowing faintly. She took a few steps downstream and the glow
faded, brightening again when she returned to her original
position. When she continued walking upstream, the glow
got even brighter. She watched it carefully and stopped
when it started to fade again. Obviously this was as close
to Quaren as she could get on this side of the river. He
must be on the land opposite her, which she could see
dimly through the thin ghostly river mists. The river was
eerie, but the current wasn't particularly swift and Oriana
had never been afraid of getting wet. Still, she knew she
had better get across this water as quickly as possible; one
of the names for this river was Oblivion.

She stepped in and gasped. The water was colder than
anything she'd ever felt in her life—*probably,* she thought,
colder than anything anyone *ever felt in their life.* Gritting
her teeth so they wouldn't chatter, she slogged on. *Step,
step and another step. Come on, you can do it,* she admon-
ished herself. *Remember to keep the dagger dry. Step,
step, step . . .*

* * *

She sat in the grass, under the trees. She was wet up to
her breasts, but it didn't matter; she'd dry fast enough in
the sun, which was making lacy patterns as it shone through
the leaves. It was so peaceful and so beautiful. She was
perfectly content to sit there and watch the play of the light

and listen to the rustling of the leaves. The birds were singing, the squirrels were chattering; it was the kind of morning that made one glad to be alive.

Alive. For some reason the word bothered her. *But why? What's wrong with being alive?* Her fingers, idly tracing the dagger in her lap, touched the braid of hair around the hilt, and her memory returned with wrenching suddenness. *Quaren. My husband is dead, and I came here to save him.*

She stood up and pulled at her wet robes, which seemed determined to cling awkwardly to her body. She started to remove the layers of veiling, but stopped after the first two. The light about her was getting too bright to bear without veils. Obviously the living were not meant to wander unveiled in the land of the dead. *Is this why widows wear veils? Has someone before me done this, and succeeded?* She tucked the extra veils under her arm and started through the woods, trusting that the faint pull from the dagger was a true guide.

She was concentrating so hard on the dagger that she nearly tripped over the boy. He appeared to be about eight or nine years old and he was lying against a tree trunk, turning a leaf between his fingers. He wore a short silver-blue tunic which matched both his eyes and his hair, and his skin looked so pale as to be true white. Oriana apologized automatically, and he looked startled, as if he hadn't noticed her presence before.

"What's wrong with you?" he asked with the directness of childhood. "You're so faint I can barely see you."

Oriana thought about it. She looked normal enough to herself, but she had to admit that he looked somehow more solid than she did. "I guess it's because I'm not dead—at least I don't think I am." She looked down at the braid on the dagger. The hair was still dark, except for a few strands of silver in the hair that had come from Quaren, and Oriana felt somehow certain that it would look different if she were dead.

"You're alive? Really?" The boy seemed to find this a strange idea. "What are you doing here, then?"

"Looking for my husband."

"Oh." He frowned, puzzled. "Aren't you supposed to wait until you're dead, too?"

Oriana smiled for the first time in several days. "Maybe

that part of my education was neglected. Did your parents teach you proper etiquette for the Shadowlands?''

"My parents didn't teach me anything," he said matter-of-factly. "I was only a baby when I died."

"I'm sorry," Oriana said.

"Why? Lots of babies die. And I'd rather be here anyway."

"You'd *rather* be dead?" Oriana asked incredulously.

"Of course." To him, this was obvious. "Look, isn't this leaf beautiful?"

The leaf was indeed beautiful; in fact, everything around them was beautiful, which surprised Oriana. She had always thought that the Shadowlands were dim and dull, not at all like this—filled with a bright beauty that hurt mortal eyes. For a moment she almost wished that she were dead, too, so that she could enjoy it freely, but her sense of duty and love toward her husband drove her to press on in her search. She duly admired the leaf and continued on her way as the boy returned to his contemplation of the beauty of unnatural nature.

* * *

She found Quaren in a stone-flagged courtyard. He was sitting on a marble bench with two other men, all discussing some terribly abstract philosophical theory. All three of them wore pale blue tunics like the boy's, and the two other men had the same silver-blue hair and eyes. Quaren's hair and eyes were still dark, but the gray that had been in his hair was gone. He looked much younger than he had in life, and his face glowed with the intellectual joy a good problem had always given him. But Oriana had never seen him look quite so happy before.

The sight of him made her heart turn over within her, and she wanted to walk over to him and fling her arms around him. *Did my trip through the river make me forget how much I love him?* she wondered. But for the moment it was enough just to see him again. She sat down on another bench in the courtyard and watched him as the men continued their discussion, content just to be in his presence and to see him happy.

Presently the discussion wound down and the other men

left. Quaren sat quietly, lost in thought, Oriana walked over and sat next to him.

"Quaren?" He didn't seem to hear her. "Quaren!" Now he looked puzzled, as if he could hear a faint sound but could see nothing that could have made it.

Am I fading away? Oriana wondered anxiously. *Maybe I'm just invisible in direct sunlight—the boy was in shadow and still had trouble seeing me.*

She took one of her extra veils and draped it over his head. Yes, now he seemed to be able to see *something* when he looked at her. She added the other veil.

He blinked and looked at her. "Do I know you?"

Oriana found herself grinding her teeth. This was not the welcome she had envisioned. After all the effort she had gone through to come find him, he ought to least to remember her. "I'm your wife," she said. She took his right hand and placed it on top of her left hand, with the dagger held between their palms.

It worked; his face cleared. "Oriana." Then he frowned. "But you're not dead. What are you doing here?"

"I came to find you," she explained, "and take you back."

"Oh." Quaren didn't seem to feel any particular enthusiasm for the idea; in fact, he looked rather blank and dazed.

Probably due to the veils, Oriana thought. *Best get him out of here as quickly as possible. The legends hint at all sorts of things that can go wrong now.* She tugged at his hand, and he rose obediently and allowed her to lead him back toward the shore.

This time there was no one in the woods. The walk was silent except for the rustling of their veils. It wasn't until they reached the shore that Quaren spoke.

"Of course. The river. I don't remember coming this way before, but then I'm sure I'm not supposed to."

"I remember it," Oriana said. "It's cold!"

He chuckled softly. "When you're dead, you don't feel it. By the way, how did I die? I don't remember that part either."

"Your horse fell on you. It all happened very quickly."

"Poor Oriana." He patted her shoulder gently. "It must have been a dreadful shock for you."

Oriana found that her eyes were suddenly full of tears

and her throat was tight. "It was awful! I can't live without you!"

"Your heart will suddenly stop beating perhaps?" he chided gently. Oriana knew the tone well; it was the one he always used when she made a statement not fully supported by verifiable fact. He sighed. "I must not have taught you as well as I thought."

"Of course you taught me well!" Oriana protested. "How do you think I got here? Do other men's wives come here seeking them? Do you think it was easy?"

"No," he said sadly. "Not easy. Easier."

"Easier than what?" Why did he sound disappointed in her? You'd think he's be pleased that she loved him enough to come seek him in the Shadowlands and that she had the courage and determination to find him.

"Easier than your alternatives."

"Well," Oriana mused aloud, "it probably would have been easier to stab myself—but that wouldn't have brought me here, would it?"

"No!" he said quickly. "Killing yourself would you leave you still bound to the world until the time you should have died." He put his other hand over hers. "Don't do that, Oriana."

Oriana thought of the spirits in the rock tunnel and shuddered. "I won't," she said definitely. "Not ever." She clung to his hand. "But I don't want to live without you!"

He smiled at that. "That's better."

"What?" Oriana realized what she had said. *Don't want to* instead of *can't*. "So my choices now are to take you back with me—I *can* do that, can't I?"

"Yes," he said flatly. "You can. Even against my will."

"—or to leave you here and go back alone." She felt her stomach clench at that thought, but forced herself to think it through. *The incredibly cold river that numbs the mind, and beyond that the tunnel, and those awful spirits—and I can well imagine what they'll say if I come back alone. . . .*

She contemplated the water in front of her. It was clearer here than it had been on the other side, and it glistened jewellike in the sun. The grass was a purer green than anyone alive could imagine, and each blade of it seemed to be full of energy. Oriana suddenly felt out of place, like a smudge on the page of a book, a dark spot on the landscape. The veils she wore seemed intolerably heavy and dark.

She remembered the boy she had met in the woods, and his matter-of-fact acceptance of his state. He'd rather be dead than alive—did everyone in the Shadowlands feel that way?

She turned to face Quaren squarely. "You'd rather stay here than go back to life again." It was a statement, not a question, but he nodded anyway.

"Wouldn't you?"

Oriana looked at the trees, glittering brightly green in the pure otherwordly sunlight. She knew exactly what he meant; more than she had ever wanted anything in her life she wanted to stay in this bright land. But she was only a shadow here, and the light, for all its beauty, was painful to her. "I wish I could see it all properly. Why do they call it the Shadowlands when it's so bright here?"

"You'll be able to see it in time."

Oriana nodded, choking back the sob caught in her throat. "When my time comes." Even through her veils she could see rainbows as the sun caught her tears. "But that could be years and years!" she protested.

Quaren's reply was no comfort. "Yes. It could be."

"And I'd have to go through it all alone—I don't want to do that!"

"Would you rather drag me back, so that I can die again, possibly of some long lingering illness which would have both of us wishing I'd stayed dead?"

"You're just afraid to go back!" she accused him.

"Not afraid," he said calmly. "I know what's back there and what's here. I died, Oriana. My place is here now. You can take me back to the outer world with you, but, now that I've been here, part of me will always remain here."

Oriana burst into tears, knowing now that what he said was true. She could take him home with her, but for the rest of their lives together she would be living with a husband who wished to be elsewhere. It certainly cast a new light on the legends. Perhaps Orfeo's loss of his wife on their journey back to the land of the living had not been a mistake after all.

It would be hard enough for her to live contentedly in the world now that she knew what lay beyond: for Quaren, knowing that he truly didn't belong among the living, it would be worse. Unhappy as she would be without him, she couldn't take him back against his wish.

"You're right," she sighed. "It's not the act of a loving spouse to drag you back." Her fingers clung convulsively to his. "But oh, I'll miss you."

"You'll know where to find me."

She forced a smile. "On the terrace, debating philosophy." She reached out with a shaking hand to pull her veils off him. "Just remember that I love you." She leaned forward to hug him convulsively with her free arm, then deliberately released him and lifted the dagger out of his hand. For a moment he glowed, even more brightly than the sun.

Then everything was gone.

* * *

It was dark, and cold, and the stone under her was hard. Gradually, as her eyes adjusted, Oriana made out her surroundings. She lay on the floor of the chapel, across the room from the bier which still held Quaren's body. Her face was wet with tears, her veils were scattered about the room as if blown by a strong wind, and Quaren's dagger was gripped tightly in her hand.

She sat up, mopped her wet face with her skirt, and walked over to the bier. Was it her imagination, or was there a peace on Quaren's face that had not been there before? She looked at the dagger she still held. Two parts of the braid around the hilt were brown; the third was a brilliant silver-blue. She smiled as she placed it between his clasped hands. Then she gathered up her veils and unlocked the door of the chapel. The priest would need to get in to prepare for the funeral.

The twentieth century is ending and the twenty-first beginning; and because of that, you may be tempted to read this as fin-de-siecle fantasy. Taking it so, you will find it stunning. "Was it really possible," you may ask yourself, "to write as wildly, as brutally, and as charmingly as this in 1900?" But you will be wrong about the date. A boy born when Jean Ingelow was writing "Mopsa" would have reached his thirties when *The Wizard of Oz* appeared. You will find much here that recalls Oz; you will also find the eeriness that L. Frank Baum set out to banish from his own fairyland. (He was thirteen when "Mopsa" was issued, and it must have frightened him.) In that quality, Neil Gaiman's *Stardust* comes closest to "Mopsa"; but Gaiman is writing for adults.

Every authority has called "Mopsa" feminist. It is not. Ingelow was writing for boys as single-mindedly as Baum ever wrote for girls; but Ingelow dared answer a question that no other such writer has even dared ask: **If there really were a fairy princess, what would she be like?**

—Gene Wolfe

MOPSA THE FAIRY
by Jean Ingelow

CHAPTER ONE

Above the Clouds

"And can this be my own world?
    'Tis all gold and snow,
Save where scarlet waves are hurled
    Down yon gulf below,"
" 'Tis thy world, 'tis my world,
    City, mead, and shore,
For he that hath his own world
    Hath many worlds more."[1]

1. 'And . . . more' Ingelow's own verses head chapters 1, 3, 4, 6, 8, 9, 12, and 16

A boy, whom I knew very well, was once going through a meadow which was full of buttercups. The nurse and his baby sister were with him; and when they got to an old hawthorn, which grew in the hedge and was covered with blossom, they all sat down in its shade, and the nurse took out three slices of plum cake, gave one to each of the children and kept one for herself.

While the boy was eating he observed that this hedge was very high and thick, and that there was a great hollow in the trunk of the old thorn tree, and he heard a twittering, as if there was a nest somewhere inside; so he thrust his head in, twisted himself round and looked up.

It was a very great thorn tree, and the hollow was so large that two or three boys could have stood upright in it; and when he got used to the dim light in that brown, still place, he saw that a good way above his head there was a nest—rather a curious one too, for it was as large as a pair of blackbirds would have built—and yet it was made of fine white wool and delicate bits of moss; in short, it was like a goldfinch's nest magnified three times.

Just then he thought he heard some little voices cry, "Jack! Jack!" His baby sister was asleep, and the nurse was reading a story book, so it could not have been either of them who called. "I must get in here," said the boy. "I wish this hole was larger." So he began to wriggle and twist himself through, and just as he pulled in his last foot he looked up, and three heads which had been peeping over the edge of the nest suddenly popped down again.

"Those heads had no beaks, I am sure," said Jack, and he stood on tiptoe and poked in one of his fingers. "And the things have no feathers," he continued; so, the hollow being rather rugged, he managed to climb up and look in.

His eyes were not used yet to the dim light; but he was sure those things were not birds—no. He poked them, and they took no notice; but when he snatched one of them out of the nest it gave a loud squeak, and said: "Oh, don't, Jack!" as plainly as possible, upon which he was so frightened that he lost his footing, dropped the thing and slipped down himself. Luckily he was not hurt, nor the thing either; he could see it quite plainly now; it was creeping about like rather an old baby, and had on a little frock and pinafore.

"It's a fairy!" exclaimed Jack to himself. "How curious! and this must be a fairy's nest. Oh, how angry the old mother will be if this little thing creeps away and gets out of the hole!" So he looked down. "Oh, the hole is on the other side," he said; and he turned round, but the hole was not on the other side; it was not on any side; it must have closed up all on a sudden, while he was looking into the nest, for, look whichever way he would, there was no hole at all, excepting a very little one high up over the nest, which let in a very small sunbeam.

Jack was very much astonished, but he went on eating his cake, and was so delighted to see the young fairy climb up the side of the hollow and scramble again into her nest that he laughed heartily; upon which all the nestlings popped up their heads and, showing their pretty white teeth, pointed at the slice of cake.

"Well," said Jack, "I may have to stay inside here for a long time, and I have nothing to eat but this cake; however, your mouths are very small, so you shall have a piece"; and he broke off a small piece and put it into the nest, climbing up to see them eat it.

These young fairies were a long time dividing and munching the cake, and before they had finished it began to be rather dark, for a black cloud came over and covered the little sunbeam. At the same time the wind rose and rocked the boughs, and made the old tree creak and tremble. Then there was thunder and rain, and the little fairies were so frightened that they got out of the nest and crept into Jack's pockets. One got into each waistcoat pocket, and the other two were very comfortable, for he took out his handkerchief and made room for them in the pocket of his jacket.

It got darker and darker, till at last Jack could only just see the hole, and it seemed to be a very long way off. Every time he looked at it, it was farther off, and at last he saw a thin crescent moon shining through it.

"I am sure it cannot be night yet," he said; and he took out one of the fattest of the young fairies and held it up towards the hole.

"Look at that," said he; "what is to be done now? The hole is so far off that it's night up there, and down here I haven't done eating my lunch."

"Well," answered the young fairy, "then why don't you whistle?"

Jack was surprised to hear her speak in this sensible manner, and in the light of the moon he looked at her very attentively.

"When first I saw you in the nest," said he, "you had a pinafore on, and now you have a smart little apron, with lace round it."

"That is because I am much older now," said the fairy; "we never take such a long time to grow up as you do."

"But your pinafore?" said Jack.

"Turned into an apron, of course," replied the fairy, "just as your velvet jacket will turn into a tail-coat when you are old enough."

"It won't," said Jack.

"Yes, it will," answered the fairy, with an air of superior wisdom. "Don't argue with me; I am older now than you are—nearly grown up in fact. Put me into your pocket again, and whistle as loudly as you can."

"Jack laughed, put her in, and pulled out another. "Worse and worse," he said; "why, this was a boy fairy, and now he has a moustache and a sword, and looks as fierce as possible!"

"I think I heard my sister tell you to whistle?" said this fairy very sternly.

"Yes, she did," said Jack. "Well, I suppose I had better do it." So he whistled very loudly indeed.

"Why did you leave off so soon?" said another of them, peeping out.

"Why, if you wish to know," answered Jack, "it was because I thought something took hold of my legs."

"Ridiculous child," cried the last of the four, "how do you think you are ever to get out, if she doesn't take hold of your legs?"

Jack thought he would rather have done a long-division sum than have been obliged to whistle; but he could not help doing it when they told him, and he felt something take hold of his legs again, and then give him a jerk, which hoisted him on to its back, where he sat astride, and wondered whether the thing was a pony; but it was not, for he presently observed that it had a very slender neck, and then that it was covered with feathers. It was a large bird, and he presently found that they were rising towards the hole, which had become so very far off, and in a few minutes she dashed through the hole, with Jack on her back and all the fairies in his pockets.

It was so dark that he could see nothing, and he twined his arms round the bird's neck, to hold on, upon which this agreeable fowl told him not to be afraid, and said she hoped he was comfortable.

"I should be more comfortable," replied Jack, "if I knew how I could get home again. I don't wish to go home just yet, for I want to see where we are flying to, but papa and mamma will be frightened if I never do."

"Oh no," replied the albatross[2] (for she was an albatross), "you need not be at all afraid about that. When boys go to Fairyland, their parents never are uneasy about them."

"Really?" exclaimed Jack.

"Quite true," replied the albatross.

"And so we are going to Fairyland?" exclaimed Jack. "How delightful!"

"Yes," said the albatross; "the back way, mind; we are only going the back way. You could go in two minutes by the usual route; but these young fairies want to go before they are summoned, and therefore you and I are taking them." And she continued to fly on in the dark sky for a very long time.

"They seem to be all fast asleep," said Jack.

"Perhaps they will sleep till we come to the wonderful river," replied the albatross; and just then she flew with a great bump against something that met her in the air.

"What craft is this that hangs out no light?" said a gruff voice.

"I might ask the same question of you," answered the albatross sullenly.

"I'm only a poor Will-o'-the-wisp,"[3] replied the voice, "and you know very well that I have but a lantern to show." Thereupon a lantern became visible, and Jack saw by the light of it a man who looked old and tired, and he

---

2. **albatross** sea-bird associated with the imagination ever since Coleridge's "The Rime of the Ancient Mariner" (1798)

3. **Will-o'-the-wisp** See note 17

was so transparent that you could see through him, lantern and all.

"I hope I have not hurt you, William," said the albatross; "I will light up immediately. Good night."

"Good night," answered the Will-o'-the-wisp. "I am going down as fast as I can; the storm blew me up, and I am never easy excepting in my native swamps."

Jack might have taken more notice of Will if the albatross had not begun to light up. She did it in this way. First one of her eyes began to gleam with a beautiful green light, which cast its rays far and near, and then, when it was as bright as a lamp, the other eye began to shine, and the light of that eye was red. In short, she was lighted up just like a vessel at sea.

Jack was so happy that he hardly knew which to look at first, there really were so many remarkable things.

"They snore," said the albatross; "they are very fast asleep, and before they wake I should like to talk to you a little."

She meant that the fairies snored, and so they did, in Jack's pockets.

"My name," continued the albatross, "is Jenny. Do you think you shall remember that? Because when you are in Fairyland and want someone to take you home again, and call 'Jenny,' I shall be able to come to you; and I shall come with pleasure, for I like boys better than fairies."

"Thank you," said Jack. "Oh yes, I shall remember your name, it is such a very easy one."

"If it is in the night that you want me, just look up," continued the albatross, "and you will see a green and red spark moving in the air; you will then call Jenny, and I will come; but remember that I cannot come unless you do call me."

"Very well," said Jack; but he was not attending, because there was so much to be seen.

In the first place all the stars excepting a few large ones were gone, and they looked frightened; and as it got lighter one after the other seemed to give a little start in the blue sky and go out. And then Jack looked down and saw, as he thought, a great country covered with very jagged snow mountains with astonishingly sharp peaks. Here and there he saw a very deep lake—at least he thought it was a lake;

but while he was admiring the mountains there came an enormous crack between two of the largest, and he saw the sun come rolling up among them, and it seemed to be almost smothered.

"Why those are clouds!" exclaimed Jack. "And, oh, how rosy they have all turned! I thought they were mountains."

"Yes, they are clouds," said the albatross; and then they turned gold color; and next they began to plunge and tumble, and every one of the peaks put on a glittering crown; and next they broke themselves to pieces and began to drift away. In fact Jack had been out all night, and now it was morning.

CHAPTER TWO

Captain Jack

It has been our lot to sail with many captains, not one of whom is fit to be a patch on your back. *Letter of the Ship's Company of H.M.S.S.* Royalist *to Captain W. T. Bate.*

All this time the albatross kept dropping down and down like a stone till Jack was quite out of breath, and they fell or flew, whichever you like to call it, straight through one of the great chasms which he had thought were lakes, and he looked down as he sat on the bird's back to see what the world is like when you hang a good way above it at sunrise.

It was a very beautiful sight; the sheep and lambs were still fast asleep on the green hills, and the sea birds were asleep in long rows upon the ledges of the cliffs, with their heads under their wings.

"Are those young fairies awake yet?" asked the albatross.

"As sound asleep as ever," answered Jack; "but, Albatross, is not that the sea which lies under us? You are a sea bird, I know, but I am not a sea boy, and I cannot live in the water."

"Yes, that is the sea," answered the albatross. "Don't you observe that it is covered with ships?"

"I see boats and vessels," answered Jack, "and all their sails are set, but they cannot sail because there is no wind."

"The wind never does blow in this great bay," said the bird; "and those ships would all lie there becalmed till they dropped to pieces if one of them was not wanted now and then to go up the wonderful river."

"But how did they come there?" asked Jack.

"Some of them had captains who ill-used their cabin-boys, some were pirate ships and others were going out on evil errands. The consequence was that when they chanced to sail within this great bay they got becalmed; the fairies came and picked all the sailors out and threw them into the water; they then took away the flags and pennons to make their best coats of, threw the ship-biscuits and other provisions to the fishes and set all the sails. Many ships which are supposed by men to have foundered lie becalmed in this quiet sea. Look at those five grand ones with high poops; they are moored close together, they were part of the Spanish Armada; and those open boats with blue sails belonged to the Romans, they sailed with Caesar when he invaded Britain."

By this time the albatross was hovering about among the vessels, making choice of one to take Jack and the fairies up the wonderful river.

"It must not be a large one," she said, "for the river in some places is very shallow."

Jack would have liked very much to have a fine three-master, all to himself; but then he considered that he did not know anything about sails and rigging, he thought it would be just as well to be contented with whatever the albatross might choose, so he let her set him down in a beautiful little open boat, with a great carved figurehead to it. There he seated himself in great state, and the albatross perched herself on the next bench and faced him.

"You remember my name?" asked the albatross.

"Oh yes," said Jack; but he was not attending—he was thinking what a fine thing it was to have such a curious boat all to himself.

"That's well," answered the bird; "then, in the next place, are those fairies awake yet?"

"No, they are not," said Jack; and he took them out of his pockets and laid them down in a row before the albatross.

"They are certainly asleep," said the bird. "Put them away again, and take care of them. Mind you don't lose any of them, for I really don't know what will happen if you do. Now I have one more thing to say to you, and that is, are you hungry?"

"Rather," said Jack.

"Then," replied the albatross, "as soon as you feel *very* hungry, lie down in the bottom of the boat and go to sleep. You will dream that you see before you a roasted fowl, some new potatoes and an apple pie. Mind you don't eat too much in your dream, or you will be sorry for it when you wake. That is all. Goodbye! I must go."

Jack put his arms round the neck of the bird and hugged her; then she spread her magnificent wings and sailed slowly away. At first he felt very lonely; but in a few minutes he forgot that, because the little boat began to swim so fast.

She was not sailing, for she had no sail, and he was not rowing, for he had no oars; so I am obliged to call her motion swimming, because I don't know of a better word. In less than a quarter of an hour they passed close under the bows of a splendid three-decker, a seventy-gun ship. The gannets[4] who live in those parts had taken possession of her, and she was so covered with nests that you could not have walked one step on her deck without treading on them. The father birds were aloft in the rigging, or swimming in the warm green sea, and they made such a clamor when they saw Jack that they nearly woke the fairies—nearly, but not quite, for the little things turned round in Jack's pockets, and sneezed, and began to snore again.

Then the boat swam past a fine brig. Some sea fairies had just flung her cargo overboard, and were playing at leapfrog on deck. These were not at all like Jack's own fairies; they were about the same height and size as himself, and they had brown faces, and red flannel shirts and red caps on. A large fleet of the pearly nautilus was collected close under the vessel's lee. The little creatures were feast-

4. **gannets** northern sea birds

ing on what the sea fairies had thrown overboard, and
Jack's boat, in its eagerness to get on, went plunging
through them so roughly that several were capsized. Upon
this the brown sea fairies looked over, and called out an-
grily: "Boat ahoy!" and the boat stopped.

"Tell that boat of yours to mind what she is about," said
the fairy sea-captain to Jack.

Jack touched his cap, and said: "Yes, sir," and then
called out to his boat: "You ought to be ashamed of yourself, running down these little live fishing-vessels so carelessly. Go at a more gentle pace."

So it swam more slowly; and Jack, being by this time
hungry, curled himself up in the bottom of the boat and
fell asleep.

He dreamt directly about a fowl and some potatoes, and
he ate a wing, and then he ate a merrythought, and then
somebody said to him that he had better not eat any more,
but he did, he ate another wing; and presently an apple pie
came, and he ate some of that, and then he ate some more,
and then he immediately woke.

"Now that bird told me not to eat too much," said Jack,
"and yet I have done it. I never felt so full in my life," and
for more than half an hour he scarcely noticed anything.

At last he lifted up his head, and saw straight before him
two great brown cliffs, and between them flowed in the
wonderful river. Other rivers flow out, but this river flowed
in, and took with it far into the land dolphins, swordfish,
mullet, sunfish and many other strange creatures; and that
is one reason why it was called the magic river, or the
wonderful river.

At first it was rather wide, and Jack was alarmed to see
what multitudes of soldiers stood on either side to guard
the banks and prevent any person from landing.

He wondered how he should get the fairies on shore.
However, in about an hour the river became much narrower, and then Jack saw that the guards were not real
soldiers, but rose-colored flamingoes.[5] There they stood in
long regiments among the reeds, and never stirred. They
are the only foot-soldiers the fairies have in their pay; they

5. **flamingoes** Carroll's Alice used flamingoes as mallets in the cro-
quet game in which soldiers formed arches

are very fierce, and never allow anything but a fairy ship to come up the river.

They guarded the banks for miles and miles, many thousands of them, standing a little way into the water among the flags and rushes; but at last there were no more reeds and no soldier guards, for the stream became narrower, and flowed between such steep rocks that no one could possibly have climbed them.

CHAPTER THREE

Winding-up Time

"Wake, baillie, wake! The crafts are out;
　　Wake!" said the knight. "Be quick!
For high street, bystreet, over the town
　　They fight with poker and stick."
Said the squire, "A fight so fell was ne'er
　　In all thy bailiewick."
What said the old clock in the tower?
　　"Tick, tick, tick!"

"Wake, daughter, wake! the hour draws on;
　　Wake!" quoth the dame. "Be quick!
The meats are set, the guests are coming,
　　The fiddler's waxing his stick."
She said, "The bridegroom waiting and waiting
　　To see thy face is sick."
What said the new clock in her bower?
　　"Tick, tick, tick!"

Jack looked at these hot brown rocks, first on the left bank and then on the right, till he was quite tired; but at last the shore on the right bank became flat, and he saw a beautiful little bay, where the water was still and where grass grew down to the brink.

He was so much pleased at this change that he cried out hastily: "Oh, how I wish my boat would swim into that bay and let me land!" He had no sooner spoken than the boat altered her course, as if somebody had been steering her, and began to make for the bay as fast as she could go.

"How odd!" thought Jack. "I wonder whether I ought to have spoken; for the boat certainly did not intend to come into this bay. However, I think I will let her alone now, for I certainly do wish very much to land here."

As they drew towards the strand the water got so shallow that you could see crabs and lobsters walking about at the bottom. At last the boat's keel grated on the pebbles; and just as Jack began to think of jumping on shore he saw two little old women approaching and gently driving a white horse before them.

The horse had panniers,[6] one on each side; and when his feet were in the water he stood still; and Jack said to one of the old women: "Will you be so kind as to tell me whether this is Fairyland?"

"What does he say?" asked one old woman of the other.

"I asked if this was Fairyland," repeated Jack, for he thought the first old woman might have been deaf. She was very handsomely dressed in a red satin gown, and did not look in the least like a washer-woman, though it afterwards appeared that she was one.

"He says, 'Is this Fairyland?' " she replied; and the other, who had a blue satin cloak, answered: "Oh, does he?" and then began to empty the panniers of many small blue and pink and scarlet shirts, and coats, and stockings; and when they had made them into two little heaps they knelt down and began to wash them in the river, taking no notice of him whatever.

Jack stared at them. They were not much taller than himself, and they were not taking the slightest care of their handsome clothes; then he looked at the old white horse, who was hanging his head over the lovely clear water with a very discontented air.

At last the blue washer-woman said: "I shall leave off now; I've got a pain in my works."

"Do," said the other. "We'll go home and have a cup of tea." Then she glanced at Jack, who was still sitting in the boat, and said: "Can you strike?"

"I can if I choose," replied Jack, a little astonished at

6. **panniers** carrying baskets placed on horses or mules

this speech. And the red and blue washer-women wrung out the clothes, put them again into the panniers and, taking the old horse by the bridle, began gently to lead him away.

"I have a great mind to land," thought Jack. "I should not wonder at all if this is Fairyland. So, as the boat came here to please me, I shall ask it to stay where it is, in case I should want it again."

So he sprang ashore, and said to the boat: "Stay just where you are, will you?" and he ran after the old women, calling to them:

"Is there any law to prevent my coming into your country?"

"Wo!" cried the red-coated old woman, and the horse stopped, while the blue-coated woman repeated: "Any law? No, not that I know of; but if you are a stranger here you had better look out."

"Why?" asked Jack.

"You don't suppose, do you," she answered, "that our Queen will wind up strangers?"

While Jack was wondering what she meant, the other said:

"I shouldn't wonder if he goes eight days. Gee!" and the horse went on.

"No, wo!" said the other.

"No, no. Gee! I tell you," cried the first.

Upon this, to Jack's intense astonishment, the old horse stopped, and said, speaking through his nose:

"Now, then, which it is to be? I'm willing to gee, and I'm agreeable to wo; but what's a fellow to do when you say them both together?"

"Why, he talks!" exclaimed Jack.

"It's because he's got a cold in his head," observed one of the washer-women; "he always talks when he's got a cold, and there's no pleasing him; whatever you say, he's not satisfied. Gee, Boney, do!"

"Gee it is, then," said the horse, and began to jog on.

"He spoke again!" said Jack, upon which the horse laughed, and Jack was quite alarmed.

"It appears that your horses don't talk?" observed the blue-coated woman.

"Never," answered Jack; "they can't."

"You mean they won't," observed the old horse; and though he spoke the words of mankind it was not in a voice like theirs. Still Jack felt that his was just the natural tone for a horse, and that it did not arise only from the length of his nose. "You'll find out some day, perhaps," he continued, "whether horses can talk or not."

"Shall I?" said Jack very earnestly.

"They'll TELL," proceeded the white horse." I wouldn't be you when they tell how you've used them."

"Have you been ill used?" said Jack, in an anxious tone.

"Yes, yes, of course he has," one of the women broke in; "but he has come here to get all right again. This is a very wholesome country for horses; isn't it, Boney?"

"Yes," said the horse.

"Well, then, jog on, there's a dear," continued the old woman. "Why, you will be young again soon, you know—young, and gamesome, and handsome; you'll be quite a colt by and by, and then we shall set you free to join your companions in the happy meadows."

The old horse was so comforted by this kind speech that he pricked up his ears and quickened his pace considerably.

"He was shamefully used," observed one washer-woman. "Look at him, how lean he is! You can see all his ribs."

"Yes," said the other, as if apologizing for the poor old horse. "He gets low-spirited when he thinks of all he has gone through; but he is a vast deal better already than he was. He used to live in London; his master always carried a long whip to beat him with, and never spoke civilly to him."

"London!" exclaimed Jack. "Why, that is my country. How did the horse get here?"

"That's no business of yours," answered one of the women. "But I can tell you he came because he was wanted, which is more than you are."

"You let him alone," said the horse in a querulous tone. "I don't bear any malice."

"No, he has a good disposition, has Boney," observed the red old woman. "Pray, are you a boy?"

"Yes," said Jack.

"A real boy, that wants no winding up?" inquired the old woman.

"I don't know what you mean," answered Jack; "but I am a real boy, certainly."

"Ah!" she replied. "Well, I thought you were, by the way Boney spoke to you. How frightened you must be! I wonder what will be done to all your people for driving, and working, and beating so many beautiful creatures to death every year that comes? They'll have to pay for it some day, you may depend."

Jack was a little alarmed, and answered that he had never been unkind himself to horses, and he was glad that Boney bore no malice.

"They worked him, and often drove him about all night in the miserable streets, and never let him have so much as a canter in a green field," said one of the women; "but he'll be all right now, only he has to begin at the wrong end."

"What do you mean?" said Jack.

"Why, in this country," answered the old woman, "they begin by being terribly old and stiff, and they seem miserable and jaded at first, but by degrees they get young again, as you heard me reminding him."

"Indeed," said Jack; "and do you like that?"

"It has nothing to do with me," she answered. "We are only here to take care of all the creatures that men have ill used. While they are sick and old, which they are when first they come to us—after they are dead, you know—we take care of them, and gradually bring them up to be young and happy again."

"This must be a very nice country to live in then," said Jack.

"For horses it is," said the old lady significantly.

"Well," said Jack, "it does seem very full of haystacks certainly, and all the air smells of fresh grass."

At this moment they came to a beautiful meadow, and the old horse stopped and, turning to the blue-coated woman, said: "Faxa, I think I could fancy a handful of clover." Upon this Faxa snatched Jack's cap off his head, and in a very active manner jumped over a little ditch, and gathering some clover, presently brought it back full, handing it to the old horse with great civility.

"You shouldn't be in such a hurry," observed the old horse, "your weights will be running down some day, if you don't mind."

"It's all zeal," observed the red-coated woman.

Just then a little man, dressed like a groom, came running up, out of breath. "Oh, here you are, Dow!" he exclaimed to the red-coated woman. "Come along, will you? Lady Betty wants you; it's such a hot day, and nobody, she says, can fan her so well as you can."

The red-coated woman, without a word, went off with the groom, and Jack thought he would go with them, for this Lady Betty could surely tell him whether the country was called Fairyland, or whether he must get into his boat and go farther. He did not like either to hear the way in which Faxa and Dow talked about their works and their weights; so he asked Faxa to give him his cap, which she did, and he heard a curious sort of little ticking noise as he came close to her, which startled him.

"Oh, this must be Fairyland, I am sure," thought Jack, "for in my country our pulses beat quite differently from that."

"Well," said Faxa, rather sharply, "do you find any fault with the way I go?"

"No," said Jack, a little ashamed of having listened. "I think you walk beautifully; your steps are so regular."

"She's machine-made," observed the old horse, in a melancholy voice, and with a deep sigh. "In the largest magnifying glass you'll hardly find the least fault with her chain. She's not like the goods they turn out in Clerkenwell."

Jack was more and more startled, and so glad to get his cap and run after the groom and Dow to find Lady Betty, that he might be with ordinary human beings again; but when he got up to them he found that Lady Betty was a beautiful brown mare! She was lying in a languid and rather affected attitude, with a load of fresh hay before her, and two attendants, one of whom stood holding a parasol over her head, while the other was fanning her.

"I'm so glad you are come, my good Dow," said the brown mare. "Don't you think I am strong enough today to set off for the happy meadows?"

"Well," said Dow, "I'm afraid not yet; you must remember that it is no use your leaving us till you have quite got over the effects of the fall."

Just then Lady Betty observed Jack, and said, "Take that boy away; he reminds me of a jockey."

The attentive groom instantly started forward, but Jack

was too nimble for him; he ran and ran with all his might, and only wished he had never left the boat. But still he heard the groom behind him; and in fact the groom caught him at last, and held him so fast that struggling was no use at all.

"You young rascal!" he exclaimed, as he recovered breath. "How you do run! It's enough to break your mainspring."

"What harm did I do?" asked Jack. "I was only looking at the mare."

"Harm!" exclaimed the groom. "Harm, indeed! Why, you reminded her of a jockey. It's enough to hold her back, poor thing!—and we trying so hard, too, to make her forget what a cruel end she came to in the old world."

"You need not hold me so tightly," said Jack. "I shall not run away again; but," he added, "if this is Fairyland, it is not half such a nice country as I expected."

"Fairyland!" exclaimed the groom, stepping back with surprise. "Why, what made you think of such a thing? This is only one of the border countries, where things are set right again that people have caused to go wrong in the world. The world, you know, is what men and women call their own home."

"I know," said Jack; "and that's where I came from." Then, as the groom seemed no longer to be angry, he went on: "And I wish you would tell me about Lady Betty."

"She was a beautiful fleet creature, of the racehorse breed," said the groom, "and she won silver cups for her master, and then they made her run a steeplechase, which frightened her, but still she won it; and then they made her run another, and she cleared some terribly high hurdles, and many gates and ditches, till she came to an awful one, and at first she would not take it, but her rider spurred and beat her till she tried. It was beyond her powers, and she fell and broke her forelegs. Then they shot her. After she had died that miserable death we had her here, to make her all right again."

"Is this the only country where you set things right?" asked Jack.

"Certainly not," answered the groom; "they lie about in all directions. Why, you might wander for years and never come to the end of this one."

"I am afraid I shall not find the one I am looking for," said Jack, "if your countries are so large."

"I don't think our world is much larger than yours," answered the groom. "But come along; I hear the bell, and we are a good way from the palace."

Jack, in fact, heard the violent ringing of a bell at some distance; and when the groom began to run, he ran beside him, for he thought he should like to see the palace. As they ran, people gathered from all sides—fields, cottages, mills—till at last there was a little crowd, among whom Jack saw Dow and Faxa, and they were all making for a large house, the wide door of which was standing open. Jack stood with the crowd and peeped in. There was a woman sitting inside upon a rocking-chair, a tall, large woman, with a gold-colored gown on, and beside her stood a table, covered with things that looked like keys.

"What is that woman doing?" said he to Faxa, who was standing close to him.

"Winding us up, to be sure," answered Faxa. "You don't suppose, surely, that we can go for ever?"

"Extraordinary!" said Jack. "Then are you wound up every evening, like watches?"

"Unless we have misbehaved ourselves," she answered; "and then she lets us run down."

"And what then?"

"What then?" repeated Faxa. "Why, then we have to stop and stand against a wall, till she is pleased to forgive us, and let our friends carry us in to be set going again."

Jack looked in, and saw the people pass in and stand close by the woman. One after the other she took by the chin with her left hand, and with her right hand found a key that pleased her. It seemed to Jack that there was a tiny keyhole in the back of their heads, and that she put the key in and wound them up.

"You must take your turn with the others," said the groom.

"There's no keyhole in my head," said Jack; "besides, I do not want any woman to wind me up."

"But you must do as others do," he persisted; "and if you have no keyhole, our Queen can easily have one made, I should think."

"Make one in my head!" exclaimed Jack. "She shall do no such thing."

"We shall see," said Faxa quietly. And Jack was so frightened that he set off, and ran back towards the river with all his might. Many of the people called to him to stop, but they could not run after him, because they wanted winding up. However, they would certainly have caught him if he had not been very quick, for before he got to the river he heard behind him the footsteps of those who had been first attended to by the Queen, and he had only just time to spring into the boat when they reached the edge of the water.

No sooner was he on board than the boat swung round, and got again into the middle of the stream; but he could not feel safe till not only was there a long reach of water between him and the shore, but till he had gone so far down river that the beautiful bay had passed out of sight and the sun was going down. By this time he began to feel very tired and sleepy; so, having looked at his fairies, and found that they were all safe and fast asleep, he laid down in the bottom of the boat, and fell into a doze, and then into a dream.

CHAPTER FOUR

Bees and other Fellow Creatures

The dove laid some little sticks,
   Then began to coo;
The gnat took his trumpet up
   To play the day through;
The pie chattered soft and long—
   But that she always does;
The bee did all he had to do,
   And only said "Buzz."

When Jack at length opened his eyes, he found that it was night, for the full moon was shining; but it was not at all a dark night, for he could see distinctly some black birds that looked like ravens. They were sitting in a row on the edge of the boat.

Now that he had fairies in his pockets he could understand bird-talk, and he heard one of these ravens saying: "There is no meat so tender; I wish I could pick their little eyes out."

"Yes," said another, "fairies are delicate eating indeed. We must speak Jack fair if we want to get at them." And she heaved up a deep sigh.

Jack lay still, and thought he had better pretend to be asleep; but they soon noticed that his eyes were open, and one of them presently walked up his leg and bowed, and asked if he was hungry.

Jack said: "No."

"No more am I," replied the raven; "not at all hungry." Then she hopped off his leg, and Jack sat up.

"And how are the sweet fairies that my young master is taking to their home?" asked another of the ravens. "I hope they are safe in my young master's pockets?"

Jack felt in his pockets. Yes, they were all safe; but he did not take any of them out, lest the ravens should snatch at them.

"Eh?" continued the raven, pretending to listen. "Did this dear young gentleman say that the fairies were asleep?"

"It doesn't amuse me to talk about fairies," said Jack; "but if you would explain some of the things in this country that I cannot make out, I should be very glad."

"What things?" asked the blackest of the ravens.

"Why," said Jack, "I see a full moon lying down there among the water-flags, and just going to set, and there is a half-moon overhead plunging among those great gray clouds, and just this moment I saw a thin crescent moon peeping out between the branches of that tree."

"Well," said all the ravens at once, "did the young master never see a crescent moon in the men and women's world?"

"Oh yes," said Jack.

"Did he never see a full moon?" asked the ravens.

"Yes, of course," said Jack; "but they are the same moon. I could never see all three of them at the same time."

The ravens were very much surprised at this, and one of them said:

"If my young master did not see the moons it must have been because he didn't look. Perhaps my young master slept in a room, and had only one window; if so, he couldn't see all the sky at once."

"I tell you, Raven," said Jack, laughing, "that I KNOW there is never more than one moon in my country, and sometimes there is no moon at all!"

Upon this all the ravens hung down their heads, and looked very much ashamed; for there is nothing that birds hate so much as to be laughed at, and they believed that Jack was saying this to mock them, and that he knew what they had come for. So first one and then another hopped to the other end of the boat and flew away, till at last there was only one left, and she appeared to be out of spirits, and did not speak again till he spoke to her.

"Raven," said Jack, "there's something very cold and slippery lying at the bottom of the boat. I touched it just now, and I don't like it at all."

"It's a water-snake,"[7] said the raven, and she stooped and picked up a long thing with her beak, which she threw out, and then looked over. "The water swarms with them, wicked, murderous creatures; they smell the young fairies, and they want to eat them."

Jack was so thrown off his guard that he snatched one fairy out, just to make sure that it was safe. It was the one with the moustache; and, alas! in one instant the raven flew at it, got it out of his hand and pecked off its head before it had time to wake or Jack to rescue it. Then, as she slowly rose, she croaked, and said to Jack: "You'll catch it for this, my young master!" and she flew to the bough of a tree, where she finished eating the fairy, and threw his little empty coat into the river.

On this Jack began to cry bitterly, and to think what a foolish boy he had been. He was the more sorry because he did not know that poor little fellow's name. But he had heard the others calling by name to their companions, and very grand names they were too. One was Jovinian—he

---

7. **water-snake** cf. "The Rime of the Ancient Mariner," lines 272–73

was a very fierce-looking gentleman; the other two were Roxaletta and Mopsa.

Presently, however, Jack forgot to be unhappy, for two of the moons went down, and then the sun rose, and he was delighted to find that however many moons there might be, there was only one sun, even in the country of the wonderful river.

So on and on they went; but the river was very wide and the waves were boisterous. On the right brink was a thick forest of trees, with such heavy foliage that a little way off they looked like a bank, green and smooth and steep; but as the light became clearer Jack could see here and there the great stems, and see creatures like foxes, wild boars, and deer come stealing down to drink in the river.

It was very hot here; not at all like the spring weather he had left behind. And as the low sunbeams shone into Jack's face he said hastily; without thinking of what would occur: "I wish I might land among those lovely glades on the left bank."

No sooner said than the boat began to make for the left bank, and the nearer they got towards it the more beautiful it became; but also the more stormy were the reaches of water they had to traverse.

A lovely country indeed! It sloped gently down to the water's edge and beautiful trees were scattered over it, soft mossy grass grew everywhere, great old laburnum trees stretched their boughs down in patches over the water, and higher up camellias, almost as large as hawthorns, grew together and mingled their red and white flowers.

The country was not so open as a park—it was more like a half-cleared woodland; but there was a wide space just where the boat was steering for that had no trees, only a few flowering shrubs. Here groups of strange-looking people were bustling about, and there were shrill fifes sounding, and drums.

Farther back he saw rows of booths or tents under the shade of the trees.

In another place some people dressed like gipsies had made fires of sticks just at the skirts of the woodland, and were boiling their pots. Some of these had very gaudy tilted carts, hung all over with goods, such as baskets, brushes, mats, little glasses, pottery and beads.

It seemed to be a kind of fair, to which people had gathered from all parts; but there was not one house to be seen. All the goods were either hung upon the trees or collected in strange-looking tents.

The people were not all of the same race; indeed, he thought the only human beings were the gipsies, for the folks who had tents were no taller than himself.

How hot it was that morning! and as the boat pushed itself into a little creek, and made its way among the beds of yellow and purple iris which skirted the brink, what a crowd of dragon-flies and large butterflies rose from them!

"Stay where you are!" cried Jack to the boat; and at that instant such a splendid moth rose slowly that he sprang on shore after it, and quite forgot the fair and the people in his desire to follow it.

The moth settled on a great red honey-flower, and he stole up to look at it. As large as a swallow, it floated on before him. Its wings were nearly black, and they had spots of gold on them.

When it rose again Jack ran after it, till he found himself close to the rows of tents where the brown people stood; and they began to cry out to him: "What'll you buy? what'll you buy, sir?" and they crowded about him, so that he soon lost sight of the moth, and forgot everything else in his surprise at the booths.

They were full of splendid things—clocks and musical boxes, strange china ornaments, embroidered slippers, red caps and many kinds of splendid silks and small carpets. In other booths were swords and dirks, glittering with jewels; and the chatter of the people when they talked together was not in a language that Jack could understand.

Some of the booths were square, and evidently made of common canvas, for when you went into them and the sun shone you could distinctly see the threads.

But scattered a little farther on in groups were some round tents which were far more curious. They were open on all sides, and consisted only of a thick canopy overhead, which was supported by one beautiful round pillar in the middle.

Outside, the canopy was white or brownish; but when Jack stood under these tents he saw that they were lined with splendid flutings of brown or pink silk—what looked like silk, at least, for it was impossible to be sure whether these were real tents or gigantic mushrooms.

They varied in size, also, as mushrooms do, and in shape: some were large enough for twenty people to stand under them, and had flat tops with a brown lining; others had dome-shaped roofs; these were lined with pink, and would only shelter six or seven.

The people who sold in these tents were as strange as their neighbors; each had a little high cap on his head, in shape just like a beehive, and it was made of straw, and had little hole in front. In fact Jack very soon saw bees flying in and out, and it was evident that these people had their honey made on the premises. They were chiefly selling country produce. They had cheeses so large as to reach to their waists, and the women trundled them along as boys do their hoops. They sold a great many kinds of seed too, in wooden bowls, and cakes and good things to eat, such as gilt gingerbread. Jack bought some of this, and found it very nice indeed. But when he took out his money to pay for it the little man looked rather strangely at it, and turned it over with an air of disgust. Then Jack saw him hand it to his wife, who also seemed to dislike it; and presently Jack observed that they followed him about, first on one side, then on the other. At last the little woman slipped her hand into his pocket, and Jack, putting his hand in directly, found his sixpence had been returned.

"Why, you've given me back my money!" he said.

The little woman put her hands behind her. "I do not like it," she said; "it's dirty; at least, it's not new."

"No, it's not new," said Jack, a good deal surprised, "but it is a good sixpence."

"The bees don't like it," continued the little woman. "They like things to be neat and new, and that sixpence is bent."

"What shall I give you then?" said Jack.

The good little woman laughed and blushed. "This young gentleman has a beautiful whistle round his neck," she observed politely, but did not ask for it.

Jack had a dog-whistle, so he took it off and gave it to her.

"Thank you, for the bees," she said. "They love to be called home when we've collected flowers for them."

So she made a pretty little curtsy, and went away to her customers.

There were some very strange creatures also, about the same height as Jack, who had no tents, and seemed there to buy, not to sell. Yet they looked poorer than the other folks and they were also very cross and discontented; nothing pleased them. Their clothes were made of moss, and their mantles of feathers; and they talked in a queer whistling tone of voice, and carried their skinny little children on their backs and on their shoulders.

They were treated with great respect by the people in the tents; and when Jack asked his friend to whom he had given the whistle what they were, and where they got so much money as they had, she replied that they lived over the hills, and were afraid to come in their best clothes. They were rich and powerful at home, and they came shabbily dressed, and behaved humbly, lest their enemies should envy them. It was very dangerous, she said, to fairies to be envied.

Jack wanted to listen to their strange whistling talk, but he could not for the noise and cheerful chattering of the brown folks, and more still for the screaming and talking of parrots.

Among the goods were hundreds of splendid gilt cages, which were hung by long gold chains from the trees. Each cage contained a parrot and his mate, and they all seemed to be very unhappy indeed.

The parrots could talk, and they kept screaming to the discontented women to buy things for them, and trying very hard to attract attention.

One old parrot made himself quite conspicuous by these efforts. He flung himself against the wires of his cage, he squalled, he screamed, he knocked the floor with his beak till Jack and one of the customers came running up to see what was the matter.

"What do you make such a fuss for?" cried the discontented woman. "You've set your cage swinging with knocking yourself about; and what good does that do? I cannot break the spell and open it for you."

"I know that," answered the parrot, sobbing; "but it hurts my feelings so that you should take no notice of me now that I have come down in the world."

"Yes," said the parrot's mate, "it hurts our feelings."

"I haven't forgotten you," answered the woman, more crossly than ever; "I was buying a measure of maize for you when you began to make such a noise."

Jack thought this was the queerest conversation he had ever heard in his life, and he was still more surprised when the bird answered:

"I would much rather you would buy me a pocket-handkerchief. Here we are, shut up, without a chance of getting out, and with nobody to pity us; and we can't even have the comfort of crying, because we've got nothing to wipe our eyes with."

"But at least," replied the woman, "you CAN cry now if you please, and when you had your other face you could not."

"Buy me a handkerchief," sobbed the parrot.

"I can't afford both," whined the cross woman, "and I've paid now for the maize." So saying, she went back to the tent to fetch her present to the parrots, and as their cage was still swinging Jack put out his hand to steady it for them, and the instant he did so they became perfectly silent, and all the other parrots on that tree, who had been flinging themselves about in their cages, left off screaming and became silent too.

The old parrot looked very cunning. His cage hung by such a long gold chain that it was just on a level with Jack's face, and so many odd things had happened that day that it did not seem more odd than usual to hear him say, in a tone of great astonishment:

"It's a BOY, if ever there was one!"

"Yes," said Jack, "I'm a boy."

"You won't go yet, will you?" said the parrot.

"No, don't," said a great many other parrots. Jack agreed to stay a little while, upon which they all thanked him.

"I had no notion you were a boy till you touched my cage," said the old parrot.

Jack did not know how this could have told him, so he only answered: "Indeed!"

"I'm a fairy," observed the parrot, in a confidential tone. "We are imprisoned here by our enemies the gipsies."

"So are we," answered a chorus of other parrots.

"I'm sorry for that," replied Jack. "I'm friends with the fairies."

"Don't tell," said the parrot, drawing a film over his eyes, and pretending to be asleep. At that moment his friend in the moss petticoat and feather cloak came up with a little measure of maize, and poured it into the cage.

"Here, neighbor," she said; "I must say goodbye now, for the gipsy is coming this way, and I want to buy some of her goods."

"Well, thank you," answered the parrot, sobbing again; "but I could have wished it had been a pocket-handkerchief."

"I'll lend you my handkerchief," said Jack. "Here!" And he drew it out and pushed it between the wires.

The parrot and his wife were in a great hurry to get Jack's handkerchief. They pulled it in very hastily; but instead of using it they rolled it up into a ball, and the parrot-wife tucked it under her wing.

"It makes me tremble all over," said she, "to think of such good luck."

"I say!' observed the parrot to Jack. "I know all about it now. You've got some of my people in your pockets—not of my own tribe, but fairies."

By this Jack was sure that the parrot really was a fairy himself, and he listened to what he had to say the more attentively.

CHAPTER FIVE

The Parrot in his Shawl

That handkerchief
Did an Egyptian to my mother give:
She was a charmer, and could almost read
The thoughts of people.
Othello[8]

"That gipsy woman who is coming with her cart," said the parrot, "is a fairy too, and very malicious.

8. *Othello* II.iv.62–66

It was she and others of her tribe who caught us and put us into these cages, for they are more powerful than we. Mind you do not let her allure you into the woods, nor wheedle you or frighten you into giving her any of those fairies."

"No," said Jack; "I will not."

"She sold us to the brown people," continued the parrot. "Mind you do not buy anything of her, for your money in her palm would act as a charm against you."

"She has a baby," observed the parrot-wife scornfully.

"Yes, a baby," repeated the old parrot; "and I hope by means of that baby to get her driven away, and perhaps get free myself. I shall try to put her in a passion. Here she comes."

There she was indeed, almost close at hand. She had a little cart; her goods were hung all about it, and a small horse drew it slowly on, and stopped when she got a customer.

Several gipsy children were with her, and as people came running together over the grass to see her goods, she sang a curious kind of song, which made them wish to buy them.

Jack turned from the parrot's cage as she came up. He had heard her singing a little way off, and now, before she began again, he felt that already her searching eyes had found him out, and taken notice that he was different from the other people.

When she began to sing her selling song he felt a most curious sensation. He felt as if there were some cobwebs before his face, and he put up his hand as if to clear them away. There were no real cobwebs, of course; and yet he again felt as if they floated from the gipsy-woman to him, like gossamer threads, and attracted him towards her. So he gazed at her, and she at him, till Jack began to forget how the parrot had warned him.

He saw her baby too, wondered whether it was heavy for her to carry and wished he could help her. I mean, he saw that she had a baby on her arm. It was wrapped in a shawl and had a handkerchief over its face. She seemed very fond of it, for she kept hushing it; and Jack softly moved nearer and nearer to the cart, till the gipsy-woman smiled, and suddenly began to sing:

"My good man—he's an old, old man—
  And my good man got a fall,
To buy me a bargain so fast he ran
  When he heard the gipsies call:
    'Buy, buy brushes,
    Baskets wrought o' rushes,
    Buy them, buy them, take them, try them,
      Buy, dames all.'

"My old man, he has money and land,
  And a young, young wife am I.
Let him put the penny in my white hand
  When he hears the gipsies cry:
    'Buy, buy laces,
    Veils to screen your faces.
    Buy them, buy them, take and try them,
      Buy, maids, buy.'"

When the gipsy had finished her song Jack felt as if he
was covered all over with cobwebs; but he could not move
away, and he did not mind them now. All his wish was to
please her, and get close to her; so when she said, in a soft
wheedling voice: "What will you please to buy, my pretty
gentleman?" he was just going to answer that he would
buy anything she recommended, when, to his astonishment
and displeasure, for he thought it very rude, the parrot
suddenly burst into a violent fit of coughing, which made
all the customers stare. "That's to clear my throat," he said,
in a most impertinent tone of voice; and then he began to
beat time with his foot, and sing, or rather scream out, an
extremely saucy imitation of the gipsy's song, and all his
parrot friends in the other cages joined in the chorus.

"My fair lady's a dear, dear lady—
  I walked by her side to woo.
In a garden alley, so sweet and shady,
  She answered, 'I love you not,
    John, John Brady,'
  Quoth my dear lady,
'Pray now, pray now, go your way now,
  Do, John, do!'"

At first the gipsy did not seem to know where that mocking song came from, but when she discovered that it was her prisoner, the old parrot, who was thus daring to imitate her, she stood silent and glared at him, and her face was almost white with rage.

When he came to the end of the verse, he pretended to burst into a violent fit of sobbing and crying, and screeched out to his wife: "Mate! mate! hand up my handkerchief. Oh! oh! it's so affecting, this song is."

Upon this the other parrot pulled Jack's handkerchief from under her wing, hobbled up and began, with a great show of zeal, to wipe his horny beak with it. But this was too much for the gipsy; she took a large brush from her cart and flung it at the cage with all her might.

This set it violently swinging backwards and forwards, but it did not stop the parrot, who screeched out: "How delightful it is to be swung!" And then he began to sing another verse in the most impudent tone possible, and with a voice that seemed to ring through Jack's head, and almost pierce it.

> "Yet my fair lady's my own, own lady,
>   For I passed another day;
> While making her moan, she sat all alone,
>   And thus and thus did she say:
>   'John, John Brady,'
>   Quoth my dear lady,
>   'Do now, do now, once more woo now,
>   Pray, John, pray!' "

"It's beautiful!" screeched the parrot-wife. "And so appro-pri-ate." Jack was delighted when she managed slowly to say this long word with her black tongue, and he burst out laughing. In the meantime a good many of the brown people came running together, attracted by the noise of the parrots and the rage of the gipsy, who flung at his cage, one after the other, all the largest things she had in her cart. But nothing did the parrot any harm; the more violently this cage swung the louder he sang, till at last the wicked gipsy seized her poor little young baby, who was lying in her arms, rushed frantically at the cage as it flew swiftly through the air towards her and struck at it with the

little creature's head. "Oh, you cruel, cruel woman!" cried
Jack, and all the small mothers who were standing near
with their skinny children on their shoulders screamed out
with terror and indignation; but only for one instant, for
the handkerchief flew off that had covered its face, and was
caught in the wires of the cage, and all the people saw that
it was not a real baby at all,[9] but a bundle of clothes, and
its head was a turnip.

Yes, a turnip! You could see that as plainly as possible,
for though the green leaves had been cut off, their stalks
were visible through the lace cap that had been tied on it.

Upon this all the crowd pressed closer, throwing her baskets, and brushes, and laces, and beads at the gipsy, and
calling out: "We will have none of your goods, you false
woman! Give us back our money, or we will drive you out
of the fair. You've stuck a stick into a turnip, and dressed
it up in baby clothes. You're a cheat! a cheat!"

"My sweet gentlemen, my kind ladies," began the gipsy;
but baskets and brushes flew at her so fast that she was
obliged to sit down on the grass and hold up the sham baby
to screen her face.

While this was going on Jack felt that the cobwebs which
had seemed to float about his face were all gone; he did
not care at all any more about the gipsy, and began to
watch the parrots with great attention.

He observed that when the handkerchief stuck between
the cage wires the parrots caught it, and drew it inside; and
then Jack saw the cunning old bird himself lay it on the
floor, fold it crosswise like a shawl, and put it on his wife.

Then she jumped upon the perch, and held it with one
foot, looking precisely like an old lady with a parrot's head.
Then he folded Jack's handkerchief in the same way, put
it on and got upon the perch beside his wife, screaming
out, in his most piercing tone:

"I like shawls; they're so becoming."

Now the gipsy did not care at all what those inferior
people thought of her, and she was calmly counting out
their money, to return it; but she was very desirous to make
Jack forget her behavior, and had begun to smile again,

---

9. **turnip** The baby whom the duchess flings with similar abandon in
Alice in Wonderland also turns out to be no real child.

and tell him she had only been joking, when the parrot spoke and, looking up, she saw the two birds sitting side by side, and the parrot-wife was screaming in her mate's ear, though neither of them was at all deaf:

"If Jack lets her allure him into the woods, he'll never come out again. she'll hang him up in a cage, as she did us. I say, how does my shawl fit?"

So saying, the parrot-wife whisked herself round on the perch, and lo! in the corner of the handkerchief were seen some curious letters, marked in red. When the crowd saw these they drew a little farther off, and glanced at one another with alarm.

"You look charming, my dear; it fits well!" screamed the old parrot in answer. "A word in your ear: 'Share and share alike' is a fine motto."

"What do you mean by all this?" said the gipsy, rising, and going with slow steps to the cage, and speaking cautiously.

"Jack," said the parrot, "do they ever eat handkerchiefs in your part of the country?"

"No, never," answered Jack.

"Hold your tongue and be reasonable," said the gipsy, trembling, "What do you want? I'll do it, whatever it is."

"But do they never pick out the marks?" continued the parrot. "Oh, Jack! are you sure they never pick out the marks?"

"The marks?" said Jack, considering. "Yes, perhaps they do."

"Stop!" cried the gipsy, as the old parrot made a peck at the strange letters. "Oh! you're hurting me. What do you want? I say again, tell me what you want, and you shall have it."

"We want to get out," replied the parrot; "you must undo the spell."

"Then give me my handkerchief," answered the gipsy, "to bandage my eyes. I dare not say the words with my eyes open. You had no business to steal it. It was woven by human hands, so that nobody can see through it; and if you don't give it to me, you'll never get out—no, never!"

"Then," said the old parrot, tossing his shawl off, "you may have Jack's handkerchief; it will bandage your eyes just as well. It was woven over the water, as yours was."

"It won't do!" cried the gipsy in terror; "give me my own."

"I tell you," answered the parrot, "that you shall have Jack's handkerchief; you can do no harm with that."

By this time the parrots all around had become perfectly silent, and none of the people ventured to say a word, for they feared the malice of the gipsy. She was trembling dreadfully, and her dark eyes, which had been so bright and piercing, had become dull and almost dim; but when she found there was no help for it, she said:

"Well, pass out Jack's handkerchief. I will set you free if you will bring out mine with you."

"Share and share alike," answered the parrot; "You must let all my friends out too."

"Then I won't let you out," answered the gipsy. "You shall come out first, and give me my handkerchief, or not one of their cages will I undo. So take your choice."

"My friends, then," answered the brave old parrot; and he poked Jack's handkerchief out to her through the wires.

The wondering crowd stood by to look, and the gipsy bandaged her eyes tightly with the handkerchief; and then, stooping low, she began to murmur something and clap her hands—softly at first, but by degrees more and more violently. The noise was meant to drown the words she muttered; but as she went on clapping, the bottom of cage after cage fell clattering down. Out flew the parrots by hundreds, screaming and congratulating one another; and there was such a deafening din that not only the sound of her spell but the clapping of her hands was quite lost in it.

But all this time Jack was very busy; for the moment the gipsy had tied up her eyes the old parrot snatched the real handkerchief off his wife's shoulders and tied it round her neck. Then she pushed out her head through the wires, and the old parrot called to Jack, and said; "Pull!"

Jack took the ends of the handkerchief, pulled terribly hard, and stopped. "Go on! go on!" screamed the old parrot.

"I shall pull her head off," cried Jack.

"No matter," cried the parrot; "no matter—only pull."

Well, Jack did pull, and he actually did pull her head off! nearly tumbling backward himself as he did it; but he saw what the whole thing meant then, for there was another head inside—a fairy's head.

Jack flung down the old parrot's head and great beak, for he saw that what he had to do was to clear the fairy of its parrot covering. The poor little creature seemed nearly dead, it was so terribly squeezed in the wires. It had a green gown or robe on, with an ermine collar; and Jack got hold of this dress, stripped the fairy out of the parrot feathers, and dragged her through—velvet robe, and crimson girdle, and little yellow shoes. She was very much exhausted, but a kind brown woman took her instantly, and laid her in her bosom. She was a splendid little creature, about half a foot long.

"There's a brave boy!" cried the parrot. Jack glanced round, and saw that not all the parrots were free yet—the gipsy was still muttering her spell.

He returned the handkerchief to the parrot, who put it round his own neck, and again Jack pulled. But oh! what a tough old parrot that was, and how Jack tugged before his cunning head would come off! It did, however, at last; and just as a fine fairy was pulled through, leaving his parrot skin and the handkerchief behind him, the gipsy untied her eyes and saw what Jack had done.

"Give me my handkerchief!" she screamed in despair.

"It's in the cage, gipsy," answered Jack; "you can get it yourself. Say your words again."

But the gipsy's spell would only open places where she had confined fairies, and no fairies were in the cage now.

"No, no, no!" she screamed; "too late! Hide me! Oh, good people, hide me!"

But it was indeed too late. The parrots had been wheeling in the air, hundreds and hundreds of them, high above her head; and as she ceased speaking she fell shuddering on the ground, drew her cloak over her face, and down they came, swooping in one immense flock, and settled so thickly all over her that she was completely covered; from her shoes to her head not an atom of her was to be seen.

All the people stood gravely looking on. So did Jack, but he could not see much for the fluttering of the parrots, nor hear anything for their screaming voices; but at last he made one of the cross people hear when he shouted to her: "What are they going to do to the poor gipsy?"

"Make her take her other form," she replied; "and then she cannot hurt us while she stays in our country. She is a fairy, as we have just found out, and all fairies have two forms."

"Oh!" said Jack; but he had no time for more questions.

The screaming, and fighting, and tossing about of little bits of cloth and cotton ceased; a black lump heaved itself up from the ground among the parrots; and as they flew aside an ugly great condor, with a bare neck, spread out its wings and, skimming the ground, sailed slowly away.

"They have pecked her so that she can hardly rise," exclaimed the parrot fairy. "Set me on your shoulder, Jack, and let me see the end of it."

Jack set him there; and his little wife, who had recovered herself, sprang from her friend the brown woman and sat on the other shoulder. He then ran on—the tribe of brown people, and mushroom people, and the feather-coated folks running too—after the great black bird, who skimmed slowly on before them till she got to the gipsy carts, when out rushed the gipsies, armed with poles, milking-stools, spades and everything they could get hold of to beat back the people and the parrots from hunting their relation, who had folded her tired wings and was skulking under a cart with ruffled feathers and a scowling eye.

Jack was so frightened at the violent way in which the gipsies and the other tribes were knocking each other about that he ran off, thinking he had seen enough of such a dangerous country.

As he passed the place where that evil-minded gipsy had been changed he found the ground strewed with little bits of her clothes. Many parrots were picking them up and poking them into the cage where the handkerchief was; and presently another parrot came with a lighted brand, which she had pulled form one of the gipsies' fires.

"That's right," said the fairy on Jack's shoulder, when he saw his friend push the brand between the wires of what had been his cage, and set the gipsy's handkerchief on fire, and all the bits of her clothes with it. "She won't find much of herself here," he observed, as Jack went on. "It will not be very easy to put herself together again."

So Jack moved away. He was tired of the noise and confusion; and the sun was just setting as he reached the little creek where his boat lay.

Then the parrot fairy and his wife sprang down, and kissed their hands to him as he stepped on board and pushed the boat off. He saw, when he looked back, that a great fight was still going on; so he was glad to get away, and he wished his two friends goodbye, and set off, the old parrot fairy calling after him: "My relations have put some of our favorite food on board for you." Then they again thanked him for his good help, and sprang into a tree, and the boat began to go down the wonderful river.

"This has been a most extraordinary day," thought Jack; "the strangest day I have had yet." And after he had eaten a good supper of what the parrots had brought he felt so tired and sleepy that he lay down in the boat, and presently fell fast asleep. His fairies were sound asleep too in his pockets, and nothing happened of the least consequence; so he slept comfortably till morning.

CHAPTER SIX

The Town with Nobody in it

> "Master," quoth the auld hound,
>   "Where will ye go?"
> "Over moss, over muir,
>   To court my new jo."
> "Master, though the night be merk,
>   I'se follow through the snow.
>
> "Court her, master, court her,
>   So shall ye do weel;
> But and ben she'll guide the house,
>   I'se get milk and meal.
> Ye'se get lilting while she sits
>   With her rock and reel."
>
> "For, oh! she has a sweet tongue,
>   And een that look down,

> A gold girdle for her waist,
>   And a purple gown.
> She has a good word forbye
>   Fra a' folk in the town."

Soon after sunrise they came to a great city, and it was
perfectly still. There were grand towers and terraces,
wharves, too, and a large market, but there was nobody
anywhere to be seen. Jack thought that might be because
it was so early in the morning; and when the boat ran itself
up against a wooden wharf and stopped, he jumped ashore,
for he thought this must be the end of his journey. A delightful town it was, if only there had been any people in
it! The market-place was full of stalls, on which were spread
toys, baskets, fruit, butter, vegetables and all the other
things that are usually sold in a market.

Jack walked about in it. Then he looked in at the open
doors of the houses, and at last, finding that they were all
empty, he walked into one, looked at the rooms, examined
the picture-books, rang the bells and set the musical-boxes
going. Then, after he had shouted a good deal, and tried
in vain to make someone hear, he went back to the edge
of the river where his boat was lying, and the water was so
delightfully clear and calm that he thought he would bathe.
So he took off his clothes, and folding them very carefully,
so as not to hurt the fairies, laid them down beside a haycock[10] and went in, and ran about and paddled for a long
time—much longer than there was any occasion for; but
then he had nothing to do.

When at last he had finished he ran to the haycock and
began to dress himself; but he could not find his stockings,
and after looking about for some time he was obliged to
put on his clothes without them, and he was going to put
his boots on his bare feet when, walking to the other side
of the haycock, he saw a little old woman about as large
as himself. She had a pair of spectacles on, and she was
knitting.

She looked so sweet tempered that Jack asked her if she
knew anything about his stockings.

"It will be time enough to ask for them when you have

10. **haycock** See note 6

had your breakfast," said she. "Sit down. Welcome to our town. How do you like it?"

"I should like it very much indeed," said Jack, "if there was anybody in it."

"I'm glad of that," said the woman. "You've seen a good deal of it; but it pleases me to find that you are a very honest boy. You did not take anything at all. I am honest too."

"Yes," said Jack, "of course you are."

"And as I am pleased with you for being honest," continued the little woman, "I shall give you some breakfast out of my basket." So she took out a saucer full of honey, a roll of bread and a cup of milk.

"Thank you," said Jack, "but I am not a beggar-boy; I have got a half-crown, a shilling, a sixpence and two pence; so I can buy this breakfast of you, if you like. You look very poor."

"Do I?" said the little woman softly; and she went on knitting, and Jack began to eat the breakfast.

"I wonder what has become of my stockings," said Jack.

"You will never see them any more," said the old woman. "I threw them into the river, and they floated away."

"Why did you?" asked Jack.

The little woman took no notice; but presently she had finished a beautiful pair of stockings, and she handed them to Jack and said:

"Is that like the pair you lost?"

"Oh no," said Jack, "these are much more beautiful stockings than mine."

"Do you like them as well?" asked the fairy woman.

"I like them much better," said Jack, putting them on. "How clever you are!"

"Would you like to wear these," said the woman, "instead of yours?"

She gave Jack such a strange look when she said this that he was afraid to take them, and answered:

"I shouldn't like to wear them if you think I had better not."

"Well," she answered, "I am very honest, as I told you; and therefore I am obliged to say that if I were you I would not wear those stockings on any account."

"Why not?" said Jack; for she looked so sweet tempered that he could not help trusting her.

"Why not?" repeated the fairy. "Why, because when you have those stockings on your feet belong to me."

"Oh!" said Jack. "Well, if you think that matters, I'll take them off again. Do you think it matters?"

"Yes," said the fairy woman; "it matters, because I am a slave, and my master can make me do whatever he pleases, for I am completely in his power. So if he found out that I had knitted those stockings for you he would make me order you to walk into his mill—the mill which grinds the corn for the town; and there you would have to grind and grind till I got free again."

When Jack heard this he pulled off the beautiful stockings and laid them on the old woman's lap. Upon this she burst out crying as if her heart would break.

"If my fairies that I have in my pocket would only wake," said Jack, "I would fight your master; for if he is no bigger than you are perhaps I could beat him, and get you away."

"No, Jack," said the little woman; "that would be of no use. The only thing you could do would be to buy me; for my cruel master has said that if ever I am late again he will sell me in the slave-market to the brown people, who work underground. And, though I am dreadfully afraid of my master, I mean to be late today, in hopes (as you are kind, and as you have some money) that you will come to the slave-market and buy me. Can you buy me, Jack, to be your slave?"

"I don't want a slave," said Jack; "and, besides, I have hardly any money to buy you with."

"But it is real money," said the fairy woman, "not like what my master has. His money has to be made every week, for if there comes a hot day it cracks, so it never has time to look old, as your half-crown does; and that is how we know the real money, for we cannot imitate anything that is old. Oh, now, now it is twelve o'clock! now I am late again! and though I said I would do it, I am so frightened!"

So saying, the little woman ran off towards the town, wringing her hands, and Jack ran beside her.

"How am I to find your master?" he said.

"Oh, Jack, buy me! buy me!" cried the fairy woman.

"You will find me in the slave-market. Bid high for me. Go back and put your boots on, and bid high."

Now Jack had nothing on his feet, so he left the poor little woman to run into the town by herself, and went back to put his boots on. They were very uncomfortable, as he had no stockings; but he did not much mind that, and he counted his money. There was the half-crown that his grandmamma had given him on his birthday, there was a shilling, a sixpence, and two pence, besides a silver four-penny-piece which he had forgotten. He then marched into the town; and now it was quite full of people—all of them little men and women about his own height. They thought he was somebody of consequence, and they called out to him to buy their goods. And he bought some stockings, and said: "What I want to buy now is a slave."

So they showed him the way to the slave-market, and there whole rows of odd-looking little people were sitting, while in front of them stood the slaves.

Now Jack had observed as he came along how very disrespectful the dogs of that town were to the people. They had a habit of going up to them and smelling at their legs, and even gnawing their feet as they sat before the little tables selling their wares; and what made this more surprising was that the people did not always seem to find out when they were being gnawed. But the moment the dogs saw Jack they came and fawned on him, and two old hounds followed him all the way to the slave-market; and when he took a seat one of them lay down at his feet, and said: "Master, set your handsome feet on my back, that they may be out of the dust."

"Don't be afraid of him," said the other hound; "he won't gnaw your feet. He knows well enough that they are real ones."

"Are the other people's feet not real?" asked Jack.

"Of course not," said the hound. "They had a feud long ago with the fairies, and they all went one night into a great cornfield which belonged to these enemies of theirs, intending to steal the corn. So they made themselves invisible, as they are always obliged to do till twelve o'clock at noon; but before morning dawn, the wheat being quite ripe, down came the fairies with their sickles, surrounded the field and cut the corn. So all their legs of course got cut off with it, for when they are invisible they cannot stir. Ever since that they have been obliged to make their legs of wood."

While the hound was telling this story Jack looked about, but he did not see one slave who was in the least like his poor little friend, and he was beginning to be afraid that he should not find her, when he heard two people talking together.

"Good day!" said one. "so you have sold that good-for-nothing slave of yours?"

"Yes," answered a very cross-looking old man. "She was late again this morning, and came to me crying and praying to be forgiven; but I was determined to make an example of her, so I sold her at once to Clink-of-the-Hole, and he has just driven her away to work in his mine."

Jack, on hearing this, whispered to the hound at his feet: "If you will guide me to Clink's hole, you shall be my dog."

"Master, I will do my best," answered the hound; and he stole softly out of the market, Jack following him.

CHAPTER SEVEN

Half A Crown

> So useful it is to have money, heigh ho!
> So useful it is to have money!
>   A. H. CLOUGH[11]

The old hound went straight through the town, smelling Clink's footsteps, till he came into a large field of barley; and there, sitting against a sheaf, for it was harvest time, they found Clink-of-the-Hole. He was a very ugly little brown man, and he was smoking a pipe in the shade; while crouched near him was the poor little woman, with her hands spread before her face.

"Good day, sir," said Clink to Jack. "You are a stranger here, no doubt?"

11. **Clough** from Clough's *Dipsychus,* act 1, scene iv

"Yes," said Jack; "I only arrived this morning."

"Have you seen the town?" asked Clink civilly. "There is a very fine market."

"Yes, I have seen the market," answered Jack. "I went into it to buy a slave, but I did not see one that I liked."

"Ah," said Clink; "and yet they had some very fine articles." Here he pointed to the poor little woman, and said: "Now that's a useful body enough, and I had her very cheap."

"What did you give for her?" said Jack, sitting down.

"Three pitchers," said Clink, "and fifteen cups and saucers, and two shillings in the money of the town."

"Is their money like this?" said Jack, taking out his shilling.

When Clink saw the shilling he changed color, and said, very earnestly: "Where did you get that, dear sir?"

"Oh, it was given me," said Jack carelessly.

Clink looked hard at the shilling, and so did the fairy woman, and Jack let them look some time, for he amused himself with throwing it up several times and catching it. At last he put it back in his pocket, and then Clink heaved a deep sigh. Then Jack took out a penny, and began to toss that up, upon which, to his great surprise, the little brown man fell on his knees, and said: "Oh, a shilling and a penny—a shilling and a penny of mortal coin! What would I not give for a shilling and a penny!"

"I don't believe you have got anything to give," said Jack cunningly. "I see nothing but that ring on your finger, and the old woman."

"But I have a great many things at home, sir," said the brown man, wiping his eyes; "and besides, that ring would be cheap at a shilling—even a shilling of mortal coin."

"Would the slave be cheap at a penny?" said Jack.

"Would you give a penny for her, dear sir?" inquired Clink, trembling with eagerness.

"She is honest," answered Jack; "ask her whether I had better buy her with this penny."

"It does not matter what she says," replied the brown man; "I would sell twenty such as she is for a penny—a real one."

"Ask her," repeated Jack; and the poor little woman wept bitterly, but she said "No."

"Why not?" asked Jack; but she only hung down her head and cried.

"I'll make you suffer for this," said the brown man. But when Jack took out the shilling, and said: "Shall I buy you with this, slave?" his eyes actually shot out sparks, he was so eager.

"Speak!" he said to the fairy woman; "and if you don't say 'Yes,' I'll strike you."

"He cannot buy me with that," answered the fairy woman, "unless it is the most valuable coin he has got."

The brown man, on hearing this, rose up in a rage, and was just going to strike her a terrible blow, when Jack cried out: "Stop!" and took out his half-crown.

"Can I buy you with this?" said he; and the fairy woman answered: "Yes."

Upon this Clink drew a long breath, and his eyes grew bigger and bigger as he gazed at the half-crown.

"Shall she be my slave for ever, and not yours," said Jack, "if I give you this?"

"She shall," said the brown man. And he made such a low bow as he took the money that his head actually knocked the ground. Then he jumped up; and, as if he was afraid Jack should repent of his bargain, he ran off towards the hole in the hill with all his might, shouting for joy as he went.

"Slave," said Jack, "that is a very ragged old apron that you have got, and your gown is quite worn out. Don't you think we had better spend my shilling in buying you some new clothes? You look so very shabby."

"Do I?" said the fairy woman gently. "Well, master, you will do as you please."

"But you know better than I do," said Jack, "though you are my slave."

"You had better give me the shilling, then," answered the little old woman; "and then I advise you to go back to the boat, and wait there till I come."

"What!" said Jack. "Can you go all the way back into the town again? I think you must be tired, for you know you are so very old."

The fairy woman laughed when Jack said this, and she had such a sweet laugh that he loved to hear it; but she took the shilling, and trudged off to the town, and he went back to the boat, his hound running after him.

He was a long time going, for he ran a good many times after butterflies, and then he climbed up several trees; and altogether he amused himself for such a long while that when he reached the boat his fairy woman was there before him. So he stepped on board, the hound followed, and the boat immediately began to swim on.

"Why, you have not bought any new clothes!" said Jack to his slave.

"No, master," answered the fairy woman; "but I have bought what I wanted." And she took out of her pocket a little tiny piece of purple ribbon, with a gold-colored satin edge, and a very small tortoiseshell comb.

When Jack saw these he was vexed, and said: "What do you mean by being so silly? I can't scold you properly, because I don't know what name to call you by, and I don't like to say 'Slave,' because that sounds so rude. Why, this bit of ribbon is such a little bit that it's of no use at all. It's not large enough even to make one mitten of."

"Isn't it?" said the slave. "Just take hold of it, master, and let us see if it will stretch."

So Jack did. And she pulled, and he pulled, and very soon the silk had stretched till it was nearly as large as a handkerchief; and then she shook it, and they pulled again. "This is very good fun," said Jack; "why, now it is as large as an apron."

So she shook it again, and gave it a twitch here and a pat there; and then they pulled again, and the silk suddenly stretched so wide that Jack was very nearly falling overboard. So Jack's slave pulled off her ragged gown and apron, and put it on. It was a most beautiful robe of purple silk, it had a gold border, and it just fitted her.

"That will do," she said. And then she took out the little tortoiseshell comb, pulled off her cap and threw it into the river. She had a little knot of soft gray hair, and she let it down and began to comb. And as she combed the hair got much longer and thicker, till it fell in waves all about her throat. Then she combed again, and it all turned gold colour, and came tumbling down to her waist; and then she stood up in the boat and combed once more, and shook out the hair, and there was such a quantity that it reached down to her feet, and she was so covered with it that you could not see one bit of her, excepting her eyes, which peeped out, and looked bright and full of tears.

Then she began to gather up her lovely locks; and when she had dried her eyes with them, she said: "Master, do you know what you have done? Look at me now!" So she threw back the hair from her face, and it was a beautiful young face; and she looked so happy that Jack was glad he had bought her with his half-crown—so glad that he could not help crying, and the fair slave cried too; and then instantly the little fairies woke, and sprang out of Jack's pockets. As they did so, Jovinian cried out: "Madam, I am your most humble servant"; and Roxaletta said: "I hope your Grace is well"; but the third got on Jack's knee and took hold of the buttons of his waistcoat, and when the lovely slave looked at her she hid her face and blushed with pretty childish shyness.

"These are fairies," said Jack's slave; "but what are you?"

"Jack kissed me," said the little thing; "and I want to sit on his knee."

"Yes," said Jack, "I took them out, and laid them in a row, to see if they were safe, and this one I kissed, because she looked such a little dear."

"Was she not like the others, then?" asked the slave.

"Yes," said Jack; "but I liked her the best; she was my favorite."

Now the instant these three fairies sprang out of Jack's pockets they got very much larger; in fact, they became fully grown—that is to say, they measured exactly one foot one inch in height, which, as most people know, is exactly the proper height for fairies of that tribe. The two who had sprung out first were very beautifully dressed. One had a green velvet coat, and a sword, the hilt of which was encrusted with diamonds. The second had a white spangled robe, and the loveliest rubies and emeralds round her neck and in her hair; but the third, the one who sat on Jack's knee, had a white frock and a blue sash on. She had soft, fat arms, and a face just like that of a sweet little child.

When Jack's slave saw this she took the little creature on her knee, and said to her: "How comes it that you are not like your companions?"

And she answered, in a pretty lisping voice: "It's because Jack kissed me."

"Even so it must be," answered the slave; "the love of a mortal works changes indeed. It is not often that we win anything so precious. Here, master, let her sit on your knee sometimes, and take care of her, for she cannot now take the same care of herself that others of her race are capable of."

So Jack let little Mopsa sit on his knee; and when he was tired of admiring his slave, and wondering at the respect with which the other two fairies treated her, and at their cleverness in getting water-lilies for her, and fanning her with feathers, he curled himself up in the bottom of the boat with his own little favorite, and taught her how to play at cat's-cradle.

When they had been playing some time, and Mopsa was getting quite clever at the game, the lovely slave said: "Master, it is a long time since you spoke to me."

"And yet," said Jack, "there is something that I particularly want to ask you about."

"Ask it, then," she replied.

"I don't like to have a slave," answered Jack; "and as you are so clever, don't you think you can find out how to be free again?"

"I am very glad you asked me about that," said the fairy woman. "Yes, master, I wish very much to be free; and as you were so kind as to give the most valuable piece of real money you possessed in order to buy me, I can be free if you can think of anything that you really like better than that half-crown, and if I can give it you."

"Oh, there are many things," said Jack. "I like going up this river to Fairyland much better."

"But you are going there, master," said the fairy woman; "you were on the way before I met with you."

"I like this little child better," said Jack; "I love this little Mopsa. I should like her to belong to me."

"She is yours," answered the fairy woman; "she belongs to you already. Think of something else."

Jack thought again, and was so long about it that at last the beautiful slave said to him: "Master, do you see those purple mountains?"

Jack turned round in the boat and saw a splendid range

of purple mountains, going up and up. They were very
great and steep, each had a crown of snow, and the sky
was very red behind them, for the sun was going down.

"At the other side of those mountains is Fairyland," said
the slave; "but if you cannot think of something that you
should like better to have than your half-crown I can never
enter in. The river flows straight up to yonder steep precipice, and there is a chasm in it which pierces it, and through
which the river runs down beneath, among the very roots
of the mountains, till it comes out at the other side. Thousands and thousands of the small people will come when
they see the boat, each with a silken thread in his hand;
but if there is a slave in it not all their strength and skill
can tow it through. Look at those rafts on the river; on
them are the small people coming up."

Jack looked, and saw that the river was spotted with
rafts, on which were crowded brown fairy sailors, each one
with three green stripes on his sleeve, which looked like
good-conduct marks. All these sailors were chattering very
fast, and the rafts were coming down to meet the boat.

"All these sailors to tow my slave!" said Jack. "I wonder,
I do wonder, what you are?" But the fairy woman only
smiled, and Jack went on: "I have thought of something
that I should like much better than my half-crown. I should
like to have a little tiny bit of that purple gown of yours
with the gold border."

Then the fairy woman said: "I thank you, master. Now
I can be free." So she told Jack to lend her his knife, and
with it she cut off a very small piece of the skirt of her
robe, and gave it to him. "Now mind," she said; "I advise
you never to stretch this unless you want to make some
particular thing of it, for then it will only stretch to the
right size; but if you merely begin to pull it for your own
amusement, it will go on stretching and stretching, and I
don't know where it will stop."

CHAPTER EIGHT

A Story

In the night she told a story,
   In the night and all night through,
While the moon was in her glory,
   And the branches dropped with dew.

'Twas my life she told, and round it
   Rose the years as from a deep;
In the world's great heart she found it,
   Cradled like a child asleep.

In the night I saw her weaving
By the misty moonbeam cold,
All the weft her shuttle cleaving
   With a sacred thread of gold.

Ah! she wept me tears of sorrow,
   Lulling tears so mystic sweet;
Then she wove my last tomorrow,
   And her web lay at my feet.

Of my life she made the story:
   I must weep—so soon 'twas told!
But your name did lend it glory,
   And your love its thread of gold!

By this time, as the sun had gone down, and none of the moons had risen, it would have been dark but that each of the rafts was rigged with a small mast that had a lantern hung on it.

By the light of these lanterns Jack saw crowds of little brown faces, and presently many rafts had come up to the boat, which was now swimming very slowly. Every sailor in every raft fastened to the boat's side a silken thread; then the rafts were rowed to shore, and the sailors jumped out and began to tow the boat along.

These crimson threads looked no stronger than the silk

that ladies sew with, yet by means of them the small people drew the boat along merrily. There were so many of them that they looked like an army as they marched in the light of the lanterns and torches. Jack thought they were very happy, though the work was hard, for they shouted and sang.

The fairy woman looked more beautiful than ever now, and far more stately. She had on a band of precious stones to bind back her hair, and they shone so brightly in the night that her features could be clearly seen.

Jack's little favorite was fast asleep, and the other two fairies had flown away. He was beginning to feel rather sleepy himself, when he was roused by the voice of his free lady, who said to him: "Jack, there is no one listening now, so I will tell you my story. I am the Fairy Queen!"

Jack opened his eyes very wide, but he was so much surprised that he did not say a word.

"One day, long, long ago," said the Queen, "I was discontented with my own happy country. I wished to see the world, so I set forth with a number of the one-foot-one fairies, and went down the wonderful river, thinking to see the world.

"So we sailed down the river till we came to that town which you know of; and there, in the very middle of the stream, stood a tower—a tall tower built upon a rock.

"Fairies are afraid of nothing but other fairies, and we did not think this tower was a fairy work, so we left our ship and went up the rock and into the tower, to see what it was like; but just as we had descended into the dungeon keep we heard the gurgling of water overhead, and down came the tower. It was nothing but water enchanted into the likeness of stone, and we all fell down with it into the very bed of the river.

"Of course, we were not drowned, but there we were obliged to lie, for we have no power out of our own element; and the next day the townspeople came down with a net and dragged the river, picked us all out of the meshes, and made us slaves. The one-foot-one fairies got away shortly; but from that day to this, in sorrow and distress, I have had to serve my masters. Luckily my crown had fallen off in the water, so I was not known to be the Queen; but till you came, Jack, I had almost forgotten that I had ever been happy and free, and I had hardly any hope of getting away."

"How sorry your people must have been," said Jack, "when they found you did not come home again."

"No," said the Queen, "they only went to sleep, and they will not wake till tomorrow morning, when I pass in again. They will think I have been absent for a day, and so will the apple-woman. You must not undeceive them; if you do, they will be very angry."

"And who is the apple-woman?" inquired Jack; but the Queen blushed; and pretended not to hear the question, so he repeated:

"Queen, who is the apple-woman?"

"I've only had her for a very little while," said the Queen evasively.

"And how long do you think you have been a slave, Queen?" asked Jack.

"I don't know," said the Queen. "I have never been able to make up my mind about that."

And now all the moons began to shine, and all the trees lighted themselves up, for almost every leaf had a glow-worm or a firefly on it, and the water was full of fishes that had shining eyes. And now they were close to the steep mountainside; and Jack looked and saw an opening in it, into which the river ran. It was a kind of cave, something like a long, long church with a vaulted roof, only the pavement of it was that magic river, and a narrow towing-path ran on either side.

As they entered the cave there was a hollow murmuring sound, and the Queen's crown became so bright that it lighted up the whole boat; at the same time she began to tell Jack a wonderful story, which he liked very much to hear, but at every fresh thing she said he forgot what had gone before; and at last, though he tried very hard to listen, he was obliged to go to sleep; and he slept soundly and never dreamed of anything till it was morning.

He saw such a curious sight when he woke. They had been going through this underground cavern all night, and now they were approaching its opening on the other side. This opening, because they were a good way from it yet, looked like a lovely little round window of blue and yellow and green glass, but as they drew on he could see far-off mountains, blue sky and a country all covered with sunshine.

He heard singing too, such as fairies make; and he saw some beautiful people, such as those fairies whom he had brought with him. They were coming along the towing-path. They were all lady fairies; but they were not very polite, for as each one came up she took a silken rope out of a brown sailor's hand and gave him a shove which pushed him into the water. In fact the water became filled with such swarms of these sailors that the boat could hardly get on. But the poor little brown fellows did not seem to mind this conduct, for they plunged and shook themselves about, scattering a good deal of spray. Then they all suddenly dived, and when they came up again they were ducks—nothing but brown ducks, I assure you, with green stripes on their wings; and with a great deal of quacking and floundering they all began to swim back again as fast as they could.

Then Jack was a good deal vexed, and he said to himself: "If nobody thanks the ducks for towing us I will;" so he stood up in the boat and shouted: "Thank you, ducks; we are very much obliged to you!" But neither the Queen nor these new towers took the least notice, and gradually the boat came out of that dim cave and entered Fairyland, while the river became so narrow that you could hear the song of the towers quite easily; those on the right bank sang the first verse, and those on the left bank answered:

"Drop, drop from the leaves of lign aloes,
    O honey-dew! drop from the tree.
Float up through your clear river shallows,
    White lilies, beloved of the bee.

"Let the people, O Queen! Say, and bless thee,
    Her bounty drops soft as the dew,
And spotless in honor confess thee,
    As lilies are spotless in hue.

"On the roof stands yon white stork awaking,
    His feathers flush rosy the while,
For, lo! from the blushing east breaking,
    The sun sheds the bloom of his smile.

"Let them boast of thy word, 'It is certain;
  We doubt it no more,' let them say,
'than tomorrow that night's dusky curtain
  Shall roll back its folds for the day.' "

"Master," whispered the old hound, who was lying at Jack's feet.

"Well?" said Jack.

"They didn't invent that song themselves," said the hound; "the old apple-woman taught it to them—the woman whom they love because she can make them cry."

Jack was rather ashamed of the hound's rudeness in saying this; but the Queen took no notice. And now they had reached a little landing-place, which ran out a few feet into the river and was strewn thickly with cowslips and violets.

Here the boat stopped, and the Queen rose and got out.

Jack watched her. A whole crowd of one-foot-one fairies came down a garden to meet her, and he saw them conduct her to a beautiful tent with golden poles and a silken covering; but nobody took the slightest notice of him, or of little Mopsa, or of the hound, and after a long silence the hound said: "Well, master, don't you feel hungry? Why don't you go with the others and have some breakfast?"

"The Queen didn't invite me," said Jack.

"But do you feel as if you couldn't go?" asked the hound.

"Of course not," answered Jack; "but perhaps I may not."

"Oh yes, master," replied the hound; "whatever you *can* do in Fairyland you *may* do."

"Are you sure of that?" asked Jack.

"Quite sure, master," said the hound; "and I am hungry too."

"Well," said Jack, "I will go there and take Mopsa. She shall ride on my shoulder; you may follow."

So he walked up that beautiful garden till he came to the great tent. A banquet was going on inside. All the one-foot-one fairies sat down the sides of the table, and at the top sat the Queen on a larger chair; and there were two empty chairs, one on each side of her.

Jack blushed; but the hound whispering again: "Master, whatever you can do you may do," he came slowly up the table towards the Queen, who was saying as he drew near:

"Where is our trusty and well-beloved, the apple-woman?" And she took no notice of Jack; so, though he could not help feeling rather red and ashamed, he went and sat in the chair beside her with Mopsa still on his shoulder. Mopsa laughed for joy when she saw the feast. The Queen said: "Oh, Jack, I am so glad to see you!" and some of the one-foot-one fairies cried out: "What a delightful little creature that is! She can laugh! Perhaps she can also cry!"

Jack looked about, but there was no seat for Mopsa; and he was afraid to let her run about on the floor, lest she should be hurt.

There was a very large dish standing before the Queen; for though the people were small the plates and dishes were exactly like those we use, and of the same size.

This dish was raised on a foot, and filled with grapes and peaches. Jack wondered at himself for doing it, but he saw no other place for Mopsa; so he took out the fruit, laid it round the dish, and set his own little one-foot-one in the dish.

Nobody looked in the least surprised; and there she sat very happily, biting an apple with her small white teeth.

Then, as they brought him nothing to eat, Jack helped himself from some of the dishes before him, and found that a fairy breakfast was very nice indeed.

In the meantime there was a noise outside, and in stumped an elderly woman. She had very thick boots on, a short gown of red print, an orange cotton handkerchief over her shoulders and a black silk bonnet. She was exactly the same height as the Queen—for of course nobody in Fairyland is allowed to be any bigger than the Queen; so, if they are not children when they arrive, they are obliged to shrink.

"How are you, dear?" said the Queen.

"I am as well as can be expected," answered the apple-woman, sitting down in the empty chair. "Now, then, where's my tea? They're never ready with my cup of tea."

Two attendants immediately brought a cup of tea and set it down before the apple-woman, with a plate of bread and butter; and she proceeded to pour it out into the saucer, and blow it, because it was hot. In so doing her wandering eyes caught sight of Jack and little Mopsa, and she set down the saucer and looked at them with attention.

Now Mopsa, I am sorry to say, was behaving so badly that Jack was quite ashamed of her. First she got out of her dish, took something nice out of the Queen's plate with her fingers and ate it; and then, as she was going back, she tumbled over a melon and upset a glass of red wine, which she wiped up with her white frock; after which she got into her dish again, and there she sat smiling, and daubing her pretty face with a piece of buttered muffin.

"Mopsa," said Jack, "you are very naughty; if you behave in this way, I shall never take you out to parties again."

"Pretty lamb!" said the apple-woman; "it's just like a child." And then she burst into tears, and exclaimed, sobbing: "It's many a long day since I've seen a child. Oh dear! Oh deary me!"

Upon this, to the astonishment of Jack, every one of the guests began to cry and sob too.

"Oh dear! Oh dear!" they said to one another, "we're crying; we can cry just as well as men and women. Isn't it delightful? What a luxury it is to cry, to be sure!"

They were evidently quite proud of it; and when Jack looked at the Queen for an explanation, she only gave him a still little smile.

But Mopsa crept along the table to the apple-woman, let her take her and hug her; and seemed to like her very much; for as she sat on her knee she patted her brown face with a little dimpled hand.

"I should like vastly well to be her nurse," said the apple-woman, drying her eyes, and looking at Jack.

"If you'll always wash her, and put clean frocks on her, you may," said Jack; "for just look at her—what a figure she is already!"

Upon this the apple-woman laughed for joy, and again everyone else did the same. The fairies can only laugh and cry when they see mortals do so.

CHAPTER NINE

After the Party

Stephano. This will prove a brave kingdom to me,
Where I shall have my music for nothing.
The Tempest[12]

When breakfast was over the guests got up, one after the other, without taking the least notice of the Queen; and the tent began to get so thin and transparent that you could see the trees and the sky through it. At last it looked only like a colored mist, with blue and green and yellow stripes, and then it was gone; and the table and all the things on it began to go in the same way. Only Jack, and the apple-woman, and Mopsa were left, sitting on their chairs, with the Queen between them.

Presently the Queen's lips began to move, and her eyes looked straight before her, as she sat up right in her chair. Whereupon the apple-woman snatched up Mopsa and, seizing Jack's hand, hurried him off, exclaiming: "Come away! Come away! She is going to tell one of her stories; and if you listen you'll be obliged to go to sleep, and sleep nobody knows how long."

Jack did not want to go to sleep; he wished to go down to the river again and see what had become of his boat, for he had left his cap and several other things in it.

So he parted from the apple-woman—who took Mopsa with her, and said he would find her again when he wanted her at her apple-stall—and went down to the boat, where he saw that his faithful hound was there before him.

"It was lucky, master, that I came when I did," said the hound, "for a dozen or so of those one-foot-one fellows were just shoving it off, and you will want it at night to sleep in."

"Yes," said Jack; "and I can stretch the bit of purple silk to make a canopy overhead—a sort of awning—for I should not like to sleep in tents or palaces that are inclined to melt away."

So the hound with his teeth, and Jack with his hands, pulled and pulled at the silk till it was large enough to make a splendid canopy, like a tent; and it reached down to the water's edge, and roofed in all the after part of the boat.

So now he had a delightful little home of his own; and there was no fear of its being blown away, for no wind ever blows in Fairyland. All the trees are quite still, no leaf rustles and the flowers lie on the ground exactly where they fall.

After this Jack told the hound to watch his boat, and went himself in search of the apple-woman. Not one fairy was to be seen, any more than if he had been in his own country, and he wandered down the green margin of the river till he saw the apple-woman sitting at a small stall with apples on it, and cherries tied to sticks, and some dry-looking nuts. She had Mopsa on her knee, and had washed her face, and put a beautiful clean white frock on her.

"Where are all the fairies gone to?" asked Jack.

"I never take any notice of that common trash and their doings," she answered. "When the Queen takes to telling her stories they are generally frightened, and go and sit in the tops of the trees."

"But you seem very fond of Mopsa," said Jack, "and she is one of them. You will help me to take care of her, won't you, till she grows a little older?"

"Grows!" said the apple-woman, laughing. "Grows! Why you don't think, surely, that she will ever be any different from what she is now!"

"I thought she would grow up," said Jack.

"They never change so long as they last," answered the apple-woman, "when once they are one-foot-one high."

"Mopsa," said Jack, "come here, and I'll measure you."

Mopsa came dancing towards Jack, and he tried to measure her, first with a yard measure that the apple-woman took out of her pocket, and then with a stick, and then with a bit of string; but Mopsa would not stand steady, and at last it ended in their having a good game of romps together, and a race; but when he carried her back, sitting on his shoulder, he was sorry to see that the apple-woman was crying again, and he asked her kindly what she did it for.

"It is because," she answered, "I shall never see my own country any more, nor any men and women and children, excepting such as by a rare chance stray in for a little while as you have done."

"I can go back whenever I please," said Jack. "Why don't you?"

"Because I came in of my own good will, after I had had fair warning that if I came at all it would end in my staying always. Besides, I don't know that I exactly wish to go home again—I should be afraid."

"Afraid of what?' asked Jack.

"Why, there's the rain and the cold, and not having anything to eat excepting what you earn. And yet," said the apple-woman, "I have three boys of my own at home; one of them must be nearly a man by this time, and the youngest is about as old as you are. If I went home I might find one or more of those boys in jail, and then how miserable I should be."

"But you are not happy as it is," said Jack. "I have seen you cry."

"Yes," said the apple-woman; "but now I live here I don't care about anything so much as I used to do. 'May I have a satin gown and a coach?' I asked when first I came. 'You may have a hundred and fifty satin gowns if you like,' said the Queen, 'and twenty coaches with six cream-colored horses to each.' But when I had been here a little time, and found I could have everything I wished for, and change it as often as I pleased, I began not to care for anything; and at last I got so sick of all their grand things that I dressed myself in my own clothes that I came in, and made up my mind to have a stall and sit at it, as I used to do, selling apples. And I used to say to myself: 'I have but to wish with all my heart to go home, and I can go, I know that;' but oh dear! oh dear! I couldn't wish enough, for it would come into my head that I should be poor, or that my boys would have forgotten me, or that my neighbors would look down on me, and so I always put off wishing for another day.[13] Now here is the Queen coming. Sit down

---

13. **and so . . . for another day** The apple-woman's rationale for not wanting to return to her human world bears comparing with the reasons adduced by the captive slave woman in Ewing's "Amelia and the Dwarfs."

on the grass and play with Mopsa. Don't let her see us talking together, lest she should think I have been telling you things which you ought not to know."

Jack looked, and saw the Queen coming slowly towards them, with her hands held out before her, as if it was dark. She felt her way, yet her eyes were wide open, and she was telling her stories all the time.

"Don't you listen to a word she says," whispered the apple-woman, and then, in order that Jack might not hear what the Queen was talking about, she began to sing.

She had no sooner begun than up from the river came swarms of one-foot-one fairies to listen, and hundreds of them dropped down from the trees. The Queen, too, seemed to attend as they did, though she kept murmuring her story all the time; and nothing that any of them did appeared to surprise the apple-woman—she sang as if nobody was taking any notice at all:

"When I sit on market-days amid the comers and the goers,
　　Oh! full oft I have a vision of the days without alloy,
And a ship comes up the river with a jolly gang of towers,
　　And a 'pull'e haul'e, pull'e haul'e, yoy! heave, hoy!'

"There is busy talk around me, all about mine ears it hummeth,
　　But the wooden wharves I look on, and a dancing heaving buoy,
For 'tis tidetime in the river, and she cometh—oh, she cometh!
　　With a 'pull'e haul'e, pull'e haul'e, yoy! heave, hoy!'

"Then I hear the water washing, never golden waves were brighter,
　　And I hear the capstan creaking—'tis a sound that cannot cloy.
Bring her to, to ship her lading, brig or schooner, sloop or lighter,
　　With a 'pull'e haul'e, pull'e haul'e, yoy! heave, hoy!'

" 'Will ye step aboard, my dearest? for the high seas lie before us.'
　　So I sailed adown the river in those days without alloy.
We are launched! But when, I wonder, shall a sweeter sound float o'er us
　　Than yon 'pull'e haul'e, pull'e haul'e, yoy! heave, hoy!' "

As the apple-woman left off singing the Queen moved away, still murmuring the words of her story, and Jack said:

"Does the Queen tell stories of what has happened, or of what is going to happen?"

"Why, of what is going to happen, of course," replied the woman. "Anybody could tell the other sort."

"Because I heard a little of it," observed Jack. "I thought she was talking of me. She said: 'So he took the measure, and Mopsa stood still for once, and he found she was only one foot high, and she grew a great deal after that. Yes, she can grow.' "

"That's a fine hearing, and a strange hearing," said the apple-woman; "and what did she mutter next?"

"Of how she heard me sobbing," replied Jack; "and while you went on about stepping on board the ship, she said: 'He was very good to me, dear little fellow! But Fate is the name of my old mother, and she reigns here.[14] Oh, she reigns! The fatal F is in her name, and I cannot take it out!' "

"Ah!" replied the apple-woman, "they all say that, and that they are fays, and that mortals call their history fable; they are always crying out for an alphabet without the fatal F."

"And then she told how she heard Mopsa sobbing too," said Jack; "sobbing among the reeds and rushes by the river side."

"There are no reeds and no rushes either here," said the apple-woman, "and I have walked the river from end to end. I don't think much of that part of the story. But you are sure she said that Mopsa was short of her proper height?"

"Yes, and that she would grow; but that's nothing. In my country we always grow."

"Hold your tongue about your country!" said the apple-woman sharply. "Do you want to make enemies of them all?"

Mopsa had been listening to this, and now she said: "I

14. **But Fate . . . reigns here.** The words "fay" and "fairy" actually do derive from the Latin *fata* or fate, a connection Ingelow will exploit in her later characterization of old Mother Fate and her daughters.

don't love the Queen. She slapped my arm as she went by, and it hurts."

Mopsa showed her little fat arm as she spoke, and there was a red place on it.

"That's odd too," said the apple-woman; "there's nothing red in a common fairy's veins. They have sap in them: that's why they can't blush."

Just then the sun went down, and Mopsa got up on the apple-woman's lap and went to sleep; and Jack, being tired, went to his boat and lay down under the purple canopy, his old hound lying at his feet to keep guard over him.

The next morning, when he woke, a pretty voice called to him: "Jack! Jack!" and he opened his eyes and saw Mopsa. The apple-woman had dressed her in a clean frock and blue shoes, and her hair was so long! She was standing on the landing-place, close to him. "Oh, Jack! I'm so big," she said. "I grew in the night; look at me."

Jack looked. Yes, Mopsa had grown indeed; she had only just reached to his knee the day before, and now her little bright head, when he measured her, came as high as the second button on his waistcoat.

"But I hope you will not go on growing so fast as this," said Jack, "or you will be as tall as my mamma is in a week or two—much too big for me to play with."

CHAPTER TEN

Mopsa Learns her Letters

A—apple-pie.
B—bit it.

"How ashamed I am," Jack said, "to think that you don't know even your letters!"

Mopsa replied that she thought that did not signify, and then she and Jack began to play at jumping from the boat on to the bank and back again; and afterwards, as not a single fairy could be seen, they had breakfast with the apple-woman.

"Where is the Queen?" asked Jack.

The apple-woman answered: "It's not the fashion to ask questions in Fairyland."

"That's a pity," said Jack, "for there are several things that I particularly want to know about this country. Mayn't I even ask how big it is?"

"How big?" said Mopsa—little Mopsa looking as wise as possible. "Why, the same size as your world, of course."

Jack laughed. "It's the same world that you call yours," continued Mopsa; "and when I'm a little older I'll explain it all to you."

"If it's our world," said Jack, "why are none of us in it, excepting me and the apple-woman?"

"That's because you've got something in your world that you call TIME," said Mopsa; "so you talk about NOW, and you talk about THEN."

And don't you?" asked Jack.

"I do if I want to make you understand," said Mopsa.

The apple-woman laughed, and said: "To think of the pretty thing talking so queen-like already! Yes, that's right, and just what the grown-up fairies say. Go on, and explain it to him if you can."

"You know," said Mopsa, "that your people say there was a time when there were none of them in the world— a time before they were made. Well, THIS is that time. This IS long ago."

"Nonsense!" said Jack. "Then how do I happen to be here?"

"Because," said Mopsa, "when the albatross brought you she did not fly with you a long way off, but a long way back—hundreds and hundreds of years. This is your world, as you can see; but none of your people are here, because they are not made yet. I don't think any of them will be made for a thousand years."

"But I saw the old ships," answered Jack, "in the enchanted bay."

"That was a border country," said Mopsa. "I was asleep while you went through those countries; but these are the real Fairylands."

Jack was very much surprised when he heard Mopsa say these strange things; and as he looked at her he felt that a sleep was coming over him, and he could not hold up his head. He felt how delightful it was to go to sleep; and though the apple-woman sprang to him when she observed that he was shutting his eyes, and though he heard her begging and entreating him to keep awake, he did not want to do so; but he let his head sink down on the mossy grass, which was as soft as a pillow, and there under the shade of a Guelder rose tree,[15] that kept dropping its white flowerets all over him, he had this dream.

He thought that Mopsa came running up to him, as he stood by the river, and that he said to her: "Oh, Mopsa, how old we are! We have lived back to the times before Adam and Eve!"

"Yes," said Mopsa; "but I don't feel old. Let us go down the river, and see what we can find."

So they got into the boat, and it floated into the middle of the river, and then made for the opposite bank, where the water was warm and very muddy, and the river became so very wide that it seemed to be afternoon when they got near enough to see it clearly; and what they saw was a boggy country, green, and full of little rills, but the water—which, as I told you, was thick and muddy—the water was full of small holes! You never saw water with eyelet-holes in it; but Jack did. On all sides of the boat he saw holes moving about in pairs, and some were so close that he looked and saw their lining; they were lined with pink, and they snorted! Jack was afraid, but he considered that this was such a long time ago that the holes, whatever they were, could not hurt him; but it made him start, notwithstanding, when a huge flat head reared itself up close to the boat, and he found that the holes were the nostrils of creatures who kept all the rest of themselves under water.

In a minute or two, hundreds of ugly flat-heads popped up, and the boat danced among them as they floundered about in the water.

"I hope they won't upset us," said Jack. "I wish you would land."

Mopsa said she would rather not, because she did not like the hairy elephants.

"There are no such things as hairy elephants," said Jack, in his dream; but he had hardly spoken when out of a

15. **Guelder rose tree** white-flowered bush, also called "snowball"

wood close at hand some huge creatures, far larger than
our elephants, came jogging down to the water. There were
forty or fifty of them, and they were covered with what
looked like tow. In fact, so coarse was their shaggy hair
that they looked as if they were dressed in door-mats; and
when they stood still and shook themselves such clouds of
dust flew out, as it swept over the river, that it almost stifled
Jack and Mopsa.

"Odious!" exclaimed Jack, sneezing. "What terrible creatures these are!"

"Well," answered Mopsa, at the other end of the boat
(but he could hardly see her for the dust), "then why do
you dream of them?"

Jack had just decided to dream of something else when,
with a noise greater than fifty trumpets, the elephants, having shaken out al the dust, came thundering down to the
water to bathe in the liquid mud. They shook the whole
country as they plunged; but that was not all. The awful
river-horses rose up and, with shrill screams, fell upon
them, and gave them battle; while up from every rill peeped
above the rushes frogs as large as oxen, and with blue and
green eyes that gleamed like the eyes of cats.

The frogs' croaking and the shrill trumpeting of the elephants, together with the cries of the river-horses, as all
these creatures fought with horn and tusk, and fell on one
another, lashing the water into whirlpools, among which
the boat danced up and down like a cork, the blinding
spray, and the flapping about of great bats over the boat
and in it—so confused Jack that Mopsa had spoken to him
several times before he answered.

"Oh, Jack!" she said at last; "if you can't dream any
better, I must call the Craken."

"Very well," said Jack. "I'm almost wrapped up and
smothered in bats' wings, so call anything you please."

Thereupon Mopsa whistled softly, and in a minute or two
he saw, almost spanning the river, a hundred yards off, a
thing like a rainbow, or a slender bridge, or still more like
one ring or coil of an enormous serpent; and presently the
creature's head shot up like a fountain, close to the boat,
almost as high as a ship's mast. It was the Craken;[16] and

16. **Craken** The sea-monster of Scandinavian mythology was the subject of Tennyson's short poem "The Kraken" (1830).

when Mopsa saw it she began to cry, and said: "We are caught in this crowd of creatures, and we cannot get away from the land of dreams. Do help us, Craken."

Some of the bats that hung to the edges of the boat had wings as large as sails, and the first thing the Craken did was to stoop its lithe neck, pick two or three of them off, and eat them.

"You can swim your boat home under my coils where the water is calm," the Craken said, "for she is so extremely old now that if you do not take care she will drop to pieces before you get back to the present time."

Jack knew it was of no use saying anything to this formidable creature, before whom the river-horses and the elephants were rushing to the shore; but when he looked and saw down the river rainbow behind rainbow—I mean coil behind coil—glittering in the sun, like so many glorious arches that did not reach to the banks, he felt extremely glad this was a dream, and besides that, he thought to himself: "It's only a fabled monster."

"No, it's only a fable to these times," said Mopsa, answering his thought; "but in spite of that we shall have to go through all the rings."

They went under one—silver, green, and blue, and gold. The water dripped from it upon them, and the boat trembled, either because of its great age or because it felt the rest of the coil underneath.

A good way off was another coil, and they went so safely under that that Jack felt himself getting used to Crakens, and not afraid. Then they went under thirteen more. These kept getting nearer and nearer together, but, besides that, the fourteenth had not quite such a high span as the former ones; but there were a great many to come, and yet they got lower and lower.

Both Jack and Mopsa noticed this, but neither said a word. The thirtieth coil brushed Jack's cap off, then they had to stoop to pass under the two next, and then they had to lie down in the bottom of the boat, and they got through with the greatest difficulty; but still before them was another! The boat was driving straight towards it, and it lay so close to the water that the arch it made was only a foot high. When Jack saw it, he called out: "No! that I cannot bear. Somebody else may do the rest of this dream. I shall jump overboard!"

Mopsa seemed to answer in quite a pleasant voice, as if she was not afraid:

"No, you'd much better wake." And then she went on: "Jack! Jack! why don't you wake?"

Then all on a sudden Jack opened his eyes, and found that he was lying quietly on the grass, that little Mopsa really had asked him why he did not wake. He saw the Queen too, standing by, looking at him, and saying to herself: "*I* did not put him to sleep. *I* did not put him to sleep."

"We don't want any more stories to-day, Queen," said the apple-woman, in a disrespectful tone, and she immediately began to sing, clattering some tea-things all the time, for a kettle was boiling on some sticks, and she was going to make tea out of doors:

> "The marten flew to the finch's nest,
>   Feathers, and moss, and a wisp of hay:
> 'The arrow it sped to thy brown mate's breast;
>   Low in the broom is thy mate today.'
>
> " 'Liest thou low, love? low in the broom?
>   Feathers and moss, and a wisp of hay,
> Warm the white eggs till I learn his doom.'
>   She beateth her wings, and away, away.
>
> " 'Ah, my sweet singer, thy days are told
>   (Feathers and moss, and a wisp of hay)!
> Thine eyes are dim, and the eggs grow cold.
>   O mournful morrow! O dark today!'
>
> "The finch flew back to her cold, cold nest,
>   Feathers and moss, and a wisp of hay.
> Mine is the trouble that rent her breast,
>   And home is silent, and love is clay."

Jack felt very tired indeed—as much tired as if he had really been out all day on the river, and gliding under the coils of the Craken. He, however, rose up when the apple-woman called him, and drank his tea, and had some fairy bread with it, which refreshed him very much.

After tea he measured Mopsa again, and found that she had grown up to a higher button. She looked much wiser too, and when he said she must be taught to read she made no objection, so he arranged daisies and buttercups into the forms of the letters, and she learnt nearly all of them that one evening, while crowds of the one-foot-one fairies looked on, hanging from the boughs and sitting in the grass, and shouting out the names of the letters as Mopsa said them. They were very polite to Jack, for they gathered all these flowers for him, and emptied them from their little caps at his feet as fast as he wanted them.

CHAPTER ELEVEN

Good Morning Sister

Sweet is childhood—childhood's over,
    Kiss and part.
Sweet is youth; but youth's a rover—
    So's my heart.
Sweet is rest; but by all showing
    Toil is nigh.
We must go. Alas! the going,
    Say "goodbye."

Jack crept under his canopy, went to sleep early that night and did not wake till the sun had risen, when the apple-woman called him, and said breakfast was nearly ready.

The same thing never happens twice in Fairyland, so this time the breakfast was not spread in a tent, but on the river. The Queen had cut off a tiny piece of her robe, the one-foot-one fairies had stretched it till it was very large, and then they had spread it on the water, where it floated and lay like a great carpet of purple and gold. One corner of it was moored to the side of Jack's boat; but he had not observed this, because of his canopy. However, that was now looped up by the apple-woman, and Jack and Mopsa saw what was going on.

Hundreds of swans had been towing the carpet along,

and were still holding it with their beaks, while a crowd of
doves walked about on it, smoothing out the creases and
patting it with their pretty pink feet till it was quite firm and
straight. The swans then swam away, and they flew away.

Presently troops of fairies came down to the landing-
place, jumped into Jack's boat without asking leave, and so
got on to the carpet, while at the same time a great tree
which grew on the bank began to push out fresh leaves, as
large as fans, and shoot out long branches, which again shot
out others, till very soon there was shade all over the carpet—a thick shadow as good as a tent, which was very
pleasant, for the sun was already hot.

When the Queen came down the tree suddenly blossomed out with thousands of red and white flowers.

"You must not go on to that carpet," said the apple-
woman; "let us sit still in the boat, and be served here."
She whispered this as the Queen stepped into the boat.

"Good morning, Jack," said the Queen. "Good morning,
dear." This was to the apple-woman; and then she stood
still for a moment and looked earnestly at little Mopsa,
and sighed.

"Well," she said to her, "don't you mean to speak to
me?" Then Mopsa lifted up her pretty face and blushed
very rosy red, and said, in a shy voice: "Good morning—
sister."

"I said so!" exclaimed the Queen; "I said so!" and she
lifted up her beautiful eyes, and murmured out: "What is
to be done now?"

"Never mind, Queen dear," said Jack. "If it was rude of
Mopsa to say that, she is such a little young thing that she
does not know better."

"It was not rude," said Mopsa, and she laughed and
blushed again. "It was not rude, and I am not sorry."

As she said this the Queen stepped on to the carpet, and
all the flowers began to drop down. They were something
like camellias, and there were thousands of them.

The fairies collected them in little heaps. They had no
tables and chairs, nor any plates and dishes for this breakfast; but the Queen sat down on the carpet close to Jack's
boat, and leaned her cheek on her hand, and seemed to be
lost in thought. The fairies put some flowers into her lap,

then each took some, and they all sat down and looked at the Queen, but she did not stir.

At last Jack said: "When is the breakfast coming?"

"This is the breakfast," said the apple-woman; "these flowers are most delicious eating. You never tasted anything so good in your life; but we don't begin till the Queen does."

Quantities of blossoms had dropped into the boat. Several fairies tumbled into it almost head over heels, they were in such a hurry, and they heaped them into Mopsa's lap, but took no notice of Jack, nor of the apple-woman either.

At last, when everyone had waited some time, the Queen pulled a petal off one flower, and began to eat, so everyone else began; and what the apple-woman had said was quite true. Jack knew that he never had tasted anything half so nice, and he was quite sorry when he could not eat any more. So, when everyone had finished, the Queen leaned her arm on the edge of the boat and, turning her lovely face towards Mopsa, said: "I want to whisper to you, sister."

"Oh!" said Mopsa. "I wish I was in Jack's waistcoat pocket again; but I'm so big now." And she took hold of the two sides of his velvet jacket, and his her face between them.

"My old mother sent a message last night," continued the Queen, in a soft, sorrowful voice. "She is much more powerful than we are."

"What is the message?" asked Mopsa; but she still hid her face.

So the queen moved over, and put her lips close to Mopsa's ear, and repeated it: "There cannot be two queens in one hive."

"If Mopsa leaves the hive, a fine swarm will go with her," said the apple-woman. "I shall, for one; that I shall!"

"No!" answered the Queen. "I hope not, dear; for you know well that this is my old mother's doing, not mine."

"Oh!" said Mopsa. "I feel as if I must tell a story too, just as the Queen does." But the apple-woman broke out in a very cross voice: "It's not at all like Fairyland, if you go on in this way, and I would as lief be out of it as in it." Then she began to sing, that she and Jack might not hear Mopsa's story:

"On the rocks by Aberdeen.
Where the whistlin' wave had been,
As I wanted and at e'en
      Was eerie;
There I saw thee sailing west,
And I ran with joy opprest—
Ay, and took out all my best,
      My dearie.

"Then I busked mysel' wi speed,
And the neighbors cried, What need?
'Tis a lass in any weed
      Aye bonny!'
Now my heart, my heart is sair.
What's the good, though I be fair,
For thou'lt never see me mair,
      Man Johnnie!"

While the apple-woman sang Mopsa finished her story; and the Queen untied the fastening which held her carpet to the boat, and went floating upon it down the river.

"Goodbye," she said, kissing her hand to them. "I must go and prepare for the deputation."

So Jack and Mopsa played about all the morning, sometimes in the boat and sometimes on the shore, while the apple-woman sat on the grass, with her arms folded, and seemed to be lost in thought. At last she said to Jack: "What was the name of the great bird that carried you two here?"

"I have forgotten," answered Jack. "I've been trying to remember ever since we heard the Queen tell her first story, but I cannot."

"I remember," said Mopsa.

"Tell it then," replied the apple-woman; but Mopsa shook her head.

"I don't want Jack to go," she answered.

"I don't want to go, nor that you should," said Jack.

"But the Queen said, 'There cannot be two Queens in one hive,' and that means that you are going to be turned out of this beautiful country."

"The other fairy lands are just as nice," answered Mopsa. "She can only turn me out of this one."

"I never heard of more than one Fairyland," observed Jack.

"It's my opinion," said the apple-woman, "that there are hundreds! And those one-foot-one fairies are such a saucy set that if I were you I should be very glad to get away from them. You've been here a very little while as yet, and you've no notion what goes on when the leaves begin to drop."

"Tell us," said Jack.

"Well, you must know," answered the apple-woman, "that fairies cannot abide cold weather; so, when the first rime frost comes, they bury themselves."

"Bury themselves?" repeated Jack.

"Yes, I tell you, they bury themselves. You've seen fairy rings, of course, even in your own country; and here the fields are full of them. Well, when it gets cold a company of fairies forms itself into a circle, and every one digs a little hole. The first that has finished jumps into his hole, and his next neighbor covers him up, and then jumps into his own little hole, and he gets covered up in his turn, till at last there is only one left, and he goes and joins another circle, hoping he shall have better luck than to be last again. I've often asked them why they do that, but no fairy can ever give a reason for anything. They always say that old Mother Fate makes them do it. When they come up again they are not fairies at all, but the good ones are mushrooms, and the bad ones are toadstools."

"Then you think there are no one-foot-one fairies in the other countries?" said Jack.

"Of course not," answered the apple-woman; "all the fairy lands are different. It's only the queens that are like."

"I wish the fairies would not disappear for hours," said Jack. "They all seem to run off and hide themselves."

"That's their ways," answered the apple-woman. "All fairies are part of their time in the shape of human creatures, and the rest of it in the shape of some animal. These can turn themselves, when they please, to Guinea-fowl. In the heat of the day they generally prefer to be in that form, and they sit among the leaves of the trees.

"A great many are now with the Queen, because there is a deputation coming: but if I were to begin to sing, such a flock of Guinea-hens would gather round that the boughs of the trees would bend with their weight, and they would light on the grass all about so thickly that not a blade of grass would be seen as far as the song was heard."

So she began to sing, and the air was darkened by great flocks of these Guinea-fowl. They alighted just as she had said, and kept time with their heads and their feet, nodding like a crowd of mandarins; and yet it was nothing but a stupid old song that you would have thought could have no particular meaning for them.

Like A Laverock in the Lift

I

It's we two, it's we two, it's we two for aye,
All the world and we two, and Heaven be our stay.
Like a laverock in the lift, sing, O bonny bride!
All the world was Adam once, with Eve by his side.

II

What's the world, my lass, my love! what can it do?
I am thine, and thou art mine; life is sweet and new.
If the world have missed the mark, let it stand by,
For we two have gotten leave, and once more we'll try.

III

Like a laverock in the lift,[17] sing, O bonny bride!
It's we two, it's we two, happy side by side.
Take a kiss from me thy man; now the song begins:
"All is made afresh for us, and the brave heart wins."

IV

When the darker days come, and no sun will shine,
Thou shalt dry my tears, lass, and I'll dry thine.
It's we two, it's we two, while the world's away,
Sitting by the golden sheaves on our wedding-day.

17. **Laverock in the Lift** Sky-larks (known as "lavericks" in the North) are noted for their airy acrobatic lifts.

CHAPTER TWELVE

They Run Away from Old Mother Fate

> A land that living warmth disowns,
>   It meets my wondering ken;
> A land where all the men are stones,
>   Or all the stones are men.

Before the apple-woman had finished, Jack and Mopsa saw the Queen coming in great state, followed by thousands of the one-foot-one fairies, and leading by a ribbon round its neck a beautiful brown doe. A great many pretty fawns were walking among the fairies.

"Here's the deputation," said the apple-woman; but as the Guinea-fowl rose like a cloud at the approach of the Queen, and the fairies and fawns pressed forward, there was a good deal of noise and confusion, during which Mopsa stepped up close to Jack and whispered in his ear: "Remember, Jack, whatever you can do you may do."

Then the brown doe lay down at Mopsa's feet, and the Queen began:

"Jack and Mopsa, I love you both. I had a message last night from my old mother, and I told you what it was."

"Yes, Queen," said Mopsa, "you did."

"And now," continued the Queen, "she has sent this beautiful brown doe from the country beyond the lake, where they are in the greatest distress for a queen, to offer Mopsa the crown; and, Jack, it is fated that Mopsa is to reign there, so you had better say no more about it."

"I don't want to be a queen," said Mopsa, pouting; "I want to play with Jack."

"You are a queen already," answered the real Queen; "at least, you will be in a few days. You are so much grown, even since the morning, that you come up nearly to Jack's shoulder. In four days you will be as tall as I am; and it is quite impossible that anyone of fairy birth should be as tall as a queen in her own country."

"But I don't see what stags and does can want with a queen," said Jack.

"They were obliged to turn into deer," said the Queen, "when they crossed their own border; but they are fairies when they are at home, and they want Mopsa, because they are always obliged to have a queen of alien birth."

"If I go," said Mopsa, "shall Jack go too?"

"Oh, no," answered the Queen; "Jack and the apple-woman are my subjects."

"Apple-woman," said Jack, "tell us what you think; shall Mopsa go to this country?"

"Why, child," said the apple-woman, "go away from here she must; but she need not go off with the deer, I suppose, unless she likes. They look gentle and harmless; but it is very hard to get at the truth in this country, and I've heard queer stories about them."

"Have you?" said the Queen. "Well, you can repeat them if you like; but remember that the poor brown doe cannot contradict them."

So the apple-woman said: "I have heard, but I don't know how true it is, that in that country they shut up their queen in a great castle, and cover her with a veil, and never let the sun shine on her; for if by chance the least little sunbeam should light on her she would turn into a doe directly, and all the nation would turn with her, and stay so."

"I don't want to be shut up in a castle," said Mopsa.

"But is it true?" asked Jack.

"Well," said the apple-woman, "as I told you before, I cannot make out whether it's true or not, for all these stags and fawns look very mild, gentle creatures."

"I won't go," said Mopsa; "I would rather run away."

All this time the Queen with the brown doe had been gently pressing with the crowd nearer and nearer to the brink of the river, so that now Jack and Mopsa, who stood facing them, were quite close to the boat; and while they argued and tried to make Mopsa come away, Jack suddenly whispered to her to spring into the boat, which she did, and he after her, and at the same time he cried out:

"Now, boat, if you are my boat, set off as fast as you can, and let nothing of fairy birth get on board of you."

No sooner did he begin to speak than the boat swung itself away from the edge, and almost in a moment it was in the very middle of the river, and beginning to float gently down with the stream.

Now, as I have told you before, that river runs up the country instead of down to the sea, so Jack and Mopsa floated still farther up into Fairyland; and they saw the Queen, and the apple-woman, and all the crowd of fawns and fairies walking along the bank of the river, keeping exactly to the same pace that the boat went; and this went on for hours and hours, so that there seemed to be no chance that Jack and Mopsa could land; and they heard no voices at all, nor any sound but the baying of the old hound, who could not swim out to them, because Jack had forbidden the boat to take anything of fairy birth on board of her.

Luckily the bottom of the boat was full of those delicious flowers that had dropped into it at breakfast time, so there was plenty of nice food for Jack and Mopsa; and Jack noticed, when he looked at her towards evening, that she was now nearly as tall as himself, and that her lovely brown hair floated down to her ankles.

"Jack," she said, before it grew dusk, "will you give me your little purse that has the silver fourpence in it?"

Now Mopsa had often played with this purse. It was lined with a piece of pale green silk, and when Jack gave it to her she pulled the silk out, and shook it, and patted it, and stretched it, just as the queen had done, and it came into a most lovely cloak, which she tied round her neck. Then she twisted up her long hair into a coil, and fastened it round her head, and called to the fireflies which were beginning to glitter on the trees to come, and they came and alighted in a row upon the coil, and turned into diamonds directly. So now Mopsa had got a crown and a robe, and she was so beautiful that Jack thought he should never be tired of looking at her; but it was nearly dark now, and he was so sleepy and tired that he could not keep his eyes open, though he tried very hard, and he began to blink, and then he began to nod, and at last he fell fast asleep, and did not awake till morning.

Then he sat up in the boat, and looked about him. A wonderful country, indeed!—no trees, no grass, no houses, nothing but red stones and red sand—and Mopsa was gone. Jack jumped on shore, for the boat had stopped, and was close to the brink of the river. He looked about for some time, and at last, in the shadow of a pale brown rock, he found her; and oh! delightful surprise, the apple-woman was there too. She was saying: "Oh, my bones! Dearie, dearie me, how they do ache!" That was not surprising, for she had been out all night. She had walked beside the river with the Queen and her tribe till they came to a little tinkling stream, which divides their country from the sandy land, and there they were obliged to stop; they could not cross it. But the apple-woman sprang over, and, though the Queen told her she must come back again in twenty-four hours, she did not appear to be displeased. Now the Guinea-hens, when they had come to listen, the day before, to the apple-woman's song, had brought each of them a grain of maize in her beak, and had thrown it into her apron; so when she got up she carried it with her gathered up there, and now she had been baking some delicious little cakes on a fire of dry sticks that the river had drifted down, and Mopsa had taken a honeycomb from the rock, so they all had a very nice breakfast. And the apple-woman gave them a great deal of good advice, and told them if they wished to remain in Fairyland, and not be caught by the brown doe and her followers, they must cross over the purple mountains.

"For on the other side of those peaks," she said, "I have heard that fairies live who have the best of characters for being kind and just. I am sure they would never shut up a poor queen in a castle."

"But the best thing you could do, dear," she said to Mopsa, "would be to let Jack call the bird, and make her carry you back to his own country."

"The Queen is not at all kind," said Jack; "I have been very kind to her, and she should have let Mopsa stay."

"No, Jack; she could not," said Mopsa; "but I wish I had not grown so fast, and I don't like to go to your country. I would rather run away."

"But who is to tell us where to run?" asked Jack.

"Oh," said Mopsa, "some of these people."

"I don't see anybody," said Jack, looking about him.

Mopsa pointed to a group of stones, and then to another group, and as Jack looked he saw that in shape they were something like people—stone people. One stone was a little like an old man with a mantle over him, and he was sitting on the ground with his knees up nearly to his chin. Another was like a woman with a hood on, and she seemed to be leaning her chin on her hand. Close to these stood something very much like a cradle in shape; and beyond were stones that resembled a flock of sheep lying down on the bare sand, with something that reminded Jack of the figure of a man lying asleep near them, with his face to the ground.

That was a very curious country; all the stones reminded you of people or of animals, and the shadows that they cast were much more like things than the stones themselves. There were blocks with things that you might have mistaken for stone ropes twisted round them; but, looking at the shadows, you could see distinctly that they were trees, and that what coiled round were snakes. Then there was a rocky prominence, at one side of which was something like a sitting figure, but its shadow, lying on the ground, was that of a girl with a distaff. Jack was very much surprised at all this; Mopsa was not. She did not see, she said, that one thing was more wonderful than another. All the fairy lands were wonderful, but the men-and-women world was far more so. She and Jack went about among the stones all day, and as the sun got low both the shadows and the blocks themselves became more and more like people, and if you went close you could now see features, very sweet, quiet features, but the eyes were all shut.

By this time the apple-woman began to feel very sad. She knew she would soon have to leave Jack and Mopsa, and she said to Mopsa, as they finished their evening meal: "I wish you would ask the inhabitants a few questions, dear, before I go, for I want to know whether they can put you in the way of how to cross the purple mountains."

Jack said nothing, for he thought he would see what Mopsa was going to do; so when she got up, and went towards the shape that was like a cradle he followed, and the apple-woman too. Mopsa went to the figure that sat by the cradle. It was a stone yet, but when Mopsa laid her little warm hand on its bosom it smiled.

"Dear," said Mopsa, "I wish you would wake."

A curious little sound was now heard, but the figure did not move, and the apple-woman lifted Mopsa on to the lap of the statue; then she put her arms round its neck, and spoke to it again very distinctly: "Dear! why don't you wake? You had better wake now; the baby's crying."

Jack now observed that the sound he had heard was something like the crying of a baby. He also heard the figure answering Mopsa. It said: "I am only a stone!"

"Then," said Mopsa, "I am not a queen yet. I cannot wake her. Take me down."

"I am not warm," said the figure; and that was quite true, and yet she was not a stone now which reminded one of a woman, but a woman that reminded one of a stone.

All the west was very red with the sunset, and the river was red too, and Jack distinctly saw some of the coils of rope glide down from the trees and slip into the water; next he saw the stones that had looked like sheep raise up their heads in the twilight, and then lift themselves and shake their woolly sides. At that instant the large white moon heaved up her pale face between two dark blue hills, and upon this the statue put out its feet and gently rocked the cradle.

Then it spoke again to Mopsa: "What was it that you wished me to tell you?"

"How to find the way over those purple mountains," said Mopsa.

"You must set off in an hour, then," said the woman, and she had hardly anything of the stone about her now. "You can easily find it by night without any guide, but nothing can ever take you to it by day."

"But we would rather stay a few days in this curious country," said Jack; "let us wait at least till tomorrow night."

The statue at this moment rubbed her hands together as if they still felt cold and stiff. "You are quite welcome to stay," she observed; "but you had better not."

"Why not?" persisted Jack.

"Father," said the woman, rising and shaking the figure next to her by the sleeve. "Wake up!" what had looked like an old man was a real old man now, and he got up and began to gather sticks to make a fire, and to pick up the little brown stones which had been scattered about all day, but which now were berries of coffee; the larger ones,

which you might find here and there, were rasped rolls.[18]
Then the woman answered Jack: "Why not? Why, because
it's full moon tonight at midnight, and the moment the
moon is past the full your Queen, whose country you have
just left, will be able to cross over the little stream, and she
will want to take you and that other mortal back. She can
do it, of course, if she pleases; and we can afford you no
protection, for by that time we shall be stones again. We
are only people two hours out of the twenty-four."

"That is very hard," observed Jack.

"No," said the women, in a tone of indifference; "it
comes to the same thing, as we live twelve times as long
as others do."

By this time the shepherd was gently driving his flock
down to the water, and round fifty little fires groups of
people were sitting roasting coffee, while cows were lowing
to be milked, and girls with distaffs were coming to them
slowly, for no one was in a hurry there. They say in that
country that they wish to enjoy their day quietly, because
it is so short.

"Can you tell us anything of the land beyond the mountains?" asked Jack.

"Yes," said the woman. "Of all fairy lands it is the best;
the people are the gentlest and kindest."

"Then I had better take Mopsa there than down the
river?" said Jack.

"You can't take her down the river," replied the woman;
and Jack thought she laughed and was glad of that.

"Why not?" asked Jack. "I have a boat."

"Yes, sir," answered the woman, "but where is it now?"

---

18. **rasped rolls** breakfast buns with a rough exterior

CHAPTER THIRTEEN

Melon Seeds

Rosalind. Well, this is the forest of Arden.
Touchstone. Ay, now am I in Arden: the more fool I;
when I was at home I was in a better place; but travellers
must be content.

As You Like It[19]

"Where is it now?" said the stone woman; and when
Jack heard that he ran down to the river, and
looked right and looked left. At last he saw his boat—a
mere speck in the distance, it had floated so far.

He called it, but it was far beyond the reach of his voice;
and Mopsa, who had followed him, said:

"It does not signify, Jack, for I feel that no place is the
right place for me but that country beyond the purple
mountains, and I shall never be happy unless we go there."

So they walked back towards the stone people hand in
hand, and the apple-woman presently joined them. She was
crying gently, for she knew that she must soon pass over the
little stream and part with these whom she called her dear
children. Jack had often spoken to her that day about going
home to her own country, but she said it was too late to think
of that now, and she must end her days in the land of Faery.

The kind stone people asked them to come and sit by their
little fire; and in the dusk the woman whose baby had slept
in a stone cradle took it up and began to sing to it. She
seemed astonished when she heard that the apple-woman had
power to go home if she could make up her mind to do it;
and as she sang she looked at her with wonder and pity.

"Little babe, while burns the west,
Warm thee, warm thee in my breast;
While the moon doth shine her best,
    And the dews distil not.

19. *As You Like It* II.iv.15–18

"All the land so sad, so fair—
Sweet its toils are, blest its care.
Child, we may not enter there!
  Some there are that will not.

"Fain would I thy margins know,
Land of work, and land of snow;
Land of life, whose rivers flow
  On, and on, and stay not.

"Fain would I thy small limbs fold,
While the weary hours are told,
Little babe in cradle cold.
  Some there are that may not."

"You are not exactly fairies, I suppose?" said Jack. "If you were, you could go to our country when you pleased."

"No," said the woman; "we are not exactly fairies; but we shall be more like them when our punishment is over."

"I am sorry you are punished," answered Jack, "for you seem very nice, kind people."

"We were not always kind," answered the woman; "and perhaps we are only kind now because we have no time and no chance of being otherwise. I'm sure I don't know about that. We were powerful once, and we did a cruel deed. I must not tell you what it was. We were told that our hearts were all as cold as stones—and I suppose they were—and we were doomed to be stones all our lives, excepting for the two hours of twilight. There was no one to sow the crops, or water the grass, so it all failed, and the trees died, and our houses fell, and our possessions were stolen from us."

"It is a very sad thing," observed the apple-woman; and then she said that she must go, for she had a long way to walk before she would reach the little brook that led to the country of her own queen; so she kissed the two children, Jack and Mopsa, and they begged her again to think better of it, and return to her own land. But she said No; she had no heart for work now, and could not bear either cold or poverty.

Then the woman who was hugging her little baby, and keeping it cosy and warm, began to tell Jack and Mopsa that it was time they should begin to run away to the country over the purple mountains, or else the Queen would overtake them and be very angry with them; so, with many promises that they would mind her directions, they set off hand in hand to run; but before they left her they could see plainly that she was beginning to turn again into stone. However, she had given them a slice of melon with the seeds in it. It had been growing on the edge of the river, and was stone in the day-time, like everything else. "When you are tired," she said, "eat the seeds, and they will enable you to go running on. You can put the slice into this little red pot, which has string handles to it, and you can hang it on your arm. While you have it with you it will not turn to stone, but if you lay it down it will, and then it will be useless."

So, as I said before, Jack and Mopsa set off hand in hand to run; and as they ran all the things and people gradually and softly settled themselves to turn into stone again. Their cloaks and gowns left off fluttering, and hung stiffly; and then they left off their occupations, and sat down, or lay themselves down; and the sheep and cattle turned stiff and stonelike too, so that in a very little while all that country was nothing but red stones and red sand, just as it had been in the morning.

Presently the full moon, which had been hiding behind a cloud, came out, and they saw their shadows, which fell straight before them; so they ran on hand in hand very merrily till the half-moon came up, and the shadows she made them cast fell sideways. This was rather awkward, because as long as only the full moon gave them shadows they had but to follow them in order to go straight towards the purple mountains. Now they were not always sure which were her shadows; and presently a crescent moon came, and still further confused them; also the sand began to have tufts of grass in it; and then, when they had gone a little farther, there were beautiful patches of anemones, and hyacinths, and jonquils, and crown imperials, and they stopped to gather them; and they got among some trees, and then, as they had nothing to guide them but the shadows, and these went all sorts of ways, they lost a great deal of time, and the trees became of taller growth; but they still ran on and on till they got into a thick forest where it was quite dark, and there Mopsa began to cry, for she was tired.

"If I could only begin to be a queen," she said to Jack, "I could go wherever I pleased. I am not a fairy, and yet I am not a proper queen. Oh, what shall I do? I cannot go any farther."

So Jack gave her some of the seeds of the melon, though it was so dark that he could scarcely find the way to her mouth, and then he took some himself, and they both felt that they were rested, and Jack comforted Mopsa.

"If you are not a queen yet," he said, "you will be by tomorrow morning; for when our shadows danced on before us yours was so very nearly the same height as mine that I could see hardly any difference."

When they reached the end of that great forest, and found themselves out in all sorts of moonlight, the first thing they did was to laugh—the shadows looked so odd, sticking out in every direction; and the next thing they did was to stand back to back, and put their heels together, and touch their heads together, to see by the shadow which was the taller; and Jack was still the least bit in the world taller than Mopsa; so they knew she was not a queen yet, and they ate some more melon seeds, and began to climb up the mountain.

They climbed till the trees of the forest looked no bigger than gooseberry bushes, and then they climbed till the whole forest looked only like a patch of moss; and then, when they got a little higher, they saw the wonderful river, a long way off, and the snow glittering on the peaks overhead; and while they were looking and wondering how they should find a pass, the moons all went down, one after the other, and, if Mopsa had not found some glow-worms, they would have been quite in the dark again. However, she took a dozen of them, and put them round Jack's ankles, so that when he walked he could see where he was going; and he found a little sheep-path, and she followed him.

Now they had noticed during the night how many shooting stars kept darting about from time to time, and at last one shot close by them, and fell in the soft moss on before. There it lay shining; and Jack, though he began to feel tired again, made haste to it, for he wanted to see what it was like.

It was not what you would have supposed. It was soft and round, and about the color of a ripe apricot; it was covered with fur, and in fact it was evidently alive, and had curled itself up into a round ball.

"The dear little thing!" said Jack, as he held it in his hand, and showed it to Mopsa. "How its hearts beats! Is it frightened?"

"Who are you?" said Mopsa to the thing. "What is your name?"

The little creature made a sound that seemed like "Wisp."

"Uncurl yourself, Wisp," said Mopsa. "Jack and I want to look at you."

So Wisp unfolded himself, and showed two little black eyes, and spread out two long filmy wings. He was like a most beautiful bat, and the light he shed out illuminated their faces.

"It is only one of the air fairies," said Mopsa. "Pretty creature! It never did any harm, and would like to do us good if it knew how, for it knows that I shall be a queen very soon. Wisp, if you like, you may go and tell your friends and relations that we want to cross over the mountains, and if they can they may help us."

Upon this Wisp spread out his wings, and shot off again; and Jack's feet were so tired that he sat down and pulled off one of his shoes, for he thought there was a stone in it. So he set the little red jar beside him, and quite forgot what the stone woman had said, but went on shaking his shoe, and buckling it, and admiring the glow-worms round his ankle, till Mopsa said: "Darling Jack, I am so dreadfully tired! Give me some more melon seeds." Then he lifted up the jar, and thought it felt very heavy; and when he put in his hand, jar, and melon, and seeds were all turned to stone together.

They were both very sorry, and they sat still for a minute or two, for they were much too tired to stir; and then shooting stars began to appear in all directions. The fairy bat had told his friends and relations, and they were coming. One fell at Mopsa's feet, another in her lap; more, more, all about, behind, before and over them. And they spread out long filmy wings, some of them a yard long, till Jack and Mopsa seemed to be enclosed in a perfect network of the rays of shooting stars, and they were both a good deal frightened. Fifty or sixty shooting stars, with black eyes that could stare, were enough, they thought, to frighten anybody.

"If we had anything to sit upon," said Mopsa, "they could carry us over the pass." She had no sooner spoken than the largest of the bats bit off one of his own long wings, and laid it at Mopsa's feet. It did not seem to matter much to him that he had parted with it, for he shot out another wing directly, just as a comet shoots out a ray of light sometimes when it approaches the sun.

Mopsa thanked the shooting fairy and, taking the wing, began to stretch it, till it was large enough for her and Jack to sit upon. Then all the shooting fairies came round it, took its edges in their mouths and began to fly away with it over the mountains. They went slowly; for Jack and Mopsa were heavy, and they flew very low, resting now and then; but in the course of time they carried the wing over the pass, and half way down the other side. Then the sun came up; and the moment he appeared all their lovely apricot-colored light was gone, and they only looked like common bats, such as you can see every evening.

They set down Jack and Mopsa, folded up their long wings and hung down their heads.

Mopsa thanked them, and said they had been useful; but still they looked ashamed, and crept into little corners and crevices of the rock, to hide.

CHAPTER FOURTEEN

Reeds and Rushes

'Tis merry, 'tis merry in Fairyland,
　When Fairy birds are singing;
When the court doth ride by their monarch's side,
　With bit and bridle ringing.
                                   WALTER SCOTT

There were many fruit-trees on that slope of the mountain, and Jack and Mopsa, as they came down, gathered some fruit for breakfast, and did not feel very tired, for the long ride on the wing had rested them.

They could not see the plain, for a slight blue mist hung over it; but the sun was hot already, and as they came down they saw a beautiful bed of high reeds, and thought they would sit awhile and rest in it. A rill of clear water ran beside the bed, so when they had reached it they sat down, and began to consider what they should do next.

"Jack," said Mopsa, "did you see anything particular as you came down with the shooting stars?"

"No, I saw nothing so interesting as they were," answered Jack. "I was looking at them and watching how they squeaked to one another, and how they had little hooks in their wings, with which they held the large wing that we sat on."

"But I saw something," said Mopsa. "Just as the sun rose I looked down, and in the loveliest garden I ever saw, and all among trees and woods, I saw a most beautiful castle. Oh, Jack! I am sure that castle is the place I am to live in, and now we have nothing to do but to find it. I shall soon be a queen, and there I shall reign."

"Then I shall be king there," said Jack; "shall I?"

"Yes, if you can," answered Mopsa. "Of course, whatever you can do you may do. And, Jack, this is a much better fairy country than either the stony land or the other that we first came to, for this castle is a real place! It will not melt away. There the people can work, they know how to love each other: common fairies cannot do that, I know. They can laugh and cry, and I shall teach them several things that they do not know yet. Oh, do let us make haste and find the castle!''

So they arose; but they turned the wrong way, and by mistake walked farther and farther in among the reeds, whose feathery heads puffed into Mopsa's face, and Jack's coat was all covered with the fluffy seed.

''This is very odd,'' said Jack. ''I thought this was only a small bed of reeds when we stepped into it; but really we must have walked a mile already.''

But they walked on and on, till Mopsa grew quite faint, and her sweet face became very pale, for she knew that the beds of reeds were spreading faster than they walked, and then they shot up so high that it was impossible to see over their heads; so at last Jack and Mopsa were so tired that they sat down, and Mopsa began to cry.

However, Jack was the braver of the two this time, and he comforted Mopsa, and told her that she was nearly a queen, and would never reach her castle by sitting still. So she got up and took his hand, and he went on before, parting the reeds and pulling her after him, till all on a sudden they heard the sweetest sound in the world: it was like a bell, and it sounded again and again.

It was the castle clock, and it was striking twelve at noon.

As it finished striking they came out at the farther edge of the great bed of reeds, and there was the castle straight before them—a beautiful castle, standing on the slope of a hill. The grass all about it was covered with beautiful flowers; two of the taller turrets were overgrown with ivy, and a flag was flying on a staff; but everything was so silent and lonely that it made one sad to look on. As Jack and Mopsa drew near they trod as gently as they could, and did not say a word.

All the windows were shut, but there was a great door in the center of the building, and they went towards it, hand in hand.

What a beautiful hall! The great door stood wide open, and they could see what a delightful place this must be to live in: it was paved with squares of blue and white marble, and here and there carpets were spread, with chairs and tables upon them. They looked and saw a great dome overhead, filled with windows of colored glass, and they cast down blue and golden and rosy reflections.

"There is my home that I shall live in," said Mopsa; and she came close to the door, and they both looked in, till at last she let go of Jack's hand, and stepped over the threshold.

The bell in the tower sounded again more sweetly than ever, and the instant Mopsa was inside there came from behind the fluted columns, which rose up on every side, the brown doe, followed by troops of deer and fawns!

"Mopsa! Mopsa!" cried Jack. "Come away! come back!" But Mopsa was too much astonished to stir, and something seemed to hold Jack from following; but he looked and looked, till, as the brown doe advanced, the door of the castle closed—Mopsa was shut in, and Jack was left outside.

So Mopsa had come straight to the place she thought she had run away from.

"But I am determined to get her away from those creatures," thought Jack; "she does not want to reign over deer." And he began to look about him, hoping to get in. It was of no use: all the windows in the front of the castle were high, and when he tried to go round, he came to a high wall with battlements. Against some parts of this wall the ivy grew, and looked as if it might have grown there for ages; its stems were thicker than his waist, and its branches were spread over the surface like network; so by means of them he hoped to climb to the top.

He immediately began to try. Oh, how high the wall was! First he came to several sparrows' nests, and very much frightened the sparrows were; then he reached the starlings' nests, and very angry the starlings were; but at last, just under the coping, he came to jackdaws' nests, and these birds were very friendly, and pointed out to him the best little holes for him to put his feet into. At last he reached the top, and found to his delight that the wall was three feet thick, and he could walk upon it quite comfortably, and look down into a lovely garden, where all the trees were in blossom, and creepers tossed their long tendrils from tree to tree, covered with puffs of yellow, or bells of white, or bunches and knots of blue or rosy bloom.

He could look down into the beautiful empty rooms of the castle, and he walked cautiously on the wall till he came to the west front, and reached a little casement window that had latticed panes. Jack peeped in; nobody was there. He took his knife and cut away a little bit of lead to let out the pane, and it fell with such a crash on the pavement below that he wondered it did not bring the deer over to look at what he was about. Nobody came.

He put in his hand and opened the latchet, and with very little trouble got down into the room. Still nobody was to be seen. He thought that the room, years ago, might have been a fairies' schoolroom, for it was strewn with books, slates and all sorts of copybooks. A fine soft dust had settled down over everything—pens, papers and all. Jack opened a copybook: its pages were headed with maxims, just as ours are, which proved that these fairies must have been superior to such as he had hitherto come among. Jack read some of them:

Turn your back on the light, and you'll follow a shadow.
The deaf queen Fate has dumb courtiers.
If the hound is your foe, don't sleep in his kennel.
That that is, is.

And so on; but nobody came, and no sound was heard, so he opened the door, and found himself in a long and most splendid gallery, all hung with pictures, and spread with a most beautiful carpet, which was as soft and white as a piece of wool, and wrought with a beautiful device. This was the letter M, with a crown and sceptre, and underneath a beautiful little boat, exactly like the one in which he had come up the river. Jack felt sure that this carpet had been made for Mopsa, and he went along the gallery upon it till he reached a grand staircase of oak that was almost black with age, and he stole gently down it, for he began to feel rather shy, more especially as he could now see the great hall under the dome, and that it had a beautiful lady in it, and many other people, but no deer at all.

These fairy people were something like the one-foot-one fairies, but much larger and more like children, and they had very gentle, happy faces, and seemed to be extremely glad and gay. But seated on a couch, where lovely painted windows threw down all sorts of rainbow colors on her, was a beautiful fairy lady, as large as a woman. She had

Mopsa in her arms, and was looking down upon her with eyes full of love, while at her side stood a boy, who was exactly and precisely like Jack himself. He had rather long light hair and grey eyes, and a velvet jacket. That was all Jack could see at first, but as he drew nearer the boy turned, and then Jack felt as if he was looking at himself in the glass.

Mopsa had been very tired, and now she was fast asleep, with her head on that lady's shoulder. The boy kept looking at her, and he seemed very happy indeed; so did the lady, and she presently told him to bring Jack something to eat.

It was rather a curious speech that she made to him: it was this:

"Jack, bring Jack some breakfast."

"What!" thought Jack to himself. "Has he got a face like mine, and a name like mine too?"

So that other Jack went away, and presently came back with a golden plate full of nice things to eat.

"I know you don't like me," he said, as he came up to Jack with the plate.

"Not like him?" repeated the lady; "and pray, what reason have you for not liking my royal nephew?"

"Oh, dame!" exclaimed the boy, and laughed.

The lady, on hearing this, turned pale, for she perceived that she herself had mistaken the one for the other.

"I see you know how to laugh," said the real Jack. "You are wiser people than those whom I went to first; but the reason I don't like you is that you are so exactly like me."

"I am not!" exclaimed the boy. "Only hear him, dame! You mean, I suppose, that you are so exactly like me. I am sure I don't know what you mean by it."

"Nor I either," replied Jack, almost in a passion.

"It couldn't be helped, of course," said the other Jack.

"Hush! hush!" said the fairy woman. "Don't wake our dear little Queen. Was it you, my royal nephew, who spoke out last?"

"Yes, dame," answered the boy, and again he offered the plate; but Jack was swelling with indignation, and he gave the plate a push with his elbow, which scattered the fruit and bread on the ground.

"I won't eat it," he said; but when he other Jack went and picked it up again, and said: "Oh yes, do, old fellow;

it's not my fault, you know," he began to consider that it was no use being cross in Fairyland; so he forgave his double, and had just finished his breakfast when Mopsa woke.

CHAPTER FIFTEEN

The Queen's Wand

One, two, three, four; one, two, three four;
  'Tis still one, two, three, four.
Mellow and silvery are the tones,
  But I wish the bells were more.

SOUTHEY

Mopsa woke: she was rather too big to be nursed, for she was the size of Jack, and looked like a sweet little girl of ten years, but she did not always behave like one; sometimes she spoke as wisely as a grown-up woman, and sometimes she changed again and seemed like a child.

Mopsa lifted up her head and pushed back her long hair: her coronet had fallen off while she was in the bed of reeds; and she said to the beautiful dame:

"I am a queen now."

"Yes, my sweet Queen," answered the lady, "I know you are."

"And you promise that you will be kind to me till I grow up," said Mopsa, "and love me, and teach me how to reign?"

"Yes," repeated the lady; " and I will love you too, just as if you were a mortal and I your mother."

"For I am only ten years old yet," said Mopsa, "and the throne is too big for me to sit upon; but I am a queen." And then she paused, and said: "Is it three o'clock?"

As she spoke the sweet clear bell of the castle sounded three times, and then chimes began to play; they played such a joyous tune that it made everybody sing. The dame sang, the crowd of fairies sang, the boy who was Jack's double sang and Mopsa sang—only Jack was silent—and this was the song:

"The prince shall to the chase again,
The dame has got her face again,
The king shall have his place again
   Aneath the fairy dome.

"And all the knights shall woo again,
And all the doves shall coo again,
And all the dreams come true again,
   And Jack shall go home."

"We shall see about that!" thought Jack to himself. And Mopsa, while she sang those last words, burst into tears, which Jack did not like to see; but all the fairies were so very glad, so joyous and so delighted with her for having come to be their queen, that after a while she dried her eyes, and said to the wrong boy:

"Jack, when I pulled the lining out of your pocket-book there was a silver fourpence in it."

"Yes," said the real Jack, "and here it is."

"Is it real money?" asked Mopsa. "Are you sure you brought it with you all the way from your own country?"

"Yes," said Jack, "quite sure."

"Then, dear Jack," answered Mopsa, "will you give it to me?"

"I will," said Jack, "if you will send this boy away."

"How can I?" answered Mopsa, surprised. "Don't you know what happened when the door closed? Has nobody told you?"

"I did not see anyone after I got into the place," said Jack. "There was no one to tell anything—not even a fawn, nor the brown doe. I have only seen down here these fairy people, and this boy, and this lady."

"The lady is the brown doe," answered Mopsa; "and this boy and the fairies were the fawns." Jack was so astonished at this that he stared at the lady and the boy and the fairies with all his might.

"The sun came shining in as I stepped inside," said Mopsa, "and a long beam fell down from the fairy dome across my feet. Do you remember what the apple-woman told us—how it was reported that the brown doe and her nation had a queen whom they shut up, and never let the sun shine on her? That was not a kind or true report, and yet it came from something that really happened."

"Yes, I remember," said Jack; "and if the sun did shine they were all to be turned into deer."

"I dare not tell you all that story yet," said Mopsa; "but, Jack, as the brown doe and all the fawns came up to greet me, and passed by turns into the sunbeam, they took their own forms, every one of them, because the spell was broken. They were to remain in the disguise of deer till a queen of alien birth should come to them against her will. I am a queen of alien birth, and did not I come against my will?"

"Yes, to be sure," answered Jack. "We thought all the time that we were running away."

"If ever you come to Fairyland again," observed Mopsa, "you can save yourself the trouble of trying to run away from the old mother."

"I shall not 'come,' " answered Jack, "because I shall not go—not for a long while, at least. But the boy—I want to know why this boy turned into another ME?"

"Because he is the heir, of course," answered Mopsa.

"But I don't see that this is any reason at all," said Jack. Mopsa laughed." That's because you don't know how to argue," she replied. "Why, the thing is as plain as possible."

"It may be plain to you," persisted Jack, "but it's no reason."

"No reason!" repeated Mopsa. "No reason! when I like you the best of anything in the world, and when I am come here to be queen! Of course, when the spell was broken he took exactly your form on that account; and very right too."

"But why?" asked Jack.

Mopsa, however, was like other fairies in this respect—that she knew all about Old Mother Fate, but not about causes and reasons. She believed, as we do in this world, that

That that is, is,

but the fairies go further than this; they say:

That that is, is; and when it is, that is the reason that it is.

This sounds like nonsense to us, but it is all right to them.

So Mopsa, thinking she had explained everything, said again:

"And, dear Jack, will you give the silver fourpence to me?"

Jack took it out; and she got down from the dame's knee and took it in the palm of her hand, laying the other palm upon it.

"It will be very hot," observed the dame.

"But it will not burn me so as really to hurt, if I am a real queen," said Mopsa.

Presently she began to look as if something gave her pain.

"Oh, it's so hot!" she said to the other Jack; "so very hot!"

"Never mind, sweet Queen," he answered; "it will not hurt you long. Remember my poor uncle and all his knights."

Mopsa still held the little silver coin; but Jack saw that it hurt her, for two bright tears fell from her eyes; and in another moment he saw that it was actually melted, for it fell in glittering drops from Mopsa's hand to the marble floor, and there it lay as soft as quicksilver.

"Pick it up," said Mopsa to the other Jack; and he instantly did so, and laid it in her hand again; and she began gently to roll it backwards and forwards between her palms till she had rolled it into a very slender rod, two feet long, and not nearly so thick as a pin; but it did not bend, and it shone so brightly that you could hardly look at it.

Then she held it out towards the real Jack, and said: "Give this a name."

"I think it is a—" began the other Jack; but the dame suddenly stopped him. "Silence, sire! Don't you know that what it is first called that it will be?"

Jack hesitated; he thought if Mopsa was a queen the thing ought to be a sceptre; but it was certainly not at all like a sceptre.

"That thing is a wand," said he.

"You are a wand," said Mopsa, speaking to the silver stick, which was glittering now in a sunbeam almost as if it were a beam of light itself. Then she spoke again to Jack:

"Tell me, Jack, what can I do with a wand?"

Again the boy king began to speak, and the dame stopped him, and again Jack considered. He had heard a great deal in his own country about fairy wands, but he could not remember that the fairies had done anything particular with them, so he gave what he thought was true, but what seemed to him a very stupid answer:

"You can make it point to anything that you please."

The moment he said this, shouts of ecstasy filled the hall, and all the fairies clapped their hands with such hurrahs of delight that he blushed for joy.

The dame also looked truly glad, and as for the other Jack, he actually turned head over heels, just as Jack had often done himself on his father's lawn.

Jack had merely meant that Mopsa could point with the wand to anything that she saw; but he was presently told that what he had meant was nothing, and that his words were everything.

"I can make it point now," said Mopsa, "and it will point aright to anything I please, whether I know where the thing is or not."

Again the hall was filled with those cries of joy, and the sweet childlike fairies congratulated each other with "The Queen has got a wand—a wand! and she can make it point wherever she pleases!"

Then Mopsa rose and walked towards the beautiful staircase, the dame and all the fairies following. Jack was going too, but the other Jack held him.

"Where is Mopsa going? and why am I not to follow?" inquired Jack.

"They are going to put on her robes, of course," answered the other Jack.

"I am so tired of always hearing you say 'of course,'" answered Jack; "and I wonder how it is that you always seem to know what is going to be done without being told. However, I suppose you can't help being odd people."

The boy king did not make a direct answer; he only said: "I like you very much, though you don't like me."

"Why do you like me?" asked Jack.

The other opened his eyes wide with surprise. "Most boys say Sire to me," he observed; "at least they used to when there were any boys here. However, that does not signify. Why, of course I like you, because I am so tired of being always a fawn, and you brought Mopsa to break the spell. You cannot think how disagreeable it is to have no

hands, and to be all covered with hair. Now look at my
hands; I can move them and turn them everywhere, even
over my head if I like. Hoofs are good for nothing in com-
parison: and we could not talk."

"Do tell me about it," said Jack. "How did you become fawns?"

"I dare not tell you," said the boy; "and listen—I hear
Mopsa."

Jack looked, and certainly Mopsa was coming, but very
strangely, he thought. Mopsa, like all other fairies, was
afraid to whisper a spell with her eyes open; so a handkerchief was tied across them, and as she came on she felt her
way, holding by the banister with one hand, and with the
other, between her finger and thumb, holding out the silver
wand. She felt with her foot for the edge of the first stair;
and Jack heard her say: I am much older—ah! so much
older, now I have got my wand. I can feel sorrow too, and
their sorrow weighs down my heart."

Mopsa was dressed superbly in a white satin gown, with
a long, long train of crimson velvet which was glittering
with diamonds; it reached almost from one end of the great
gallery to the other, and had hundreds of fairies to hold it
and keep it in its place. But in her hair were no jewels,
only a little crown made of daisies, and on her shoulders
her robe was fastened with the little golden image of a
boat. These things were to show the land she had come
from and the vessel she had come in.

So she came slowly, slowly downstairs blindfold, and
muttering to her wand all the time.

> "Though the sun shine brightly,
> Wand, wand, guide rightly."

So she felt her way down to the great hall. There the wand
turned half round in the hall towards the great door, and
she and Jack and the other Jack came out on to the lawn
in front with all the followers and train-bearers; only the
dame remained behind.

Jack noticed now for the first time that, with the one
exception of the boy-king, all these fairies were lady-fairies;
he also observed that Mopsa, after the manner of fairy

queens, though she moved slowly and blindfold, was beginning to tell a story. This time it did not make him feel sleepy. It did not begin at the beginning: their stories never do.

These are the first words he heard, for she spoke softly and very low, while he walked at her right hand, and the other Jack on her left:

"And so now I have no wings. But my thoughts can go up (Jovinian and Roxaletta could not think). My thoughts are instead of wings; but they have dropped with me now, as a lark among the clods of the valley. Wand, do you bend? Yes, I am following, wand.

"And after that the bird said: 'I will come when you call me.' I have never seen her moving overhead; perhaps she is out of sight. Flocks of birds hover over the world, and watch it high up where the air is thin. There are zones, but those in the lowest zone are far out of sight.

"I have not been up there. I have no wings.

"Over the highest of the birds if the place where angels float and gather the children's souls as they are set free.

"And so that woman told me—(Wand, you bend again, and I will turn at your bending)—that woman told me how it was: for when the new king was born, a black fairy with a smiling face came and sat within the doorway. She had a spindle, and would always spin. She wanted to teach them how to spin, but they did not like her, and they loved to do nothing at all. So they turned her out.

"But after her came a brown fairy, with a grave face, and she sat on the black fairy's stool and gave them much counsel. They liked that still less; so they got spindles and spun, for they said: 'She will go now, and we shall have the black fairy again.' When she did not go they turned her out also, and after her came a white fairy, and sat in the same seat. She did nothing at all, and she said nothing at all; but she had a sorrowful face, and she looked up. So they were displeased. They turned her out also; and she went and sat by the edge of the lake with her two sisters.

"And everything prospered over all the land; till, after shearing-time, the shepherds, because the king was a child, came to his uncle, and said: 'Sir, what shall we do with the old wool, for the new fleeces are in the bales, and there is no storehouse to put them in?' So he said: 'Throw them into the lake.'

"And while they threw them in, a great flock of finches flew to them, and said: 'Give us some of the wool that you do not want; we should be glad of it to build our nests with.'

"They answered: 'Go and gather for yourselves; there is wool on every thorn.'

"Then the black fairy said: 'They shall be forgiven this time, because the birds should pick wool for themselves.'

"So the finches flew away.

"Then the harvest was over, and the reapers came and said to the child king's uncle: 'Sir, what shall we do with the new wheat, for the old is not half eaten yet, and there is no room in the granaries?'

"He said: 'Throw that into the lake also.'

"While they were throwing it in, there came a great flight of the wood fairies, fairies of passage from over the sea. They were in the form of pigeons, and they alighted and prayed them: 'O cousins! we are faint with our long flight; give us some of that corn which you do not want, that we may peck it and be refreshed.'

"But they said: 'You may rest on our land, but our corn is our own. Rest awhile, and go and get food in your own fields.'

"Then the brown fairy said: 'They may be forgiven this once, but yet it is a great unkindness.'

"And as they were going to pour in the last sackful, there passed a poor mortal beggar, who had strayed in from the men and women's world, and she said: 'Pray give me some of that wheat, O fairy people! for I am hungry, I have lost my way, and there is no money to be earned here. Give me some of that wheat, that I may bake cakes, lest I and my baby should starve.'

"And they said: 'What is starve? We never heard that word before, and we cannot wait while you explain it to us.'

"So they poured it all into the lake; and then the white fairy said: 'This cannot be forgiven them;' and she covered her face with her hands and wept. Then the black fairy rose and drove them all before her—the prince, with his chief shepherd and his reapers, his courtiers and his knights; she drove them into the great bed of reeds, and

no one had ever set eyes on them since. Then the brown
fairy went into the palace where the king's aunt sat, with
all her ladies and her maids about her, and with the child
king on her knee.

"It was a very gloomy day.

"She stood in the middle of the hall, and said: 'Oh, you
cold-hearted and most unkind! my spell is upon you, and
the first ray of sunshine shall bring it down. Lose your
present forms, and be of a more gentle and innocent race,
till a queen of alien birth shall come to reign over you
against her will.'

"As she spoke they crept into corners, and covered the
dame's head with a veil. And all that day it was dark and
gloomy, and nothing happened, and all the next day it
rained and rained; and they thrust the dame into a dark
closet, and kept her there for a whole month, and still not
a ray of sunshine came to do them any damage; but the
dame faded and faded in the dark, and at last they said:
'She must come out, or she will die; and we do not believe
the sun will ever shine in our country any more.' So they
let the poor dame come out; and lo! as she crept slowly
forth under the dome, a piercing ray of sunlight darted
down upon her head, and in an instant they were all
changed into deer, and the child king too.

"They are gentle now, and kind; but where is the prince?
Where are the fairy knights and fairy men?

"Wand! why do you turn?"

Now while Mopsa told her story the wand continued to
bend, and Mopsa, following, was slowly approaching the
foot of a great precipice, which rose sheer up for more than
a hundred feet. The crowd that followed looked dismayed
at this: they thought the wand must be wrong; or even if it
was right, they could not climb a precipice.

But still Mopsa walked on blindfold, and the wand
pointed at the rock till it touched it, and she said: "Who is
stopping me?"

They told her, and she called to some of her ladies to
untie the handkerchief. Then Mopsa looked at the rock,
and so did the two Jacks. There was nothing to be seen
but a very tiny hole. The boy-king thought it led to a bees'
nest, and Jack thought it was a keyhole, for he noticed in

the rock a slight crack which took the shape of an arched
door. Mopsa looked earnestly at the hole. "It may be a
keyhole," she said, "but there is no key."

CHAPTER SIXTEEN

Failure

We are much bound to them that do succeed;
   But, in a more pathetic sense, are bound
   To such as fail. They all our loss expound;
They comfort us for work that will not speed,
And life—itself a failure. Ay, his deed,
   Sweetest in story, who the dusk profound
   Of Hades flooded with entrancing sound,
Music's own tears, was failure. Doth it read
Therefore the worse? Ah, no! So much to dare,
   He fronts the regnant Darkness on its throne.—
So much to do; impetuous even there,
   He pours out love's disconsolate sweet moan—
He wins; but few for that his deed recall:
Its power is in the look which costs him all.[20]

At this moment Jack observed that a strange woman
was standing among them, and that the train-bearing
fairies fell back, as if they were afraid of her. As no one
spoke, he did, and said: "Good morning!"

"Good afternoon!" she answered, correcting him. 'I am
the black fairy. Work is a fine thing. Most people in your
country can work."

"Yes," said Jack.

"There are two spades," continued the fairy woman;
"one for you, and one for your double."

Jack took one of the spades—it was small, and was made
of silver; but the other Jack said with scorn:

20. **costs him all** Orpheus, the son of a Muse, managed to rescue his
wife Eurydice through the power of his lyre, but lost her by looking
back at Hades before they had reached the safety of the upper world.

"I shall be a king when I am old enough, and must I dig like a clown?"

"As you please," said the black fairy, and walked away.

Then they all observed that a brown woman was standing there; and she stepped up and whispered in the boy king's ear. As he listened his sullen face became good tempered, and at last he said, in a gentle tone: "Jack, I'm quite ready to begin if you are."

"But where are we to dig?" asked Jack.

"There," said a white fairy, stepping up and setting her foot on the grass just under the little hole. "Dig down as deep as you can."

So Mopsa and the crowd stood back, and the two boys began to dig; and greatly they enjoyed it, for people can dig so fast in Fairyland.

Very soon the hole was so deep that they had to jump into it, because they could not reach the bottom with their spades. "This is very jolly indeed," said Jack, when they had dug so much deeper that they could only see out of the hole by standing on tiptoe.

"Go on," said the white fairy; so they dug till they came to a flat stone, and then she said: "Now you can stamp. Stamp on the stone, and don't be afraid." So the two Jacks began to stamp, and in such a little time that she had only half turned her head round, the flat stone gave way, for there was a hollow underneath it, and down went the boys, and utterly disappeared.

Then, while Mopsa and the crowd silently looked on, the white fairy lightly pushed the clods of earth towards the hole with the side of her foot, and in a very few minutes the hole was filled in, and that so completely and so neatly that when she had spread the turf on it, and given it a pat with her foot, you could not have told where it had been. Mopsa said not a word, for no fairy ever interferes with a stronger fairy; but she looked on earnestly, and when the white stranger smiled she was satisfied.

Then the white stranger walked away, and Mopsa and the fairies sat down on a bank under some splendid cedar trees. The beautiful castle looked fairer than ever in the afternoon sunshine; a lovely waterfall tumbled with a tinkling noise near to hand, and the bank was covered with beautiful wild flowers.

They sat for a long while, and no one spoke: what they were thinking of is not known, but sweet Mopsa often sighed.

At last a noise—a very, very slight noise, as of footsteps of people running—was heard inside the rock, and then a little quivering was seen in the wand. It quivered more and more as the sound increased. At last that which had looked like a door began to shake as if someone was pushing it from within. Then a noise was distinctly heard as of a key turning in the hole, and out burst the two Jacks, shouting for joy, and a whole troop of knights and squires and serving-men came rushing wildly forth behind them.

Oh, the joy of that meeting! Who shall describe it? Fairies by dozens came up to kiss the boy king's hand, and Jack shook hands with everyone that could reach him. Then Mopsa proceeded to the castle between the two Jacks, and the king's aunt came out to meet them, and welcomed her husband with tears of joy; for these fairies could laugh and cry when they pleased, and they naturally considered this a great proof of superiority.

After this a splendid feast was served under the great dome. The other fairy feasts that Jack had seen were nothing to it. The prince and his dame sat at one board, but Mopsa sat at the head of the great table, with the two Jacks one on each side of her.

Mopsa was not happy, Jack was sure of that, for she often sighed; and he thought this strange. But he did not ask her any questions, and he, with the boy king, related their adventures to her: how, when the stone gave way, they tumbled in and rolled down a sloping bank till they found themselves at the entrance of a beautiful cave, which was all lighted up with torches, and glittering with stars and crystals of all the colours in the world. There was a table spread with what looked like a splendid luncheon in this great cave, and chairs were set round, but Jack and the boy-king felt no inclination to eat anything, though they were hungry, for a whole nation of ants were creeping up the honey-pots. There were snails walking about over the tablecloth, and toads peeping out of some of the dishes.

So they turned away and, looking for some other door to lead them farther in, they at last found a very small one—so small that only one of them could pass through at a time.

They did not tell Mopsa all that had occurred on this occasion. It was thus:

The boy-king said: "I shall go in first, of course, because of my rank."

"Very well," said Jack, "I don't mind. I shall say to myself that you've gone in first to find the way for me, because you're my double. Besides, now I think of it, our Queen always goes last in a procession; so it's grand to go last. Pass in, Jack."

"No," answered the other Jack; "now you have said that, I will not. You may go first."

So they began to quarrel and argue about this, and it is impossible to say how long they would have gone on if they had not begun to hear a terrible and mournful sort of moaning and groaning, which frightened them both and instantly made them friends. They took tight hold of one another's hand, and again there came a loud sighing, and a noise of all sorts of lamentation, and it seemed to reach them through the little door.

Each of the boys would now have been very glad to go back, but neither liked to speak. At last Jack thought anything would be less terrible than listening to those dismal moans, so he suddenly dashed through the door, and the other Jack followed.

There was nothing terrible to be seen. They found themselves in a place like an immensely long stable; but it was nearly dark, and when their eyes got used to the dimness they saw that it was strewn with quantities of fresh hay, from which curious things like sticks stuck up in all directions. What were they?

"They are dry branches of trees," said the boy-king.

"They are table legs turned upside down," said Jack, but then the other Jack suddenly perceived the real nature of the thing, and he shouted out: "No; they are antlers!"

The moment he said this the moaning ceased, hundreds of beautiful antlered heads were lifted up and the two boys stood before a splendid herd of stags; but they had had hardly time to be sure of this when the beautiful multitude rose and fled away into the darkness, leaving the two boys to follow as well as they could.

They were sure they ought to run after the herd, and
they ran, but they soon lost sight of it, though they heard
far on in front what seemed at first like a pattering of deers'
feet, but the sound changed from time to time. It became
heavier and louder, and then the clattering ceased, and it
was evidently the tramping of a great crowd of men. At
last they heard words, very glad and thankful words; people
were crying to one another to make haste, lest the spell
should come upon them again. Then the two Jacks, still
running, came into a grand hall, which was quite full of
knights and all sorts of fairy men, and there was the boy
king's uncle, but he looked very pale. "Unlock the door!"
they cried. "We shall not be safe till we see our new Queen.
Unlock the door; we see light coming through the
keyhole."

The two Jacks came on to the front, and felt and shook
the door. At last the boy-king saw a little golden key glittering on the floor, just where the one narrow sunbeam fell
that came through the keyhole; so he snatched it up. It
fitted, and out they all came, as you have been told.

When they had done relating their adventures, the new
Queen's health was drunk. And then they drank the health
of the boy-king, who stood up to return thanks, and, as is
the fashion there, he sang a song. Jack thought it the most
ridiculous song he had ever heard; but as everybody else
looked extremely grave, he tried to be grave too. It was
about Cock Robin and Jenny Wren, how they made a wedding feast,[21] and how the wren said she should wear her
brown gown, and the old dog brought a bone to the feast.

> " 'He had brought them,' he said, 'some meat on a bone:
> They were welcome to pick it or leave it alone.' "

The fairies were very attentive to this song; they seemed,
if one may judge by their looks, to think it was rather a
serious one. Then they drank Jack's health, and afterwards
looked at him as if they expected him to sing too; but as

21. **wedding feast** Jack fails to see that the "ridiculous" song is directed at himself; the nursery rhyme is intended to remind Jack of
"Jenny," the name he is trying to repress, and to prepare him for
his displacement.

he did not begin, he presently heard them whispering, and one asking another: "Do you think he knows manners?"

So he thought he had better try what he could do, and he stood up and sang a song that he had often heard his nurse sing in the nursery at home.

"One morning, oh! so early, my beloved, my beloved,
All the birds were singing blithely, as if never they
   would cease;
'Twas a thrush sang in my garden, 'Hear the story, hear
   the story!'
      And the lark sang, 'Give us glory!'
      And the dove said, 'Give us peace!'

"Then I listened, Oh! so early, my beloved, my beloved,
To that murmur from the woodland of the dove, my
   dear, the dove;
When the nightingale came after, 'Give us fame to
   sweeten duty!'
      When the wren sang, 'Give us beauty!'
      She made answer, 'Give us love!'

"Sweet is spring, and sweet the morning, my beloved,
   my beloved;
Now for us doth spring, doth morning, wait upon the
   year's increase,
And my prayer goes up, 'Oh, give us, crowned in youth
   with marriage glory,
      Give for all our life's dear story,
      Give us love, and give us peace!' "

"A very good song too," said the dame, at the other end of the table, "only you made a mistake in the first verse. What the dove really said was, no doubt, 'Give us peas.' All kinds of doves and pigeons are very fond of peas."

"It isn't peas, though," said Jack. However, the court historian was sent for to write down the song, and he came with a quill pen, and wrote it down as the dame said it ought to be.

Now all this time Mopsa sat between the two Jacks, and she looked very mournful—she said hardly a word.

When the feast was over, and everything had vanished,

the musicians came in, for there was to be dancing; but while they were striking up the white fairy stepped in, and, coming up, whispered something in Jack's ear; but he could not hear what she said, so she repeated it more slowly, and still he could neither hear nor understand it.

Mopsa did not seem to like the white fairy: she leaned her face on her hand and sighed; but when she found that Jack could not hear the message, she said: "That is well. Cannot you let things alone for this one day?" The fairy then spoke to Mopsa, but she would not listen; she made a gesture of dislike and moved away. So then this strange fairy turned and went out again, but on the doorstep she looked round, and beckoned to Jack to come to her. So he did; and then, as they two stood together outside, she made him understand what she had said. It was this:

"Her name was Jenny, her name was Jenny."

When Jack understood what she said he felt so sorrowful; he wondered why she had told him, and he longed to stay in that great place with Queen Mopsa—his own little Mopsa, whom he had carried in his pocket, and taken care of, and loved.

He walked up and down, up and down, outside, and his heart swelled and his eyes filled with tears. The bells had said he was to go home, and the fairy had told him how to go. Mopsa did not need him, she had so many people to take care of her now; and then there was that boy, so exactly like himself that she would not miss him. Oh, how sorrowful it all was! Had he really come up the fairy river, and seen those strange countries, and run away with Mopsa over those dangerous mountains, only to bring her to the very place she wished to fly from, and there to leave her, knowing that she wanted him no more, and that she was quite content?

No; Jack felt that he could not do that. "I will stay," he said; "they cannot make me leave her. That would be too unkind."

As he spoke he drew near to the great yawning door, and looked in. The fairy folk were singing inside; he could hear their pretty chirping voices, and see their beautiful faces, but he could not bear it, and he turned away.

The sun began to get low, and all the west was dyed with

crimson. Jack dried his eyes, and, not liking to go in, took
one turn more.

"I will go in," he said; "there is nothing to prevent me."
He set his foot on the step of the door, and while he hesitated Mopsa came out to meet him.

"Jack," she said, in a sweet mournful tone of voice. But
he could not make any answer; he only looked at her earnestly, because her lovely eyes were not looking at him,
but far away towards the west.

"He lives there," she said, as if speaking to herself. "He
will play there again, in his father's garden."

Then she brought her eyes down slowly from the rose-
flush in the cloud, and looked at him and said: "Jack."

"Yes," answered Jack; "I am here. What is it that you
wish to say?"

She answered: "I am come to give you back your kiss."

So she stooped forward as she stood on the step, and
kissed him, and her tears fell on his cheek.

"Farewell!" she said, and she turned and went up the
steps and into the great hall; and while Jack gazed at her
as she entered, and would fain have followed, but could
not stir, the great doors closed together again, and he was
left outside.

Then he knew, without having been told, that he should
never enter them any more. He stood gazing at the castle;
but it was still—no more fairy music sounded.

How beautiful it looked in the evening sunshine, and
how Jack cried!

Suddenly he perceived tat reeds were growing up between him and the great doors: the grass, which had all day
grown about the steps, was getting taller; it had long spear-
like leaves, it pushed up long pipes of green stem, and
they whistled.

They were up to his ankles, they were presently up to
his waist; soon they were as high as his head. He drew back
that he might see over them; they sprang up faster as he
retired, and again he went back. It seemed to him that the
castle also receded; there was a long reach of these great
reeds between it and him, and now they were growing behind also, and on all sides of him. He kept moving back
and back: it was of no use, they sprang up and grew yet

more tall, till very shortly the last glimpse of the fairy castle was hidden from his sorrowful eyes.

The sun was just touching the tops of the purple mountains when Jack lost sight of Mopsa's home; but he remembered how he had penetrated the bed of reeds in the morning, and he hoped to have the same good fortune again. So on and on he walked, pressing his way among them as well as he could, till the sun went down behind the mountains, and the rosy sky turned gold color, and the gold began to burn itself away, and then all on a sudden he came to the edge of the reed-bed, and walked out upon a rising ground.

Jack ran up it, looking for the castle. He could not see it, so he climbed a far higher hill; still he could not see it. At last, after a toilsome ascent to the very top of the green mountain, he saw the castle lying so far, so very far off, that its peaks and battlements were on the edge of the horizon, and the evening mist rose while he was gazing, so that all its outlines were lost, and very soon they seemed to mingle with the shapes of the hill and the forest, till they had utterly vanished away.

Then he threw himself down on the short grass. The words of the white fairy sounded in his ears: "Her name was Jenny," and he burst into tears again, and decided to go home.

He looked up into the rosy sky, and held out his arms, and called: "Jenny! O Jenny! come."

In a minute or two he saw a little black mark overhead, a small speck, and it grew larger, and larger, and larger still, as it fell headlong down like a stone. In another instant he saw a red light and a green light, then he heard the winnowing noise of the bird's great wings, and she alighted at his feet, and said: "Here I am."

"I wish to go home," said Jack, hanging down his head and speaking in a low voice, for his heart was heavy because of his failure.

"That is well," answered the bird. She took Jack on her back, and in three minutes they were floating among the clouds.

As Jack's feet were lifted up from Fairyland he felt a little consoled. He began to have a curious feeling, as if this had all happened a good while ago, and then half the sorrow he had felt faded into wonder, and the feeling still grew upon him that these things had passed some great while since, so that he repeated to himself: "It was a long time ago."

Then he fell asleep, and did not dream at all, nor know anything more till the bird woke him.

"Wake up now, Jack," she said; "we are at home."

"So soon!" said Jack, rubbing his eyes. "But it is evening; I thought it would be morning."

"Fairy time is always six hours in advance of your time," said the bird. "I see glow-worms down in the hedge, and the moon is just rising."

They were falling so fast that Jack dared not look; but he saw the church, and the wood, and his father's house, which seemed to be starting up to meet him. In two seconds more the bird alighted, and he stepped down from her back into the deep grass of his father's meadow.

"Goodbye!" she said. "Make haste and run in, for the dews are falling," and before he could ask her one question, or even thank her, she made a wide sweep over the grass, beat her magnificent wings, and soared away.

It was all very extraordinary, and Jack felt shy and ashamed; but he knew he must go home, so he opened the little gate that led into the garden, and stole through the shrubbery, hoping that his footsteps would not be heard.

Then he came out on the lawn, where the flower-beds were, and he observed that the drawing-room window was open, so he came softly towards it and peeped in.

His father and mother were sitting there. Jack was delighted to see them, but he did not say a word, and he wondered whether they would be surprised at his having stayed away so long. His mother sat with her back to the open window, but a candle was burning, and she was reading aloud. Jack listened as she read, and knew that this was not in the least like anything that he had seen in Fairyland, nor the reading like anything that he had heard, and he began to forget the boy-king, and the apple-woman, and even his little Mopsa, more and more.

At last his father noticed him. He did not look at all surprised, but just beckoned to him with his finger to come in. So Jack did, and got upon his father's knee, where he curled himself up comfortably, laid his head on his father's

waistcoat and wondered what he would think if he should
be told about the fairies in somebody else's waistcoat
pocket. He thought, besides, what a great thing a man was;
he had never seen anything so large in Fairyland, nor so
important; so, on the whole, he was glad he had come back,
and felt very comfortable. Then his mother, turning over
the leaf, lifted up her eyes and looked at Jack, but not as
if she was in the least surprised, or more glad to see him
than usual; but she smoothed the leaf with her hand, and
began again to read, and this time it was about the Shepherd Lady

I

"Who pipes upon the long green hill,
  Where meadow grass is deep?
The white lamb bleats but followeth on—
  Follow the clean white sheep.
The dear white lady in yon high tower,
  She hearkeneth in her sleep.

"All in long grass the piper stands,
  Goodly and grave is he:
Outside the tower, at dawn of day,
  The notes of his pipe ring free.
A thought from his heart doth reach to hers:
  'Come down, O lady! to me.'

"She lifts her head, she dons her gown:
  Ah! the lady is fair;
She ties the girdle on her waist,
  And binds her flaxen hair,
And down she stealeth, down and down,
  Down the turret stair.

"Behold him! With the flock he wons
  Along yon grassy lea.
'My shepherd lord, my shepherd love,
  What wilt thou, then, with me?
My heart is gone out of my breast,
  And followeth on to thee.'

II

" 'The white lambs feed in tender grass:
  With them and thee to bide,
How good it were,' she saith at noon;
  'Albeit the meads are wide.
Oh! well is me,' she saith when day
  Draws on to eventide.

"Hark! hark! the shepherd's voice. Oh, sweet!
  Her tears drop down like rain.
'Take now this crook, my chosen, my fere,
  And tend the flock full fain:
Feed them, O lady, and lose not one,
  Till I shall come again.'

"Right soft her speech: 'My will is thine,
  And my reward thy grace!'
Gone are his footsteps over the hill,
  Withdrawn his goodly face;
The mournful dusk begins to gather,
  The daylight wanes apace.

III

"On sunny slopes, ah! long the lady
  Feedeth her flock at noon;
She leads them down to drink at eve
  Where the small rivulets croon.
All night her locks are wet with dew,
  Her eyes outwatch the moon.

"Over the hills her voice is heard,
  She sings when light doth wane:
'My longing heart is full of love.
  When shall my loss be gain?
My shepherd lord, I see him not,
  But he will come again.' "

When she had finished Jack lifted his face and said,
"Mamma!" Then she came to him and kissed him, and his

father said: "I think it must be time this man of ours was in bed."

So he looked earnestly at them both, and as they still asked him no questions, he kissed and wished them good-night; and his mother said there were some strawberries on the sideboard in the dining-room, and he might have them for his supper.

So he ran out into the hall, and was delighted to find all the house just as usual, and after he had looked about him he went into his own room, and said his prayers. Then he got into his little white bed, and comfortably fell asleep.

That's all.

In a field where all too many writers sound alike, Jack Vance's voice has always been unique. I first encountered Vance back in the '50s, in an Ace Double that I bought for thirty-five cents. These days his work is published in beautiful hardcover limited editions that cost somewhat more, but I buy every one the moment I can get my hands on it, and devour them almost before I get them home.

He is a storyteller, a stylist, a poet; you can get drunk on his names alone.

Vance has written more science fiction than fantasy, but he is one of the rare writers who excels at both forms (and at mysteries as well, as his Edgar Award gives proof). His *Lyonesse* novels of the 1980s rank as one of the great fantasy trilogies, and in the *Dying Earth* series he created one of the most memorable imaginary settings of all time, a world to rank with Tolkien's Middle Earth, Fritz Leiber's Nehwon, and Robert E. Howard's Hyborian Age. To populate his haunted ruins, tired hills, and ancient cities, he gave us a cast of characters just as wonderfully varied and colorful: Cugel the Clever, Rhialto the Marvelous, the Laughing Magician, and all the rest.

Liane the Wayfarer was one of the first. *The Dying Earth* began back in 1950 with a slim little volume of stories from an obscure publishing house. Half a century later, every story in that book remains fresh and vivid in my mind. Picking one favorite was no easy task. Turjan of Miir, T'sain and T'sais, Ulan Dhor . . . Guyal of Sfere's haunting quest for the Museum of Man . . . any of them would have been just as worthy of the nod. But in the end I had to choose the tale of Liane the Wayfarer.

It was simply . . . well . . . unavoidable.

—George R. R. Martin

LIANE THE WAYFARER
by Jack Vance

Through the dim forest came Liane the Wayfarer, passing along the shadowed glades with a prancing light-footed gait. He whistled, he caroled, he was plainly in high

spirits. Around his finger he twirled a bit of wrought
bronze—a circlet graved with angular crabbed characters,
now stained black.

By excellent chance he had found it, banded around the
root of an ancient yew. Hacking it free, he had seen the
characters on the inner surface—rude forceful symbols,
doubtless the cast of a powerful antique rune. . . . Best
take it to a magician and have it tested for sorcery.

Liane made a wry mouth. There were objections to the
course. Sometimes it seemed as if all living creatures con-
spired to exasperate him. Only this morning, the spice merchant—what a tumult he had made dying! How carelessly
he had spewed blood on Liane's cockscomb sandals! Still,
thought Liane, every unpleasantness carried with it com-
pensation. While digging the grave he had found the
bronze ring.

And Liane's spirits soared; he laughed in pure joy. He
bounded, he leapt. His green cape flapped behind him, the
red feather in his cap winked and blinked. . . . But still—
Liane slowed his step—he was no whit closer to the mystery
of the magic, if magic the ring possessed.

Experiment, that was the word!

He stopped where the ruby sunlight slanted down without hindrance from the high foliage, examined the ring,
traced the glyphs with his fingernail. He peered through. A
faint film, a flicker? He held it at arm's length. It was
clearly a coronet. He whipped off his cap, set the band on
his brow, rolled his great golden eyes, preened himself. . . .
Odd. It slipped down on his ears. It tipped across his eyes.
Darkness. Frantically Liane clawed it off. . . . A bronze
ring, a hand's-breadth in diameter. Queer.

He tried again. It slipped down over his head, his shoulders. His head was in the darkness of a strange separate
space. Looking down, he saw the level of the outside light
dropping as he dropped the ring.

Slowly down. . . . Now it was around his ankles—and in
sudden panic, Liane snatched the ring up over his body,
emerged blinking into the maroon light of the forest.

He saw a blue-white, green-white flicker against the foliage. It was a Twk-man, mounted on a dragon-fly, and light
glinted from the dragon-fly's wings.

Liane called sharply, "Here, sir! Here, sir!"

The Twk-man perched his mount on a twig. "Well, Liane, what do you wish?"

"Watch now, and remember what you see." Liane pulled the ring over his head, dropped it to his feet, lifted it back. He looked up to the Twk-man, who was chewing a leaf. "And what did you see?"

"I saw Liane vanish from mortal sight—except for the red curled toes of his sandals. All else was as air."

"Ha!" cried Liane. "Think of it! Have you ever seen the like?"

The Twk-man asked carelessly, "Do you have salt? I would have salt."

Liane cut his exultations short, eyed the Twk-man closely.

"What news do you bring me?"

"Three erbs killed Florejin the Dream-builder, and burst all his bubbles. The air above the manse was colored for many minutes with the flitting fragments."

"A gram."

"Lord Kandive the Golden has built a barge of carven mo-wood ten lengths high, and it floats on the River Scaum for the Regatta, full of treasure."

"Two grams."

"A golden witch named Lith has come to live on Thamber Meadow. She is quiet and very beautiful."

"Three grams."

"Enough," said the Twk-man, and leaned forward to watch while Liane weighed out the salt in a tiny balance. He packed it in small panniers hanging on each side of the ribbed thorax, then twitched the insect into the air and flicked off through the forest vaults.

Once more Liane tried his bronze ring, and this time brought it entirely past his feet, stepped out of it and brought the ring up into the darkness beside him. What a wonderful sanctuary! A hole whose opening could be hidden inside the hole itself! Down with the ring to his feet, step through, bring it up his slender frame and over his shoulders, out into the forest with a small bronze ring in his hand.

Ho! and off to Thamber Meadow to see the beautiful golden witch.

Her hut was a simple affair of woven reeds—a low dome

with two round windows and a low door. He saw Lith at
the pond bare-legged among the water shoots, catching
frogs for her supper. A white kirtle was gathered up tight
around her thighs; stock-still she stood and the dark water
rippled rings away from her slender knees.

She was more beautiful than Liane could have imagined,
as if one of Florejin's wasted bubbles had burst here on
the water. Her skin was pale creamed stirred gold, her hair
a denser, wetter gold. Her eyes were like Liane's own, great
golden orbs, and hers were wide apart, tilted slightly.

Liane strode forward and planted himself on the bank.

She looked up startled, her ripe mouth half-open.

"Behold, golden witch, here is Liane. He has come to
welcome you to Thamber; and he offers you his friendship,
his love . . ."

Lith bent, scooped a handful of slime from the bank and
flung it into his face.

Shouting the most violent curses, Liane wiped his eyes
free, but the door to the hut had slammed shut.

Liane strode to the door and pounded it with his fist.

"Open and show your witch's face, or I burn the hut!"

The door opened, and the girl looked forth, smiling.
"What now?"

Liane entered the hut and lunged for the girl, but twenty
thin shafts darted out, twenty points pricking his chest. He
halted, eyebrows raised, mouth twitching.

"Down, steel," said Lith. The blades snapped from view.
"So easily could I seek your vitality," said Lith, "had I
willed."

Liane frowned and rubbed his chin as if pondering. "You
understand," he said earnestly, "what a witless thing you
do. Liane is feared by those who fear fear, loved by those
who love love. And you—" his eyes swam the golden glory
of her body—"you are ripe as a sweet fruit, you are eager,
you glisten and tremble with love. You please Liane, and
he will spend much warmness on you."

"No, no," said Lith, with a slow smile. "You are too
hasty."

Liane looked at her in surprise. "Indeed?"

"I am Lith," said she. "I am what you say I am. I fer-
ment, I burn, I seethe. Yet I may have no lover but him
who has served me. He must be brave, swift, cunning."

"I am he," said Liane. He chewed at his lip. "It is not usually thus. I detest this indecision." He took a step forward. "Come, let us—"

She backed away. "No, no. You forget. How have you served me, how have you gained the right to my love?"

"Absurdity!" stormed Liane. "Look at me! Note my perfect grace, the beauty of my form and feature, my great eyes, as golden as your own, my manifest will and power. . . . It is you who should serve me. That is how I will have it." He sank upon a low divan. "Woman, give me wine."

She shook her head. "In my small domed hut I cannot be forced. Perhaps outside on Thamber Meadow—but in here, among my blue and red tassels, with twenty blades of steel at my call, you must obey me. . . . So choose. Either arise and go, never to return, or else agree to serve me on one small mission, and then have me and all my ardor."

Liane sat straight and stiff. An odd creature, the golden witch. But, indeed, she was worth some exertion, and he would make her pay for her impudence.

"Very well, then," he said blandly. "I will serve you. What do you wish? Jewels? I can suffocate you in pearls, blind you with diamonds. I have two emeralds the size of your fist, and they are green oceans, where the gaze is trapped and wanders forever among vertical green prisms . . ."

"No, no jewels—"

"An enemy, perhaps. Ah, so simple. Liane will kill you ten men. Two steps forward, thrust—*thus!*" He lunged. "And souls go thrilling up like bubbles in a beaker of mead."

"No. I want no killing."

He sat back, frowning. "What, then?"

She stepped to the back of the room and pulled at a drape. It swung aside, displaying a golden tapestry. The scene was a valley bounded by two steep mountains, a broad valley where a placid river ran, past a quiet village and so into a grove of trees. Golden was the river, golden the mountains, golden the trees—golds so various, so rich, so subtle that the effect was like a many-colored landscape. But the tapestry had been rudely hacked in half.

Liane was entranced. "Exquisite, exquisite . . ."

Lith said, "It is the Magic Valley of Ariventa so depicted. The other half has been stolen from me, and its recovery is the service I wish of you."

"Where is the other half?" demanded Liane. "Who is the dastard?"

Now she watched him closely. "Have you ever heard of Chun? Chun the Unavoidable?"

Liane considered. "No."

"He stole the half to my tapestry, and hung it in a marble hall, and this hall is in the ruins to the north of Kaiin."

"Ha!" muttered Liane.

"The hall is by the Place of Whispers, and is marked by a leaning column with a black medallion of a phoenix and a two-headed lizard."

"I go," said Liane. He rose. "One day to Kaiin, one day to steal, one day to return. Three days."

Lith followed him to the door. "Beware of Chun the Unavoidable," she whispered.

And Liane strode away whistling, the red feather bobbing in his green cap. Lith watched him, then turned and slowly approached the golden tapestry. "Golden Ariventa," she whispered, "my heart cries and hurts with longing for you . . ."

* * *

The Derna is a swifter, thinner river than the Scaum, its bosomy sister to the south. And where the Scaum wallows through a broad dale, purple with horse-blossom, pocked white and gray with crumbling castles, the Derna has sheered a steep canyon, overhung by forested bluffs.

An ancient flint road long ago followed the course of the Derna, but now the exaggeration of the meandering has cut into the pavement, so that Liane, treading the road to Kaiin, was occasionally forced to leave the road and make a detour through banks of thorn and the tube-grass which whistled in the breeze.

The red sun, drifting across the universe like an old man creeping to his death-bed, hung low to the horizon when Liane breasted Porphiron Scar, looked across white-walled Kaiin and the blue bay of Sanreale beyond.

Directly below was the market-place, a medley of stalls selling fruits, slabs of pale meat, molluscs from the slime banks, dull flagons of wine. And the quiet people of Kaiin moved among the stalls, buying their sustenance, carrying it loosely to their stone chambers.

Beyond the market-place rose a bank of ruined columns, like broken teeth—legs to the arena built two hundred feet from the ground by Mad King Shin; beyond, in a grove of bay trees, the glassy dome of the palace was visible, where Kandive the Golden ruled Kaiin and as much of Ascolais as one could see from a vantage on Porphiron Scar.

The Derna, no longer a flow of clear water, poured through a network of dank canals and subterranean tubes, and finally seeped past rotting wharves into the Bay of Sanreale.

A bed for the night, thought Liane; then to his business in the morning.

He leapt down the zig-zag steps—back, forth, back, forth—and came out into the market-place. And now he put on a grave demeanor. Liane the Wayfarer was not unknown in Kaiin, and many were ill-minded enough to work him harm.

He moved sedately in the shade of the Pannone Wall, turned through a narrow cobbled street, bordered by old wooden houses glowing the rich brown of old stump-water in the rays of the setting sun, and so came to a small square and the high stone face of the Magician's Inn.

The host, a small fat man, sad of eye, with a small fat nose the identical shape of his body, was scraping ashes from the hearth. He straightened his back and hurried behind the counter of his little alcove.

Liane said, "A chamber, well-aired, and a supper of mushrooms, wine and oysters."

The innkeeper bowed humbly.

"Indeed, sir—and how will you pay?"

Liane flung down a leather sack, taken this very morning. The innkeeper raised his eyebrows in pleasure at the fragrance.

"The ground buds of the spase-bush, brought from a far land," said Liane.

"Excellent, excellent. . . . Your chamber, sir, and your supper at once."

As Liane ate, several other guests of the house appeared and sat before the fire with wine, and the talk grew large, and dwelt on wizards of the past and the great days of magic.

"Great Phandaal knew a lore now forgot," said one old man with hair dyed orange. "He tied white and black strings to the legs of sparrows and sent them veering to his direction. And where they wove their magic woof, great trees appeared, laden with flowers, fruits, nuts, or bulbs of rare liqueurs. It is said that thus he wove Great Da Forest on the shores of Sanra Water."

"Ha," said a dour man in a garment of dark blue, brown and black, "this I can do." He brought forth a bit of string, flicked it, whirled it, spoke a quiet word, and the vitality of the pattern fused the string into a tongue of red and yellow fire, which danced, curled, darted back and forth along the table till the dour man killed it with a gesture.

"And this I can do," said a hooded figure in a black cape sprinkled with silver circles. He brought forth a small tray, laid it on the table and sprinkled therein a pinch of ashes from the hearth. He brought forth a whistle and blew a clear tone, and up from the tray came glittering motes, flashing the prismatic colors red, blue, green, yellow. They floated up a foot and burst in coruscations of brilliant colors, each a beautiful star-shaped pattern, and each burst sounded a tiny repetition of the original tone—the clearest, purest sound in the world. The motes became fewer, the magician blew a different tone, and again the motes floated up to burst in glorious ornamental spangles. Another time—another swarm of motes. At last the magician replaced his whistle, wiped off the tray, tucked it inside his cloak and lapsed back to silence.

Now the other wizards surged forward, and soon the air above the table swarmed with visions, quivered with spells. One showed the group nine new colors of ineffable charm and radiance; another caused a mouth to form on the landlord's forehead and revile the crowd, much to the landlord's discomfiture, since it was his own voice. Another displayed a green glass bottle from which the face of a demon peered and grimaced; another a ball of pure crystal which rolled back and forward to the command of the sorcerer who owned it, and who claimed it to be an earring of the fabled master Sankaferrin.

Liane had attentively watched all, crowing in delight at the bottled imp, and trying to cozen the obedient crystal from its owner, without success.

And Liane became pettish, complaining that the world

was full of rock-hearted men, but the sorcerer with the crystal earring remained indifferent, and even when Liane spread out twelve packets of rare spice he refused to part with his toy.

Liane pleaded, "I wish only to please the witch Lith."

"Please her with the spice, then."

Liane said ingenuously, "Indeed, she has but one wish, a bit of tapestry which I must steal from Chun the Unavoidable."

And he looked from face to suddenly silent face.

"What causes such immediate sobriety? Ho, Landlord, more wine!"

The sorcerer with the earring said, "If the floor swam ankle-deep with wine—the rich red wine of Tanvilkat—the leaden print of that name would still ride the air."

"Ha," laughed Liane, "let only a taste of that wine pass your lips, and the fumes would erase all memory."

"See his eyes," came a whisper. "Great and golden."

"And quick to see," spoke Liane. "And these legs—quick to run, fleet as starlight on the waves. And this arm—quick to stab with steel. And my magic—which will set me to a refuge that is out of all cognizance." He gulped wine from a beaker. "Now behold. This is magic from antique days." He set the bronze band over his head, stepped through, brought it up inside the darkness. When he deemed that sufficient time had elapsed, he stepped through once more.

The fire glowed, the landlord stood in his alcove, Liane's wine was at hand. But of the assembled magicians, there was no trace.

Liane looked about in puzzlement. "And where are my wizardly friends?"

The landlord turned his head: "They took to their chambers; the name you spoke weighed on their souls."

And Liane drank his wine in frowning silence.

* * *

Next morning he left the inn and picked a roundabout way to the Old Town—a gray wilderness of tumbled pillars, weathered blocks of sandstone, slumped pediments with crumbled inscriptions, flagged terraces overgrown with rusty moss. Lizards, snakes, insects crawled the ruins; no other life did he see.

Threading a way through the rubble, he almost stumbled on a corpse—the body of a youth, one who stared at the sky with empty eye-sockets.

Liane felt a presence. He leapt back, rapier half-bared. A stooped old man stood watching him. He spoke in a feeble, quavering voice: "And what will you have in the Old Town?"

Liane replaced his rapier. "I seek the Place of Whispers. Perhaps you will direct me."

The old man made a croaking sound at the back of his throat. "Another? Another? When will it cease? . . ." He motioned to the corpse. "This one came yesterday seeking the Place of Whispers. He would steal from Chun the Unavoidable. See him now." He turned away. "Come with me." He disappeared over a tumble of rock.

Liane followed. The old man stood by another corpse with eye-sockets bereft and bloody. "This one came four days ago, and he met Chun the Unavoidable. . . . And over there behind the arch is still another, a great warrior in cloison armor. And there—and there—" he pointed, pointed. "And there—and there—like crushed flies."

He turned his watery blue gaze back to Liane. "Return, young man, return—lest your body lie here in its green cloak to rot on the flagstones."

Liane drew his rapier and flourished it. "I am Liane the Wayfarer; let them who offend me have fear. And where is the Place of Whispers?"

"If you must know," said the old man, "it is beyond that broken obelisk. But you go to your peril."

"I am Liane the Wayfarer. Peril goes with me."

The old man stood like a piece of weathered statuary as Liane strode off.

And Liane asked himself, suppose this old man were an agent of Chun, and at this minute were on his way to warn him? . . . Best to take all precautions. He leapt up on a high entablature and ran crouching back to where he had left the ancient.

Here he came, muttering to himself, leaning on his staff. Liane dropped a block of granite as large as his head. A thud, a croak, a gasp—and Liane went his way.

He strode past the broken obelisk, into a wide court—the Place of Whispers. Directly opposite was a long wide hall, marked by a leaning column with a big black medallion, the sign of a phoenix and a two-headed lizard.

Liane merged himself with the shadow of a wall, and stood watching like a wolf, alert for any flicker of motion.

All was quiet. The sunlight invested the ruins with dreary splendor. To all sides, as far as the eye could reach, was broken stone, a wasteland leached by a thousand rains, until now the sense of man had departed and the stone was one with the natural earth.

The sun moved across the dark-blue sky. Liane presently stole from his vantage-point and circled the hall. No sight nor sign did he see.

He approached the building from the rear and pressed his ear to the stone. It was dead, without vibration. Around the side—watching up, down, to all sides; a breach in the wall. Liane peered inside. At the back hung half a golden tapestry. Otherwise the hall was empty.

Liane looked up, down, this side, that. There was nothing in sight. He continued around the hall.

He came to another broken place. He looked within. To the rear hung the golden tapestry. Nothing else, to right or left, no sight or sound.

Liane continued to the front of the hall and sought into the eaves; dead as dust.

He had a clear view of the room. Bare, barren, except for the bit of golden tapestry.

Liane entered, striding with long soft steps. He halted in the middle of the floor. Light came to him from all sides except the rear wall. There were a dozen openings from which to flee and no sound except the dull thudding of his heart.

He took two steps forward. The tapestry was almost at his fingertips.

He stepped forward and swiftly jerked the tapestry down from the wall.

And behind was Chun the Unavoidable.

Liane screamed. He turned on paralyzed legs and they were leaden, like legs in a dream which refused to run.

Chun dropped out of the wall and advanced. Over his

shiny black back he wore a robe of eyeballs threaded on silk.

Liane was running, fleetly now. He sprang, he soared. The tips of his toes scarcely touched the ground. Out the hall, across the square, into the wilderness of broken statues and fallen columns. And behind came Chun, running like a dog.

Liane sped along the crest of a wall and sprang a great gap to a shattered fountain. Behind came Chun.

Liane darted up a narrow alley, climbed over a pile of refuse, over a roof, down into a court. Behind came Chun.

Liane sped down a wide avenue lined with a few stunted old cypress trees, and he heard Chun close at his heels. He turned into an archway, pulled his bronze ring over his head, down to his feet. He stepped through, brought the ring up inside the darkness. Sanctuary. He was alone in a dark magic space, vanished from earthly gaze and knowledge. Brooding silence, dead space . . .

He felt a stir behind him, a breath of air. At his elbow a voice said, "I am Chun the Unavoidable."

* * *

Lith sat on her couch near the candles, weaving a cap from frogskins. The door to her hut was barred, the windows shuttered. Outside, Thamber Meadow dwelled in darkness.

A scrape at her door, a creak as the lock was tested. Lith became rigid and stared at the door.

A voice said, "Tonight, O Lith, tonight it is two long bright threads for you. Two because the eyes were so great, so large, so golden . . ."

Lith sat quiet. She waited an hour; then, creeping to the door, she listened. The sense of presence was absent. A frog croaked nearby.

She eased the door ajar, found the threads and closed the door. She ran to her golden tapestry and fitted the threads into the ravelled warp.

And she stared at the golden valley, sick with longing for Ariventa, and tears blurred out the peaceful river, the quiet golden forest. "The cloth slowly grows wider . . . One day it will be done, and I will come home. . . ."

Some writers are given a great gift: the ability to weave words of
jewel-color into perfect shapes. Manly Wade Wellman was a master of such craft. John the Balladeer is one of his most beloved
creations: a good man armed with faith, who brings hope to, and
support for, those who deserve his aid. John stands for the Light
against the Dark and, by the power of his singing silver strings,
draws sweet and healing waters from mud and choking weeds.
His magic music shouts to the "mountains so high" and soothes
in the "valley so low." Long may he wander among us to keep
The Spring ever flowing for years to come.

—Andre Norton

THE SPRING
by Manly Wade Wellman

Time had passed, two years of it, when I got back to
those mountains again and took a notion to visit the
spring.

When I was first there, there'd been just a muddy, weedy
hole amongst rocks. A young fellow named Zeb Gossett
lay there, a-burning with fever, a-trying to drink at it. I
pulled him onto some ferns and put my blanket over him.
Then I knelt down and dragged out the mud with my
hands, picked weeds away and bailed with a canteen cup.
Third time I emptied the hole to the bottom, water came
clear and sweet. I let Zeb Gossett have some, and then I
built us a fire and stirred up a hoecake. By the time it was
brown on both sides, he was able to sit up and eat half of it.

Again and again that night, I fetched him water, and it
did him good. When I picked my silver-strung guitar, he
even joined in to sing. Next day he allowed he was well,
and said he'd stay right where such a good thing happened
to him. I went on, for I had something else to do. But I
left Zeb a little sack of meal and a chunk of bacon and
some salt in a tin can. Now, returned amongst mountains
named Hark and Wolter and Dogged, not far from Yandro,

I went up the trail I recollected to see how the spring came on.

The high slope caved in there, to make a hollow grown with walnut and pine and hickory, and the spring showed four feet across, with stones set in all the way round. Beside the shining water hung a gourd ladle. Across the trail was a cabin, and from the cabin door came Zeb Gossett. "John." he called my name, "how you come on?"

We shook hands. He was fine-looking, young, about as tall as I am. His face was tanned and he'd grown a short brown beard. He wore jeans and a home-sewn blue shirt. "Who'd expect I'd find Zeb Gossett here?" I said.

"I live here, John. Built that cabin myself, and I've got title to two acres of land. A corn patch, potatoes and cabbages and beans and tomatoes. It's home. When you knelt down to make that spring give the water that healed me, I knew this was where I'd live. But come on in. I see you still tote that guitar."

His cabin was small but rightly made, of straight poles with neat-notched corner joints, whitewash on the clay chinking. There was glass in the windows to each side of the split-slab door. He led me into a square room with a stone fireplace and two chairs and a table. Three-four books on a shelf. The bed had a blazing-star quilt. Over the fire bubbled an iron pot with what smelled like stewing deer meat.

"Yes, I live here, and the neighborhood folks make me welcome," he said when we sat down. "I knew that spring had holy power. I watch over it and let others heal their ills with it."

"It was just a place I scooped out," I reminded him. "We had to have water for you, so I did it."

"It's cured hundreds of sick folks," he said. "I carried some to the Fleming family when they had flu, then others heard tell of it and came here. They come all the time. I don't take pay. I tell them, 'Kneel down before you drink, the way John did while he was a-digging. And pray before you drink, and give thanks afterwards.' "

"You shouldn't ought to give me such credit, Zeb."

"John," he said, "that's healing water. It washes away air bad thing whatsoever. It helps mend up broken bones even. Why, I've known folks drink it and settle family quarrels and lawsuits. It's a miracle, and you did it."

I wouldn't have that. I said, "Likely the power was in the water before you and I came here. I just cleaned the mud out."

"I know better, and so do you," Zeb grinned at me.

Outside, a sweet voice: "Hello, the house," it spoke. "Hello, Zeb, might could I take some water?"

He jumped up and went out like as if he expected to see angels. I followed him out, and I reckon it was an angel he figured he saw.

She was a slim girl, but not right small. In her straight blue dress and canvas shoes, with her yellow curls water-falled down her back, she was pretty to see. In one hand she toted a two-gallon bucket. She smiled, and that smile made Zeb's knees buck.

"Tilda"—he said her name like a song—"you don't have to ask for water, just dip it. Somebody in your family ailing?"

"No, not exactly." Then her blue eyes saw me and she waited.

"This is my friend John, Tilda," said Zeb. "He dug the spring. John, this is Tilda Fleming. Her folks neighbor with me just round the trail bend."

"Proud to be known to you, ma'am," I made my manners, but she was a-looking at Zeb, half nervous, half happy.

"Who's the water for, then?" he inquired her.

"Why," she said, shy with every word, "that's why I wondered if you'd let me have it. You see, our chickens—" and she stopped again, like as if she felt shamed to tell it.

"Ailing chickens should ought to have whatever will help them, Zeb." I put in a word.

"That's a fact," said Zeb, "and a many a fresh egg your folks have given me, Tilda. So take water for them, please."

She dropped down on her knees and bowed her head above the spring. She was a pretty sight, a-doing that. I could tell that Zeb thought so.

But somebody else watched. I saw a stir beyond some laurel, and looked hard thataway.

It was another girl, older than Tilda, taller. Her hair was blacker than storm, and her pointy-chinned, pale face was lovely. She looked at Tilda a-kneeling by the spring and she sneered, and it showed her teeth as bright as glass beads.

Zeb didn't see her. He bent over Tilda where she knelt, was near about ready to kneel with her. I walked through the yard toward the laurel. That tall, black-haired girl moved into the open and waited for me.

She wore a long dress of tawny, silky stuff, hardly what you'd look for in the mountains. It hung down to her feet, but it held to her figure, and the figure was fine. She looked at me, impudent-faced. "I declare," she said in a sugary-deep voice, "this is the John we hear so much about. A fine-looking man, no doubt in the world about that. But that's a common name."

"I always reckoned it's been borne by a many a good man," I said. "How come you to know me?"

"I heard you and Zeb Gossett a-talking. I can hear at a considerable distance." Her wide, dark eyes crawled over me like spiders. "My name's Craye Sawtelle, John. You and I might could be profitable acquaintances to each other."

"I'm proud to be on good terms with most folks," I said. "You come to visit with Zeb, yonder?"

"Maybe, when that little snip trots her water bucket home." Craye Sawtelle looked at Tilda a-filling the pail, and for a second those bright teeth showed. "I have business to talk with Zeb. Maybe he'll find the wit to hark to it."

Zeb walked Tilda to the trail. Craye Sawtelle had come into the yard with me, and when Tilda walked on and Zeb turned back, Craye said, "Good day to you, Zeb Gossett," and he jumped like as if he'd been stuck with a pin.

"What can I do for you, Miss Craye?" he said.

She ran her eyes over him, too. "You know the answer to that. I'll make you a good offer for this house and this spring."

He shook his head till his young beard flicked in the air. "You know the place isn't for sale, and the spring water's free to all."

"Only if they kneel and pray by it." She smiled a chilly smile. "I'm not a praying sort, Zeb."

"Nobody's heart to kneel before God," said Zeb.

"I don't kneel to your God," she said.

"What god do you kneel to?" I inquired her, and her black eyes blazed round to me.

"You make what educated folks call an educated guess," she said to me. "If you know so much, why should I answer you?"

She turned back to Zeb. "What if I told you there's a question about your title here, that I could gain possession?"

"I'd say, let's go to the court house and find out."

"You're impossible," she shrilled at him. "But I'm reasonable. I'll give you time to think it over. Like sundown tomorrow."

Then she went off away, the other direction from Tilda. In that tawny dress, air line of her swayed.

Just then, the sun looked murkier over us. Here and there amongst the trees, the leaves showed their pale undersides, like before a storm comes.

"Let's go in and have something to eat," Zeb said to me.

It was a good deer-meat stew, with cornmeal dumplings. I had two helps. Zeb said he'd put in onions and garlic and thyme and bay leaf, with a dollop of wine from a bottle he kept for that. We finished up and drank black coffee. While we sipped, a sort of lonesome whinnying sound rose outside.

"That's an owl," said Zeb. "Bad luck this time of day."

"I figured this was the sort of place where owls hoot in the daytime and they have possums for yard dogs." I tried to crack the old joke, but Zeb didn't laugh.

"Let me say what's been here," he said. "The trouble's with that witch-girl, Craye Sawtelle. She makes profit by this and that—says strings of words supposed to make your crops grow, allows she can turn your cows or pigs sick unless you pay her. What she wants is this spring, this holy spring. Naturally, she figures it would make her rich."

"And you won't give it over."

"It's not mine to give, John. I reckon it saved my life— I'd have died without you knelt to scoop it clear for me. So I owe it to folks to let them cure themselves with it. Oh, Craye's tried everything. You've seen what sort she is. First off, she wanted us to be partners—in the spring and other things. That didn't work with me, and she got ugly. I'll banter you she's done things to the Flemings, like those

sick chickens you heard tell of from Tilda. And she told
me she'd put a curse on my corn patch. Things don't go
right well there just now."

I picked my guitar. "Hark at this," I said:

> *Three holy kings, four holy saints,*
> *At heaven's high gate that stand,*
> *Speak out to bid all evil wait*
> *And stir no foot or hand . . .*

"Where'd you catch that song, John?"

"Long ago, from old Uncle T. P. Hinnard. He allowed it
was a good song against bad stuff."

Zeb crinkled his eyes. "Like enough it is, but it sort of
chills the blood. You know one of a different kind?"

The owl quivered its voice outside as I touched the
strings again.

> *Her hair is of a brightsome color*
> *And her cheeks are rosy red,*
> *On her breast are two white lilies*
> *Where you long to lay your head.*

"Tilda," said Zeb, a-brightening up. "You made that
song about Tilda."

"It's older than Tilda's great-grandsire," I told him, "but
it'll do for her. I saw how she and you lean to one another."

"If it wasn't for Craye Sawtelle—" And he stopped.

"Tell me about her," I bade him, and he did.

She'd lived thereabouts before Zeb built his cabin. She
followed witchcraft and didn't care a shuck who knew it.
Some folks went to her for charms and helps, others were
scared to say her name out loud. When Zeb began a-letting
sick folks drink from the spring, she tried air way she knew
to cut herself in. She'd tried to sweet-talk Zeb, even tried
to move into his cabin with him. But by then he'd met
Tilda Fleming and couldn't think of air girl but her.

"When she saw I wouldn't love her, she started in to
make me fear her," he said. "She's done that thing, pretty
much. You wonder yourself why I don't speak up to Tilda.
I've got it in mind that if I did, Craye would do something

awful to her. I don't know what it would be, likely I don't want to know."

I made the guitar string whisper to drown out the owl's voice. "What would she do with the spring if she had it?"

"Make folks pay for its water, I told you. Maybe turn its power round to do bad instead of good. I can't rightly say."

I leaned my guitar on the wall. "Maybe I'll just go out and walk round your place before the sun goes down."

"Be careful, John."

"Shoo," I said, "I'll do that. I may not be the smartest man in these mountains, but I'm sure enough the carefullest."

I went out at the door. The sun had dropped to a fold of the mountains. I walked back and looked at Zeb's rows of corn, his bean patch with pods a-coming on, the other beds of vegetables. Past his garden grew up trees, tall and close together, with shadowy dark amongst them.

"We meet again, John," said a voice I'd come to know.

"I reckoned we might, Miss Craye," I said, and out she came from betwixt two pines. She carried a stick of fresh wood, its bark peeled off.

"If I pointed this wand at you and said a spell," she said, "what would happen?"

"We'll never know without you try it."

She tossed her hair, black as a yard up a chimney on a dark night. Her teeth showed, bright and sharp. "That means you figure you've got help against spells," she said. "I'm not without help myself. I don't go air place without help."

"Then you must be hard pushed when it's not nigh."

I felt the presence of what she talked about. Back in the thicket, I knew, were gathered things. I couldn't see them, just felt them. A stir and a sigh back yonder.

"John," she said, "you could go farther and fare worse than by making a friend of me. You understand things these country hodges nair dreamt of. You've been up and down the world and grabbed onto truths here and there."

"I've done that thing," I agreed her, "and the poet wasn't right all the time when he said beauty was truth and truth was beauty. Truth can be right ugly now and then."

"Suppose Zeb Gossett was shown a quick way out of

here," she said. "Suppose you and I got to be partners in the spring and other matters."

"What kind of partners?"

She winnowed close then. I made out she didn't have on air stitch under her silky dress. She was proudly made, and well she knew it. She stood so close she near about touched me.

"What kind of partners would you like us to be?" she whispered.

"Miss Craye," said I, "no, thank you. No partnerships in the spring or in you, either one."

If she'd had the power to kill me with a look, I'd have died then and there. For hell's worst fury is a woman scorned, says another poet.

"I don't know why I don't raise my voice and set my pack on you," she breathed out in my face, and drew off a step.

"Maybe I can make one of those educated guesses," I said. "Your pack might not be friendly to you, not when you've just failed at something."

"You're the failure!" she squeaked like a bat.

"A failure for you, like Zeb Gossett. Isn't the third time the charm? If it doesn't work the third time, where will the charm put you?"

"I gave you and Zeb Gossett till sundown tomorrow," she gritted out with her pointy teeth. "Just about twenty-four hours."

"We'll be here," I said.

She backed off amongst the trees. They tossed their branches, like as if in a high wind. I turned and went back to the cabin. As I helped Zeb do the dishes, I related him what had passed.

"You bluffed her out of something she might try on you," said Zeb.

"I wasn't a-bluffing. If she's got the power of evil, I've been up against that in my time, and folks will say evil nair truly won over me. I hope some power of good is in me."

"Sure it is," he said. "Look out yonder at that healing spring. But she says bad will fall on us by sundown tomorrow. How can we go all right against that?"

"I don't rightly know how to answer that," I made con-

fession. "We'll play it by ear, same as I play this guitar."
And I picked it up to change the subject.

Out yonder was a sound, like a whisper, but too soft and
sneaky to be a real voice. And a shadow passed outside
a window.

I stopped my picking. Zeb had taken a dark-covered
book from the shelf and was opening it. "What's that?"
I asked.

"The Bible." He flung the covers wide and stabbed down
his finger. "I'm a-going to cast a sign for us."

I knew about that, open the Bible anywhere and put your
finger on a text and look for guidance in it.

"Here, the last verse in thirteenth Mark." Zeb read it
out: " 'And what I say unto you I say unto all, Watch.' "

"Watch," I repeated. "That's what we'll do tonight."

Shadows at the window again. Zeb looked in the Bible,
but didn't read from it anymore. I picked my guitar, the
tune of "Never Trust a Stranger." Outside rose a rush of
wind, and when I looked out it was darkened. Night, and,
from what I could judge, no moon. The owl hooted. On
the hearth, the fire burnt blue. Zeb got up and lit a candle.
Its flame fluttered like a yellow leaf.

Then a scratchy peck at the door. Zeb looked at me, his
eyes as wide as sunflowers. I put down the guitar and went
to the door.

It opened by hiking the latch on a string. I cracked it
inward a tad and looked at what was out there. A dog? It
was as big as a big one, black and bristly-haired. Its eyes
shone, likewise its teeth. It looked to be a-getting up on its
hind legs, and for a second I thought its front paws were
hairy hands.

"Thanks," I said to it, "whatever you got to sell, we don't
want any."

I closed the door and the latch fell into place. I heard
that big body a-pressing against the wood. A whiney little
sound, then the wind again. Zeb put more wood on the
fire, though it wasn't cold. "What must we do?" he asked.

"Watch, the way the Bible told us," I replied him.

Things moved heavily all round the cabin. A scratch at
a windowpane. Feet tippy-toed on the roof.

"I reckon it's up to you, John," said Zeb, his Bible back

in his hand. "Up to you to see us through this night. You've got good in you to stand off the bad."

I thought of saying that Craye had given us to sundown the next day, which should ought to mean we'd last till then. As to the good in me, I hoped it was there. But it's not a right thing to claim aught for yourself, just be thankful if it helps.

Zeb gave us both a whet out of a jug of good blockade, and again I picked guitar. He joined in with me to sing "Lonesome River Shore" and "Call Me from the Valley," and wanted me to do the one that had minded him of Tilda. Things quietened outside while we sang. The devil's afraid of music, I'd heard tell from a preacher in a church house one time.

But when I put the guitar by, I heard another kind of singing. It was outside, it was a moanish tune and a woman's voice a-doing it. I tried to make out the words:

> *Cummer, go ye before, cummer, go ye,*
> *Gif ye not go before, cummer, let me . . .*

And I'd heard that same song before. It was sung, folks said, near about four hundred years back, at North Berwick, in Scotland, to witch a king on his throne and the princess he wanted to marry. I didn't reckon I'd tell Zeb that.

"Sounds like Craye Sawtelle's voice," he said as he listened. "What does cummer mean, John?"

"I think that's an old-timey word for a chum, a friend," I replied him.

"Then what cummers are out there with Craye?" His face was white—so white I never mentioned the dog-thing that had come to the door.

"She'd better not fetch her cummers in here," I said to hearten him. "They might could hear what wouldn't please them."

"Hear what?"

I had to tell him something, so I took the guitar and sang:

> *Lights in the valley outshine the sun,*
> *Look away beyond the blue . . .*

He looked to feel better. Outside, the other singing died out.

"Would it help if we had crosses at the windows?" he asked, and I nodded him it wouldn't hurt. He tied splinters of firewood crosswise with twine string and put two at the windows and hung another to the latch of the door. Out yonder, somebody moaned like as if the somebody had felt a pain somewhere. Zeb actually grinned at that.

Time dragged by, and the wind sighed round the cabin, or anyway something with a voice like wind. I yawned and stretched, and told him I felt like sleep.

"Take the bed yonder," Zeb bade me. "I'll sit up. I won't be able to sleep."

"That's what you think," I said. "Get into your bed. I'll put down this blanket I fetched with me, just inside the door."

And I did, and wropped up in it. I didn't stay awake long, though once it sounded like as if something sniffed at where the door came down to the bottom. Shoo, gentlemen, you can sleep if you're tired enough.

What woke me up was the far-off crow of a rooster. I was glad to hear that, because a rooster's crow makes bad spirits leave. I rolled over and got up. Zeb was at the fireplace, with an iron fork to toast pieces of bread. A saucepan was a-boiling eggs.

"We're still here," he said. "It wonders me what Craye Sawtelle was up to last night."

"Just a try at scaring us," I said. "She gave us till sundown tonight, you recollect."

Somehow, that pestered him. He didn't talk much while we ate. I said I'd fetch a pail of water, and out I went with it to the spring. There, at the spring but not right close up beside it, stood Craye Sawtelle. This time she wore a long black dress, with black sandals on her bare feet, and her hair was tied up with a string of red beads.

"Good day, ma'am," I said. "How did you fare last night?"

"I was a trifle busy," she answered. "A-getting ready for sundown."

I dipped my bucket in the spring. The water looked sweet.

"I note by your tracks that you've been round and round

here," I said, "but you nair once got close enough to dip in the spring."

"That will come," she promised me. "It will come when the spring's mine, when there's no bar against me. How does that sound to you, John?"

"Why, since you ask, it sounds like the same old song by the same old mockingbird. Like a try at scaring us out. Miss Craye, I've been a-figuring on you since we met up yesterday, and I'll give you my straight-out notion. There's nothing you can do to me or Zeb Gossett, no matter how you try."

"You'll be sorry you said that." ·

"I'm already sorry," I said. "I hate to talk thisaway to lady-folks, but some things purely have to be said."

"And yonder comes Zeb Gossett," she said, pointing. "He'll do like you, try to talk himself out of being afraid."

Zeb came along to where I stood with the bucket in my hand. He looked tight-mouthed and pale yonder his brown beard.

"Have you come to talk business?" Craye inquired him, and showed him her pointy teeth.

"I talk no business with you," he said.

"Wait until the sun slides down behind the mountain," she mocked at him. "Wait until dark. See what I make happen then."

"I don't have to wait," he said. "I've made my mind up."

"Then why should J wait, either?" she snarled out. "Why not do the thing now?"

She lifted up her hands, crooked like claws. She began to say a string of wild words, in whatever language I don't know. Zeb gave back from her.

"I hate things like this, folks," I said, and I upped with the bucket and flung that water from the spring all over her.

She screamed like an animal caught in a trap. I saw yellow foam come a-slathering out of her mouth. She whirled round and whirled round again and slammed down, and by then you couldn't see her on account of the thick dark steam that rose.

Zeb ran buck off a dozen steps, but I stood there to watch, the empty bucket in my hand.

The steam thinned, but you couldn't see Craye Sawtelle. She was gone.

Only that black dress, twisted and empty, and only those two black sandals on the soaked ground, with no feet in them. Naught else. Not a sigh of Craye Sawtelle. The last of the steam drifted off, and Zeb and I stared at each other.

"She's gone," Zeb gobbled in his throat. "Gone. How did you—"

"Well"—I steadied my voice—"yesterday you said it washed away air bad thing whatever. So I thought I'd see if it would do that. No doubt about it, Craye Sawtelle was badness through and through."

He looked down at the empty dress and empty sandals.

"Blessed water," he said. "Holy water. You made it so."

"I can't claim that, Zeb. More likely it was your doing, when you started in to use it for help to sick and troubled folks."

"But you knew that if you threw it on her—"

"No." I shook my head. "I just only hoped it would work, and it did. Wherever Craye Sawtelle's been washed to, I don't reckon she'll be back from there."

He looked up along the trail. Yonder came Tilda Fleming.

"Tilda," he said her name. "What shall I tell Tilda?"

"Why not tell her what's in your heart for her?" I asked. "I reckon she's plumb ready to hark at you."

He started to walk toward her and I headed back to the cabin.

There are masters, and then there are *Masters;* and no one will disagree, I'm sure, when I say that Robert Bloch was a *MASTER.* In fact, I think it's safe to say that he pioneered a thoroughly modern approach to horror/fantasy literature that has led many other writers to successful careers. A lot of us are doing nothing more than exploring and filling in the details of territories he carved out of his vast and vivid imagination.

It's difficult to pick one favorite story, but I've settled on "That Hell-Bound Train" (instead of, say "Yours Truly, Jack the Ripper" or "Enoch") simply because this "deal with the devil" story is so damned charming and filled to overflowing with humanity.

I only met Mr. Bloch once, and I'll admit that I was totally intimidated at the time. What surprised me was to find that the author of *Psycho* and so many other stories that impressed and influenced me was such a kind, sweet, gentle person.

It may be risky to say this, but I do think he was *underappreciated* . . . or maybe *undervalued* is a better word. While he was alive, he certainly garnered plenty of awards and recognition from countless writers' groups and organization as well the respect and love of personal friends. But when you read and feel the humanity in such stories as "That Hell-Bound Train," maybe you'll agree that Robert Bloch—the man and the writer—could *never* have been overvalued.

I miss his voice and his vision.

—Rick Hautala

THAT HELL-BOUND TRAIN
by Robert Bloch

When Martin was a little boy, his Daddy was a Railroad Man. Daddy never rode the high iron, but he walked the tracks for the CB&Q, and he was proud of his job. And every night when he got drunk, he sang this old song about *That Hell-Bound Train.*

Martin didn't quite remember any of the words, but he couldn't forget the way his Daddy sang them out. And when Daddy made the mistake of getting drunk in the afternoon and got squeezed between a Pennsy tank-car and an AT&SF gondola, Martin sort of wondered why the Brotherhood didn't sing the song at his funeral.

After that, things didn't go so good for Martin, but somehow he always recalled Daddy's song. When Mom up and ran off with a traveling salesman from Keokuk (Daddy must have turned over in his grave, knowing she'd done such a thing, and with a *passenger,* too!) Martin hummed the tune to himself every night in the Orphan Home. And after Martin himself ran away, he used to whistle the song softly at night in the jungles, after the other bindlestiffs were asleep.

Martin was on the road for four-five years before he realized he wasn't getting anyplace. Of course he'd tried his hand at a lot of things—picking fruit in Oregon, washing dishes in a Montana hash-house, stealing hubcaps in Denver and tires in Oklahoma City—but by the time he'd put in six months on the chain-gang down in Alabama he knew he had no future drifting around this way on his own.

So he tried to get on the railroad like his Daddy had and they told him that times were bad.

But Martin couldn't keep away from the railroads. Wherever he traveled, he rode the rods; he'd rather hop a freight heading north in sub-zero weather than lift his thumb to hitch a ride with a Cadillac headed for Florida. Whenever he managed to get hold of a can of Sterno, he'd sit there under a nice warm culvert, think about the old days, and often as not he'd hum the song about *That Hell-Bound Train.* That was the train the drunks and the sinners rode—the gambling men and the drifters, the big-time spenders, the skirt-chasers, and all the jolly crew. It would be really fine to take a trip in such good company, but Martin didn't like to think of what happened when that train finally pulled into the Depot Way Down Yonder. He didn't figure on spending eternity stoking boilers in Hell, without even a Company Union to protect him. Still, it would be a lovely ride. If there was *such* a thing as a Hell-Bound Train. Which, of course, there wasn't.

At least Martin didn't *think* there was, until that evening when he found himself walking the tracks heading south, just outside of Appleton Junction. The night was cold and dark, the way November nights are in the Fox River Valley,

and he knew he'd have to work his way down to New
Orleans for the winter, or maybe even Texas. Somehow he
didn't much feel like going, even though he'd heard tell that
a lot of those Texas automobiles had solid gold hubcaps.

No sir, he just wasn't cut out for petty larceny. It was
worse than a sin—it was unprofitable, too. Bad enough to
do the Devil's work, but then to get such miserable pay
on top of it! Maybe he'd better let the Salvation Army
convert him.

Martin trudged along humming Daddy's song, waiting for
a rattler to pull out of the Junction behind him. He'd have
to catch it—there was nothing else for him to do.

But the first train to come along came from the other
direction, roaring toward him along the track from the
south.

Martin peered ahead, but his eyes couldn't match his
ears, and so far all he could recognize was the sound. It
was a train, though; he felt the steel shudder and sing beneath his feet.

And yet, how could it be? The next station south was
Neenah-Menasha, and there was nothing due out of there
for hours.

The clouds were thick overhead, and the field-mists
rolled like a cold fog in a November midnight. Even so,
Martin should have been able to see the headlight as the
train rushed on. But there was only the whistle, screaming
out of the black throat of the night. Martin could recognize
the equipment of just about any locomotive ever built, but
he'd never heard a whistle that sounded like this one. It
wasn't signaling; it was screaming like a lost soul.

He stepped to one side, for the train was almost on top
of him now. And suddenly there it was, looming along the
tracks and grinding to a stop in less time than he'd believed
possible. The wheels hadn't been oiled, because they
screamed too, screamed like the damned. But the train slid
to a halt and the screams died away into a series of low,
groaning sounds, and Martin looked up and saw that this
was a passenger train. It was big and black, without a single
light shining in the engine cab or any of the long string of
cars; Martin couldn't read any lettering on the sides, but
he was pretty sure this train didn't belong on the North-
western Road.

He was even more sure when he saw the man clamber down out of the forward car. There was something wrong about the way he walked, as though one of his feet dragged, and about the lantern he carried. The lantern was dark, and the man held it up to his mouth and blew, and instantly it glowed redly. You don't have to be a member of the Railway Brotherhood to know that this is a mighty peculiar way of lighting a lantern.

As the figure approached, Martin recognized the conductor's cap perched on his head, and this made him feel a little better for a moment—until he noticed that it was worn a bit too high, as though there might be something sticking up on the forehead underneath it.

Still, Martin knew his manners, and when the man smiled at him, he said, "Good evening, Mr. Conductor."

"Good evening, Martin."

"How did you know my name?"

The man shrugged. "How did you know I was the Conductor?"

"You *are,* aren't you?"

"To you, yes. Although other people, in other walks of life, may recognize me in different roles. For instance, you ought to see what I look like to the folks out in Hollywood." The man grinned. "I travel a great deal," he explained.

"What brings you here?" Martin asked.

"Why, you ought to know the answer to that, Martin. I came because you needed me. Tonight, I suddenly realized you were backsliding. Thinking of joining the Salvation Army, weren't you?"

"Well—" Martin hesitated.

"Don't be ashamed. To err is human, as somebody-or-other once said. *Reader's Digest,* wasn't it? Never mind. The point is, I felt you needed me. So I switched over and came your way."

"What for?"

"Why, to offer you a ride, of course. Isn't it better to travel comfortably by train than to march along the cold streets behind a Salvation Army band? Hard on the feet, they tell me, and even harder on the eardrums."

"I'm not sure I'd care to ride your train, sir," Martin said. "Considering where I'm likely to end up."

"Ah, yes. The old argument." The Conductor sighed. "I suppose you'd prefer some sort of bargain, is that it?"

"Exactly," Martin answered.

"Well, I'm afraid I'm all through with that sort of thing. There's no shortage of prospective passengers any more. Why should I offer you any special inducements?"

"You must want me, or else you wouldn't have bothered to go out of your way to find me."

The Conductor sighed again. "There you have a point. Pride was always my besetting weakness, I admit. And somehow I'd hate to lose you to the competition, after thinking of you as my own all these years." He hesitated. "Yes, I'm prepared to deal with you on your own terms, if you insist."

"The terms?" Martin asked.

"Standard proposition. Anything you want."

"Ah," said Martin.

"But I warn you in advance, there'll be no tricks. I'll grant you any wish you can name—but in return, you must promise to ride the train when the time comes."

"Suppose it never comes?"

"It will."

"Suppose I've got the kind of a wish that will keep me off forever?"

"There is no such wish."

"Don't be too sure."

"Let me worry about that," the Conductor told him. "No matter what you have in mind, I warn you that I'll collect in the end. And there'll be none of this last-minute hocus-pocus, either. No last-hour repentances, no blonde *frauleins* or fancy lawyers showing up to get you off. I offer a clean deal. That is to say, you'll get what you want, and I'll get what I want."

"I've heard you trick people. They say your worse than a used-car salesman."

"Now, wait a minute—"

"I apologize," Martin said, hastily. "But it *is* supposed to be a fact that you can't be trusted."

"I admit it. On the other hand, you seem to think you have found a way out."

"A surefire proposition."

"Surefire? Very funny!" The man began to chuckle, then halted. "But we waste valuable time, Martin. Let's get down to cases. What do you want from me?"

Martin took a deep breath. "I want to be able to stop Time."

"Right now?"

"No. Not yet. And not for everybody. I realize that would be impossible, of course. But I want to be able to stop Time for myself. Just once, in the future. Whenever I get to a point where I know I'm happy and contented, that's where I'd like to stop. So I can just keep on being happy forever."

"That's quite a proposition," the Conductor mused. "I've got to admit I've never heard anything just like it before—and believe me, I've listened to some lulus in my day." He grinned at Martin. "You've really been thinking about this, haven't you?"

"For years," Martin admitted. Then he coughed. "Well, what do you say?"

"It's not impossible, in terms of your own *subjective* time-sense," the Conductor murmured. "Yes, I think it could be arranged."

"But I mean *really* to stop. Nor for me just to *imagine* it."

"I understand. And it can be done."

"Then you'll agree?"

"Why not? I promised you, didn't I? Give me your hand."

Martin hesitated. "Will it hurt very much? I mean, I don't like the sight of blood, and—"

"Nonsense! You've been listening to a lot of poppycock. We already have made our bargain, my boy. I merely intend to put something into your hand. The ways and means of fulfilling your wish. After all, there's no telling at just what moment you may decide to exercise the agreement, and I can't drop everything and come running. So it's better if you can regulate matters for yourself."

"You're going to give me a Time-stopper?"

"That's the general idea. As soon as I can decide what would be practical." The Conductor hesitated. "Ah, the very thing! Here, take my watch."

He pulled it out of his vest-pocket; a railroad watch in a

silver case. He opened the back and made a delicate adjustment; Martin tried to see just exactly what he was doing, but the fingers moved in a blinding blur.

"There we are," the Conductor smiled. "It's all set, now. When you finally decide where you'd like to call a halt, merely turn the stem in reverse and unwind the watch until it stops. When it stops, Time stops, for you. Simple enough?" And the Conductor dropped the watch into Martin's hand.

The young man closed his fingers tightly around the case. "That's all there is to it, eh?"

"Absolutely. But remember—you can stop the watch only once. So you'd better make sure that you're satisfied with the moment you choose to prolong. I caution you in all fairness, make very certain of your choice."

"I will." Martin grinned. "And since you've been so fair about it, I'll be fair, too. There's one thing you seem to have forgotten. It doesn't really matter *what* moment I choose. Because once I stop Time for myself, that means I stay where I am forever. I'll never have to get any older. And if I don't get any older, I'll never die. And if I never die, then I'll never have to take a ride on your train."

The Conductor turned away. His shoulders shook, convulsively, and he may have been crying. "And you said *I* was worse than a used-car salesman," he gasped, in a strangled voice.

Then he wandered off into the fog, and the train-whistle gave an impatient shriek, and all at once it was moving swiftly down the track, rumbling out of sight in the darkness.

Martin stood there, blinking down at the silver watch in his hand. If it wasn't that he could actually see it and feel it there, and if he couldn't smell that peculiar odor, he might have thought he'd imagined the whole thing from start to finish—train, Conductor, bargain, and all.

But he had the watch, and he could recognize the scent left by the train as it departed, even though there aren't many locomotives around that use sulphur and brimstone as fuel.

And he had no doubts about his bargain. That's what came of thinking things through to a logical conclusion.

Some fools would have settled for wealth, or power, or Kim Novak. Daddy might have sold out for a fifth of whiskey.

Martin knew that he'd made a better deal. Better? It was foolproof. All he needed to do now was choose his moment.

He put the watch in his pocket and started back down the railroad track. He hadn't really had a destination in mind before, but he did now. He was going to find a moment of happiness. . . .

* * *

Now young Martin wasn't altogether a ninny. He realized perfectly well that happiness is a relative thing; there are conditions and degrees of contentment, and they vary with one's lot in life. As a hobo, he was often satisfied with a warm handout, a double-length bench in the park, or a can of Sterno made in 1957 (a vintage year). Many a time he had reached a state of momentary bliss through such simple agencies, but he was aware that thee were better things. Martin determined to seek them out.

Within two days he was in the great city of Chicago. Quite naturally, he drifted over to West Madison Street, and there he took steps to elevate his role in life. He became a city bum, a panhandler, a moocher. Within a week he had risen to the point where happiness was a meal in a regular one-arm luncheon joint, a two-bit flop on a real army cot in a real flophouse, and a full fifth of muscatel.

There was a night, after enjoying all three of these luxuries to the full, when Martin thought of unwinding his watch at the pinnacle of intoxication. But he also thought of the faces of the honest johns he'd braced for a handout today. Sure, they were squares, but they were prosperous. They wore good clothes, held good jobs, drove nice cars. And for them, happiness was even more ecstatic—they ate dinner in fine hotels, they slept on innerspring mattresses, they drank blended whiskey.

Square or no, they had something there. Martin fingered his watch, put aside the temptation to hock it for another bottle of muscatel, and went to sleep determined to get himself a job and improve his happiness-quotient.

When he awoke he had a hangover, but the determination was still with him. Before the month was out Martin was working for a general contractor over on the South Side, at one of the big rehabilitation projects. He hated the grind, but the pay was good, and pretty soon he got himself a one-room apartment out on Blue Island Avenue. He was accustomed to eating in decent restaurants now, and he bought himself a comfortable bed, and every Saturday night he went down to the corner tavern. It was all very pleasant, but—

The foreman liked his work and promised him a raise in a month. If he waited around, the raise would mean that he could afford a secondhand car. With a car, he could even start picking up a girl for a date now and then. Other fellows on the job did, and they seemed pretty happy.

So Martin kept on working, and the raise came through and the car came through and pretty soon a couple of girls came through.

The first time it happened, he wanted to unwind his watch immediately. Until he got to thinking about what some of the older men always said. There was a guy named Charlie, for example, who worked alongside him on the hoist. "When you're young and don't know the score, maybe you get a kick out of running around with those pigs. But after a while, you want something better. A nice girl of your own. That's the ticket."

Martin felt he owned it to himself to find out. If he didn't like it better, he could always go back to what he had.

Almost six months went by before Martin met Lillian Gillis. By that time he'd had another promotion and was working inside, in the office. They made him go to night school to learn how to do simple bookkeeping, but it meant another fifteen bucks extra a week, and it was nicer working indoors.

And Lillian *was* a lot of fun. When she told him she'd marry him, Martin was almost sure that the time was now. Except that she was sort of—well, she was a *nice* girl, and she said they'd have to wait until they were married. Of course, Martin couldn't expect to marry her until he had a little more money saved up, and another raise would help, too.

That took a year. Martin was patient, because he knew it was going to be worth it. Every time he had any doubts, he took out his watch and looked at it. But he never showed it to Lillian, or anybody else. Most of the other men wore expensive wristwatches, and the old silver railroad watch looked just a little cheap.

Martin smiled as he gazed at the stem. Just a few twists and he'd have something none of these other poor working slobs would ever have. Permanent satisfaction, with his blushing bride—

Only getting married turned out to be just the beginning. Sure, it was wonderful, but Lillian told him how much better things would be if they could move into a new place and fix it up. Martin wanted decent furniture, a TV set, a nice car.

So he started taking night courses and got a promotion to the front office. With the baby coming, he wanted to stick around and see his son arrive. And when it came, he realized he'd have to wait until it got a little older, started to walk and talk and develop a personality of its own.

About this time the company sent him out on the road as a troubleshooter on some of those other jobs, and now he *was* eating at those good hotels, living high on the hog and the expense account. More than once he was tempted to unwind his watch. This was the good life. . . . Of course, it would be even better if he just didn't have to *work*. Sooner or later, if he could cut in on one of the company deals, he could make a pile and retire. Then everything would be ideal.

It happened, but it took time. Martin's son was going to high school before he really got up there into the chips. Martin got a strong hunch that it was now or never, because he wasn't exactly a kid any more.

But right about then he met Sherry Westcott, and she didn't seem to think he was middlepaged at all, in spite of the way he was losing hair and adding stomach. She taught him that a *toupee* would cover the bald spot and a cummerbund could cover the potgut. In fact, she taught him quite a lot and he so enjoyed learning that he actually took out his watch and prepared to unwind it.

Unfortunately, he chose the very moment that the private detectives broke down the door of the hotel room, and then there was a long stretch of time when Martin was so busy fighting the divorce action that he couldn't honestly say he was enjoying any given moment.

When he made the final settlement with Lil he was broke again, and Sherry didn't seem to think he was so young, after all. So he squared his shoulders and went back to work.

He made his pile, eventually, but it took longer this time, and there wasn't much chance to have fun along the way. The fancy dames in the fancy cocktail lounges didn't seem to interest him any more, and neither did the liquor. Besides, the Doc had warned him off that.

But there were other pleasures for a rich man to investigate. Travel, for instance—and not riding the rods from one hick burg to another, either. Martin went around the world by plane and luxury liner. For a while it seemed as though he would find his moment after all, visiting the Taj Mahal by moonlight. Martin pulled out the battered old watchcase, and got ready to unwind it. Nobody else was there to watch him—

And that's why he hesitated. Sure, this was an enjoyable moment, but he was alone. Lil and the kid were gone, Sherry was gone, and somehow he'd never had time to make any friends. Maybe if he found new congenial people, he'd have the ultimate happiness. That must be the answer—it wasn't just money or power or sex or seeing beautiful things. The real satisfaction lay in friendship.

So on the boat trip home, Martin tried to strike up a few acquaintances at the ship's bar. But all these people were much younger, and Martin had nothing in common with them. Also they wanted to dance and drink, and Martin wasn't in condition to appreciate such pastimes. Nevertheless, he tried.

Perhaps that's why he had the little accident the day before they docked in San Francisco. "Little accident" was the ship's doctor's way of describing it, but Martin noticed he looked very grave when he told him to stay in bed, and he'd called an ambulance to meet the liner at the dock and take the patient right to the hospital.

At the hospital, all the expensive treatment and the expensive smiles and the expensive words didn't fool Martin any. He was an old man with a bad heart, and they thought he was going to die.

But he could fool them. He still had the watch. He found it in his coat when he put on his clothes and sneaked out of the hospital.

He didn't have to die. He could cheat death with a single gesture—and he intended to do it as a free man, out there under a free sky.

That was the real secret of happiness. He understood it now. Not even friendship meant as much as freedom. This was the best thing of all—to be free of friends or family or the furies of the flesh.

Martin walked slowly beside the embankment under the night sky. Come to think of it, he was just about back where he'd started, so many years ago. But the moment was good, good enough to prolong forever. Once a bum, always a bum.

He smiled as he thought about it, and then the smile twisted sharply and suddenly, like the pain twisting sharply and suddenly in his chest. The world began to spin and he fell down on the side of the embankment.

He couldn't see very well, but he was still conscious, and he knew what had happened. Another stroke, and a bad one. Maybe this was it. Except that he wouldn't be a fool any longer. He wouldn't wait to see what was still around the corner.

Right now was his chance to use his power and save his life. And he was going to do it. He could still move, nothing could stop him.

He groped in his pocket and pulled out the old silver watch, fumbling with the stem. A few twists and he'd cheat death, he'd never have to ride that Hell-Bound Train. He could go on forever.

Forever.

Martin had never really considered the word before. To go on forever—but *how?* Did he *want* to go on forever, like this; a sick old man, lying helplessly here in the grass?

No. He couldn't do it. He wouldn't do it. And suddenly he wanted very much to cry, because he knew that somewhere along the line he'd outsmarted himself. And now it was too late. His eyes dimmed, there was a roaring in his ears . . .

He recognized the roaring, of course, and he wasn't at all surprised to see the train come rushing out of the fog up there on the embankment. He wasn't surprised when it stopped, either, or when the Conductor climbed off and walked slowly towards him.

The Conductor hadn't changed a bit. Even his grin was still the same.

"Hello, Martin," he said. "All aboard."

"I know," Martin whispered. "But you'll have to carry me. I can't walk. I'm not even really talking any more, am I?"

"Yes you are," the Conductor said. "I can hear you fine. And you can walk, too." He leaned down and placed his hand on Martin's chest. There was a moment of icy numbness, and then, sure enough, Martin could walk after all.

He got up and followed the Conductor along the slope, moving to the side of the train.

"In here?" he asked.

"No, the next car," the Conductor murmured. "I guess you're entitled to ride Pullman. After all, you're quite a successful man. You've tasted the joys of wealth and position and prestige. You've known the pleasures of marriage and fatherhood. You've sampled the delights of dining and drinking and debauchery, too, and you traveled high, wide and handsome. So let's not have any last-minute recriminations."

"All right," Martin sighed. "I can't blame you for my mistakes. On the other hand, you can't take credit for what happened, either. I worked for everything I got. I did it all on my own. I didn't even need your watch."

"So you didn't." the Conductor said, smiling. "But would you mind giving it back to me now?"

"Need it for the next sucker, eh?" Martin muttered.

"Perhaps."

Something about the way he said it made Martin look up. He tried to see the Conductor's eyes, but the brim of his cap cast a shadow. So Martin looked down at the watch instead.

"Tell me something," he said, softly. "If I give you the watch, what will you do with it?"

"Why, throw it into the ditch," the Conductor told him. "That's all I'll do with it." And he held out his hand.

"What if somebody comes along and finds it? And twists the stem backwards, and stops Time?"

"Nobody would do that," the Conductor murmured. "Even if they knew."

"You mean, it was all a trick? This is only an ordinary, cheap watch?"

"I didn't say that," whispered the Conductor. "I only said that no one has ever twisted the stem backwards. They've all been like you, Martin—looking ahead to find that perfect happiness. Waiting for the moment that never comes."

The Conductor held out his hand again.

Martin sighed and shook his head. "You cheated me after all."

"You cheated yourself, Martin. And now you're going to ride that Hell-Bound Train."

He pushed Martin up the steps and into the car ahead. As he entered, the train began to move and the whistle screamed. And Martin stood there in the swaying Pullman, gazing down the aisle at the other passengers. He could see them sitting there, and somehow it didn't seem strange at all.

Here they were; the drunks and the sinners, the gambling men and the grifters, the big-time spenders, the skirt-chasers, and all the jolly crew. They knew where they were going, of course, but they didn't seem to give a damn. The blinds were drawn on the windows, yet it was light inside, and they were all living it up—singing and passing the bottle and roaring with laughter, throwing the dice and telling their jokes and bragging their big brags, just the way Daddy used to sing about them in the old song.

"Mighty nice traveling companions," Martin said. "Why, I've never seen m such a pleasant bunch of people. I mean, they seem to be really enjoying themselves!"

The Conductor shrugged. "I'm afraid things won't be quite so jazzy when we pull into that Depot Way Down Yonder."

For the third time, he held out his hand. "Now, before you sit down, if you'll just give me that watch. A bargain's a bargain—"

Martin smiled. "A bargain's a bargain," he echoed. "I agreed to ride your train if I could stop Time when I found the right moment of happiness. And I think I'm about as happy right here as I've ever been."

Very slowly, Martin took hold of the silver watch-stem.
"No!" gasped the Conductor. "No!"

But the watch-stem turned.

"Do you realize what you've done?" the Conductor
yelled. "Now we'll never reach the Depot! We'll just go on
riding, all of us—forever!"

Martin grinned. "I know," he said. "But the fun is in the
trip, not the destination. You taught me that. And I'm looking forward to a wonderful trip. Look, maybe I can even
help. If you were to find me another one of those caps,
now, and let me keep this watch— "

And that's the way it finally worked out. Wearing his cap
and carrying his battered old silver watch, there's no happier person in or out of this world—now and forever—than
Martin. Martin, the new Brakeman on That Hell-Bound
Train.

The watchman rubbed his hands and looked round for a minute or two, as if he expected something else to happen. "Eleven o'clock," he called at last; and though he couldn't commit himself to a description which seemed so subject to qualification as to be in bad faith, added: "And all's all."

It's difficult to describe the effect such prose had on me when I first read it. Or rather, heard it. Truth to tell, I'd never heard of Mr. John Harrison when I had the pleasure of making his acquaintance at a science fiction convention in, of all places, Oslo, Norway. (We were both rather far afield at the time, I more than he.) In the name of that pleasure, I went to hear him read "The Dancer from the Dance"—which for me was yet another form of being far afield, since as a rule I don't enjoy listening to anyone read aloud.

Standing at a lab table in a chemistry classroom before an audience of earnest, intelligent, and cruelly shy Norwegians, flanked by bunsen burners and sinks, Harrison proceeded to weave an enchantment the likes of which I'd never encountered before. In almost every sentence, he astonished me with images, names, and locutions that seemed to reach far beyond their literal grasp.

The people who live in them believe that insects the size of horses infest the Heath.

The Plaza of Realized Time.

If you approached them properly one of them would always tuck her chalk down her grubby white drawers, lick the snot off her upper lip, and lead you to Orves.

In less than a page, Harrison had entranced me. I forgot that I sat on a hard wooden chair in a tiered gallery plainly intended for lectures of numbing impersonality. I forgot that I didn't like readings. Half the time, I forgot to squirm, which for me is as natural as breathing, and at least as necessary. When I met *Vera Ghillera, Vriko's immortal ballerina, Egon Rhys, leader of the Blue Anemone Ontological Association,* and *The greatest clown of his day, called by the crowd "Kiss-O-Suck,"* I had the dreamlike sensation, at once languid and exhilarating, that they played out their oblique drama on the black surface of the lab table below me.

> *He had come originally from the bone-white hinterlands of the Mingulay Littoral, where the caravans seem to float like yellow birdcages at midday across the violet lakes of the mirage "while inside them women consult feverishly their grubby packs of cards."*

> *Egon Rhys blundered across the entangled grain of the watershed, one peat hag to the next, until it brought him to a standstill. The very inconclusiveness of his encounter with his rivals, perhaps, had exhausted him.*

I couldn't keep up with it all. Every sentence—sometimes every word—meant more than I knew how to absorb. When the watchman finally announced, *"And all's all,"* I felt dazed and somehow humbled, as if I'd been touched by the ineffable while I slept.

Since then, "The Dancer from the Dance" has haunted my memory. And I've read everything by M. John Harrison that I could get my hands on. Of tales set in the world of this story there are both quite a few and nowhere near enough. However, he has also published novels which on the surface have little to do with conventional fantasy, but which transcend the page and obsess the mind as only the most "fantastic" narratives can— among them *Climbers, The Course of the Heart,* and my personal favorite, *Signs of Life.*

Perhaps the truest thing I can say about Harrison's work is that every story he writes is one which could have come from nobody else. Each is *sui generis,* unique in the most important sense of the word.

—Stephen R. Donaldson

THE DANCER FROM THE DANCE
by M. John Harrison

"I'll be your dog!"
—*KIA-ORA* ADVERTISEMENT

The city has always been full of little strips and triangles of unused land. A row of buildings falls down in Chenaniaguine—the ground is cleared for further use—elder and nettle spring up—nothing is ever built. Or else the New Men set aside some park for a municipal estate, then quarrel among themselves: a few shallow trenches and low brick courses are covered in a season by couch-grass and "fat hen." Allmans Heath, bounded on two sides by empty warehouses, an abattoir, and a quarantine hospital, and on its third by a derelict reach of the canal, looks like any of them.

A few houses stare morosely at it from the city side of the canal. The people who live in them believe that insects the size of horses infest the Heath. Nobody has ever seen one, nevertheless once a year the large wax effigy of a locust, freshly varnished and with a knot of reed-grasses in its mouth, is brought out from the houses and paraded up and down the towpath. In the background of this ceremony the Heath seems to stretch away forever. It is the same if you go and look from the deserted pens of the cattle market, or one of the windows of the old hospital. To walk round it takes about an hour.

Every winter years ago, little girls would chalk the ground for "blind michael" in a courtyard off the Plaza of Realized Time. (It was on the left as you came to the Plain Moon Cafe where even in February the tables were arranged on the pavement, their planished copper tops gleaming in the weak sun. You turned down by an ornamental apple tree.) Generally they were the illegitimate children of midinettes, laundry women who worked in

Minnet-Saba, or the tradesmen from the Rivelin Market. They preserved a fierce independence and wore short stiff blouses which bared the hollow of their backs to the grimmest weather. If you approached them properly one of them would always tuck her chalk down her grubby white drawers, lick the snot off her upper lip, and lead you to Orves; it was hard work to keep up with her in the steep winding streets.

Most sightseers changed their minds as soon as they saw the shadow of the observatory falling across the houses, and went back to drink hot genever in the Plain Moon. Those who kept on under the black velvet banners of the New Men, which in those days hung heavily from every second-floor window, would find themselves on the bank of the canal at Allmans Reach.

There was not much to see. The cottages were often boarded up at that time of year. A few withered dock plants lined the water's edge where the towpath had collapsed. No one was in sight. The wind from the Heath made your eyes water until you turned away and found the girl standing quite still next to you, her hands hanging at her sides. She would hardly look at you, or the Heath; she might glance at her feet. If you offered her money she would scratch her behind, screech with laughter, and run off down the hill. Later you might see her kneeling on the pavement in some other part of the Quarter, the wet chalk in her mouth, staring with a devout expression at something she had drawn.

Vera Ghillera, Vriko's immortal ballerina, had herself taken to Allmans Reach the day she arrived in the city from Sour Bridge. She was still a provincial and not more than a child herself, as thin and fierce and naïve as any of them in the courtyard off the Plaza, but determined to succeed; long in the muscle for classical dance, perhaps, but with a control already formidable and a sharp technical sense. It was the end of a winter afternoon when she got there. She stood away from her guide and looked over the canal. After a minute her eyes narrowed as if she could see something moving a great distance away. "Wait," she said. "Can you—? No. It's gone." The sun was red across the ice. Long before the city knew her lyrical port de bras, she knew the city. Long, long before she crossed the canal she had seen Allmans Heath and acknowledged it.

Everyone has read how Vera Ghillera, choreographed by Madame Chevigne, costumed by Audsley King, and dancing against sets designed by Paulinus Rack from sketches attributed to Ens Laurin Ashlyme, achieved overnight fame at the Prospekt Theater as Lucky Parminta in *The Little Hump-backed Horse;* how she was courted by Rack and Ingo Lympany amongst others, but did not marry; and how she kept her place as principal dancer for forty years despite the incurable fugues which compelled her to attend regularly and in secret the asylum at Wergs.

Less of her early life is public. In her autobiography, *The Constant Imago,* she is not frank about her illness or how it came about. And few of her contemporaries, were ever aware of the helplessness of her infatuation with Egon Rhys, leader of the Blue Anemone Ontological Association.

Rhys was the son of a trader in fruit and vegetables at Rivelin—one of those big, equivocally natured women whose voice or temper dominate the Market Quarter for years on end, and whose absence leaves it muted and empty. He had been in and out of the market since her death, a man enclosed, not much used to the ordinary emotions, not interested in anything but his own life. He tended to act in good faith.

He was shorter than Vera Ghillera. As a boy, first selling crystallized flowers round the combat rings, then as the apprentice of Osgerby Practal, he had learned to walk with a shambling gait that diverted attention from his natural balance and energy. This he retained. (Later in life, though his limbs thickened, his energy seemed to increase rather than abate—at seventy, they said, he could hardly stand still to talk to you.) He had large hands and a habit of looking at them intently, with a kind of amused indulgence, as if he wanted to see what they would do next.

His heavy, pleasant face was already well-known about the rings when Vera came to the city. Under the aegis of the Blue Anemone he had killed forty men. As a result the other "mutual" associations often arranged a truce among themselves in order to bring about his death. The Feverfew Anschluss had a special interest in this, as did the Fourth

of October and the Fish Head Men from Austonley. At
times even his relations with the Anemone were difficult.
He took it calmly, affecting an air of amusement which—
as in other notorious bravos—seems to have masked not
anxiety but an indifference of which he was rather
ashamed, and which in itself sometimes frightened him. He
let himself be seen about the Quarter unaccompanied; and
walked openly about in the High City, where Vera first
observed him from an upper room.

The Little Hump-backed Horse was history by then: she
had carried a lamp in *Mariana Natesby,* overcome with furious concentration the debilitating danse d'école work and
formalism of Lympany's *The Ginger Boy*. She had danced
with de Cuevas, then past the height of his powers, and
been his lover; she had had her portrait painted once a
year for the oleograph trade, as "Delphine," "Manalas,"
and—looking over a parapet or smiling mysteriously under
a hat—as the unnamed girl in *The Fire Last Wednesday at
Lowth*. She had got her full growth. At work, though she
was so tall, her body seemed compacted, pulled in on itself
like the spring of a humane killer: but she looked exhausted
when the makeup came off, and somehow underfed as she
slumped awkwardly, legs apart, on a low chair in her sweat-
stained practice clothes. She had forgotten how to sit. She
was "all professional deformity in body and soul." Her
huge eyes gave you their attention until she thought you
were looking at someone else, then became blank and tired.

She never lost her determination, but an unease had
come over her.

In the morning before practice she could be seen in the
workmen's cafes down by the market, huddled and fragile-
looking in an expensive woolen coat. She listened to the
sad-sounding traders' calls in the early fog; hearing them
as remote, and as urgent as the cries of lookouts in the
bows of a ship. "Two fathoms and shelving!" She watched
the girls playing blind michael in the courtyard off the Plaza
of Realized Time; but as soon as they recognized her
walked quickly away. "One fathom!"

The first time she saw Egon Rhys she ran down into the
street without thinking and found him face to face with two
or three members of the Yellow Paper College. It was a
fraught moment; razors were already out in the weird

Minnet-Saba light, which lay across the paving stones the
color of mercury. Rhys had his back to some iron railings,
and a line of blood ran vertically down his jaw from a nick
under one eye.

"Leave that man alone!" she said. At ten years old in
the depressed towns of the Midland Level she had seen
unemployed boys fighting quietly under the bridges; building fires on waste ground. "Can't you find anything better
to do?"

Rhys stared at her in astonishment and jumped over
the railings.

"Don't ask me who she was," he said later in the Dryad's
Saddle. "I legged it out of there faster than you could say,
right through someone's front garden. They're hard fuckers,
those Yellow Paper men." He touched the cut they had
given him. "I think they've chipped my cheekbone."

He laughed.

"Don't ask me anything!"

But after that Vera seemed to be everywhere. He had
quick glimpses of a white face with heavily made-up eyes
among the crowds that filled the Market Quarter at the
close of every short winter afternoon. He thought he saw
her in the audience at the ring behind the Dryad's Saddle.
(She was blinking in the fumes from the naphtha lamps.)
Later she followed him from venue to venue in the city and
brought him great bunches of sol d'or whenever he won.

With the flower-boys she sent her name, and tickets to
the Prospekt Theater. There he was irritated by the orches-
tra, confused by the constant changes of scene, and embarrassed by the revealing costumes of the dancers. The smell
of dust and sweat and the thud of their feet on the stage
spoiled the illusion for him: he had always understood
dancing to be graceful. When Vera had him brought up to
her dressing room afterwards he found her wearing an old
silk practice top rotting away under the arms, and a pair
of loose, threadbare woolen stockings out of which someone had cut the feet. "I have to keep my calves warm,"
she explained when she caught him staring at them. He was
horrified by the negligent way she sprawled, watching him
intently in the mirrors, and he thought her face seemed as
hard and tired as a man's; he left as soon as he could.

Vera went home and stood irresolutely near her bed. The

geranium on the window sill was like an artificial flower on a curved stem, its white petals more or less transparent as the clouds covered and uncovered the moon. She imagined saying to him,

"You smell of geraniums."

She began to buy him the latest novels. Just then, too, a new kind of music was being played everywhere, so she took him to concerts. She commissioned Ens Laurin Ashlyme to paint his portrait. He couldn't be bothered to read, he said; he listened distractedly to the whine of the cor anglais then stared over his shoulder all evening as if he had seen someone he knew; he frightened the artist by showing him how good an edge his palette knife would take. "Don't send so many flowers," he told her. Nothing she could offer seemed to interest him, not even his own notoriety.

Then he watched a cynical turn called *Insects* at the Allotrope Cabaret in Cheminor. One of the props used in this was a large yellow locust. When they first dragged it onto the cramped Allotrope stage it appeared to be a clever waxwork. But soon it moved, and even waved one of its hands, and the audience discovered among the trembling antennae and gauze wings a naked woman, painted with wax, lying on her back with her knees raised to simulate the bent rear legs of the insect. She wore to represent its head a stylized, highly varnished mask. Fascinated, Rhys leaned forward to get a better view. Vera heard his breath go in with a hiss. He said loudly, "What's that? What is that animal?" People began to laugh at his enthusiasm; they couldn't see that the double entendre of the act meant nothing to him. "Does anyone know?" he asked them.

"Hush!" said Vera. "You're spoiling it for everyone else."

Poor lighting and a smell of stale food made the Allotrope a cheerless place to perform; it was cold. The woman in the insect mask, having first adjusted it on her shoulders so that it would face the audience when she did, stood up and made the best she could of an "expressive" dance, crossing and uncrossing her thick forearms in front of her while her breath steamed into the chilly air and her feet slapped one two three, one two three on the unchalked boards. But Rhys would not leave until the bitter end, when the mask came off and under it was revealed the triumphant smile, disarranged chestnut hair and tired puffy face of some local artiste hardly sixteen years old, to whistles of delight.

Outside, their shadows fell huge and black on the wall that runs, covered with peeling political cartoons, the length of Endingall Street. "It doesn't seem much to stand in front of an audience for," said Vera, imitating the barren, oppressive little steps. "I would be frightened to go on." She shuddered sympathetically. "Did you see her poor ankles?"

Rhys made an impatient gesture.

"I thought it was very artistic," he said. Then: "That animal! *Do* things like that exist anymore?"

Vera laughed.

"Go on Allmans Heath and see for yourself. Isn't that where you're supposed to go to see them? What would you do if you were face to face with it now? A thing as big as that?"

He caught her hands to stop her from dancing. "I'd kill it," he said seriously. "I'd—" What he might do he had to think for a moment, staring into Vera's face. She stood dead still. "Perhaps it would kill me," he said wonderingly. "I never thought. I never thought things like that might really exist." He was shivering with excitement: she could feel it through his hands. She looked down at him. He was as thick-necked and excitable as a little pony. All of a sudden she was sharply aware of his life, which had somehow assembled for itself like a lot of eccentric furniture the long perspective of Endingall Street, the open doors of the Allotrope Cabaret, that helpless danseuse with her overblocked shoes and ruined ankles, to what end he couldn't see.

"Nothing could kill you," she said shyly.

Rhys shrugged and turned away.

For a week or two after that she seemed to be able to forget him. The weather turned wet and mild, the ordinary vigor of their lives kept them apart.

His relations with the Blue Anemone had never been more equivocal: factions were out for him in High City and Low. If Vera had known he was so hard put to it in the alleys and waste ground around Chenaniaguine and Lowth, who can say what she might have done. Luckily, while he ran for it with an open razor in one hand and a bunch of

dirty bandages coming unraveled from the other, she was
at the barre ten hours a day for her technique. Lympany
had a new production, *Whole Air:* it would be a new *kind*
of ballet, he believed. Everyone was excited by the idea,
but it would mean technique, technique, technique. "The
surface is dead!" he urged his dancers: "Surface is only the
visible part of *technique*!"

Ever since she came up from the Midlands Vera had hated
rest-days. At the end of them she was left sleepless
and irritated in her skin, and as she lay in bed the city sent
granular smoky fingers in through her skylight, unsettling
her and luring her out so that late at night she had to go
to the arena and, hollow-eyed, watch the clowns. There
while thinking about something else she remembered Rhys
again, so completely and suddenly that he went across
her—snap!—like a crack in glass. Above the arena the air
was purple with Roman candles bursting and by their urgent intermittent light she saw him quite clearly standing
in Endingall Street shivering in the grip of his own enthusiasm, driven yet balked by it like all nervous animals. She
also remembered the locust of the Allotrope Cabaret. She
thought,

" 'Artistic!' "

Though on a good night you could still hear the breathy
whisper of twenty-five thousand voices wash across the pan-
tile roofs of Montrouge like a kind of invisible firework,
the arena by then was really little more than a great big
outdoor circus, and all the old burnings and quarterings
had given place to acrobatics, horse-racing, trapeze acts,
etc. The New Men liked exotic animals. They did not seem
to execute their political opponents—or each other—in
public, though some of the aerial acts looked like murder.
Every night there was a big, stupid lizard or a megatherium
brought in to blink harmlessly and even a bit sadly up at
the crowd until they had convinced themselves of its rapac-
ity. And there were more fireworks than ever: to a blast of
maroons full of magnesium and a broad falling curtain of
cerium rain, the clowns would erupt bounding and cart-
wheeling into the circular sandy space—jumping up, falling
down, building unsteady pyramids, standing nine or ten
high on one another's shoulders, active and erratic as grass-

hoppers in the sun. They fought, with rubber knives and whitewash. They wore huge shoes. Vera loved them.

The greatest clown of his day, called by the crowd "Kiss-O-Suck," was a dwarf of whose real name no one was sure. Some people knew him as "Morgante," others as "Rotgob" or "The Grand Pan." His legs were frail-looking and twisted, but he was a fierce gymnast, often able to perform four separate somersaults in the air before landing bent-kneed, feet planted wide apart, rock steady in the black sand. He would alternate cartwheels with handsprings at such a speed he seemed to be two dwarfs, while the crowd egged him on with whistles and cheers. He always ended his act by reciting verses he had made up himself:

> *Codpoorlie—tah*
> *Codpoorrrlie—tah!*
> *Codpoorlie—tah! tah! tah!*
> *Dog pit.*
> > *Dog pit pooley*
> > *Dog pit pooley*
> > *Dog pit have-a-rat*
> > *tah tah tah*
> > *(ta ta).*

For a time his vogue was so great he became a celebrity on the Unter-Main-Kai, where he drank with the intellectuals and minor princes in the Bistro Californium, strutted up and down in a padded doublet of red velvet with long scalloped sleeves, and had himself painted as "The Lord of Misrule." He bought a large house in Montrouge.

He had come originally from the hot bone-white hinterlands of the Mingulay Littoral, where the caravans seem to float like yellow bird cages at midday across the violet lakes of the mirage "while inside them women consult feverishly their grubby packs of cards." If you are born in that desert, its inhabitants often boast, you know all deserts. Kiss-O-Suck was not born a dwarf but chose it as his career, having himself confined for many years in the black oak box, the gloottokoma, so as to stunt his growth. Now he was at the peak of his powers. When he motioned peremptorily the other clowns sprang up into the air around him. His voice echoed to Vera over the arena. "Dog pit pooley!" he chanted, and the crowd gave it him back: but Vera, still somehow on Endingall Street with Egon Rhys trembling beside her, heard, "Born in a desert, knows all deserts!" The next day she sent him her name with a great bunch of anemones. "I admire your act." They met in secret in Montrouge.

At the Bistro Californium, Ansel Verdigris, poet of the city, lay with his head sideways on the table; a smell of lemon gin rose from the tablecloth bunched up under his cheek. Some way away from him sat the Marquis de M——, pretending to write a letter. They had quarreled earlier, ostensibly about the signifier and the signified, and then Verdigris had tried to eat his glass. At that time of night everyone else was at the arena. Without them the Californium was only a few chairs and tables someone had arranged for no good reason under the famous frescoes. De M——would have gone to the arena himself but it was cold outside with small flakes of snow falling through the lights on the Unter-Main-Kai. "Discovering this about itself," he wrote, "the place seems stunned and quiet. It has no inner resources."

Egon Rhys came in with Vera, who was saying:

"—was sure he could be here."

She pulled her coat anxiously about her. Rhys made her sit where it was warm. "I'm tired tonight," she said. "Aren't you?" As she crossed the threshold she had looked up and seen a child's face smile obliquely out at her from a grimy patch in the frescoes. "I'm tired." All day long, she complained, it had been the port de bras: Lympany wanted something different—something that had never been done before. " 'A new *kind* of port de bras'!" she mimicked, " 'A whole new *way* of dancing'! But I have to be so careful in the cold. You can hurt yourself if you work too hard in weather like this."

She would drink only tea, which at the Californium is always served in wide china cups as thin and transparent as a baby's ear. When she had had some she sat back with a laugh. "I feel better now!"

"He's late," said Rhys.

Vera took his arm and pressed her cheek briefly against his shoulder.

"You're so warm! When you were young did you ever

touch a cat or a dog just to feel how warm it was? I did. I used to think: 'It's alive! It's alive!' ''

When he didn't respond she added, "In two or three days' time you could have exactly what you want. Don't be impatient."

"It's already midnight."

She let his arm go.

"He was so sure he would be here. We lose nothing if we wait."

There things rested. Fifteen minutes passed; perhaps half an hour. De M——, certain now that Verdigris was only pretending to be asleep to taunt him, crumpled a sheet of paper suddenly and dropped it on the floor. At this Rhys, whose affairs had made him nervous, jumped to his feet. The Marquis's mouth dropped open weakly. When nothing else happened Rhys sat down again. He thought, "After all I'm as safe here as anyone else in the city." He was still wary, though, of the poet, whom he thought he recognized. Vera glanced once or twice at the frescoes (they were old; no one could agree on what was represented), then quickly down at her cup. All this time Kiss-O-Suck the dwarf had been sitting slumped on a corner of the mantelpiece behind them like a great doll someone had put there for effect years before.

His legs dangled. He wore red tights, and yellow shoes with a bell on each toe; his doublet was made of some thick black stuff quilted like a leather shin-guard and sewn all over with tiny glass mirrors. Immobility was as acceptable to him as motion: in repose his body would remember the gloottokoma and the hours he had spent there, while his face took on the look of varnished papier-mâché, shiny but as if dust had settled in the lines down the side of his hooked nose down to his mouth, which was set in a strange but extraordinarily sweet smile.

He had been watching Vera since she came in. When she repeated eventually, "He was so sure he could be here," he whispered to himself: "I was! Oh, I was!" A moment later he jumped down off the mantelpiece and blew lightly in Egon Rhys's ear.

Rhys threw himself across the room, smashing into the tables as he tried to get at his razor, which he kept tucked up the sleeve of his coat. He fetched up against the Marquis

de M——and screamed, "Get out of the fucking way!" But
the Marquis could only stare and tremble, so they rocked
together for a moment, breathing into one another's faces,
until another table went over. Rhys, who was beginning to
have no idea where he was, knocked de M——down and
stood over him. "Don't kill me," said de M——. The razor,
Rhys found, was tangled up with the silk lining of his
sleeve: in the end he got two fingers into the seam and
ripped the whole lot down from the elbow so that the
weapon tumbled out already open, flickering in the light.
Up went Rhys's arm, with the razor swinging at the end of
it, high in the air.

"Stop!" shouted Vera. "Stop that!"

Rhys stared about him in confusion; blinked. By now he
was trembling too. When he saw the dwarf laughing at him
he realized what had happened. He let the Marquis go.
"I'm sorry," he said absentmindedly. He went over to
where Kiss-O-Suck had planted himself rock-steady on his
bent legs in the middle of the floor, and caught hold of
his wrist.

"What if I cut your face for that?" he asked, stroking
the dwarf's cheek as if to calm him down. "Here. Or say
here. What if I did that?"

The dwarf seemed to consider it. Suddenly his little wrist
slipped and wriggled in Rhys's grip like a fish; however
hard Rhys held on, it only twisted and wriggled harder,
until he had let go of it almost without knowing. (All night
after that his fingers tingled as if they had been rubbed
with sand.)

I don't think she would like that," said Kiss-O-Suck.
"She wouldn't like you to cut someone as small as me."

He shrieked; slapped Rhys's face; jumped backwards
from where he stood, without so much as a twitch of intent,
right over the table and into the hearth. Out of his doublet
he brought a small jam jar, which he put down in the center
of the table. It contained half a dozen grasshoppers, a gray
color, with yellowish legs. At first they were immobile, but
the firelight dancing on the glass around them seemed to
invigorate them and after a moment or two they started to
hop about in the jar at random.

"Look!" said the dwarf.

"Aren't they lively?" cried Vera.

She smiled with delight. The dwarf chuckled. They were so pleased with themselves that eventually Egon Rhys was forced to laugh too. He tucked his razor back up his sleeve and stuffed the lining in after it as best he could. Thereafter strips of red silk hung down round his wrist, and he sometimes held the seam together with his fingers. "You must be careful with that," said Vera. When she tapped the side of their jar, one or two of the grasshoppers seemed to stare at her seriously for a moment, their enigmatic, horsey little heads quite still, before they renewed their efforts to get out, popping and ticking against the lid.

"I love them!" she said, which made Egon Rhys look sidelong at the dwarf and laugh even louder. "I love them! Don't you?"

The Marquis watched incredulously. He got himself to his feet and with a look at Ansel Verdigris as if to say "This is all your fault," ran out on to the Unter-Main-Kai. A little later Rhys, Vera, and the dwarf followed. They were still laughing; Vera and Rhys were arm in arm. As they went out into the night, Verdigris, who really had been asleep, woke up.

"Fuck off then," he sneered. His dreams had been confused.

The day they crossed the canal they were followed all the way up to Allmans Reach from the Plain Moon Cafe. The mutual associations were out: it was another truce. Rhys could distinguish the whistles of the Fish Head Men, January the Twelfth, the Yellow Paper College (now openly calling itself a "schism" of the Anemone and publishing its own broadsheet from the back room of a pie shop behind Red Hart Lane). This time, he was afraid, the Anemone was out too. He had no credit anywhere. At Orves he made the dwarf watch one side of the road while he watched the other. "Pay most attention to doorways." Faces appeared briefly in the cobbled mouths of alleys. Vera Ghillera shivered and pulled the hood of her cloak round her face.

"Don't speak," warned Egon Rhys.

He had a second razor with him, one that he no longer used much. That morning he had thought, "It's old but it will do," and taken it down off the dusty windowsill where it lay—its handle as yellow as bone—between a ring of his

mother's and a glass of cloudy water through which the
light seemed to come suddenly when he picked it up.

Though he was careful to walk with his hands turned in
to the sides of his body in such a way as to provoke no
one, he had all the way up the hill a curious repeating
image of himself as somebody who had *already* run mad
with the two razors—hurtling after his enemies across the
icy treacherous setts while they stumbled into dark corners
or flung themselves over rotting fences, sprinting from one
feeble refuge to another. "I'll pen them up," he planned,
"in the observatory. They won't stop me now. Those bastards from Austonley . . ." It was almost as if he had done
it. He seemed to be watching himself from somewhere behind his own back; he could hear himself yelling as he went
for them, a winter gleam at the end of each wildly swinging arm.

"We'll see what happens then," he said aloud, and the
dwarf glanced up at him in surprise. "We'll see what happens
then." But the observatory came and went and nothing
happened at all.

By then some of the Austonley men were no longer both-
ering to hide, swaggering along instead with broad grins.
Other factions soon fell in with them, until they formed a
loose, companionable half-circle ten or fifteen yards back
along the steep street. Their breath mingled in the cold air,
and after a few minutes there was even some laughter and
conversation between the different parties. As soon as they
saw he was listening to them they came right up to Rhys's
heels, watching his hands warily and nudging each other.
The Yellow Paper kept itself apart from this: there was no
sign of the Anemone at all. Otherwise it was like a holiday.

Someone touched his shoulder and, stepping deftly away
in the same movement, asked him in a soft voice hardly
older than a boy's, "Still got that old ivory bugger of Osgerby's up your sleeve, Egon? That old slasher of Osgerby
Practal's?"

"Still got her there, have you?" repeated someone else.
"Let's have a look at her, Egon."

Rhys shrugged with fear and contempt.

It was bitterly cold on the canal bank. Vera stood listening to the rush of the broken weir a hundred yards up
the reach. Sprays of scarlet rose hips hung over the water

like necklaces tossed into the frozen air; a wren was bobbing and dipping among the dry reeds and withered dock plants beneath them.

"I can't see what such a little thing would find to eat," she said. "Can you?" No one answered.

The sound of the weir echoed off the boarded-up housefronts. Men from a dozen splinter groups and minor factions now filled the end of the lane to Orves, sealing it off. More were arriving all the time. They scraped heavily to and fro on the cinder path, avoiding the icy puddles, blowing into their cupped hands for warmth, giving Rhys quick shy looks as if to say, "We're going to have you this time." Some were sent to block the towpath. Presently the representatives of the Blue Anemone Ontological Association came out of one of the houses, where they had spent the morning playing black-and-red in a single flat ray of light that slanted between the boards and fell on a wooden chair. They had some trouble with the door.

Rhys brandished his razors at them.

"Where's the sense in this? Orcer Pust's a month dead; I put Ingarden down there with him not four nights ago—where was the sense in that?"

Sense was not at issue, they said.

"How many of you will I get before you get me?"

The representatives of the Anemone shrugged. It was all one to them.

"Come on then! Come on!" Rhys shouted to the bravos in the lane. "I can see some bastards I know over there. How would they like it? In the eyes? In the neck? Facedown in the bath-house tank with Orcer Pust?"

Kiss-O-Suck the dwarf sat down suddenly and unlaced his boots. When he had rolled his voluminous black trousers up as far as they would go he made a comical face and stepped into the canal, which submerged him to the thighs. He then waded out a few yards, turned round, and said quietly to Rhys, "As far as they're concerned you're as good as dead already." Further out, where it was deeper, probing gingerly in the mud with his toes, he added, "You're as good as dead on Allmans Heath." He slipped: swayed for a moment: waved his arms. "Oops." Shivering and blowing he climbed out onto the other side and began to rub his legs vigorously. "Foo. That's cold. Foo. Tah."

He called, "Why should they fight when they've only to make sure you go across?"

Rhys stared at him; then at the men from the Anemone. "You were none of you anything until I pulled you out of the gutter," he told them. He ran his hands through his hair.

When it was Vera's turn, the water was so cold she thought it would stop her heart.

Elder grew in thickets on the edge of the Heath as if some attempt at habitation had been made a long time ago. Immediately you got in among it, Vriko began to seem quiet and distant; the rush of the weir died away. There were low mounds overgrown with nettle and matted couch-grass; great brittle white-brown stems of cow parsley followed the line of a foundation or a wall; here and there a hole had been scraped by the dogs that swam over in the night from the city—bits of broken porcelain lay revealed in the soft black soil. Where brambles had colonized the open ground water could be heard beneath them, trickling away from the canal down narrow, aimless runnels and trenches.

It was hard for the dwarf to force his way through this stuff, and after about half an hour he fell on his back in a short rectangular pit like an empty cistern, from which he stared up sightlessly for a moment with arms and legs rigid in some sort of paralytic fit. "Get me out," he said in a low, urgent voice. "Pull me out."

Later he admitted to Vera:

"When I was a boy in the gloottokoma I would sometimes wake in the dark not knowing if it was night or day; or where I was; or what period of my life I was in. I could have been a baby in an unlit caravan. Or had I already become Kiss-O-Suck, Morgante, 'the Grand Little Man with the crowd in the palm of his hand'? It was impossible to tell: my ambitions were so clear to me, my disorientation so complete."

"I could never get enough to eat," said Vera. "Until I was ten years old I ate and ate."

The dwarf looked at her whitely for a moment.

"Anyway, that was how it felt," he said, "to live in a box. What a blaze of light when you were able to open the lid!"

Elder soon gave way to stands of emaciated birch, in a region of shallow valleys and long spurs between which the streams ran in beds of honey-colored stone as even as formal paving; a few oaks grew in sheltered positions among boulders the size of houses on an old alluvial bench. "It seems so empty!" said Vera. The dwarf laughed. "In the south they would call this the 'plaza,' " he boasted. "If they knew about it they'd come here for their holidays." But after a mile or so of rising ground they reached the edge of a plateau, heavily dissected into a fringe of peaty gullies each with steep black sides above a trickle of orange water. Stones like bits of tile littered the watershed, sorted into curious polygonal arrays by the frost. There was no respite from the wind that blew across it. And though when you looked back you could still see Vriko, it seemed to be fifteen or twenty miles away, a handful of spires tiny and indistinct under a setting sun.

"This is more like it," said Kiss-O-Suck.

Egon Rhys blundered across the entangled grain of the watershed, one peat hag to the next, until it brought him to a standstill. They very inconclusiveness of his encounter with his rivals, perhaps, had exhausted him. He showed no interest in his surroundings, but whenever she would let him he leaned on Vera's arm, describing to her as if she had never been there the Allotrope Cabaret—how pretty its little danseuse had been, how artistically she had danced, how well she had counterfeited an animal he had never imagined could exist. "I was amazed!" he kept saying. Every so often he stood still and looked down at his clothes as though he wondered how they had got dirty. "At least try and help yourself," said Vera, who thought he was ill.

The moment it got dark he was asleep; but he must have heard Kiss-O-Suck talking in the night because he woke up and said,

"In the market when my mother was alive it was always, 'Run and fetch a box of sugared anemones. Run, Egon, and fetch it now.' " Just when he seemed to have gone back to sleep again, his mouth hanging open and his head on one side, he began repeating with a kind of infantile resentment and melancholy, " 'Run and fetch it now! Run and fetch it now! Run and fetch it now!' "

He laughed.

In the morning, when he opened his eyes and saw he was on Allmans Heath, he remembered none of this. "Look!" he said, pulling Vera to her feet. "Just look at it!" He was already quivering with excitement.

"Did you ever feel the wind so cold?"

A cindery plain stretched level and uninterrupted to the horizon, smelling faintly of the rubbish pit on a wet day. The light that came and went across it was like the light falling through rainwater in empty tins; and the city could no longer be seen, even in the distance. To start with it was loose uncompacted stuff, ploughed up at every step to reveal just beneath the surface millions of bits of small rusty machinery like the insides of clocks; but soon it became as hard and gray as the sky, so that Vera could hardly tell where cinders left off and air began.

Rhys strode along energetically. He made the dwarf tell him about the other deserts he had visited. How big were they? What animals had he seen there? He would listen for a minute or two to the dwarf's answers, then say with satisfaction, "None of those places were as cold as this, I expect," or: "You get an albino sloth in the south, I've heard." Then, stopping to pick up what looked like a very long thin spring, coiled on itself with such brittle delicacy it must have been the remains of some terrific but fragile dragonfly: "What do you think of this, as a sign? I mean, from your experience?" The dwarf, who had not slept well, was silent.

"I could go on walking forever!" Rhys exclaimed, throwing the spring into the air. But later he seemed to tire again, and he complained that they had walked all day for nothing. He looked intently at the dwarf.

"How do you explain that?"

"What I care about," the dwarf said, "is having a piss." He walked off a little way and gasping with satisfaction sent a thick yellow stream into the ground. "Foo!" Afterwards he poked the cinders with his foot and said, "It takes it up, this stuff. Look at that. You could water it all day and never tell. Hallo, I think I can see something growing there already! Dwarfs are more fertile than ordinary people." (That night he sat awake again, slumped sideways, his arms wrapped round his tucked-up knees, watching Vera Ghillera with an unidentifiable expression on his face.

When he happened to look beyond her, or feel the wind on his back, he shuddered and closed his eyes.)

"When I first saw you," Vera told Egon Rhys, "you had cut your check. Do you remember? A line of blood ran down, and at the end of it I could see one perfect drop ready to fall."

"That excited you, did it?"

She stared at him.

He turned away in annoyance and studied the Heath. They had been on it now for perhaps three, perhaps four days. He had welcomed the effort, and gone to sleep worn out; he had woken up optimistic and been disappointed. Nothing was moving. The dwarf. did not seem to be able to give him a clear idea of what to look for. He had thought sometimes that he could see something out of the corner of his eye; but this was only a kind of rapid, persistent fibrillating movement, never so much an insect as its ghost or preliminary illusion. Though at first it had aggravated him, now that it was wearing off he wished it would come back.

"My knee was damaged practicing to dance Fyokla in *The Battenberg Cake.* That was chain after chain of the hardest steps Lympany could devise, they left your calves like blocks of wood. It hurt to run down all those stairs to help you."

"Help me!" jeered Rhys.

"I'm the locust that brought you here," she said suddenly.

She stood back on the hard cinders. One two three, one two three, she mimicked the poverty-stricken skips and hops that pass for dance at the Allotrope Cabaret; the pain and lassitude of the dancer who performs them. Her feet made a faint dry scraping sound.

"I'm the locust you came to see. After all, it's as much as *she* could do."

Rhys looked alertly from Vera to the dwarf. Ribbons of frayed red silk fluttered from his sleeve in the wind.

"I meant a real insect," he said. "You knew that before we started."

"We haven't been lucky," Kiss-O-Suck agreed.

When Rhys took hold of his wrist he stood as still and

compliant as a small animal and added, "Perhaps we came
at the wrong time of year."

Something had gone out of him: Rhys gazed down into his
lined face as if he was trying to recognize what. Then he
pushed the dwarf tenderly onto the cinders and knelt over
him. He touched each polished check, then ran his fingertips
in bemusement down the sides of the jaw. He seemed to be
about to say something: instead he flicked the razor into his
hand with a quick snaky motion so that light shot off the
hollow curve of the blade. The dwarf watched it; he nodded.
"I've never been in a desert in my life," he admitted. "I made
that up for Vera. It sounded more exotic."

He considered this. "Yet how could I refuse her anything? She's the greatest dancer in the world."

"You were the greatest clown," Rhys said.

He laid the flat of the razor delicately against the dwarf's
cheekbone, just under the eye, where there were faint veins
in a net beneath the skin.

"I believed all that."

Kiss-O-Suck's eyes were china-blue. "Wait," he said. Look!"

Vera, who had given up trying to imitate locust or danseuse or indeed anything, was en pointe and running chains
of steps out across the ash, complicating and recomplicating
them in a daze of technique until she felt exactly like one
of the ribbons flying from Rhys's sleeve. It was a release
for her, they were always saying at the Prospekt Theater, to
do the most difficult things, all kinds of allegro and batterie
bewilderingly entangled, then suddenly the great turning
jump forbidden to female dancers for more than a hundred
years. As she danced she reduced the distinction between
Heath and sky. The horizon, never convinced of itself,
melted. Vera was left crossing and recrossing a space steadily less definable. A smile came to Kiss-O-Suck's lips; he
pushed the razor away with one fat little hand and cried:

"She's floating!"

"That won't help you, you bastard," Egon Rhys
warned him.

He made the great sweeping cut which a week before
had driven the razor through the bone and gristle at the
base of Toni Ingarden's throat.

It was a good cut. He liked it so much he let it pass over
the dwarf's head; stopped the weapon dead; and, tossing it

from one hand to the other, laughed. The dwarf looked surprised. "Ha!" shouted Rhys. Suddenly he spun around on one bent leg as if he had heard another enemy behind him. He threw himself sideways, cutting out right and left faster than you could see. "And this is how I do it," he panted, "when it comes down to the really funny business." The second razor appeared magically in his other hand and between them they parceled up the emptiness, slashing wildly about with a life of their own while Rhys wobbled and ducked across the surface of the desert with a curious, shuffling, buckle-kneed, bent-elbowed gait. "Now I'll show you how I can kick!" he called.

But Kiss-O-Suck, who had watched this performance with an interested air, murmuring judicially at some difficult stroke, only smiled and moved away. He had the idea—it had never been done before—to link in sequence a medley of cartwheels, "flying Dementos," and handsprings, which would bounce him so far into the smoky air of the arena, spinning over and over himself with his knees tucked into his stomach, that eventually he would be able to look *down* on the crowd, like a firework before it burst. "Tah!" he whispered, as he nerved himself up. "Codpoorlie, tah!"

Soon he and Rhys were floating too, leaping and twirling and wriggling higher and higher, attaining by their efforts a space that had no sense of limit or closure. But Vera Ghillera was always ahead of them, and seemed to generate their rhythm as she went.

* * *

Deserts spread to the northeast of the city, and in a wide swathe to its south.

They are of all kinds, from peneplains of disintegrating metallic dust—out of which rise at intervals lines of bony incandescent hills—to localized chemical sumps, deep, tarry and corrosive, over whose surfaces glitter small flies with papery wings and perhaps a pair of legs too many. These regions are full of old cities that differ from Vriko only in the completeness of their deterioration. The traveler in them may be baked to death; or, discovered with his eyelids frozen together, leave behind only a journal which ends in the middle of a sentence.

The Metal Salt Marches, Fenlen Island, the Great Brown Waste: the borders of regions as exotic as this are drawn differently on the maps of competing authorities: but they are at least bounded in the conventional sense. Allmans Heath, whose borders can be agreed on by everyone, does not seem to be. Neither does it seem satisfactory now to say that while those deserts lie outside the city, Allmans Heath lies within it.

* * *

The night was quiet.

Five to eleven, and except where the weir agitated its surface, the canal at Allmans Reach was covered with the lightest and most fragile web of ice. A strong moon cast its blue and gamboge light across the boarded-up fronts of the houses by the towpath. "They don't look as if much life ever goes on in them," thought the watchman, an unimaginative man at the beginning of his night's work, which was to walk from there up to the back of the Atteline Quarter (where he could get a cup of tea if he wanted one) and down again. He banged his hands together in the cold. As he stood there he saw three figures wade into the water on the other side of the canal.

They were only ten yards upstream, between him and the weir, and the moonlight fell on them clearly. They were wrapped up in cloaks and hoods, "like brown paper parcels, or statues tied up in sacks," he insisted later; and under these garments their bodies seemed to be jerking and writhing in a continual rhythmic motion, though for him it was too disconnected to be called a dance. The new ice parted for them like damp sugar floating on the water. They paid no attention to the watchman, but forded the canal, tallest first, shortest last, and disappeared down the cinder lane that goes via Orves and the observatory to the courtyard near the Plain Moon Cafe.

The watchman rubbed his hands and looked round for a minute or two, as if he expected something else to happen. "Eleven o'clock," he called at last; and though he couldn't commit himself to a description which seemed so subject to qualification as to be in bad faith, added: "And all's all."

In my house, there are a number of key jobs that fall to me. Some involve brute strength—like twisting lids off recalcitrant jars, or breaking up ice on the driveway that I didn't shovel, or hauling the garbage can to the side of the road for the trusty professional trash service to pick up with their usual air of what-the-hey bonhomie. But another job I have is spider killer.

Not bug killer. Everyone's cool with just about any other kind of insect. Spiders though . . . are special. What is it . . . with spiders? Too many legs? The web? Or something else? It's obviously a question John Wyndham has thought about. Everyone knows Wyndham's classic novel, *Day of the Triffids*. It showed that even house plants could be the stuff of nightmares. But it was a short dark fantasy story of Wyndham's that really helped shape my own twisted world view. In "More Spinned Against," the subject is a very special spider and—as in so many great tales—a "deal." And just maybe this is why I'm always getting asked to kill the little guys. . . .

—Matt Costello

MORE SPINNED AGAINST . . .
by John Wyndham

One of the things about her husband that displeased Lydia Charters more as the years went by was the shape of him; another was his hobby. There were other displeasures, of course, but it was these in particular that aroused her sense of failure.

True, he had been much the same shape when she had married him, but she had looked for improvement. She had envisioned the development, under her domestic influence, of a more handsome, suaver, better filled type. Yet after nearly twelve years of her care and feeding there was scarcely any demonstrable improvement. The torso, the main man, looked a little more solid, and the scales endorsed that it was so, but unfortunately this simply seemed to emphasize the knobby, gangling, loosely-hinged effect of the rest.

Once, in a mood of more than usual dissatisfaction, Lydia had taken a pair of his trousers and measured them carefully. Inert and empty, they seemed all right—long in the leg, naturally, but not abnormally so, and the usual width that people wore—but put to use, they immediately achieved the effect of being too narrow and full of knobs, just as his sleeves did. After the failure of several ideas to soften this appearance, she had realized that she would have to put up with it. Reluctantly, she had told herself: "Well, I suppose it can't be helped. It must be just one of those things—like horsy women getting to look more like horses, I mean," and thereby managed a dig at the hobby, as well.

Hobbies are convenient in the child, but an irritant in the adult; which is why women are careful never to have them, but simply to be interested in this or that. It is perfectly natural for a woman—and Lydia was a comely demonstration of the art of being one—to take an interest in semiprecious and, when she can afford them, precious stones: Edward's hobby, on the other hand, was not really natural to anyone.

Lydia had known about the hobby before they were married, of course. No one could know Edward for long without being aware of the way his eyes hopefully roved the corners of any room he chanced to be in, or how, when he was out of doors, his attention would be suddenly snatched away from any matter in hand by the sight of a pile of dead leaves, or a piece of loose bark. It had been irritating at times, but she had not allowed it to weigh too much with her, since it would naturally wither from neglect later. For Lydia held the not uncommon opinion that though, of course, a married man should spend a certain amount of his time assuring an income, beyond that there ought to be only one interest in his life—from which it followed that the existence of any other must be slightly insulting to his wife, since everybody knows that a hobby is really just a form of sublimation.

The withering, however, had not taken place.

Disappointing as this was in itself, it would have been a lot more tolerable if Edward's hobby had been the collection of objects of standing—say, old prints, or first editions, or oriental pottery. That kind of thing could not only be displayed for envy, it had value; and the collector himself had status. But no one achieved the status of being any more than a crank for having even a very extensive collection of spiders.

Even over butterflies or moths, Lydia felt without actually putting the matter to the test, one could perhaps have summoned up the appearance of some enthusiasm. There was a kind of nature's-living-jewels line that one could take if they were nicely mounted. But for spiders—a lot of nasty, creepy-crawly, leggy horrors, all getting gradually more pallid in tubes of alcohol—she could find nothing to be said at all.

In the early days of their marriage Edward had tried to give her some of his own enthusiasm, and Lydia had listened as tactfully as possible to his explanations of the complicated lives, customs, and mating habits of spiders, most of which seemed either disgusting, or very short on morals, or frequently both, and to his expatiations on the beauties of coloration and marking which her eye lacked the affection to detect. Luckily, however, it had gradually become apparent from some of her comments and questions that Edward was not awakening the sympathetic understanding he had hoped for, and when the attempt lapsed Lydia had been able to retreat gratefully to her former viewpoint that all spiders were undesirable, and the dead only slightly less horrible than the living.

Realizing that frontal opposition to spiders would be poor tactics, she had attempted a quiet and painless weaning. It had taken her two or three years to appreciate that this was not going to work; after that, the spiders had settled down to being one of those bits of the rough that the wise take with the smooth and leave unmentioned except on those occasions of extreme provocation when the whole catalog of one's dissatisfactions is reviewed.

Lydia entered Edward's spider room about once a week, partly to tidy and dust it, and partly to enjoy detesting its inhabitants in a pleasantly masochistic fashion. This she could do on at least two levels. There was the kind of generalized satisfaction that anyone might feel, in looking along the rows of test tubes, that at any rate here were a whole lot of displeasing creepies that would creep no more. And then there was the more personal sense of compensa-

tion in the reflection that though they had to some extent
succeeded in diverting a married man's attention from its
only proper target, they had had to die to do it.

There was an astonishing number of test tubes ranged in
the racks along the walls; so many that at one time she had
hopefully inquired whether there could be many more
kinds of spiders. His first answer of five hundred and sixty
in the British Isles had been quite encouraging, but then
he had gone on to speak of twenty thousand or so different
kinds in the world, not to mention the allied orders, whatever they might be, in a way that was depressing.

There were other things in the room besides the test
tubes: a shelf of reference books, a card index, a table holding his carefully hooded miscroscope. There was also a long
bench against one wall supporting a variety of bottles, packets of slides, boxes of new test tubes, as well as a number
of glass-topped boxes in which specimens were preserved
for study alive before they went into the alcohol.

Lydia could never resist peeping into these condemned
cells with a satisfaction which she would scarcely have
cared to admit, or, indeed, even have felt in the case of
other creatures, but somehow with spiders it just served
them right for being spiders. As a rule there would be five
or six of them in similar boxes, and it was with surprise
one morning that she noticed a large bell jar ranged neatly
in the line. After she had done the rest of the dusting,
curiosity took her over to the bench. It should, of course,
have been much easier to observe the occupant of the bell
jar than those of the boxes, but in fact it was not, because
the inside, for fully two-thirds of its height, was obscured
by web. A web so thickly woven as to hide the occupant
entirely from the sides. It hung in folds, almost like a drap-
ery, and on examining it more closely, Lydia was impressed
by the ingenuity of the work; it looked surprisingly like a
set of Nottingham lace curtains—though reduced greatly in
scale, of course, and perhaps not quite in the top flight of
design. Lydia went closer to look over the top edge of
the web, and down upon the occupant. "Good gracious!"
she said.

The spider, squatting in the center of its web-screened
circle, was quite the largest she had ever seen. She stared
at it. She recalled that Edward had been in a state of some

excitement the previous evening, but she had paid little attention except to tell him, as on several previous occasions, that she was much too busy to go and look at a horrible spider: she also recalled that he had been somewhat hurt about her lack of interest. Now, seeing the spider, she could understand that: she could even understand for once how it was possible to talk of a beautifully colored spider, for there could be no doubt at all that this specimen deserved a place in the nature's-living-jewels class.

The ground color was a pale green with a darker stippling, which faded away toward the under side. Down the center of the back ran a pattern of blue arrowheads, bright in the center and merging almost into the green at the points. At either side of the abdomen were bracket-shaped squiggles of scarlet. Touches of the same scarlet showed at the joints of the green legs, and there were small markings of it, too, on the upper part of what Edward resoundingly called the cephalothorax, but which Lydia thought of as the part where the legs were fastened on.

Lydia leaned closer. Strangely, the spider had not frozen into immobility in the usual spiderish manner. Its attention seemed to be wholly taken up by something held out between its front pair of legs, something that flashed as it moved. Lydia thought that the object was an aquamarine, cut and polished. As she moved her head to make sure, her shadow fell across the bell jar. The spider stopped twiddling the stone, and froze. Presently a small, muffled voice said:

"Hullo! Who are you?" with a slight foreign accent.

Lydia looked round. The room was as empty as before.

"No. Here!" said the muffled voice.

She looked down again at the jar, and saw the spider pointing to itself with its number two leg on the right.

"My name," said the voice, sociably, "is Arachne. What's yours?"

"Er—Lydia," said Lydia, uncertainly.

"Oh, dear! Why?" asked the voice.

Lydia felt a trifle nettled. "What do you mean, why?" she asked.

"Well, as I recall it, Lydia was sent to hell as a punishment for doing very nasty things to her lover. I suppose you aren't given to—?"

"Certainly not," Lydia said, cutting the voice short.

"Oh," said the voice, doubtfully. "Still, they can't have given you the name for nothing. And, mind you, I never really blamed Lydia. Lovers, in my experience, usually deserve—" Lydia lost the rest as she looked around the room again, uncertainly.

"I don't understand," she said. "I mean, is it really—?"

"Oh, it's me, all right," said the spider. And to make sure, it indicated itself again, this time with the third leg on the left.

"But—but spiders can't—"

"Of course not. Not real spiders, but I'm Arachne—I told you that."

A hazy memory stirred at the back of Lydia's mind.

"You mean *the* Arachne?" she inquired.

"Did you ever hear of another?" the voice asked, coldly.

"I mean, the one who annoyed Athene—though I can't remember just how?" said Lydia.

"Certainly. I was technically a spinster, and Athene was jealous and—"

"I should have thought it would be the other way—oh, I see, you mean you spun?"

"That's what I said. I was *the* best spinner and weaver, and when I won the all-Greece open competition and beat Athene she couldn't take it; she was so furiously jealous that she turned me into a spider. It's very unfair to let gods and goddesses go in for competitions at all, I always say. They're spitefully bad losers, and then they go telling lies about you to justify the bad-tempered things they do in revenge. You've probably heard it differently?" the voice added, on a slightly challenging note.

"No, I think it was pretty much like that," Lydia told her, tactfully. "You must have been a spider a very long time now," she added.

"Yes, I suppose so, but you give up counting after a bit." The voice paused, then it went on: "I say, would you mind taking this glass thing off? It's stuffy in here; besides, I shouldn't have to shout."

Lydia hesitated.

"I never interfere with anything in this room. My husband gets so annoyed if I do."

"Oh, you needn't be afraid I shall run away. I'll give you my word on that, if you like."

But Lydia was still doubtful.

"You're in a pretty desperate position, you know," she said, with an involuntary glance at the alcohol bottle.

"Not really," said the voice in a tone that suggested a shrug. "I've often been caught before. Something always turns up—it *has* to. That's one of the few advantages of of having a really permanent curse on you. It makes it impossible for anything really fatal to happen."

Lydia looked round. The window was shut, the door, too, and the fireplace was blocked up.

"Well, perhaps for a few minutes, if you promise," she allowed.

She lifted the jar, and put it down to one side. As she did so the curtains of web trailed out, and tore.

"Never mind about them. Phew! That's better," said the voice, still small, but now quite clear and distinct.

The spider did not move. It still held the aquamarine, catching the light and shining, between its front legs.

On a sudden thought, Lydia leaned down and looked at the stone more closely. She was relieved to see that it was not one of her own.

"Pretty, isn't it?" said Arachne. "Not really my color, though. I rather kill it, I think. One of the emeralds would have been more suitable—even though they were smaller."

"Where did you get it?" Lydia asked.

"Oh, a house just near here. Next door but one, I think it was."

"Mrs. Ferris's—yes, of course, that would be one of hers."

"Possibly," agreed Arachne. "Anyway, it was in a cabinet with a lot of others, so I took it, and I was just coming through the hedge out of the garden, looking for a comfortable hole to enjoy it in, when I got caught. It was the stone shining that made him see me. A funny sort of man, rather like a spider himself, if he had had more legs."

Lydia said, somewhat coldly:

"He was smarter than you were."

"H'm," said Arachne, noncommittally.

She laid the stone down and started to move about, trailing several threads from her spinnerets. Lydia drew away a little. For a moment she watched Arachne, who appeared to be engaged in a kind of doodling, then her eyes returned to the aquamarine.

"I have a little collection of stones myself. Not as good as Mrs. Ferris's, of course, but one or two nice ones amongst them," she remarked.

"Oh," said Arachne, absent-minded as she worked out her pattern.

"I—I should rather like a nice aquamarine," said Lydia. "Suppose the door happened to have been left open just a little. . . ."

"There!" said Arachne, with satisfaction. "Isn't that the prettiest doily you ever saw?"

She paused to admire her work.

Lydia looked at it, too. The pattern seemed to her to show a lack of subtlety, but she agreed tactfully. "It's delightful! Absolutely charming! I wish I could—I mean, I don't know how you do it."

"One has just a little talent, you know," said Arachne, with undeceiving modesty. "You were saying something?" she added.

Lydia repeated her earlier remark.

"Not really worth my while," said Arachne. "I told you something *has* to happen, so why should I bother?"

She began to doodle again. Rapidly, though with a slightly abstracted air, she constructed another small lace mat suitable for the lower-income-bracket trade, and pondered over it for a moment. Presently she said:

"Of course, if it were to be *made* worth my while . . ."

"I couldn't afford very much—" began Lydia, with caution.

"Not money," said Arachne. "What on earth would I do with money? But I am a bit overdue for a holiday."

"Holiday?" Lydia repeated, blankly.

"There's a sort of alleviation clause," Arachne explained. "Lots of good curses have them. It's often something like being uncursed by a prince's kiss—you know, something so improbable that it's a real outside chance, but gets the god a reputation for not being such a Shylock after all. Mine is that I'm allowed twenty-four hours' holiday in the year— but I've scarcely ever had it." She paused, doodling an inch or two of lace edging. "You see," she added, "the difficult thing is to find someone willing to change places for twenty-four hours."

"Er—yes, I can see it would be," said Lydia, detachedly.

Arachne put out one foreleg and spun the aquamarine round so that it glittered.

"Someone willing to change places," she repeated.

"Well—er—I—er—I don't think—" Lydia tried.

"It's not at all difficult to get in and out of Mrs. Ferris's house—not when you're my size," Arachne observed.

Lydia looked at the aquamarine. It wasn't possible to stop having a mental picture of the other stones that were lying bedded on black velvet in Mrs. Ferris's cabinet.

"Suppose one got caught?" she suggested.

"One need not bother about that—except as an inconvenience. I should have to take over in twenty-four hours again, in any case," Arachne told her.

"Well—I don't know—" said Lydia, unwillingly.

Arachne spoke in a ruminative manner:

"I remember thinking how easy it would be to carry them out one by one, and hide them in a convenient hole," she said.

Lydia was never able to recall in detail the succeeding stages of the conversation, only that at some point where she was still intending to be tentative and hypothetical Arachne must have thought she was more definite. Anyway, one moment she was still standing beside the bench, and the next, it seemed, she was on it, and the thing had happened.

She didn't really feel any different, either. Six eyes did not seem any more difficult to manage than two, though everything looked exceedingly large, and the opposite wall very far away. The eight legs seemed capable of managing themselves without getting tangled, too.

"How do you? —Oh, I see," she said.

"Steady on," said a voice from above. "That's more than enough for a pair of curtains you've wasted there. Take it gently, now. Always keep the word 'dainty' in mind. Yes, that's much better—a little finer still. That's it. You'll soon get the idea. Now all you have to do is walk over the edge, and let yourself down on it."

"Er—yes," said Lydia, dubiously. The edge of the bench seemed a long way from the floor.

The figure towering above turned as if to go, and then turned back on a thought that occurred to her.

"Oh, there's just one thing," she said. "About men."

"Men?" said Lydia.

"Well, male spiders. I mean, I don't want to come back and find that—"

"No, of course not," agreed Lydia. "I shall be pretty busy, I expect. And I don't—er—think I feel much interested in male spiders, as a matter of fact."

"Well, I don't know. There's this business of like calling to like."

"I think it sort of probably depends on how long you have been like," suggested Lydia.

"Good. Anyway, it's not very difficult. He'll only be about a sixteenth of your size, so you can easily brush him off. Or you can eat him, if you like."

"*Eat* him!" exclaimed Lydia. "Oh, yes, I remember my husband said something—no, I think I'll just brush him off, as you said."

"Just as you like. There's one thing about spiders, they're much better arranged to the female advantage. You don't have to go on being cumbered up with a useless male just because. You simply find a new one when you want him. It simplifies things a lot, really."

"I suppose so," said Lydia. "Still, in only twenty-four hours—"

"Quite," said Arachne. "Well, I'll be off. I mustn't waste my holiday. You'll find you'll be quite all right once you get the hang of it. Goodbye till tomorrow." And she went out, leaving the door slightly ajar.

Lydia practiced her spinning a little more until she could be sure of keeping a fairly even thread. Then she went to the edge of the bench. After a slight hesitation she let herself over. It turned out to be quite easy, really.

* * *

Indeed, the whole thing turned out to be far easier than she had expected. She found her way to Mrs. Ferris's drawing-room, where the door of the cabinet had been carelessly left unlatched, and selected a nice fire-opal. There was no difficulty in discovering a small hole on the road side of the front bank in which the booty could be deposited for collection later. On the next trip she chose a small ruby, and the next time an excellently cut square zircon, and the operation settled down to an industrious routine which was interrupted by nothing more than the advances of a couple of male spiders who were easily bowled over with a flip of the front leg, and became discouraged.

By the late afternoon Lydia had accumulated quite a nice little hoard in the hole in the bank. She was in the act of adding a small topaz, and wondering whether she would make just one more trip, when a shadow fell across her. She froze quite still, looking up at a tall gangling form with knobbly joints, which really did look surprisingly spidery from that angle.

"Well, I'm damned," said Edward's voice, speaking to itself. "Another of them! Two in two days. Most extraordinary."

Then, before Lydia could make up her mind what to do, a sudden darkness descended over her, and presently she found herself being joggled along in a box.

A few minutes later she was under the bell jar that she had lifted off Arachne, with Edward bending over her, looking partly annoyed at finding that his specimen had escaped, and partly elated that he had recaptured it.

After that, there didn't seem to be much to do but doodle a few lace curtains for privacy, in the way Arachne had. It was a consoling thought that the stones were safely cached away, and that any time after the next twelve or thirteen hours she would be able to collect them at her leisure. . . .

* * *

No one came near the spider room during the evening. Lydia could distinguish various domestic sounds taking place in more or less their usual succession, and culminating in two pairs of footfalls ascending the stairs. And but for physical handicaps, she might have frowned slightly at this point. The ethics of the situation were somewhat obscure. Was Arachne really entitled? Oh, well, there nothing one could do about it, anyway.

Presently the sound of movement ceased, and the house settled down for the night.

She had half expected that Edward would look in to assure himself of her safety before he went to work in the morning. She remembered that he had done so in the case of other and far less spectacular spiders, and she was a trifle piqued that when at last the door did open, it was simply to admit Arachne. She noticed, also, that Arachne had not succeeded in doing her hair with just that touch that suited Lydia's face.

Arachne gave a little yawn, and came across to the bench.

"Hullo," she said, lifting the jar, "had an interesting time?"

"Not this part of it," Lydia said. "Yesterday was very satisfactory, though. I hope you enjoyed your holiday."

"Yes," said Arachne. "Yes, I had a nice time—though it did somehow seem less of a change than I'd hoped." She looked at the watch on her wrist. "Well, time's nearly up. If I don't get back, I'll have that Athene on my tail. You ready?"

"Certainly," said Lydia, feeling more than ready.

"Well, here we are again," said Arachne's small voice. She stretched her legs in pairs, starting at the front and working astern. Then she doodled a capital A in a debased Gothic script to assure herself that her spinning faculties were unimpaired.

"You know," she said, "habit is a curious thing. I'm not sure that by now I'm not more comfortable like this, after all. Less inhibited, really."

She scuttered over to the side of the bench and let herself down, looking like a ball of brilliant feathers sinking to the floor. As she reached it, she unfolded her legs and ran across to the open door. On the threshold she paused.

"Well, goodbye, and thanks a lot," she said. "I'm sorry about your husband. I'm afraid I rather forgot myself for the moment."

Then she scooted away down the passage as if she were a ball of colored wools blowing away in the draught.

"Goodbye," said Lydia, by no means sorry to see her go.

The intention of Arachne's parting remark was lost on her: in fact, she forgot it altogether until she discovered the collection of extraordinarily knobbly bones that someone had recently put in the dustbin.

Charles Dickens has always been my favorite writer. This fantasy tale, which is embedded in *The Pickwick Papers,* is one of my favorites. To me, this story illustrates Dickens' genius, for he not only imbues his people with life, but he even manages to transform an old chair into a believable, lovable, rascally character.

I have loved this story from the first time I ever read it and I've never looked at an old "queer" chair quite the same since!

—Margaret Weis

THE BAGMAN'S STORY
by Charles Dickens

"One winter's evening, about five o'clock, just as it began to grow dusk, a man in a gig might have been seen urging his tired horse along the road which leads across Marlborough Downs, in the direction of Bristol. I say he might have been seen, and I have no doubt he would have been, if anybody but a blind man had happened to pass that way; but the weather was so bad, and the night so cold and wet, that nothing was out but the water, and so the traveller jogged along in the middle of the road, lonesome and dreary enough. If any bagman of that day could have caught sight of the little neck-or-nothing sort of gig, with a clay-colored body and red wheels, and the vixen-ish ill-tempered, fast-going bay mare that looked like a cross between a butcher's horse and a two-penny post-office pony, he would have known at once, that this traveller could have been no other than Tom Smart, of the great house of Bilson and Slum, Cateaton Street, City. However, as there was no bagman to look on, nobody knew anything at all about the matter; and so Tom Smart and his clay-colored gig with the red wheels, and the vixenish mare with the fast pace, went on together, keeping the secret among them: and nobody was a bit the wiser.

"There are many pleasanter places even in this dreary world, than Marlborough Downs when it blows hard; and if you throw in beside, a gloomy winter's evening, a miry and sloppy road, and a pelting fall of heavy rain, and try the effect, by way of experiment, in your own proper person, you will experience the full force of this observation.

"The wind blew—not up the road or down it, through that's bad enough, but sheer across it, sending the rain slanting down like the lines they used to rule in the copybooks at school, to make the boys slope well. For a moment it would die away, and the traveller would begin to delude himself into the belief that, exhausted with its previous fury, it had quietly lain itself down to rest, when, whoo! he would hear it growling and whistling in the distance, and on it would come rushing over the hill-tops, and sweeping along the plain, gathering sound and strength as it drew nearer, until it dashed with a heavy gust against horse and man, driving the sharp rain into their ears, and its cold damp breath into their very bones; and past them it would scour, far, far away, with a stunning roar, as if in ridicule of their weakness, and triumphant in the consciousness of its own strength and power.

"The bay mare splashed away, through the mud and water with drooping ears; now and then tossing her head as if to express her disgust at this very ungentlemanly behavior of the elements, but keeping a good place notwithstanding, until a gust of wind, more furious than any that had yet assailed them, caused her to stop suddenly and plant her four feet firmly against the ground, to prevent her being blown over. It's a special mercy that she did this, for if she *had* been blown over, the vixenish mare was so light, and the gig was so light, and Tom Smart such a light weight into the bargain, that they must infallibly have all gone rolling over and over together until they reached the confines of earth, or until the wind fell; and in either case the probability is, that neither the vixenish mare, nor the clay-colored gig with the red wheels, nor Tom Smart, would ever have been fit for service again.

" 'Well, damn my straps and whiskers,' says Tom Smart (Tom sometimes had an unpleasant knack of swearing), 'Damn my straps and whiskers,' says Tom, 'if this ain't pleasant, blow me!'

"You'll very likely ask me why, as Tom Smart had been pretty well blown already, he expressed this wish to be submitted to the same process again. I can't say—all I know is, that Tom Smart said so—or at least he always told my uncle he said so, and it's just the same thing.

" 'Blow me,' says Tom Smart; and the mare neighed as if she were precisely of the same opinion.

" 'Cheer up, old girl,' said Tom, patting the bay mare on the neck with the end of his whip. 'It won't do pushing on, such a night as this; the first house we come to we'll put up at, so the faster you go the sooner it's over. Soho, old girl—gently—gently.'

"Whether the vixenish mare was sufficiently well acquainted with the tones of Tom's voice to comprehend his meaning, or whether she found it colder standing still than moving on, of course I can't say. But I can say that Tom had no sooner finished speaking, than she pricked up her ears, and started forward at a speed which made the clay-colored gig rattle till you would have supposed every one of the red spokes were going to fly out on the turf of Marlborough Downs; and even Tom, whip as he was, couldn't stop or check her pace, until she drew up, of her own accord, before a road-side inn on the right hand side of the way, about half a quarter of a mile from the end of the Downs.

"Tom cast a hasty glance at the upper part of the house as he threw the reins to the hostler, and stuck the whip in the box. It was a strange old place, built of a kind of shingle, inlaid, as it were, with cross-beams, with gabled-topped windows projecting completely over the pathway, and a low door with a dark porch, and a couple of steep steps leading down into the house, instead of the modern fashion of half a dozen shallow ones leading up to it. It was a comfortable-looking place though, for there was a strong cheerful light in the bar-window, which shed a bright ray across the road, and even lighted up the hedge on the other side; and there was a red flickering light in the opposite window, one moment but faintly discernible, and the next gleaming strongly through the drawn curtains, which intimated that a rousing fire was blazing within. Marking these little evidences with the eye of an experienced traveller, Tom dismounted with as much agility as his half-frozen limbs would permit, and entered the house.

"In less than five minutes' time, Tom was ensconced in the room opposite the bar—the very room where he had imagined the fire blazing—before a substantial matter-of-fact roaring fire, composed of something short of a bushel of coals, and wood enough to make half a dozen decent gooseberry bushes, piled half way up the chimney, and roaring and crackling with a sound that of itself would have warmed the heart of any reasonable man. This was comfortable, but this was not all, for a smartly-dressed girl, with a bright eye and a neat ankle, was laying a very clean white cloth on the table; and as Tom sat with his slippered feet on the fender, and his back to the open door, he saw a charming prospect of the bar reflected in the glass over the chimney-piece, with delightful rows of green bottles and gold labels, together with jars of pickles and preserves, and cheeses and boiled hams, and rounds of beef, arranged on shelves in the most tempting and delicious array. Well, this was comfortable too; but even this was not all—for in the bar, seated at tea at the nicest possible little table, drawn close up before the brightest possible little fire, was a buxom widow of somewhere about eight and forty or thereabouts, with a face as comfortable as the bar, who was evidently the landlady of the house, and the supreme ruler over all these agreeable possessions. There was only one drawback to the beauty of the whole picture, and that was a tall man—a very tall man—in a brown coat and bright basket buttons, and black whiskers, and wavy black hair, who was seated at tea with the widow, and who it required no great penetration to discover was in a fair way of persuading her to be a widow no longer, but to confer upon him the privilege of sitting down in that bar for and during the whole remainder of the term of his natural life.

"Tom Smart was by no means of an irritable or envious disposition, but somehow or other the tall man with the brown coat and the bright basket buttons did rouse what little gall he had in his composition, and did make him feel extremely indignant; the more especially as he could now and then observe, from his seat before the glass, certain little affectionate familiarities passing between the tall man and the widow, which sufficiently denoted that the tall man was as high in favor as he was in size. Tom was fond of hot punch—I may venture to say he was *very* fond of hot punch—and after he had seen the vixenish mare well fed and well littered down, and eaten every bit of the nice little hot dinner which the widow tossed up for him with her own hands, he just ordered a tumbler of it, by way of experiment. Now, if there was one thing in the whole range of domestic art, which the widow could manufacture better than another it was this identical article; and the first tumbler was adapted to Tom Smart's taste with such peculiar nicety, that he ordered a second with the least possible delay. Hot punch is a pleasant thing, gentlemen—an extremely pleasant thing under any circumstances—but in that snug old parlor, before the roaring fire, with the wind blowing outside till every timber in the old house creaked again, Tom Smart found it perfectly delightful. He ordered another tumbler, and then another—I am not quite certain whether he didn't order another after that—but the more he drank of the hot punch, the more he thought of the tall man.

" 'Confound his impudence!' said Tom to himself, 'what business has he in that snug bar? Such an ugly villain too!' said Tom. 'If the widow had any taste, she might surely pick up some better fellow than that.' Here Tom's eye wandered from the glass on the chimney-piece, to the glass on the table; and as he felt himself become gradually sentimental, he emptied the fourth tumbler of punch and ordered a fifth.

"Tom Smart, gentlemen, had always been very much attached to the public line. It had long been his ambition to stand in a bar of his own, in a green coat, knee-cords, and tops. He had a great notion of taking the chair at convivial dinners, and he had often thought how well he could preside in a room of his own in the talking way, and what a capital example he could set to his customers in the drinking department. All these things passed rapidly through Tom's mind as he sat drinking the hot punch by the roaring fire, and he felt very justly and properly indignant that the tall man should be in a fair way of keeping such an excellent house, while he, Tom Smart, was as far from it as ever. So, after deliberating over the last two tumblers, whether he hadn't a perfect right to pick a quarrel with the tall man for having contrived to get into the good graces of the buxom widow, Tom Smart at last arrived at the satisfactory conclusion that he was a very ill-used and persecuted individual, and had better go to bed.

"Up a wide and ancient staircase the smart girl preceded Tom, shading the chamber candle with her hand, to protect it from the currents of air which in such a rambling old place might have found plenty of room to disport themselves in, without blowing the candle out, but which did blow it out nevertheless; thus affording Tom's enemies an opportunity of asserting that it was he, and not the wind, who extinguished the candle, and that while he pretended to be blowing it alight again, he was in fact kissing the girl. Be this as it may, another light was obtained, and Tom was conducted through a maze of rooms, and a labyrinth of passages, to the apartment which had been prepared for his reception, where the girl bade him good night, and left him alone.

"It was a good large room with big closets, and a bed which might have served for a whole boarding-school, to say nothing of a couple of oaken presses that would have held the baggage of a small army; but what struck Tom's fancy most was a strange, grim-looking high-backed chair, carved in the most fantastic manner, with a flowered damask cushion, and the round knobs at the bottom of the legs carefully tied up in red cloth, as if it had got the gout in its toes. Of any other queer chair, Tom would only have thought it *was* a queer chair, and there would have been an end of the matter; but there was something about this particular chair, and yet he couldn't tell what it was, so odd and so unlike any other piece of furniture he had ever seen, that it seemed to fascinate him. He sat down before the fire, and stared at the old chair for half an hour;—Deuce take the chair, it was such a strange old thing, he couldn't take his eyes off it.

" 'Well,' said Tom, slowly undressing himself, and staring at the old chair all the while, which stood with a mysterious aspect by the bed-side, 'I never saw such a rum concern as that in my days. Very odd,' said Tom, who had got rather sage with the hot punch, 'Very odd.' Tom shook his head with an air of profound wisdom, and looked at the chair again. He couldn't make anything of it though, so he got into bed, covered himself up warm, and fell asleep.

"In about half an hour, Tom woke up, with a start, from a confused dream of tall men and tumblers of punch: and the first object that presented itself to his waking imagination was the queer chair.

" 'I won't look at it any more,' said Tom to himself, and he squeezed his eyelids together, and tried to persuade himself he was going to sleep again. No use; nothing but queer chairs danced before his eyes, kicking up their legs, jumping over each other's backs, and playing all kinds of antics.

" 'I may as well see one real chair, as two or three complete sets of false ones,' said Tom, bringing out his head from under the bed-clothes. There it was, plainly discernible by the light of the fire, looking as provoking as ever.

"Tom gazed at the chair; and, suddenly as he looked at it, a most extraordinary change seemed to come over it. The carving of the back gradually assumed the lineaments and expression of an old shrivelled human face; the damask cushion became an antique, flapped waistcoat; the round knobs grew into a couple of feet, encased in red cloth slippers; and the old chair looked like a very ugly old man, of the previous century, with his arms a-kimbo. Tom sat up in bed, and rubbed his eyes to dispel the illusion. No. The chair was an ugly old gentleman; and what was more, he was winking at Tom Smart.

"Tom was naturally a headlong, careless sort of dog, and he had had five tumblers of hot punch into the bargain; so, although he was a little startled at first, he began to grow rather indignant when he saw the old gentleman winking and leering at him with such an impudent air. At length he resolved that he wouldn't stand it; and as the old face still kept winking away as fast as ever, Tom said, in a very angry tone:

" 'What the devil are you winking at me for?'

" 'Because I like it, Tom Smart,' said the chair; or the old gentleman, whichever you like to call him. He stopped winking though, when Tom spoke, and began grinning like a superannuated monkey.

" 'How do you know my name, old nut-cracker face!' inquired Tom Smart, rather staggered;—though he pretended to carry it off so well.

" 'Come, come, Tom,' said the old gentleman, 'that's not the way to address solid Spanish Mahogany. Dam'me, you couldn't treat me with less respect if I was veneered.' When

the old gentleman said this, he looked so fierce that Tom
began to be frightened.

" 'I didn't mean to treat you with any disrespect, sir,'
said Tom; in a much humbler tone than he had spoken in
at first.

" 'Well, well,' said the old fellow, 'perhaps not—perhaps
not. Tom—'

" 'Sir—'

" 'I know everything about you, Tom; everything. You're
very poor, Tom.'

" 'I certainly am,' said Tom Smart. 'But how came you
to know that?'

" 'Never mind that,' said the old gentleman; 'you're much
too fond of punch, Tom.'

"Tom Smart was just on the point of protesting that he
hadn't tasted a drop since his last birth-day, but when his
eye encountered that of the old gentleman, he looked so
knowing that Tom blushed, and was silent.

" 'Tom,' said the old gentleman, 'the widow's a fine
woman—remarkably fine woman—eh, Tom?' Here the old
fellow screwed up his eyes, cocked up one of his wasted
little legs, and looked altogether so unpleasantly amorous,
that Tom was quite disgusted with the levity of his behavior;—at his time of life, too!

" 'I am her guardian, Tom,' said the old gentleman.

" 'Are you?' inquired Tom Smart.

" 'I knew her mother, Tom," said the old fellow; 'and
her grandmother. She was very fond of me—made me this
waistcoat, Tom.'

" 'Did she?' said Tom Smart.

" 'And these shoes,' said the old fellow, lifting up one of
the red-cloth mufflers; 'but don't mention it, Tom. I
shouldn't like to have it known that she was so much
attached to me. It might occasion some unpleasantness in
the family.' When the old rascal said this; he looked so
extremely impertinent, that, as Tom Smart afterwards declared, he could have sat upon him without remorse.

" 'I have been a great favorite among the women in my
time, Tom,' said the profligate old debauchee; 'hundreds of
fine women have sat in my lap for hours together. What
do you think of that, you dog, eh!' The old gentleman was
proceeding to recount some other exploits of his youth,

when he was seized with such a violent fit of creaking that he was unable to proceed.

" 'Just serves you right, old boy,' thought Tom Smart; but he didn't say anything.

" 'Ah!' said the old fellow, 'I am a good deal troubled with this now. I am getting old, Tom, and have lost nearly all my rails. I have had an operation performed, too—a small piece let into my back—and I found it a severe trial, Tom.'

" 'I daresay you did, sir,' said Tom Smart.

" 'However,' said the old gentleman, 'that's not the point. Tom! I want you to marry the widow.'

" 'Me, sir!' said Tom.

" 'You'; said the old gentleman.

" 'Bless your reverend locks,' said Tom—(he had a few scattered horse-hairs left), 'bless your reverend locks, she wouldn't have me.' And Tom sighed involuntarily, as he thought of the bar.

" 'Wouldn't she?' said the old gentleman, firmly.

" 'No, no,' said Tom; 'there's somebody else in the wind. A tall man—a confoundedly tall man—with black whiskers.'

" 'Tom,' said the old gentleman; 'she will never have him.'

" 'Won't she?' said Tom. 'If you stood in the bar, old gentleman, you'd tell another story.'

" 'Pooh, pooh,' said the old gentleman. 'I know all about that.'

" 'About what?' said Tom.

" 'The kissing behind the door, and all that sort of thing, Tom,' said the old gentleman. And here he gave another impudent look, which made Tom very wroth, because as you all know, gentlemen, to hear an old fellow, who ought to know better, talking about these things, is very unpleasant—nothing more so.

" 'I know all about that, Tom,' said the old gentleman. 'I have seen it done very often in my time, Tom, between more people than I should like to mention to you; but it never came to anything after all.'

" 'You must have seen some queer things,' said Tom, with an inquisitive look.

"You may say that, now,' replied the old fellow, with a

very complicated wink. 'I am the last of my family, Tom,' said the old gentleman, with a melancholy sigh.

" 'Was it a large one?' inquired Tom Smart.

" 'There were twelve of us, Tom,' said the old gentleman, 'fine, straight-backed, handsome fellows as you'd wish to see. None of your modern abortions—all with arms, and with a degree of polish, though I say it that should not, which would have done your heart good to behold.'

" 'And what's become of the others, sir?' asked Tom Smart.

"The old gentleman applied his elbow to his eye as he replied, 'Gone, Tom gone. We had hard service, Tom, and they hadn't all my constitution. They got rheumatic about the legs and arms, and went into kitchens and other hospitals; and one of 'em, with long service and hard usage, positively lost his senses:—he got so crazy that he was obliged to be burnt. Shocking thing that, Tom.'

" 'Dreadful!' said Tom Smart.

"The old fellow paused for a few minutes, apparently struggling with his feelings of emotion, and then said:

" 'However, Tom, I am wandering from the point. This tall man, Tom, is a rascally adventurer. The moment he married the widow, he would sell off all the furniture, and run away. What would be the consequence? She would be deserted and reduced to ruin, and I should catch my death of cold in some broker's shop.'

" 'Yes, but—'

" 'Don't interrupt me,' said the old gentleman. 'Of you, Tom, I entertain a very different opinion; for I well know that if you once settled yourself in a public-house, you would never leave it, as long as there was anything to drink within its walls.'

" 'I am very much obliged to you for your good opinion, sir,' said Tom Smart.

" 'Therefore,' resumed the old gentleman, in a dictatorial tone; 'you shall have her, an he shall not.'

" 'What is to prevent it?' said Tom Smart, eagerly.

" 'This disclosure,' replied the old gentleman: 'he is already married.'

" 'How can I prove it?' said Tom, starting half out of bed.

"The old gentleman untucked his arm from his side, and

having pointed to one of the oaken presses, immediately replaced it in its old position.

" 'He little thinks,' said the old gentleman, 'that in the right-hand pocket of a pair of trousers in that press, he has left a letter, entreating him to return to his disconsolate wife, with six—mark me, Tom—six babes, and all of them small ones.'

"As the old gentleman solemnly uttered these words, his features grew less and less distinct, and his figure more shadowy. A film came over Tom Smart's eyes. The old man seemed gradually blending into the chair, the damask waistcoat to resolve into a cushion, the red slippers to shrink into little red cloth bags. The light faded gently away, and Tom Smart fell back on his pillow, and dropped asleep.

"Morning aroused Tom from the lethargic slumber, into which he had fallen on the disappearance of the old man. He sat up in bed, and for some minutes vainly endeavored to recall the events of the preceding night. Suddenly they rushed upon him. He looked at the chair; it was a fantastic and grim-looking piece of furniture, certainly, but it must have been a remarkably ingenious and lively imagination, that could have discovered any resemblance between it and an old man.

" 'How are you, old boy?' said Tom. He was bolder in the daylight—most men are.

"The chair remained motionless, and spoke not a word.

" 'Miserable morning,' said Tom. No. The chair would not be drawn into conversation.

" 'Which press did you point to?—you can tell me that,' said Tom. Devil a word, gentlemen, the chair would say.

"It's not much trouble to open it, anyhow,' said Tom, getting out of bed very deliberately. He walked up to one of the presses. The key was in the lock; he turned it, and opened the door. There *was* a pair of trousers there. He put his hand into the pocket, and drew forth the identical letter the old gentleman had described!

" 'Queer sort of thing, this,' said Tom Smart; looking first at the chair and then at the press, and then at the letter, and then at the chair again. 'Very queer,' said Tom. But, as there was nothing in either, to lessen the queerness, he thought he might as well dress himself, and settle the tall man's business at once—just to put him out of his misery.

"Tom surveyed the rooms he passed through, on his way down-stairs, with the scrutinizing eye of a landlord; thinking it not impossible, that before long, they and their contents would be his property. The tall man was standing in the snug little bar, with his hands behind him, quite at home. He grinned vacantly at Tom. A casual observer might have supposed he did it, only to show his white teeth; but Tom Smart thought that a consciousness of triumph was passing through the place where the tall man's mind would have been, if he had had any. Tom laughed in his face; and summoned the landlady.

" 'Good morning, ma'am,' said Tom Smart, closing the door of the little parlor as the widow entered.

" 'Good morning, sir,' said the widow. 'What will you take for breakfast, sir?'

"Tom was thinking how he should open the case, so he made no answer.

" 'There's a very nice ham,' said the widow, 'and a beautiful cold larded fowl. Shall I send 'em in, sir?'

"These words roused Tom from his reflections. His admiration of the widow increased as she spoke. Thoughtful creature! Comfortable provider!

" 'Who is that gentleman in the bar, ma'am?' inquired Tom.

" 'His name is Jinkins, sir,' said the widow, slightly blushing.

" 'He's a tall man,' said Tom.

" 'He is a very fine man, sir,' replied the widow, 'and a very nice gentleman.'

" 'Ah!' said Tom.

" 'Is there anything more you want, sir?' inquired the widow, rather puzzled by Tom's manner.

" 'Why, yes,' said Tom. 'My dear ma'am, will you have the kindness to sit down for one moment?'

"The widow looked much amazed, but she sat down, and Tom sat down too, close beside her. I don't know how it happened, gentlemen—indeed my uncle used to tell me that Tom Smart said *he* didn't know how it happened either—but somehow or other the palm of Tom's hand fell upon the back of the widow's hand, and remained there while he spoke.

" 'My dear ma'am,' said Tom Smart—he had always a great notion of committing the amiable— 'My dear ma'am, you deserve a very excellent husband;—you do indeed.'

" 'Lor', sir,' said the widow—as well she might: Tom's made of commencing the conversation being rather un-usual, not to say startling; the fact of his never having set eyes upon her before the previous night, being taken into consideration. 'Lor', sir.'

" 'I scorn to flatter, my dear ma'am,' said Tom Smart. 'You deserve a very admirable husband, and whoever he is, he'll be a very lucky man.' As Tom said this his eye involuntarily wandered from the widow's face, to the com-forts around him.

"The widow looked more puzzled than ever, and made an effort to rise. Tom gently pressed her hand, as if to detain her, and she kept her seat. Widows, gentlemen, are not usually timorous, as my uncle used to say.

" 'I am sure I am very much obliged to you, sir, for your good opinion,' said the buxom landlady, half laughing; 'and if ever I marry again—'

" '*If,*' said Tom Smart, looking very shrewdly out of the right-hand corner of his left eye. '*If*—'

" 'Well,' said the widow, laughing outright this time. '*When* I do, I hope I shall have as good a husband as you describe.'

" 'Jinkins to wit,' said Tom.

" 'Lor', sir!' exclaimed the widow.

" 'Oh, don't tell me,' said Tom, 'I know him.'

" 'I am sure nobody who knows him, knows anything bad of him,' said the widow, bridling up at the mysterious air with which Tom had spoken.

" 'Hem!' said Tom Smart.

"The widow began to think it was high time to cry, so she took out her handkerchief and inquired whether Tom wished to insult her: whether he thought it like a gentleman to take away the character of another gentleman behind his back: why, if he had got anything to say, he didn't say it to the man, like a man, instead of terrifying a poor weak woman in that way; and so forth.

" 'I'll say it to him fast enough,' said Tom, 'only I want you to hear it first.'

" 'What is it?' inquired the widow, looking intently in Tom's countenance.

" 'I'll astonish you,' said Tom, putting his hand in his pocket.

" 'If it is, that he wants money,' said the widow, 'I know that already, and you needn't trouble yourself.'

" 'Pooh, nonsense, that's nothing,' said Tom Smart. '*I* want money. 'Tan't that.'

" 'Oh, dear, what can it be?' exclaimed the poor widow.

" 'Don't be frightened,' said Tom Smart. He slowly drew forth the letter, and unfolded it. 'You won't scream?' said Tom, doubtfully.

" 'No, no,' replied the widow; 'let me see it.'

" 'You won't go fainting away, or any of that nonsense?' said Tom.

" 'No, no,' returned the widow, hastily.

" 'And don't run out, and blow him up,' said Tom, because I'll do all that for you; you had better not exert yourself.'

" 'Well, well,' said the widow, 'let me see it.'

" 'I will,' replied Tom Smart; and, with these words, he placed the letter in the widow's hand.

"Gentlemen, I have heard my uncle say, that Tom Smart said the widow's lamentations when she heard the disclosure would have pierced a heart of stone. Tom was certainly very tender-hearted, but they pierced his, to the very core. The widow rocked herself to and fro, and wrung her hands.

" 'Oh, the deception and villainy of man!' said the widow.

" 'Frightful, my dear ma'am; but compose yourself,' said Tom Smart.

" 'Oh, I can't compose myself,' shrieked the widow. 'I shall never find any one else I can love so much!'

" 'Oh yes, you will, my dear soul,' said Tom Smart, letting fall a shower of the largest sized tears, in pity for the widow's misfortunes. Tom Smart, in the energy of his compassion, had put his arm round the widow's waist; and the widow, in a passion of grief, had clasped Tom's hand. She looked up in Tom's face and smiled through her tears. Tom looked down in hers, and smiled through his.

"I could never find out, gentlemen, whether Tom did or did not kiss the widow at that particular moment. He used to tell my uncle he didn't, but I have my doubts about it. Between ourselves, gentlemen, I rather think he did.

"At all events, Tom kicked the very tall man out at the front door half an hour after, and married the widow a month after. And he used to drive about the country, with the clay-colored gig with red wheels, and the vixenish mare with the fast pace, till he gave up business many years afterwards, and went to France with his wife; and then the old house was pulled down."

I think all Zelazny stories tend to be special, but some more so
than others. In the early Eighties I was putting together an anthology having to do with chess, or chesslike games, and naturally
(hopefully) I asked Roger to contribute something new.

What I didn't know was that two other anthologists had made
similar requests at almost the same time—one seeking a story
about unicorns, the other a tale set in a bar. Roger, being a
practical man, wondered if one story might satisfy all three of us;
and being a considerate gentleman, he was careful to clear the
idea with all of us before proceeding.

So here it is—a unicorn who plays chess in a bar.

—Fred Saberhagen

UNICORN VARIATIONS
by Roger Zelazny

A bizarrerie of fires, cunabulum of light, it moved with a
deft, almost dainty deliberation, phasing into and out
of existence like a storm-shot piece of evening; or perhaps
the darkness between the flares was more akin to its truest
nature—swirl of black ashes assembled in prancing cadence
to the lowing note of desert wind down the arroyo behind
buildings as empty yet filled as the pages of unread books
or stillnesses between the notes of a song.

Gone again. Back again. Again.

Power, you said? Yes. It takes considerable force of iden-
tity to manifest before or after one's time. Or both.

As it faded and gained it also advanced, moving through
the warm afternoon, its tracks erased by the wind. That is,
on those occasions when there were tracks.

A reason. There should always be a reason. Or reasons.

It knew why it was there—but not why it was *there,* in
that particular locale.

It anticipated learning this shortly, as it approached the
desolation-bound line of the old street. However, it knew
that the reason may also come before, or after. Yet again,

the pull was there and the force of its being was such that it had to be close to something.

The buildings were worn and decayed and some of them fallen and all of them drafty and dusty and empty. Weeds grew among floorboards. Birds nested upon rafters. The droppings of wild things were everywhere, and it knew them all as they would have known it, were they to meet face to face.

It froze, for there had come the tiniest unanticipated sound from somewhere ahead and to the left. At that moment, it was again phasing into existence and it released its outline which faded as quickly as a rainbow in hell, that but the naked presence remained beyond subtraction.

Invisible, yet existing, strong, it moved again. The clue. The cue. Ahead. *A gauche.* Beyond the faded word SALOON on weathered board above. Through the swinging doors. (One of them pinned atop.)

Pause and assess.

Bar to the right, dusty. Cracked mirror behind it. Empty bottles. Broken bottles. Brass rail, black, encrusted. Tables to the left and rear. In various states of repair.

Man seated at the best of the lot. His back to the door. Levi's. Hiking boots. Faded blue shirt. Green backpack leaning against the wall to his left.

Before him, on the tabletop, is the faint, painted outline of a chessboard, stained, scratched, almost obliterated.

The drawer in which he had found the chessmen is still partly open.

He could no more have passed up a chess set without working out a problem or replaying one of his better games, than he could have gone without breathing, circulating his blood or maintaining a relatively stable body temperature.

It moved nearer, and perhaps there were fresh prints in the dust behind it, but none noted them.

It, too, played chess.

It watched as the man replayed what had perhaps been his finest game, from the world preliminaries of seven years past. He had blown up after that—surprised to have gotten even as far as he had—for he never could perform well under pressure. But he had always been proud of that one game, and he relieved it as all sensitive beings do certain turning points in their lives. For perhaps twenty minutes, no one could have touched him. He had been shining and pure and hard and clear. He had felt like the best.

It took up a position across the board from him and stared. The man completed the game, smiling. Then he set up the board again, rose and fetched a can of beer from his pack. He popped the top.

When he returned, he discovered that White's King's Pawn had been advanced to K4. His brow furrowed. He turned his head, searching the bar, meeting his own puzzled gaze in the grimy mirror. He looked under the table. He took a drink of beer and seated himself.

He reached out and moved his Pawn to K4. A moment later, he saw White's King's Knight rise slowly into the air and drift forward to settle upon KB3. He stared for a long while into the emptiness across the table before he advanced his own Knight to his KB3.

White's Knight moved to take his Pawn. He dismissed the novelty of the situation and moved his Pawn to Q3. He all but forgot the absence of a tangible opponent as the White Knight dropped back to its KB3. He paused to take a sip of beer, but no sooner had he placed the can upon the tabletop than it rose again, passed across the board and was upended. A gurgling noise followed. Then the can fell to the floor, bouncing, ringing with an empty sound.

"I'm sorry," he said, rising and returning to his pack. "I'd have offered you one if I'd thought you were something that might like it."

He opened two more cans, returned with them, placed one near the far edge of the table, one at his own right hand.

"Thank you," came a soft, precise voice from a point beyond it.

The can was raised, tilted slightly, returned to the tabletop.

"My name is Martin," the man said.

"Call me Tlingel," said the other. "I had thought that perhaps your kind was extinct. I am pleased that you at least have survived to afford me this game."

"Huh?" Martin said. "We were all still around the last time that I looked—a couple of days ago."

"No matter. I can take care of that later," Tlingel replied. "I was misled by the appearance of this place."

"Oh. It's a ghost town. I backpack a lot."

"Not important. I am near the proper point in your career as a species. I can feel that much."

"I am afraid that I do not follow you."

"I am not at all certain that you would wish to. I assume that you intend to capture that pawn?"

"Perhaps. Yes, I do wish to. What are you talking about?"

The beer can rose. The invisible entity took another drink.

"Well," said Tlingel, "to put it simply, your—sucessors—grow anxious. Your place in the scheme of things being such an important one, I had sufficient power to come and check things out."

" 'Successors'? I do not understand."

"Have you seen any griffins recently?"

Martin chuckled.

"I've heard the stories," he said, "seen the photos of the one supposedly shot in the Rockies. A hoax, of course."

"Of course it must seem so. That is the way with mythical beasts."

"You're trying to say that it was real?"

"Certainly. Your world is in bad shape. When the last grizzly bear died recently, the way was opened for the griffins—just as the death of the last aepyornis brought in the yeti, the dodo the Loch Ness creature, the passenger pigeon the sasquatch, the blue whale the kraken, the American eagle, the cockatrice—"

"You can't prove it by me."

"Have another drink."

Martin began to reach for the can, halted his hand and stared.

A creature approximately two inches in length, with a human face, a lionlike body and feathered wings was crouched next to the beer can.

"A mini-sphinx," the voice continued. "They came when you killed off the last smallpox bacillus."

"Are you trying to say that whenever a natural species dies out a mythical one takes its place?" he asked.

"In a word—yes. Now. It was not always so, but you have destroyed the mechanisms of evolution. The balance is now redressed by those others of us, from the morning land—we, who have never truly been endangered. We return, in our time."

"And you—whatever you are. Tlingel—you say that humanity is now endangered?"

"Very much so. But there is nothing that you can do about it, is there? Let us get on with the game."

The sphinx flew off. Martin took a sip of beer and captured the Pawn.

"Who," he asked then, "are to be our successors?"

"Modesty almost forbids," Tlingel replied. "In the case of a species as prominent as your own, it naturally has to be the loveliest, most intelligent, most important of us all."

"And what are you? Is there any way that I can have a look?"

"Well—yes. If I exert myself a trifle."

The beer can rose, was drained, fell to the floor. There followed a series of rapid rattling sounds retreating from the table. The air began to flicker over a large area opposite Martin, darkening within the glowing framework. The outline continued to brighten, its interior growing jet black. The form moved, prancing about the saloon, multitudes of tiny, cloven hoofprints scoring and cracking the floorboards. With a final, near-blinding flash it came into full view and Martin gasped to behold it.

A black unicorn with mocking, yellow eyes sported before him, rising for a moment onto its hind legs to strike a heraldic pose. The fires flared about it a second longer, then vanished.

Martin had drawn back, raising one hand defensively.

"Regard me!" Tlingel announced. "Ancient symbol of wisdom, valor and beauty, I stand before you!"

"I thought your typical unicorn was white," Martin finally said.

"I am archetypical," Tlingel responded, dropping to all fours, "and possessed of virtues beyond the ordinary."

"Such as?"

"Let us continue our game."

"What about the fate of the human race? You said—"

". . . And save the small talk for later."

"I hardly consider the destruction of humanity to be small talk."

"And if you've any more beer . . ."

"All right," Martin said, retreating to his pack as the creature advanced, its eyes like a pair of pale suns. "There's some lager."

* * *

Something had gone out of the game. As Martin sat before the ebon horn on Tlingel's bowed head, like an insect about to be pinned, he realized that his playing was off. He had felt the pressure the moment he had seen the beast—and there was all that talk about an imminent doomsday. Any run-of-the-mill pessimist could say it without troubling him, but coming from a source as peculiar as this . . .

His earlier elation had fled. He was no longer in top form. And Tlingel was good. Very good. Martin found himself wondering whether he could manage a stalemate.

After a time, he saw that he could not and resigned.

The unicorn looked at him and smiled.

"You don't really play badly—for a human," it said.

"I've done a lot better."

"It is no shame to lose to me, mortal. Even among mythical creatures there are very few who can give a unicorn a good game."

"I am pleased that you were not wholly bored," Martin said. "Now will you tell me what you were talking about concerning the destruction of my species?"

"Oh, that," Tlingel replied. "In the morning land where those such as I dwell, I felt the possibility of your passing come like a gentle wind to my nostrils, with the promise of clearing the way for us—"

"How is it supposed to happen?"

Tlingel shrugged, horn writing on the air with a toss of the head.

"I really couldn't say. Premonitions are seldom specific. In fact, that is what I came to discover. I should have been about it already, but you diverted me with beer and good sport."

"Could you be wrong about this?"

"I doubt it. That is the other reason I am here."

"Please explain."

"Are there any beers left?"

"Two, I think."

"Please."

Martin rose and fetched them.

"Damn! The tab broke off this one," he said.

"Place it upon the table and hold it firmly."

"All right."

Tlingel's horn dipped forward quickly, piercing the can's top.

". . . Useful for all sorts of things," Tlingel observed, withdrawing it.

"The other reason you're here . . ." Martin prompted.

"It is just that I am special. I can do things that the others cannot."

"Such as?"

"Find your weak spot and influence events to exploit it, to—hasten matters. To turn the possibility into a probability, and then—"

"*You* are going to destroy us? Personally?"

"That is the wrong way to look at it. It is more like a game of chess. It is as much a matter of exploiting your opponent's weaknesses as of exercising your own strengths. If you had not already laid the groundwork I would be powerless. I can only influence that which already exists."

"So what will it be? World War III? An ecological disaster? A mutated disease?"

"I do not really know yet, so I wish you wouldn't ask me in that fashion. I repeat that at the moment I am only observing. I am only an agent—"

"It doesn't sound that way to me."

Tlingel was silent. Martin began gathering up the chessmen.

"Aren't you going to set up the board again?"

"To amuse my destroyer a little more? No thanks."

"That's hardly the way to look at it—"

"Besides, those are the last beers."

"Oh." Tlingel stared wistfully at the vanishing pieces, then remarked, "I would be willing to play you again without additional refreshment . . ."

"No thanks."

"You are angry."

"Wouldn't you be, if our situations were reversed?"

"You are anthropomorphizing."

"Well?"

"Oh, I suppose I would."

"You could give us a break, you know—at least, let us make our own mistakes."

"You've hardly done that yourself, though, with all the creatures my fellows have succeeded."

Martin reddened.

"Okay. You just scored one. But I don't have to like it."

"You are a good player. I know that . . ."

"Tlingel, if I were capable of playing at my best again, I think I could beat you."

The unicorn snorted two tiny wisps of smoke.

"Not *that* good," Tlingel said.

"I guess you'll never know."

"Do I detect a proposal?"

"Possibly. What's another game worth to you?"

Tlingel made a chuckling noise.

"Let me guess: You are going to say that if you beat me you want my promise not to lay my will upon the weakest link in mankind's existence and shatter it."

"Of course."

"And what do I get for winning?"

"The pleasure of the game. That's what you want, isn't it?"

"The terms sound a little lopsided."

"Not if you are going to win anyway. You keep insisting that you will."

"All right. Set up the board."

"There is something else that you have to know about me first."

"Yes?"

"I don't play well under pressure, and this game is going to be a terrific strain. You want my best game, don't you?"

"Yes, but I'm afraid I've no way of adjusting your own reactions to the play."

"I believe I could do that myself if I had more than the usual amount of time between moves."

"Agreed."

"I mean a lot of time."

"Just what do you have in mind?"

"I'll need time to get my mind off it, to relax, to come back to the positions as if they were only problems. . . ."

"You mean to go away from here between moves?"

"Yes."

"All right. How long?"

"I don't know. A few weeks, maybe."

"Take a month. Consult your experts, put your computers onto it. It may make for a slightly more interesting game."

"I really didn't have that in mind."

"Then it's time that you're trying to buy."

"I can't deny that. On the other hand, I will need it."

"In that case, I have some terms. I'd like this place cleaned up, fixed up, more lively. It's a mess. I also want beer on tap."

"Okay. I'll see to that."

"Then I agree. Let's see who goes first."

Martin switched a black and a white pawn from hand to hand beneath the table. He raised his fists then and extended them. Tlingel leaned forward and tapped. The black horn's tip touched martin's left hand.

"Well, it matches my sleek and glossy hide," the unicorn announced.

Martin smiled, setting up the white for himself, the black pieces for his opponent. As soon as he had finished, he pushed his Pawn to K4.

Tlingel's delicate, ebon hoof moved to advance the Black King's Pawn to K4.

"I take it that you want a month now, to consider your next move?"

Martin did not reply but moved his knight to KB3. Tlingel immediately moved a Knight to QB3.

Martin took a swallow of beer and then moved his Bishop to N5. The unicorn moved the other Knight to B3. Martin immediately castled and Tlingel moved the Knight to take his Pawn.

"I think we'll make it," Martin said suddenly, "if you'll just let us alone. We do learn from our mistakes, in time."

"Mythical things do not exactly exist in time. Your world is a special case."

"Don't you people ever make mistakes?"

"Whenever we do they're sort of poetic."

Martin snarled and advanced his Pawn to Q4. Tlingel immediately countered by moving the Knight to Q3.

"I've got to stop," Martin said, standing. "I'm getting mad, and it will affect my game."

"You will be going, then?"

"Yes."

He moved to fetch his pack.

"I will see you here in one month's time?"

"Yes."

"Very well."

The unicorn rose and stamped upon the floor and lights began to play across its dark coat. Suddenly, they blazed and shot outward in all directions like a silent explosion. A wave of blackness followed.

Martin found himself leaning against the wall, shaking. When he lowered his hand from his eyes, he saw that he was alone, save for the knights, the bishops, the kings, the queens, their castles and both the kings' men.

He went away.

* * *

Three days later Martin returned in a small truck, with a generator, lumber, windows, power tools, paint, stain, cleaning compounds, wax. He dusted and vacuumed and replaced rotted wood. He installed the windows. He polished the old brass until it shone. He stained and rubbed. He waxed the floors and buffed them. He plugged holes and washed glass. He hauled all the trash away.

It took him the better part of a week to turn the old place from a wreck back into a saloon in appearance. Then he drove off, returned all of the equipment he had rented and bought a ticket for the Northwest.

The big, damp forest was another of his favorite places for hiking, for thinking. And he was seeking a complete change of scene, a total revision of outlook. Not that his next move did not seem obvious, standard even. Yet, something nagged . . .

He knew that it was more than just the game. Before that he had been ready to get away again, to walk drowsing among shadows, breathing clean air.

Resting, his back against the bulging root of a giant tree, he withdrew a small chess set from his pack, set it up on a rock he'd moved into position nearby. A fine, mistlike rain was settling, but the tree sheltered him, so far. He reconstructed the opening through Tlingel's withdrawal of the

Knight to Q3. The simplest thing would be to take the Knight with the Bishop. But he did not move to do it.

He watched the board for a time, felt his eyelids dropping, closed them and drowsed. It may only have been for a few minutes. He was never certain afterwards.

Something aroused him. He did not know what. He blinked several times and closed his eyes again. Then he reopened them hurriedly.

In his nodded position, eyes directed downward, his gaze was fixed upon an enormous pair of hairy, unshod feet—the largest pair of feet that he had ever beheld. They stood unmoving before him, pointed toward his right.

Slowly—very slowly—he raised his eyes. Not very far, as it turned out. The creature was only about four and a half feet in height. As it was looking at the chessboard rather than at him, he took the opportunity to study it.

It was unclothed but very hairy, with a dark brown pelt, obviously masculine, possessed of low brow ridges, deep-set eyes that matched its hair, heavy shoulders, five-fingered hands that sported opposing thumbs.

It turned suddenly and regarded him, flashing a large number of shining teeth.

"White's pawn should take the pawn," it said in a soft, nasal voice.

"Huh? Come on," Martin said. "Bishop takes knight."

"You want to give me black and play it that way? I'll walk all over you."

Martin glanced again at its feet.

". . . Or give me white and let me take that pawn. I'll still do it."

"Take white," Martin said, straightening. "Let's see if you know what you're talking about." He reached for his pack. "Have a beer?"

"What's a beer?"

"A recreational aid. Wait a minute."

Before they had finished the six-pack, the sasquatch—whose name, he had learned, was Grend—had finished Martin. Grend had quickly entered a ferocious midgame, backed him into a position of swindling security and pushed him to the point where he had seen the end and resigned.

"That was one hell of a game," Martin declared, leaning back and considering the apelike countenance before him.

"Yes, we Bigfeet are pretty good, if I do say it. It's our one big recreation, and we're so damned primitive we don't have much in the way of boards and chessmen. Most of the time, we just play it in our heads. There're not many can come close to us."

"How about unicorns?" Martin asked.

Grend nodded slowly.

"They're about the only ones can really give us a good game. A little dainty, but they're subtle. Awfully sure of themselves, though, I must say. Even when they're wrong. Haven't seen any since we left the morning land, of course. Too bad. Got any more of that beer left?"

"I'm afraid not. But listen, I'll be back this way in a month. I'll bring some more if you'll meet me here and play again."

"Martin, you've got a deal. Sorry. Didn't mean to step on your toes."

* * *

He cleaned the saloon again and brought in a keg of beer which he installed under the bar and packed with ice. He moved in some bar stools, chairs and tables which he had obtained at a Goodwill store. He hung red curtains. By then it was evening. He set up the board, ate a light meal, unrolled his sleeping bag behind the bar and camped there that night.

The following day passed quickly. Since Tlingel might show up at any time, he did not leave the vicinity, but took his meals there and sat about working chess problems. When it began to grow dark, he lit a number of oil lamps and candles.

He looked at his watch with increasing frequency. He began to pace. He couldn't have made a mistake. This was the proper day. He—

He heard a chuckle.

Turning about, he saw a black unicorn head floating in the air above the chessboard. As he watched, the rest of Tlingel's body materialized.

"Good evening, Martin." Tlingel turned away from the board. "The place looks a little better. Could use some music . . .

Martin stepped behind the bar and switched on the transistor radio he had brought along. The sounds of a string quartet filled the air. Tlingel winced.

"Hardly in keeping with the atmosphere of the place."

He changed stations, located a Country & Western show.

"I think not," Tlingel said. "It loses something in transmission."

He turned it off.

"Have we a good supply of beverage?"

Martin drew a gallon stein of beer—the largest mug that he could locate, from a novelty store—and set it upon the bar. He filled a much smaller one for himself. He was determined to get the beast drunk if it were at all possible.

"Ah! Much better than those little cans," said Tlingel, whose muzzle dipped for but a moment. "Very good."

The mug was empty. Martin refilled it.

"Will you move it to the table for me?"

"Certainly."

"Have an interesting month?"

"I suppose I did."

"You've decided upon your next move?"

"Yes."

"Then let's get on with it."

Martin seated himself and captured the Pawn.

"Hm. Interesting."

Tlingel stared at the board for a long while, then raised a cloven hoof which parted in reaching for the piece.

"I'll just take that bishop with this little knight. Now I suppose you'll be wanting another month to make up your mind what to do next."

Tlingel leaned to the side and drained the mug.

"Let me consider it," Martin said, "while I get you a refill."

Martin sat and stared at the board through three more refills. Actually, he was not planning. He was waiting. His response to Grend had been Knight takes Bishop, and he had Grend's next move ready.

"Well?" Tlingel finally said. "What do you think?"

Martin took a small sip of beer.

"Almost ready," he said. "You hold your beer awfully well."

Tlingel laughed.

"A unicorn's horn is a detoxicant. Its possession is a universal remedy. I wait until I reach the warm glow stage, then I use my horn to burn off any excess and keep me right there.''

"Oh," said Martin. "Neat trick, that."

". . . If you've had too much, just touch my horn for a moment and I'll put you back in business."

"No, thanks. That's all right. I'll just push this little pawn in front of the queen's rook two steps ahead."

"Really . . ." said Tlingel. "That's interesting. You know, what this place really needs is a piano—rinkytink, funky . . . Think you could manage it?"

"I don't play."

"Too bad."

"I suppose I could hire a piano player."

"No. I do not care to be seen by other humans."

"If he's really good, I suppose he could play blindfolded."

"Never mind."

"I'm sorry."

"You are also ingenious. I am certain that you will figure something out by next time."

Martin nodded.

"Also, didn't those old places used to have sawdust all over the floors?"

"I believe so."

"That would be nice."

"Check."

Tlingel searched the board frantically for a moment.

"Yes. I meant 'yes.' I said 'check.' It means 'yes' sometimes, too."

"Oh. Rather. Well, while we're here . . ."

Tlingel advanced the Pawn to Q3.

Martin stared. That was not what Grend had done. For a moment he considered continuing on his own from here. He had tried to think of Grend as a coach up until this point. He had forced away the notion of crudely and crassly pitting one of them against the other. Until P-Q3. Then he recalled the game he had lost to the sasquatch.

"I'll draw the line here," he said, "and take my month."

"All right. Let's have another drink before we say good night. Okay?"

"Sure. Why not?"

They sat for a time and Tlingel told him of the morning

land, of primeval forests and rolling plains, of high craggy mountains and purple seas, of magic and mythic beasts.

Martin shook his head.

"I can't quite see why you're so anxious to come here," he said, "with a place like that to call home."

Tlingel sighed.

"I suppose you'd call it keeping up with the griffins. It's the thing to do these days. Well. Till next month . . ."

Tlingel rose and turned away.

"I've got complete control now. Watch!"

The unicorn form faded, jerked out of shape, grew white, faded again, was gone, like an afterimage.

Martin moved to the bar and drew himself another mug. It was a shame to waste what was left. In the morning, he wished the unicorn were there again. Or at least the horn.

* * *

It was a gray day in the forest and he held an umbrella over the chessboard upon the rock. The droplets fell from the leaves and made dull, plopping noises as they struck the fabric. The board was set up again through Tlingel's P-Q3. Martin wondered whether Grend had remembered, had kept proper track of the days . . .

"Hello," came the nasal voice from somewhere behind him and to the left.

He turned to see Grend moving about the tree, stepping over the massive roots with massive feet.

"You remembered," Grend said. "How good! I trust you also remembered the beer?"

"I've lugged up a whole case. We can set up the bar right here."

"What's a bar?"

"Well, it's a place where people go to drink—in out of the rain—a bit dark, for atmosphere—and they sit up on stools before a big counter, or else at little tables—and they talk to each other—and sometimes there's music—and they drink."

"We're going to have all that here?"

"No. Just the dark and the drinks. Unless you count the rain as music. I was speaking figuratively."

"Oh. It does sound like a very good place to visit, though."

"Yes. If you will hold this umbrella over the board, I'll set up the best equivalent we can have here."

"All right. Say, this looks like a version of that game we played last time."

"It is. I got to wondering what would happen if it had gone this way rather than the way that it went."

"Hmm. Let me see . . ."

Martin removed four six-packs from his pack and opened the first.

"Here you go."

"Thanks."

Grend accepted the beer, squatted, passed the umbrella back to Martin.

"I'm still white?"

"Yeah."

"Pawn to King six."

"Really?"

"Yep."

"About the best thing for me to do would be to take this pawn with this one."

"I'd say. Then I'll just knock off your knight with this one."

"I guess I'll just pull this knight back to K2."

". . . And I'll take this one over to B3. May I have another beer?"

An hour and a quarter later, Martin resigned. The rain had let up and he had folded the umbrella.

"Another game?" Grend asked.

"Yes."

The afternoon wore on. The pressure was off. This one was just for fun. Martin tried wild combinations, seeing ahead with great clarity, as he had that one day . . .

"Stalemate," Grend announced much later. "That was a good one, though. You picked up considerably."

"I was more relaxed. Want another?"

"Maybe in a little while. Tell me more about bars now."

So he did. Finally. "How is all that beer affecting you?" he asked.

"I'm a bit dizzy. But that's all right. I'll still cream you the third game."

And he did.

"Not bad for a human, though. Not bad at all. You coming back next month?"

"Yes."

"Good. You'll bring more beer?"

"So long as my money holds out."

"Oh. Bring some plaster of paris then. I'll make you some nice footprints and you can take casts of them. I understand they're going for quite a bit."

"I'll remember that."

Martin lurched to his feet and collected the chess set.

"Till then."

"Ciao."

* * *

Martin dusted and polished again, moved in the player piano and scattered sawdust upon the floor. He installed a fresh keg. He hung some reproductions of period posters and some atrocious old paintings he had located in a junk shop. He placed cuspidors in strategic locations. When he was finished, he seated himself at the bar and opened a bottle of mineral water. He listened to the New Mexico wind moaning as it passed, to grains of sand striking against the windowpanes. He wondered whether the whole world would have that dry, mournful sound to it if Tlingel found a means of doing away with humanity, or—disturbing thought—whether the successors to his own kind might turn things into something resembling the mythical morning land.

This troubled him for a time. Then he went and set up the board through Black's P-Q3. When he turned back to clear the bar he saw a line of cloven hoofprints advancing across the sawdust.

"Good evening, Tlingel," he said. "What is your pleasure?"

Suddenly, the unicorn was there, without preliminary pyrotechnics. It moved to the bar and placed one hoof upon the brass rail.

"The usual."

As Martin drew the beer, Tlingel looked about.

"The place has improved, a bit."

"Glad you think so. Would you care for some music?"

"Yes."

Martin fumbled at the back of the piano, locating the

switch for the small, battery-operated computer which controlled the pumping mechanism and substituted its own memory for rolls. The keyboard immediately came to life.

"Very good," Tlingel stated. "Have you found your move?"

"I have."

"Then let us be about it."

He refilled the unicorn's mug and moved it to the table, along with his own.

"Pawn to King six," he said, executing it.

"What?"

"Just that."

"Give me a minute. I want to study this."

"Take your time."

"I'll take the pawn," Tlingel said, after a long pause and another mug.

"Then I'll take this knight."

Later, "Knight to K2," Tlingel said.

"Knight to B3."

An extremely long pause ensued before Tlingel moved the Knight to N3.

The hell with asking Grend, Martin suddenly decided. He'd been though this part any number of times already. He moved his Knight to N5.

"Change the tune on that thing!" Tlingel snapped.

Martin rose and obliged.

"I don't like that one either. Find a better one or shut it off!"

"And get me another beer!"

He refilled their mugs.

"All right."

Tlingel moved the Bishop to K2.

Keeping the unicorn from castling had to be the most important thing at the moment. So Martin moved his Queen to R5. Tlingel made a tiny, strangling noise, and when Martin looked u smoke was curling from the unicorn's nostrils.

"More beer?"

"If you please."

As he returned with it, he saw Tlingel move the Bishop to capture the Knight. There seemed no choice for him at that moment, but he studied the position for a long while anyhow.

Finally, "Bishop takes bishop," he said.

"Of course."

"How's the warm glow?"

Tlingel chuckled.

"You'll see."

The wind rose again, began to howl. The building creaked.

"Okay," Tlingel finally said, and moved the Queen to Q2.

Martin stared. What was he doing? So far, it had gone all right, but— He listened again to the wind and thought of the risk he was taking.

"That's all, folks," he said, leaning back in his chair. "Continued next month."

Tlingel sighed.

"Don't run off. Fetch me another. Let me tell you of my wanderings in your world this past month."

"Looking for weak links?"

"You're lousy with them. How do you stand it?"

"They're harder to strengthen than you might think. Any advice?"

"Get the beer."

They talked until the sky paled in the east, and Martin found himself taking surreptitious notes. His admiration for the unicorn's analytical abilities increased as the evening advanced.

When they finally rose, Tlingel staggered.

"You all right?"

"Forgot to detox, that's all. Just a second. Then I'll be fading."

"Wait!"

"Whazzat?"

"I could use one, too."

"Oh. Grab hold, then."

Tlingel's head descended and Martin took the tip of the horn between his fingertips. Immediately, a delicious, warm sensation flowed through him. He closed his eyes to enjoy it. His head cleared. An ache which had been growing within his frontal sinus vanished. The tiredness went out of his muscles. He opened his eyes again.

"Thank—"

Tlingel had vanished. He held but a handful of air.

"—you."

* * *

"Rael here is my friend," Grend stated. "He's a griffin."

"I'd noticed."

Martin nodded at the beaked, golden-winged creature.

"Pleased to meet you, Rael."

"The same," cried the other in a high-pitched voice. "Have you got the beer?"

"Why—uh—yes."

"I've been telling him about beer," Grend explained, half-apologetically. "He can have some of mine. He won't kibitz or anything like that."

"Sure. All right. Any friend of yours . . ."

"The beer!" Rael cried. "Bars!"

"He's not real bright," Grend whispered. "But he's good company. I'd appreciate your humoring him."

Martin opened the first six-pack and passed the griffin and the sasquatch a beer apiece. Rael immediately punctured the can with his beak, chugged it, belched and held out his claw.

"Beer!" he shrieked. "More beer!"

Martin handed him another.

"Say, you're still into that first game, aren't you?" Grend observed, studying the board. "Now, *that* is an interesting position."

Grend drank and studied the board.

"Good thing it's not raining," Martin commented.

"Oh, it will. Just wait a while."

"More beer!" Rael screamed.

Martin passed him another without looking.

"I'll move my pawn to N6," Grend said.

"You're kidding."

"Nope. Then you'll take that pawn with your bishop's pawn. Right?"

"Yes . . ."

Martin reached out and did it.

"Okay. Now I'll just swing this knight to Q5."

Martin took it with the Pawn.

Grend moved his Rook to K1.

"Check," he announced.

"Yes. That *is* the way to go," Martin observed.

Grend chuckled.

"I'm going to win this game another time," he said.

"I wouldn't put it past you."

"More beer?" Rael said softly.

"Sure."

As Martin poured him another, he noticed that the griffin was now leaning against the tree trunk.

After several minutes, Martin pushed his King to B1.

"Yeah, that's what I thought you'd do," Grend said. "You know something?"

"What?"

"You play a lot like a unicorn."

"Hm."

Grend moved his Rook to R3.

Later, as the rain descended gently about them and Grend beat him again, Martin realized that a prolonged period of silence had prevailed. He glanced over at the griffin. Rael had tucked his head beneath his left wing, balanced upon one leg, leaned heavily against the tree and gone to sleep.

"I told you he wouldn't be much trouble," Grend remarked.

Two games later, the beer was gone, the shadows were lengthening and Rael was stirring.

"See you next month?"

"Yeah."

"You bring my plaster of paris?"

"Yes, I did."

"Come on, then. I know a good place pretty far from here. We don't want people beating about *these* bushes. Let's go make you some money."

"To buy beer?" Rael said, looking out from under his wing.

"Next month," Grend said.

"You ride?"

"I don't think you could carry both of us," said Grend, "and I'm not sure I'd want to right now if you could."

"Bye-bye then," Rael shrieked, and he leaped into the air, crashing into branches and tree trunks, finally breaking through the overhead cover and vanishing.

"There goes a really decent guy," said Grend. "He sees everything and he never forgets. Knows how everything works—in the woods, in the air—even in the water. Generous, too, whenever he has anything."

"Hm," Martin observed.

"Let's make tracks," Grend said.

* * *

"Pawn to N6? Really?" Tlingel said. "All right. The bishop's pawn will just knock off the pawn."

Tlingel's eyes narrowed as Martin moved the Knight to Q5.

"At least this is an interesting game" the unicorn remarked. "Pawn takes Knight."

Martin moved the Rook.

"Check."

"Yes, it is. This next one is going to be a three flagon move. Kindly bring me the first."

Martin thought back as he watched Tlingel drink and ponder. He almost felt guilty for hitting it with a powerhouse like the sasquatch behind its back. He was convinced now that the unicorn was going to lose. In every variation of this game that he'd played with Black against Grend, he'd been beaten. Tlingel was very good, but the sasquatch was a wizard with not much else to do but mental chess. It was unfair. But it was not a matter of personal honor, he kept telling himself. He was laying to protect his species against a supernatural force which might well be able to precipitate World War III by some arcane mind-manipulation or magically induced computer foulup. He didn't dare give the creature a break.

"Flagon number two, please."

He brought it another. He studied it as it studied the board. It was beautiful, he realized for the first time. It was the loveliest living thing he had ever seen. Now that the pressure was on the verge of evaporating and he could regard it without the overlay of fear which had always been there in the past, he could pause to admire it. If something *had* to succeed the human race, he could think of worse choices . . .

"Number three now."

"Coming up."

Tlingel drained it and moved the King to B1.

Martin leaned forward immediately and pushed the Rook to R3.

Tlingel looked up, stared at him.

"Not bad."

Martin wanted to squirm. He was struck by the nobility of the creature. He wanted so badly to play and beat the unicorn on his own, fairly. Not this way.

Tlingel looked back at the board, then almost carelessly moved the Knight to K4.

"Go ahead. Or will it take you another month?"

Martin growled softly, advanced the Rook and captured the Knight.

"Of course."

Tlingel captured the Rook with the Pawn. This was not the way that the last variation with Grend had run. Still . . .

He moved his Rook to KB3. As he did, the wind seemed to commence a peculiar shrieking, above, amid the ruined buildings.

"Check," he announced.

The hell with it! he decided. I'm good enough to manage my own endgame. Let's play this out.

He watched and waited and finally saw Tlingel move the King to N1.

He moved his Bishop to R6. Tlingel moved the Queen to K2. The shrieking came again, sounding nearer now. Martin took the Pawn with the Bishop.

The unicorn's head came up and it seemed to listen for a moment. Then Tlingel lowered it and captured the Bishop with the King.

Martin moved his Rook to KN3.

"Check."

Tlingel returned the King to B1.

Martin moved the Rook to KB3.

"Check."

Tlingel pushed the King to N2.

Martin moved the Rook back to KN3.

"Check."

Tlingel returned the King to B1, looked up and stared at him, showing teeth.

"Looks as if we've got a drawn game," the unicorn stated. "Care for another one?"

"Yes, but not for the fate of humanity."

"Forget it. I'd given up on that a long time ago. I decided that I wouldn't care to live here after all. I'm a little more discriminating than that.

"Except for this bar." Tlingel turned away as another shriek sounded just beyond the door, followed by strange voices. "What is that?"

"I don't know," Martin answered, rising.

The doors opened and a golden griffin entered.

"Martin!" it cried. "Beer! Beer!"

"Uh—Tlingel, this is Rael, and, and—"

Three more griffins followed him in. Then came Grend, and three others of his own kind.

"—and that one's Grend," Martin said lamely. "I don't know the others."

They all halted when they beheld the unicorn.

"Tlingel," one of the sasquatches said. "I thought you were still in the morning land."

"I still am, in a way. Martin, how is it that you are acquainted with my former countrymen?"

"Well—uh—Grend here is my chess coach."

"Aha! I begin to understand."

"I am not sure that you really do. But let me get everyone a drink first."

Martin turned on the piano and set everyone up.

"How did you find this place?" he asked Grend as he was doing it. "And how did you get here?"

"Well . . ." Grend looked embarrassed. "Rael followed you back."

"Followed a jet?"

"Griffins are supernaturally fast."

"Oh."

"Anyway, he told his relatives and some of my folks about it. When we saw that the griffins were determined to visit you, we decided that we had better come along to keep them out of trouble. They brought us."

"I—see. Interesting . . ."

"No wonder you played like a unicorn, that one game with all the variations."

"Uh—yes."

Martin turned away, moved to the end of the bar.

"Welcome, all of you," he said. "I have a small announcement. Tlingel, awhile back you had a number of observations concerning possible ecological and urban disasters and lesser dangers. Also, some ideas as to possible safeguards against some of them."

"I recall," said the unicorn.

"I passed them along to a friend of mine in Washington who used to be a member of my old chess club. I told him that the work was not entirely my own."

"I should hope so."

"He has since suggested that I turn whatever group was involved into a think tank. He will then see about paying something for its efforts."

"I didn't come here to save the world," Tlingel said.

"No, but you've been very helpful. And Grend tells me that the griffins, even if their vocabulary is a bit limited, know almost all that there is to know about ecology."

"That is probably true."

"Since they have inherited a part of the Earth, it would be to their benefit as well to help preserve the place. Inasmuch as this many of us are already here, I can save myself some travel and suggest right now that we find a meeting place—say here, once a month—and that you let me have your unique viewpoints. You must know more about how species become extinct than anyone else in the business."

"Of course," said Grend, waving his mug, "but we really should ask the yeti, also. I'll do it, if you'd like. Is that stuff coming out of the big box music?"

"Yes."

"I like it. If we do this think tank thing, you'll make enough to keep this place going?"

"I'll buy the whole town."

Grend conversed in quick gutturals with the griffins, who shrieked back at him.

"You've got a think tank," he said, "and they want more beer."

Martin turned toward Tlingel.

"They were your observations. What do you think?"

"It may be amusing," said the unicorn, "to stop by occasionally." Then, "So much for saving the world. Did you say you wanted another game?"

"I've nothing to lose."

Grend took over the tending of the bar while Tlingel and Martin returned to the table.

He beat the unicorn in thirty-one moves and touched the extended horn.

The piano keys went up and down. Tiny sphinxes buzzed about the bar, drinking the spillage.

ABOUT THE AUTHORS

Charles de Lint is a full-time writer and musician who presently makes his home in Ottawa, Ontario, Canada, with his wife MaryAnn Harris, an artist and musician. His most recent books are *Somewhere to Be Flying* and the single author collection entitled *Moonlight and Vines*. For more information on his work, visit his Web site at <www.cyberus.ca/~cdl>.

Jack Vance combines elements of the mystery, fantasy, and science fiction genres into a adventure-filled style that is all his own. His strengths lie in creating detailed, imaginative yet plausible societies, complete with a noticeable lack of altruism. Along the way to garnering awards such as the Edgar, Hugo, and Nebula Awards, he has examined such far-ranging topics as the power of language and the concept and price of freedom and independence. Notable novels include *The Languages of Pao, The Dragon Masters,* and *Bildungsroman.*

Terry Pratchett is best known for *Discworld,* his humorous fantasy series set on a world supported by four elephants on the back of a giant turtle swimming through space. Through more than twenty novels, he has lampooned just about every aspect of British society, as well as Hollywood, rock music, death, and just about everything else under the sun. A former journalist for various English cities and press officer for the Central Electricity Board Western Region, he was awarded the British Science Fiction award in 1990. He lives with his wife, Lyn Pratchett, in Wilts, England.

Mention the name Poul Anderson and instantly dozens of excellent science fiction novels and short stories spring to mind. However, like many authors, he has also tried his hand at fantasy fiction, with equally impressive results. Two of his novels that deserve mention are *Three Hearts and Three Lions* and *The Broken Sword,* the latter based on the Norse elven myths. He has also written in universes as diverse as Shakespeare's comedies and Robert E. Howard's Conan mythos. A seven-time winner of the Hugo Award, he has also been awarded three Nebulas and the Tolkien Memorial Award.

Humor and hope for the future are two hallmarks of the stories of R. A. Lafferty. Outrageous yet believable characters, transformation, and elements of the eternal war between Heaven and Hell also appear in his work. He has been writing fiction unlike anything else for more than twenty-five years, and has been rewarded with a Hugo Award and a World Fantasy Lifetime Achievement Award in 1990. He lives in Tulsa, Oklahoma.

L. Sprague de Camp has been writing since the 1930s, and has more than three dozen novels, dozens of short stories, and many nonfiction works to show for his efforts. Known early on for his space opera novels, he was first critically recognized for the novel *Lest Darkness Fall,* about one man's attempt to change history during the Roman Empire. In his wide-ranging career he has written everything from Conan pastiches to books on writing science fiction. He has also edited more that a dozen fantasy anthologies and manuscripts, working with authors such as Christopher Stasheff and the late Robert E. Howard.

M. R. James (1862–1936) was the most-lauded author of the nineteenth-century ghost story in the world. A scholar of classical languages and medieval and Biblical legend, he enjoyed a successful career as the director of the Fitzwilliam Museum in Cambridge and as Provost at King's College from 1905–1918 as well as Vice-Chancellor at Cambridge from 1913–1915. He was awarded various honorary degrees during his career and received the Order of Merit in 1930. It is his supernatural fiction, however, that he will be remembered for, stories that didn't rely on overt horror or description, but rather the gently lurking terror that crept up on the usually unsuspecting protagonist, until he came face-to-face with what he most feared.

Barbara Kingsolver has been writing evocative fiction about the plight of repressed indigenous cultures for more than a decade now. A former technical writer and freelance journalist, she turned to full-time writing with the publication of her first novel *The Bean Trees,* and has since published three more novels, *Animal Dreams, Pigs in Heaven,* and *The Poisonwood Bible,* as well as a nonfiction book about the role women played in the Arizona mining strike of 1983, a book of essays, and a book of poetry. She has been critically lauded for her emotionally stirring prose and poetry, and has won the PEN fiction prize and a citation of accomplishment from the United Nations National Council of Women. Along with her fiction, she has also reviewed fiction for both *The New York Times* and the *Los Angeles Times.*

Debra Doyle and James D. Macdonald, a husband-and-wife writing team, have written a number of fantasy and science fiction novels for young readers, including the *Circle of Magic* books. They have four children, including a set of twins, and live in Colebrook, New Hampshire. Mr. Macdonald was a naval officer for many years, and is now a journalist. Dr. Doyle occasionally teaches English and composition at local colleges. Other stories by them appear in *Witch Fantastic, Werewolves, Vampires,* and *A Wizard's Dozen.*

Elisabeth Waters sold her first short story to Marion Zimmer Bradley for *The Keeper's Price,* the first of the Darkover anthologies. She has sold short stories to a variety of anthologies, including *Chicks in Chainmail* and *Sword of Ice and Other Tales of Valdemar.* Her first novel, a fantasy called *Changing Fate,* was awarded the 1989 Gryphon Award, and was published by DAW in 1994. She is a member of the Science Fiction And Fantasy Writers of America and the Authors Guild. She has also worked as a supernumerary with the San Francisco Opera, where she has appeared in *La Gioconda, Manon Lescaut, Madame Butterfly, Khovanschina, Das Rheingold, Werther,* and *Idomeneo.*

Jean Ingelow (1820–1897) wrote fantasy that many critics of her time labeled feminist, but she was writing for children, not just girls, and a closer examination of her fiction reveals this. She created a haunting, evocative wonderland that was at once eerie yet captivating, quite unlike the worlds of L. Frank Baum or Lewis Carroll. In "Mopsa the Fairy" she examines one possible permutation of a very unstereotypical fairy princess.

Manly Wade Wellman (1903–1986) got his start in the pulps, contributing science fiction and horror tales to *Weird Tales* and *Astounding Stories* in 1927. He is best known for his fantasy stories involving paranormal investigators, the most famous of which are his stories set in the Apalachian mountains featuring John the Balladeer, a wandering minstrel who battles evil with the help of magic and his silver-stringed guitar. While he wrote more than twenty adult novels, his largest body of work was in children's novels, with dozens of books published. His work was honored by critics and audiences alike, and he won awards as diverse as the Edgar Award from the Mystery Writers of America, the American Association of Local Historians Award of Merit, and the World Fantasy Award for lifetime achievement.

Robert Bloch (1917–1994) is remembered as the writer of the book *Psycho,* the basis for Alfred Hitchcock's famous film of the same name. He got his start writing stories for pulp magazines such as *Weird Tales, Fantastic Adventures,* and *Unknown.* Later in his career he wrote the novels *American Gothic, Firebug,* and *Fear and Trembling,* among many others. He also edited several anthologies, including *Psycho-paths* and *Monsters in Our Midst.*

M. John Harrison began his writing career as a critic for the magazine *New Worlds* in the late 1960s. He has since published several novels of lyrical fantasy about the city of Virconium, including *The Pastel City,* and *A Storm of Wings,* as well as three collections of short stories and several other non-series novels, including *Luck in the Head* and *Signs of Life.* He was also a regular contributor to the *New Manchester Review* in the late 1970s. He lives in London, England.

Influenced by the novels of H. G. Wells, the theme of humans dealing with catastrophe is prominent in the work of John Wyndham (1903–1969). The novel *Day of the Triffids* is his best-known work dealing with this subject. Alien invasion, telepathy, mutation, and fantastic events occurring in everyday life are also explored in his work, usually as the catalyst for change in the Earth of his novels.

As one of the leading novelists of his age, Charles Dickens (1812–1870) helped legitimize the literary use of horror and the supernatural in such novels as *The Pickwick Papers* and *Bleak House,* and the unfinished *Mystery of Edwin Drood*. He also popularized the concept of the Christmas ghost story with his seminal work *A Christmas Carol*. He is also remembered for his mainstream novels, including *Oliver Twist, David Copperfield,* and *Great Expectations*.

Roger Zelazny (1937–1995) burst onto the science-fiction writing scene as part of the "New Wave" group of writers in the mid to late 1960s. His novels *This Immortal* and *Lord of Light* met universal praise, the latter winning a Hugo Award for best novel. His work is notable for its lyrical style and innovative use of language both in description and dialogue. His most recognized series is the *Amber* novels, about a parallel universe which is the one true world, with all others, Earth included, being mere reflections of his created universe. Besides the Hugo, he was also awarded three Nebulas, three more Hugos, and two Locus Awards.

Science Fiction Anthologies

☐ **STAR COLONIES**
  Martin H. Greenberg and John Helfers, editors 0-88677-894-1—$6.99
Let Jack Williamson, Alan Dean Foster, Mike Resnick, Pamela Sargent, Dana Stabenow and others take you to distant worlds where humans seek to make new homes—or to exotic places where aliens races thrive.

☐ **ALIEN ABDUCTIONS**
  Martin H. Greenberg and Larry Segriff, editors 0-88677-856-5—$6.99
Prepare yourself for a close encounter with these eleven original tales of alien experiences and their aftermath. By authors such as Alan Dean Foster, Michelle West, Ed Gorman, Peter Crowther, and Lawrence Watt-Evans.

☐ **MOON SHOTS**
  Peter Crowther, editor   0-88677-848-4—$6.99
July 20, 1969: a date that will live in history! In honor of the destiny-altering mission to the Moon, these original tales were created by some of today's finest SF writers, such as Ben Bova, Gene Wolfe, Brian Aldiss, Alan Dean Foster, and Stephen Baxter.

☐ **MY FAVORITE SCIENCE FICTION STORY**
  Martin H. Greenberg, editor   0-88677-830-1—$6.99
Here is a truly unique volume, comprised of seminal science fiction stories specifically chosen by some of today's top science fiction names. With stories by Sturgeon, Kornbluth, Waldrop, and Zelazny, among others, chosen by such modern-day masters as Clarke, McCaffrey, Turtledove, Bujold, and Willis.

Prices slightly higher in Canada   **DAW: 104**

Payable in U.S. funds only. No cash/COD accepted. Postage & handling: U.S./CAN. $2.75 for one book, $1.00 for each additional, not to exceed $6.75; Int'l $5.00 for one book, $1.00 each additional. We accept Visa, Amex, MC ($10.00 min.), checks ($15.00 fee for returned checks) and money orders. Call 800-788-6262 or 201-933-9292, fax 201-896-8569; refer to ad #104.

Penguin Putnam Inc.	**Bill my:** ☐Visa ☐MasterCard ☐Amex_____ (expires)
P.O. Box 12289, Dept. B	Card#_____
Newark, NJ 07101-5289	
Please allow 4-6 weeks for delivery.	Signature_____
Foreign and Canadian delivery 6-8 weeks.	

Bill to:

Name_____

Address_____City_____

State/ZIP_____

Daytime Phone #_____

Ship to:

Name_____ Book Total $_____

Address_____ Applicable Sales Tax $_____

City_____ Postage & Handling $_____

State/Zip_____ Total Amount Due $_____

This offer subject to change without notice.